Anna King was born in the East End of London and grew up in Hackney. She wrote ten novels before her death in 2003.

The Ragamuffins

ANNA KING

sphere

SPHERE

First published in Great Britain by Little, Brown in 2002
Reprinted by Warner in 2003
This paperback edition published in 2011 by Sphere

A CIP catalogue record for this book
is available from the British Library.

ISBN 978-0-7515-4831-0

Printed and bound in Great Britain by
Clays Ltd, St Ives plc

Papers used by Sphere are from well-managed forests
and other responsible sources.

MIX
Paper from
responsible sources

FSC
www.fsc.org   FSC® C104740

Sphere
An imprint of
Little, Brown Book Group
100 Victoria Embankment
London EC4Y 0DY

An Hachette UK Company
www.hachette.co.uk

www.littlebrown.co.uk

Acknowledgements

To my husband, Dave, for his support during a difficult period in my life. Also to my doctor, Ian Hannah, for putting up with my weekly visits. Without them, I might not have finished this book.

And also a special thank you to my agent, David Grossman, and my editor, Barbara Boote, for their patience and understanding.

'What yer smiling about, Missus?'

Jerked out of her reverie, Ellen replied merrily, 'Nothing, Micky. At least nothing that would be of interest to you. Now then, are you going to take your wages in kind, or would you prefer money today?'

The young boy hesitated for only the briefest of seconds. The smell of the newly baked bread was like torture to his undernourished body; moreover he hadn't only himself to think about. There was someone else with an empty belly who would be waiting anxiously for his return. Hitching up his torn, soiled trousers that came to a halt just below his knees, he answered cheerfully, 'Thanks, Missus. I'll 'ave some grub, please. I'm so hungry, me belly thinks me throat's been cut.'

'Well, we can't have that, can we?' Ellen was already behind the counter putting six currant buns and a large loaf of bread into a brown paper bag. 'Here you are, Micky, you get off home while it's still hot. I'm sure your mother must be very proud to have a hard-working boy like you, though you must try and get a more permanent job now you've left school . . .' Ellen stopped in mid-flow, her hand flying to her mouth as she realised she sounded as if she was poking her nose into the boy's affairs. 'Oh, I'm sorry, Micky, it's no business of mine what you do. After all, I've only known you a few weeks.' Giving a nervous laugh, she said, 'I seem to be putting my foot in it with everyone today, and it's not even six-thirty yet.'

As she spoke, the bell over the shop door tinkled heralding the first customer of the day. Taking his chance to escape any more probing questions, Micky thanked Ellen once again, adding quickly that he would be round bright and early the next day, then quickly vanished into the cold, dark morning.

When the boy left the shop, Agnes returned saying sullenly, 'Mr Mitson wants ter see yer. I'll take over here.'

As Ellen passed through the heavy curtain to the room out back she heard Agnes make some remark about it 'being all right for some', but Ellen had heard such disparaging remarks from Agnes for so long she no longer took any notice.

A blast of heat hit her full in the face as she entered the bakehouse. Arthur Mitson was in the act of taking a batch of piping hot loaves from the oven when he became aware of his wife's presence. Tipping the six crusty loaves from the large, flat shovel on to a nearby workbench, he mopped his sweating brow with the back of his hand and smiled tenderly.

'You all right, love? I've just had Agnes giving me an earful about encouraging beggars. I take it she was referring to the young lad that's been hanging around for the last couple of weeks?'

Ellen stepped forward and placed a kiss on her husband's chubby cheek. 'Don't you worry about me. I can handle Agnes, and yes, she was referring to Micky. The poor little soul. And he's no beggar, Arthur, as you well know. When I told him there wasn't any work for him today he refused to take any form of payment from me, when it's painfully clear to see he's desperate for a decent meal. I had to invent a job for tomorrow, just so he could justify himself in taking a loaf of bread and a half dozen buns.'

Arthur appraised his wife wryly. 'And what, may I ask, is this important job you have lined up for the young lad?'

Casting her eyes over the top of her husband's thinning hair, Ellen said guiltily, 'I pretended I needed help with tomorrow's coal delivery.'

Arthur Mitson's eyebrows seemed to meet across his forehead in a worried frown. 'Oh, now, love, you shouldn't have done that. You know Mr Dobbs has always seen to the coal delivery. He's done it for the last ten years or more.' Shaking his head anxiously he added, 'You've put me in a bit of a spot now, love. I mean, how am I going to explain to the man that his job's been given away to some street urchin?'

Ellen's eyes clouded. 'Micky's no street urchin, Arthur, any more than he's a common beggar. He's just a decent young boy trying to make do the best way he knows how. As for Mr Dobbs, huh!' The mirthless laugh made Arthur flinch. 'I've hardly taken away his job; blooming hell, Arthur, he runs his own business. The only reason he carries the coal down to the basement is because of the five shilling tip you give him. He doesn't do it out of charity, and that young boy needs the money more than Mr Dobbs.' She stared hard at her husband. 'I'll tell you what, Arthur, come tomorrow, I'll tell Mr Dobbs he won't be getting his extra five bob any more, then we'll see what he says. If he still insists on carrying the coal to the basement for nothing, then I'll apologise. But if he makes a fuss, then I'm going to give the job to Micky. What do you think of that?'

The thinning head shook from side to side helplessly as Arthur tried to remember the girl he had married. A girl who had been totally dependent on him. The young woman now facing him bore no resemblance to that memory. His plump face grave, Arthur said anxiously, 'All right, all right, love. Let's not fall out over it. After all, the boy might not even turn up tomorrow.'

Even as he said the words, Arthur knew it was only wishful thinking on his part. Of course the boy would show up. Where else would he get fresh food and five bob for an hour's work? It wasn't that Arthur resented the boy, quite the contrary. He had only met him once, but the lad had seemed a decent sort – not like some of them around these parts. No, it wasn't Micky that was the trouble. If it hadn't been him, it would be someone or something else for Agnes to complain about. Now it seemed that, come tomorrow, he would have Mr Dobbs to contend with as well. Sighing loudly, Arthur Mitson reflected that life would be a lot quieter if only Ellen would act like other businessmen's wives and stay out of his place of work.

Ellen watched her husband's silent battle and felt a wave of compassion for the kindly man. She knew how Arthur loathed any form of confrontation, and was saddened that she had heaped further worries onto his shoulders. The poor man had enough on his plate dealing with Agnes on a daily basis without her adding to his troubles. If it had been anything else she would have backed down, but she had promised Micky a job tomorrow and she wasn't going to go back on her word.

'He'll turn up, Arthur,' she said softly.

'I know he will, love,' Arthur replied, the tone of his voice resigned to the inevitable. Then he had an idea. Clearing his dry throat he said carelessly, 'Tell you what. How about you having a lie-in tomorrow? I don't like you having to get up so early, especially when Agnes is here to do the work. There really is no reason for you to get up at the crack of dawn. And don't worry about the boy, I'll see to him, I promise.' He looked into his wife's face, his countenance earnest.

Ellen returned the look, then shook her head wistfully, knowing full well how her husband's mind worked. He was simply trying to get her out of the way tomorrow so that he could create another job for Micky, thereby keeping his promise to see to the boy, and thus appeasing Mr Dobbs into the bargain. Her eyes flickering, Ellen fought down a feeling of resentment. It wasn't Arthur's fault he had no gumption; some people were born that way, but that didn't mean to say she was going to encourage her husband's weakness. Keeping her voice low she said softly, 'You know I don't like lying in bed, Arthur.' Actually, that wasn't quite true. She loved her bed and would happily stay in it all morning if she could do so without feeling guilty. Though she did allow herself a full half hour after Arthur had risen. Then she would stretch out luxuriously, revelling in the opportunity of having the large four-poster bed to herself, even if it was only for a short time. 'Anyway, I like to earn my keep. Speaking of which, Agnes said you wanted to see me. Do you want me to keep an eye on the bread while you see the delivery man? He's due soon, isn't he?'

The factory where Arthur bought his supplies delivered every Tuesday morning. And such was the high regard her husband engendered, partly due to the large order he placed every week, that the owner of the factory always brought Arthur's purchases personally. And once their business was concluded, the two men would indulge in a glass of port upstairs in the drawing room above the shop where their living quarters were situated. 'I know how much you enjoy Mr Stone's weekly visit, as does he.' She paused; then, with a mischievous grin, she said playfully, 'And of course, there's always the added bonus of the usual tipple to warm him up on the journey back to his factory.'

Arthur made a face at his wife, while at the same time sliding another batch of loaves into the hot oven, followed by a large tray of currant buns which he placed on the shelf below the bread. His task completed, Arthur Mitson looked at his young wife, and as always when he saw her, his heart began to race with love – and fear. With love because he worshipped the very ground she walked on, and for the joy she had brought into his life. With fear, because he was constantly afraid she might leave him one day. Even though she had never once, in the nine months they had been married, shown any sign of discontent, Arthur feared there would come a time when she would see him for the overweight, balding, middle-aged man he was. If he had married a woman of his own age, then his fears would have been unfounded.

But Ellen was only just eighteen, and even though she wasn't what one would term beautiful, she had a pretty face and a kindly nature.

'What's the matter, Arthur? You look as if you're miles away.' Ellen was gazing at him quizzically.

Blinking the sweat out of his eyes, Arthur answered quickly, 'Oh, you know me, love. Always in a world of my own.' Taking off the coarse linen apron he always wore when baking, he carried on, 'Look, you go back into the shop while I finish tidying up.' Nodding his head towards the custom-built oven he added, 'Those last two trays should see us through the day. If we do start to run low, I can always bake some more.'

Ellen nodded, glad to get away from the stifling heat of the small room. 'I'll let you know when Mr Stone arrives. In the meantime I suppose I'll have to put up with Agnes' delightful company for a while longer.' With a wry smile, Ellen winked playfully at her husband before closing the door behind her.

Alone once more, Arthur lowered his large frame onto a three-legged stool. His face, red from the heat of the oven, was pensive as his mind travelled down a well-worn path of distant memories.

He had struck up a friendship with Eric Simms while still at school and that friendship had remained firm for over thirty years. Arthur had been best man at Eric's marriage to Mary Sumner, a childhood friend of them both. A year after the wedding, Mary had given birth to their only child, a daughter they had named Ellen. Arthur could still remember the awe he had experienced the first time he had held the tiny

bundle of humanity, and the overwhelming feeling of
love that had been generated inside his body and heart
towards the child cradled safely in his arms. Over the
years he had watched Ellen grow from a helpless
infant into a lovely, warm-hearted young girl, not realising she had taken over his life. He had only existed
from one Sunday to the next. A lonely man, with no
other friends or family, his entire world became
centred on that one day; the day he visited his friends
and their captivating daughter.

Then there had come that dreadful night, fifteen
months ago, when a fire had swept through the
terraced house he had come to look on as his second
home, killing his dear friends, and leaving their only
child an orphan.

Ellen would have suffered the same fate had she
not been staying the night at a friend's house.
Naturally distraught, Ellen had turned to Arthur for
comfort. She had been sixteen at the time of her
parents' untimely death, a very naive and trusting
sixteen. Arthur hadn't planned what had happened
next – it just had.

At first his only aim had been to comfort the young
girl in her hour of need. He was a decent, hard-
working man and the only thought in his mind was
that of caring and providing for Ellen until such time
when she would be able to fend for herself, no matter
how long it took. The idea of taking advantage of the
young girl in such circumstances would never have
entered his mind.

So he had brought her here to recover from her grief.
She had no living relatives; it was only natural that

Ellen should turn to Arthur, a man she had always known and loved, for help in the darkest moments of her young life.

The first six months had been the worst as Ellen slowly came to terms with her loss. Then Arthur had begun to notice the looks directed at him by his women customers, the same women who, when Ellen had first arrived, had applauded Arthur for his generosity in taking the orphaned girl into his home. The disapproving looks had soon escalated to open hostility and accusations at the state of affairs existing between himself, a middle-aged man, and a young, unchaperoned girl.

Arthur had been horrified. The very nature of the cruel implications had made him physically ill. He had been content just to have Ellen nearby, but he'd had to admit the whole set-up looked decidedly unsavoury to the outside world – the unfounded notions no doubt helped along by Agnes' bitter tongue.

For a brief moment, Arthur's conscience hung heavily on him. There had been a time when Agnes had been more than just an assistant to him. But that had been a long time ago, before Ellen had entered the world and his life. If he'd had any sense at all, he would have fired Agnes years ago. But, being the timid man he was, he had simply taken the line of least resistance and let life slip by. Though he had to admit Agnes hadn't caused him any trouble back then. She had seemed happy enough to continue working for him with no strings attached – until the day he had brought the distraught Ellen into his home.

Overnight, Agnes had turned from a pleasant, easy-going woman, into a hard-faced, bitter harridan. Yet even now, confronted and hounded by the woman whose wages he had paid every week for the past twenty years, Arthur still couldn't pluck up the courage to dismiss his one-time lover who was now the bane of his life.

His shoulders hunched, Arthur gave a long, shuddering sigh of self-pity. He was truly sorry he had caused Agnes so much hurt, but, oh, how he wished the blasted woman could put the past behind her and be happy for him.

The sound of raised laughter coming from the shop wrenched Arthur from his maudlin thoughts and brought a smile to his lips. That was Ellen's laughter he could hear, he would know that sound anywhere. Yet even as he smiled, a sudden stab of fear shot through him like a knife. What if she *did* leave him one day? What would he do then? She was his whole life. Without her he would be nothing.

Gripping the edge of the table for support, Arthur tried to steady his rapid breathing while he reminded himself that it was Ellen who had first brought up the idea of marriage. Faced with the prospect of having to leave her new-found stability and, like Arthur, afraid of facing life without each other, Ellen had tentatively suggested that they should marry in order to silence the wagging tongues. It had seemed the best thing to do at the time. The irony was, that if Agnes had kept her spiteful tongue quiet, he and Ellen would most likely never have even contemplated marriage. And in due course, Ellen would probably have moved out of his home and made a life for herself – a life that might not have included him.

Getting to his feet Arthur gave a wry shake of his head as he realised, for the first time, that he had Agnes to thank for his wedded state, and wondered if Agnes was aware of that fact.

'Arthur, Mr Stone's here.'

Arthur jumped. He hadn't heard Ellen enter the room. 'Oh, oh, all right, love. I'll be right out.' Glad of the diversion, Arthur planted a wet kiss on Ellen's cheek saying jovially, 'Thanks, love. I won't be long.'

When the portly figure had disappeared to meet his visitor Ellen puffed out her cheeks, her hand waving in front of her face in an effort to combat the heat of the room. Looking for something to do, she made herself a mug of tea, then realised the milkman hadn't called yet. Knowing she had used the last of the milk earlier she walked over to the back door and looked out, her ears straining for the sound of the milkman's horse and cart. After the searing heat of the kitchen, the cold February wind was a welcome relief, but only for a few seconds.

Soon shivering with cold, Ellen wrapped her arms around her waist for warmth, her eyes peering down the narrow, pitch-black alley, hoping to catch sight of the swinging lantern that would herald the arrival of the milkman.

'Morning, Mrs Mitson.'

The sound from the darkness caused Ellen to stumble back into the doorway.

'Oh, Mr Parker, you made me jump.' Feeling a little

foolish Ellen forced a smile to her face to hide her confusion.

'Sorry about that, Mrs Mitson, I didn't mean to scare you.'

The light from the bakery washed over the man standing before her, making it easy for Ellen to recognise Ted Parker, one of her regular customers.

Smothering a nervous laugh, Ellen replied, 'That's all right. I just came out to see if there was any sign of the milkman.' She heard her words come out in a high-pitched tone and silently chastised herself for acting like a fool.

'Oh, he's just turned into Shore Street, he should be here soon. I'll wait with you if you're nervous.'

The note of mockery in the man's voice caused Ellen to draw herself up to her full height, her manner now defensive. Feeling the rush of blood to her face she replied tersely, 'That won't be necessary, Mr Parker. I'm sure I'm quite safe on my own doorstep. Anyway, my husband is within calling distance if I should need any assistance.'

The man tipped his hat towards her. 'I'm sure Mr Mitson's presence is very reassuring. It would take a brave man to tackle him.'

This time there was no doubting the sarcasm in the man's tone, but before Ellen could make a suitable rejoinder, the clip clop of horses' hooves broke the silence of the early morning – and the uncomfortable atmosphere.

'Oh, here he is,' Ellen cried thankfully.

The man stepped back, a sardonic smile on his lips. 'Good morning to you, Mrs Mitson.'

16

'Good morning, Mr Parker,' Ellen said stiffly, painfully aware of her beating heart.

Some time later, as she sat with a mug of tea in her hands, Ellen went over the small incident in her mind, cringing as she recalled how stupid she must have sounded – not only stupid, but childlike. Aware of her still-shaking hands, Ellen gripped the mug tighter. She knew most women would have handled the situation with more aplomb, most of them even enjoying a bit of harmless flirting. But most women of her age had some experience of life and she'd had none.

Suddenly impatient with herself she slammed the mug down on the table with an angry thud. What was the matter with her? Letting a trivial incident upset her so much. She really was acting like a child now. But isn't that what she was? Oh, she might have a wedding ring on her finger, but that didn't make her a woman. She wasn't a woman in any sense of the word, not even in the four-poster bed she shared with Arthur.

Apart from an affectionate cuddle and a peck on the cheek, her husband had never tried to take things any further, thank God!

Appalled at her thoughts, Ellen got to her feet in confusion. She had to find something to do, something that would occupy her. Getting a bowl of water and a scrubbing brush, Ellen got down on her knees and began attacking the floor. But still her mind would give her no peace. For the first time since her wedding, Ellen was experiencing the pangs of discontent. And all because of Ted Parker!

Resting back on her heels, Ellen stared into the

empty room. She was only eighteen and married to a man old enough to be her father. She had never known the thrill of being courted by a man of her own age, never had the chance to experience the world, or the people in it. And now she never would.

Young, exciting men like Ted Parker were out of her reach for ever. She must accept that fact and learn to live with it.

Yet as she scrubbed at the scrupulously clean floor with renewed vigour, the feeling of resentment continued to surge through her body.

If only people hadn't been so nasty about her living with Arthur she wouldn't have been in such a rush to get married. But she mustn't forget what she owed to Arthur. Without him she might have ended up in the workhouse.

Her thoughts tumbling around her head she remembered the conversation she had unwittingly overheard a week before the hastily arranged wedding.

She had been rudely awoken by the sound of a fierce argument. Still half asleep she hadn't recognised Agnes' voice and when she did, she had crept out of bed, tip-toeing down the carpeted stairs, hardly able to breathe. She hadn't realised at the time why she had been so careful not to be heard, but at the back of her mind she had known there was something going on between Arthur and Agnes. Sitting on the bottom step in her nightgown, she had listened in stunned silence as Agnes had begged Arthur to call off the wedding. It had been obvious Agnes was crying by the tremor in her voice as she reminded Arthur of the love they had once shared, a love she still harboured for him. Arthur's reply had been too soft to hear. There had followed a strained silence, a silence so great that Ellen was afraid the sound of her rapidly beating heart would give her presence away. Then Agnes, her voice low and bitter, had said harshly, 'Don't give me that load of old rubbish, Arthur. If all yer wanted was to give the girl a proper home without people gossiping, yer could 'ave offered to adopt her. After all, you're old enough to be her father, ain't yer?'

Shaken and disturbed, Ellen had crept back to bed. She had never mentioned to Arthur that she had overheard the heated conversation of that night. But by God! She wished she had.

Back then, she had been so naive, so unworldly, so afraid of losing her new home and the comforting presence of Arthur. She had trusted him implicitly. Now she had to question his true intentions. It was no wonder Agnes hated her so much. Given the circumstances, Ellen didn't blame her.

It was as Agnes had said that night. If all Arthur had wanted was to provide a home for Ellen, then why hadn't he done what Agnes had suggested and adopted her?

Getting slowly to her feet, Ellen sat down at the table, her expression thoughtful.

Since her marriage she had begun working in the shop, and the experience of coming into daily contact with the colourful people of the East End had quickly opened her eyes to the ways of the world.

But by the time she had realised she could fend for herself, Arthur had already made her his wife.

* * *

Ted Parker turned at the top of the alley into Morning Lane, a wry smile on his face. He shouldn't have tormented the poor cow like that, but he hadn't been able to resist it. He had been at the end of the alley, making his way towards the tram stop when the light from the back of the bakery had caught his attention and, without thinking, he had walked towards the light. As might any man, only some men might have taken advantage of the situation. What was her husband thinking about anyway? Letting a young girl, and that's all she was, a girl, stand about in the doorway of the pitch-black alley. Good God! Anyone could have walked by. It was ten years since the last Ripper murder in 1888, but they'd never caught him, had they? For all anyone knew, the maniac could still be walking the streets. The clanking of the tram brought his mind back to the present. At such an early hour Ted easily got a seat, and, after paying his fare, settled back on the wooden slat, his face thoughtful. Old Mitson must have thought his boat had come in when Ellen had agreed to marry him. He was old enough to be her father, or grandfather come to that.

Ted gave himself a mental shake and turned his mind to other matters. But he couldn't get the image of those big, brown, trusting eyes out of his mind, nor the image of the silky chestnut hair caught up in a bun at the back of the slender neck. A girl of Ellen Mitson's age should have her hair falling naturally, not bound up like some woman twice her age. Oh! To hell with it! What was he concerning himself about anyway? It was no business of his what she did. Yet, some hours later, as he bantered good-naturedly with customers at his stall in Roman Road market, he still couldn't get Ellen's sweet face out of his mind.

CHAPTER TWO

Micky Masters hurried along the cobbled pavement clutching the hot parcel close to his chest for warmth, the heady aroma of the package wafting tantalisingly up his nostrils. Ignoring the rough pebbles that dug cruelly into the soles of his feet through his worn boots, the boy turned into a side road, his hurried steps taking him towards a derelict building that stood out amid a pile of rubble that had once been a row of terraced houses. Micky was nearing his destination when he saw the shadowy figure of a man lurking in front of the building he was heading for. With a loud cry Micky sprang forward.

'Oi, you! What yer hanging around 'ere for? Go on, piss off, yer dirty old man.' His grimy face etched with fear, Micky leapt towards the figure barely visible in the dark, winter morning. Stooping quickly he picked up a broken piece of brick and, without thinking, threw it with all his might at the figure.

Startled, the man began to back off, then, hitching up the collar of his thick coat, he hurried away.

'An' don't come back, d'yer hear me?' Micky shouted after the retreating figure. His heart beating fast, Micky waited until the man had disappeared before running into the ruin calling out fearfully, 'Molly? You all right, Moll?' Silence greeted him, causing his stomach to lurch and increasing the rapid beating of his heart. Then, out of the darkness, a soft, tremulous voice replied, 'I'm here, Micky. I'm up here.'

At the sound, Micky's heart slowed its frantic beating. With a bound he raced towards a piece of rope dangling from the rotting roof and, with the dexterity of youth, pulled himself up into what had once been a bedroom. Peering into the gloom he hissed, 'What yer doing sitting in the dark? Yer scared the living daylights outta me.'

Relief turning to anger he felt around the dirty floor for the candle and matches. Finding both he quickly struck a match and ignited the tallow wick. The flare of the candle instantly lit up the gloomy room, and the tear-stained face of the little girl crouched in the far corner, her back tight against the wall.

'I'm sorry, Micky. I . . . I had ter put the candle out, 'cos that man came again. He was calling for me . . . An' I was frightened. So I thought if I put the candle out, he might think there was nobody here. Why does he keep coming 'ere, Micky? He scares me . . . I don't want yer to leave again. Please, Micky, don't leave me on me own again.'

Averting his gaze, Micky made a great play of pulling the warm package from the inside of his jumper muttering, 'I can't, Moll. Yer know I can't. I 'ave ter look fer work, an' I can't do that with you tagging along.' Breaking off a chunk of warm bread he handed it to the forlorn figure, adding in mock cheerfulness, 'C'mon, Moll, 'ave some breakfast. I got some buns too. An' they're still hot. Go on, 'ave some.'

The little girl stretched out a grubby hand to take the food, her hunger overcoming her earlier fear. Her confidence returning now her big brother was back with her, Molly asked through a mouthful of bread, 'Yer not going out again, are yer, Micky?'

Micky lowered his head saying gruffly, 'Now, come on, Moll. We've been through this all before. Yer know I've got ter work. How we gonna get a place of our own if I don't work?'

Molly's lips began to tremble. Spraying out a spittle of dry crumbs she said tearfully, 'But what about that man, Micky? He always comes when yer not here. He must be watching all the time. What does he want, Micky? Why does he want me?'

Again Micky felt a wave of helplessness sweep over him. How could he explain to his eight-year-old sister that certain men liked little girls instead of women. Especially when he didn't understand it himself. What he did know was that his little sister was in constant danger whenever he wasn't around to protect her. Yet what else was he supposed to do? As he'd tried to explain to Molly, he had to find work. If he didn't, how would they survive? At the same time he had to look out for his sister. He was all she had now. It was up to him to provide for her and to keep her safe. But how was he to do both? If there had been work for him at the bakery, he would have been gone for hours. Suppose that man had managed to get to Molly during his absence? The very notion brought a wave of bile up from his empty stomach into his throat. Forcing the disgusting thoughts from his mind he broke off two more chunks of bread and, handing one to Molly, said, 'Look, he's gone now, ain't he? So get on with yer breakfast an' forget about him. I'm 'ere now, ain't I? And he ain't gonna come back while I'm 'ere, is he?'

Molly immediately brightened. Her childish mind eased, she forgot her earlier fears and concentrated on the food her brother had provided.

Micky too was now thinking only of his stomach. Stuffing the warm bread into his mouth with relish he thought how good it would be to have a hot mug of sweet tea to wash it down with.

Instead he filled two tin cans from a bucket of tepid water he had fetched from the stand pipe at the top of the street earlier that morning.

In the soft candlelight he gazed lovingly at Molly as she drank noisily from the tin can. Her thirst quenched, she gave a loud sigh of contentment.

'That was lovely, Micky, thanks.'

Micky shuffled awkwardly, saying gruffly, 'Don't be daft, I'm yer brother, ain't I? There's no need ter thank me fer feeding yer, that's what I'm 'ere for.'

Looking into the large, blue eyes staring at him so trustingly, Micky felt a lump gather in his throat. Then his gaze travelled to his sister's matted hair that, when washed, fell to her waist in golden curls. But it had been a long time since Molly's hair, and body, had seen any soap and water. He too was in dire need of a good wash. The nearest either of them had had recently was a quick sluice over their hands and face from the water bucket.

Their breakfast finished, Micky looked at the currant buns longingly then shook his head. He'd save them, and the rest of the bread for later. Not trusting himself to resist the delicious treat, Micky carefully put them back in the paper bag. Conscious that Molly was staring at him anxiously, he gave her a playful nudge and grinned. 'All right, I'll stay. You go back ter sleep, then later on, I'll take yer down the market. The bloke on the fish stall said he might 'ave some work fer me. Yer might as well come along.' Pushing his face close to hers he laughed, adding, 'Maybe someone might even give you a job, if we're lucky, then we could stay together all the time.'

The enormity of his words banished the smile from his face, yet the words had the opposite effect on his sister. Her pretty face lighting up, she breathed wistfully, 'Wouldn't that be wonderful, Micky? D'yer think that might happen one day?'

Micky averted his eyes, not daring to meet his sister's gaze for fear she might see the desolate look on his face. Adopting a lighter mood, he said, 'Look, seeing as how I ain't gotta go back ter the bakery today, why don't we get some sleep? I don't know about you, sis, but I could do with another couple of hours' kip.'

Her eyes stretching wide with happiness, Molly squealed, 'Oh, yes, Micky. I'd love ter go back ter sleep.'

Less than ten minutes later the young girl was fast asleep. Lying close by her side on top of a soiled mattress they had found in the ruins along with three equally filthy blankets to cover them against the cruel winter months, Micky stared up through the broken roof waiting for daylight to break. His mind, as always when there was nothing else to occupy it, returned to the reason he and Molly now found themselves in such dire circumstances. Blinking to hold back tears that threatened to flow, Micky angrily brushed the back of his hand across his eyes. Bleeding hell! He was going soft. It was lucky Molly hadn't seen him like this. In her eyes, her brother, at the grand age of fourteen, was almost a man. Composing himself, he rested his arm against the back of his head and let his mind wander.

This time last year he and Molly had been at home; home being a modest two-bedroom house in Hoxton. Their parents, like the majority of people living in the East End, had always had to struggle to make ends meet. Their father, a big, gruff man they had both idolised, had worked down the docks. His wage had varied from week to week, but Annie Masters had always boasted she could make a penny stretch further than any other woman in the street. They had been poor, but never hungry or cold, their mother had seen to that. It was only now that Micky realised how much their parents had gone without in order that he and Molly didn't suffer. Now they were both dead, their deaths occurring with such alacrity that Micky still couldn't believe he'd never see either of his parents again. Shifting restlessly he carefully turned so as not to disturb Molly who, now her mind was at peace and her belly full, was deep in slumber.

The last time they had seen their father he was going off to work. He had never returned home. One of the managers from the docks, accompanied by a police-man, had called at the house, their grave expressions giving no need for words. There had been an accident involving a crane down at the docks and their father had been killed.

Annie Masters had never been the same after her husband's early demise. In order to earn a living, she had found a cleaning job. But her health had never been good at the best of times, and she too had died. For the two children who were still grieving for their father, the death of their mother so soon after losing their father had sent them into shock.

Yet further tragedy was about to strike.

Micky, who had just finished school, had imagined himself capable of looking after his sister once he had found a job, but the authorities had thought other-wise. Despite anguished protests, the two children had been taken to the workhouse by two grim-faced offi-cials. Molly had been content enough to have some kind of stability, but Micky, independent by nature, had kicked his heels in protest against their new envi-ronment, his agile mind looking for the first oppor-tunity to escape the oppressive building. The children had been in the workhouse for three months before the chance of getting out was presented to them. Due to a severe winter, a good deal of the staff had taken to their beds with influenza, their misery resulting in a severe shortage of staff. Micky, who had been biding his time, had quickly seen the diminished staffing arrangements as a stroke of luck, and had lost no time in taking advantage of the situation. With the remaining staff struggling to keep order, it had been relatively easy to simply walk out of the workhouse with their meagre possessions tied up in a small bundle. They had walked for what seemed an age, with Micky expecting to feel the hand of the law on his shoulders at any second. And when he had realised they were free at last, Micky had been ecstatic. But he hadn't taken into account his little sister. Molly, excited at first, had soon become fretful as the early January evening began to draw in.

Micky too had become increasingly anxious as the darkness closed in around them, his earlier euphoria deserting him as stark reality set in. Alone, cold and hungry, without any money, the two children had quickly found themselves at the mercy of the elements. With Molly crying with fear, cold and hunger, Micky, who was close to tears himself, had become desperate. Then their luck had changed. Just as Micky, worn down by Molly's pitiful cries, had almost decided to go back to the workhouse, they had stumbled on the derelict house. With no light to guide them the two children had felt their way though the pitch-black house, stumbling time and time again as their feet tripped over unseen objects scattered throughout the crumbling building. Guided by touch alone, Micky had found a mattress and a pile of blankets, the filthy condition of their find not becoming apparent until the following day when the morning light had flooded their new dwelling. Even then, they had been so glad to have somewhere to stay, the appalling condition of the house had seemed a palace.

Molly, worn out by the eventful day, had quickly fallen asleep on the heavily soiled mattress. And Micky, bone-tired himself, but knowing that if he allowed himself the luxury of sleep, he and Molly, who hadn't eaten since the bowl of lumpy porridge they had consumed that morning in the workhouse, would wake up ravenous. As tired as he was, Micky knew it would be better if he went out now, while it was still early evening. While Molly slept, Micky crept out of the building, his weary footsteps trudging towards the market in Well Street where, hopefully, he could earn enough money to buy some sorely needed food.

He had managed to earn a couple of shillings by running errands and helping to clear away the stalls for several market traders. He had also been given a bag of ripe apples and pears for his hard work. Knowing the effect such food could have on an empty stomach, Micky had decided to buy a loaf of bread to supplement the impromptu supper. Once again, his luck held, guiding his footsteps towards the bakery at the top of Morning Lane.

There he had met the baker's wife, a lovely young woman who, sensing his need, had refused payment for the bread, insisting she was going to throw it out anyway due to the lateness of the day. Micky had known the young woman was just being kind. Yesterday's bread was always sought after by women eager to buy a loaf or some cakes at half price.

Beside him, Molly stirred restlessly, throwing off her

covering. Gently, so as not to disturb her, Micky pulled the blankets up around her neck, thinking as he did so how horrified his mother would have been to see her beloved children living in such filthy surroundings.

If only that was all he had to worry about! They could survive the way they were living for quite a while. At least, he could; he wasn't so sure about his sister. It would be better once summer came. And he didn't know how long the house they were occupying would remain standing. Why this house alone had escaped being demolished Micky didn't know. But what he was sure of was that, sooner or later, when the council decided what it planned to do with the vacant plot of land, they would waste no time in removing the last remaining house. In the meantime, he had to work and work hard if he wanted to get them into some kind of home where they would be safe. His plans were somewhat hazy, his mind closed to the pitfalls ahead, but one thing he couldn't shut from his mind was the man. His lips tightened, his arms automatically going around the small innocent form lying beside him as he thought about the stranger.

He had turned up ten days ago. At first Micky had feared he was an official come to take him and Molly back to the workhouse, but the man had been quick to reassure Micky that that was not his intention. The man, who had introduced himself as Kenneth Wells, had gone out of his way to be friendly to the two orphans, and for the first time since running away, the children had begun to feel safe. He had begun by bringing food and making the children feel as if they had found an ally – and Micky hadn't been too proud to admit that they needed an adult in their lives. Every day the man would turn up, always bringing some treat with him, usually food, his manner genial and sympathetic to their plight. A week later, when the children had become comfortable in his presence, the man had sent Micky off on an errand. The youth, not having any reason to distrust their new-found friend, had gone off willingly. On his return, he hadn't noticed that his normally bubbly sister was very quiet, almost subdued. The next day, when Micky, a florin clutched tightly in his hand, prepared to go off on another errand, Molly had grabbed his hand, her eyes imploring him not to go. To his everlasting shame, when Molly had needed him most, he had let her down. But something had nagged at him until, cursing himself for a fool, he'd raced back to the building. The sight that had met his eyes would remain with him until his dying day. Closing his eyes tightly, he tried not to remember the vision of the man holding Molly on his lap. His dear, sweet Molly, her tiny frame rigid with fear as the man slobbered over her face, while his hands . . . Oh, God! Those hands. Hands that had been stretched out in friendship and been gratefully accepted, had turned into vile, despicable instruments fondling and groping the young, innocent child Micky had left in his care.

The image had been burned into his brain for ever. At the time, his mind had seemed to close down. The next thing he remembered, he was on the man's back, screaming, kicking and punching with all the strength he possessed. Taken by surprise by the unexpected, ferocious assault, the man had fled. For the next two days Molly hadn't left her brother's side, nor had he wanted her to. But they'd had to come back to reality. In order to survive, Micky had to work, and he couldn't work with Molly alongside him. So he had come up with a plan.

Together they had carried the mattress and blankets to the top of the house. Then they had removed the rickety staircase, the rotten wood coming away easily in their hands. Micky had then attached a rope to the only solid beam left in the upper part of the house, enabling him and Molly to climb up to their new living quarters, and then pulling the rope up after them, thus repelling any unwanted visitors. It wasn't an ideal solution, but it was the best he could do for now. Judging by the man's presence outside the house this morning, it was obvious that Kenneth Wells, if that was his real name, wasn't going to be put off so easily. The only consolation was that Molly, innocent and trusting, simply thought the man only wanted to kiss and cuddle her, like her dad used to do before she went to bed. But even very young children knew what they did and didn't like. Molly had loved her father dearly and she knew that his loving embraces bore no resemblance to the way that horrible man had slobbered all over her. She had been badly frightened by the man's unwanted attentions, but fortunately was still oblivious of his true intentions.

Forcing his mind to other matters, Micky thought ahead to tomorrow. The baker's wife hadn't said how much he would be paid for the morning's work, but whatever she offered would be fair. He only wished he hadn't had to lie to her. Then again, he hadn't actually lied. She had assumed, quite normally, that Micky had a home and family, and Micky had simply chosen not to enlighten her on that small matter. He wondered briefly how old she was. She only looked about sixteen, but she must be older than that. Though he had nearly put his foot in it on meeting the baker himself. Seeing them together Micky had naturally assumed the baker was the girl's dad. Luckily for him, Ellen Mitson had immediately introduced the portly man as her husband.

He had been very pleasant and friendly too. Letting out a soft sigh, Micky tried to get some sleep. If only there was a proper job to be had at the bakery. No matter how menial the work, Micky would jump at the chance of having a regular wage to look forward to. That was his dream. To have somewhere for him and Molly to live without fear. To have their own front door, to sleep once again between clean sheets, to be able to have a proper bath and clean clothes to put on. There were plenty of boarding houses in the East End where he could find a room with no questions asked. All he needed was that elusive job. Flopping onto his side, his face tilted up at the hole in the roof, Micky waited for daybreak. He would give Molly another hour then take her with him around the local factories and shops. There must be somewhere that was looking for a strong, willing boy.

An idea struck him, bringing a smile to his lips. Maybe the baker's wife knew of somewhere. After all, she said he should look for a job. It was worth asking.

Excited at the notion, Micky closed his eyes, waiting for Molly to wake up. But when, some time later, Molly awoke, she found her big brother fast asleep. Smiling happily, the little girl snuggled against the warm body of the boy who, in her eyes, was her provider and protector. Nothing bad could ever happen to her while Micky was around.

CHAPTER THREE

'Five bob!' Micky looked down at the two, shiny half crowns nestling in his blackened palm, his face stretched incredulously. Shaking his head he muttered, 'This can't be right, Missus. Not just fer an hour's work. Yer must 'ave made a mistake.'

Ellen, her own face a picture of happy satisfaction, smiled. 'There's no mistake, Micky. That's the amount my husband paid the coalman – until I offered the job to you.'

Two bright blue eyes stared out of the blackened face in bewilderment. 'But yer said you always had ter shift the coal by yerself.' His voice, still quivering with excitement at the money in his hand, now held an accusation. 'Did yer just pretend yer had ter shift the coal yerself, just so yer could give me the money? 'Cos, like I told yer before, Missus, I ain't taking no charity, not even from you.'

Finding herself on the offensive, Ellen shifted

guiltily. 'Now, Micky. It isn't quite like that. It's true I did lie, and I'm sorry for that, but that money in your hand is money you worked hard for. You're entitled to it. I've always resented the money my husband insisted on paying the coalman, a man who owns his own business, when there are many people who, to my mind, need the work and the money more than he does.'

Micky held Ellen's gaze, his need for the money wrestling with his conscience. Slowly his fingers closed over the coins. He would be mad to throw it back, especially when he and Molly needed it so much. But he hated being treated as a charity case. It was only for Molly's sake that he was prepared to swallow his pride and take the money. But instead of feeling a sense of worth for a job well done, Micky felt cheated somehow. Not only because of the money, which was almost a full week's wage for some men, but because of the young woman who had given it to him. He had thought they could become friends. He had wanted to please her and had thought he was helping her by taking on the job. Now it seemed she only felt sorry for him. To her, he, Micky, was just another street urchin, and he was surprised and somewhat bewildered by the unfamiliar emotions swirling inside his chest.

'Micky?' Ellen was staring at him anxiously. They were both of the same height, and, with his entire face blackened with coaldust, the only way the young boy could be recognised was by his eyes. And for the first time, Ellen was struck by their bright, almost cobalt blue. For a few seconds they stared at each other, the boy and the young woman. No words were spoken. Ellen appeared to be mesmerised by the boy's unflinching stare. Then a jolt rippled through her body bringing her sharply back to her senses.

Good Lord! What was happening to her? First she had made a fool of herself in front of Ted Parker, now she was being intimidated by a mere youth.

'I'll be off then, Missus. Thanks ... yer know ...' Micky nodded at his closed palm. 'It was kind of yer.'

Ellen gulped. 'I wasn't being kind, Micky. The job had to be done, and I thought you deserved the work. Call by tomorrow, and I'll see if there's anything else needs doing.' Regaining her composure, Ellen gave a small laugh. 'I hope you told your mother the nature of the job you had lined up for today. Goodness, you look as if you've spent a morning up a chimney. Go on now, get yourself home. I expect your mother will have a hot bath waiting for you.'

Micky nodded, his eyes now averted. He wished he could tell Mrs Mitson the truth. But even if she seemed very young, she was still an adult, and might turn him and Molly over to the authorities, thinking she was doing it for their best interests.

'Yeah, you're right, Missus. I'd better be off.' Micky hesitated, his thoughts jumbled. Then he asked hopefully, 'I was wondering if yer knew of anyone that wanted a young lad for regular work?' Giving a nervous laugh, he added, 'Like yer said yesterday, now I've left school I should be looking for a permanent job.'

Ellen thought hard. There was nothing she would like better than to take the boy on permanently, but there simply wasn't the work. It was only a small bakery. In fact they were overstaffed since she had begun working in the shop. Arthur and Agnes could run the business perfectly well between them, as they had done for many years before she had arrived. As Agnes was always pointing out to her.

Then a thought struck her. Walking slowly with Micky to the door she said quietly, 'I can't think of anyone off hand, Micky, but I'll certainly ask around.' Conscious of Agnes' curious stare, Ellen continued. 'Look, let me have a word with my husband, and we'll see what we can do, though I can't promise anything.'

Micky nodded. 'Can't ask fer more than that, Missus. Ta. See yer in the morning.'

'Yes, all right, Micky. Take care. 'Bye.' Ellen stood at the door until the slim figure had disappeared into the morning gloom.

'If yer don't mind shutting the door, I'd be ever so grateful. Only it's bleeding freezing fer us old 'uns. The cold gets right inter me bones. That's if it ain't no trouble, like.'

The sarcasm in Agnes' voice was lost on Ellen, whose thoughts were elsewhere. Closing the door, she said absent-mindedly, 'I'm just going to make some tea. Look after things please, Agnes.'

Agnes glared after the retreating figure. 'I think I can manage, Missus. After all, I've only been doing the job fer twenty years. And I wouldn't say no ter a cuppa, if there's one going.'

Her mind still elsewhere, Ellen replied amiably, 'Yes, of course, Agnes. I'll bring one out to you.'

Taken by surprise, Agnes mumbled, 'Oh, right. Yeah, thanks.'

Arthur, as usual at this early hour, was busy baking. Glancing up, he looked at his wife and gave her a curt nod, before returning his attention to the job in hand. Ellen sighed impatiently, then shrugged. So he was still sulking, was he? Well, let him. Putting the kettle on, Ellen thought back to earlier that morning when Mr Dobbs had arrived, his sooty face wreathed in smiles. That was until Ellen informed him his services in unloading and carrying the monthly supply of coal to the basement would no longer be required. Arthur had been present at the time, but instead of backing her up, he had launched into a spate of apologies. Reliving the scene Ellen felt a fresh burst of anger. Watching and listening to the pitiful spectacle, Ellen had cringed. And when Mr Dobbs, his countenance no longer amiable, had begun a blistering attack on Ellen for what he termed an act of treachery, Arthur, instead of making a stand and taking his wife's side, as most men would have done, had quickly washed his hands of the whole affair, placing the situation squarely on Ellen's shoulders. Ellen could still feel the shame at seeing her husband, the man who was supposed to put his wife first, humiliating himself. She had thought that hearing Mr Dobbs berate her would have infused some gumption into Arthur. But he had let her down and for that she would never forgive him, nor respect him ever again. Ignoring the bulky form, Ellen set about making the morning tea.

'Well! Don't you have anything to say?' Arthur's voice cut into the silence of the stuffy room.

Turning to face him, Ellen looked at the plump, red face, filled with self-righteous indignation and immediately went on the defensive. 'Excuse me, Arthur?' she answered, her voice deceptively soft. 'I'm not sure what you mean. Unless of course you're referring to that embarrassing spectacle you made of yourself this morning.'

Still smarting after being, as he thought, put into an impossible position, Arthur flinched as the truth struck home. His lower lip quivering, he tried to restore his humiliated ego, even though, deep down, he knew full well he had disgraced himself. Not only in the eyes of Mr Dobbs, whose scathing look had said more than mere words could ever convey, but also in the eyes of the one person he so desperately wanted to impress. But instead of admitting his shame, Arthur, like most ineffectual men, tried instead to shift the blame on to the nearest person, and that person was Ellen.

Drawing himself up to his full height he said angrily, 'You made me look a right fool in front of Mr Dobbs. And all for some little guttersnipe. Huh! It says a lot for me, doesn't it? How do you think I felt with you taking over the conversation, pushing me out of the way as if I counted for nothing . . .'

Ellen rounded on her husband, her fierce anger more than a match for Arthur's feeble blusterings. 'How do I think you felt?' she shouted. 'How do you think *I* felt having to witness my husband, the one man I thought I could depend on for support, practically grovelling to the coalman, apologising over and over until I felt I would be sick with shame. Even if

41

you didn't agree with me, you should have stood by me; that's what husbands do. I wouldn't have minded you having a go at me in private, but to take Mr Dobbs' side against your own wife, well that says it all, doesn't it, Arthur?'

Her voice had risen and Arthur, already humiliated once today, didn't want everyone in the shop hearing his wife laying into him as well. Adopting a different tack, he put his hands up in a feeble attempt to stifle Ellen's tongue. 'All right, all right, love. There's no need to broadcast our private lives to everyone.'

Coming nearer he laid a tentative hand on Ellen's arm, his face now sheepish, but Ellen, who once would have relented, now shook off the offending hand with disdain. 'There you go again, Arthur. Thinking of yourself as usual. All you're worried about is saving face, but I think it's a bit late for that, don't you?'

The colour in Arthur's face deepened, and it had nothing to do with the heat of the kitchen. His stomach churning, he tried once again to pacify Ellen. 'Please, love, let's leave it, eh? I mean . . .' He uttered a small, nervous laugh. 'There's no point in going on about it, is there? I mean, it's done now, so let's forget about it, all right, love?'

Ellen's gaze remained stony. In their short married life, there had been plenty of times she had kept quiet, or given in, just to keep the peace and to keep Arthur happy. But that had been when she was still in awe of the man who had saved her from the workhouse and was willing to be a pliable and good wife. But things had changed. *She* had changed. With a sudden start of awareness, Ellen knew that her life would never be the same again.

Arthur, too, was experiencing the same emotions, and felt a surge of blinding panic. What he had always feared now seemed to be in danger of happening. His feverish mind turning this way and that, he tried to think of the best way of defusing the situation. Should he be compliant and ask Ellen's forgiveness? Or should he do what he should have done that morning and make a stand? To be the strong man Ellen wanted him to be. The silence in the stifling room was becoming unbearable, then Arthur made his decision. Unfortunately it was the wrong one. Adopting a manly stance, he said firmly, 'Now then, Ellen. I think I've been very patient with you over this sorry affair. I let you humiliate me in front of a very close friend, just to keep you happy, but no more. In future the running of the business will be mine and mine alone. You may continue to serve in the shop, if you wish, but you will disassociate yourself from making any decisions and you will also sever all ties with the boy. There'll be no more encouraging the boy to come here for hand outs in return for some small job that could easily be done by either you or Agnes.' Well into his stride, Arthur began to pace the room, his hands clasped behind his back.

He should have looked instead at his young wife to see her reaction to his words. But he was too far into his new persona to notice the danger signs in Ellen's face. 'I know it will be difficult for you, so I think it would be wiser if you stayed upstairs tomorrow and let me deal with the lad. Don't worry,

I'll let the boy down gently. Now then, why don't we kiss and make up.' Stretching his arms wide he smiled, 'Come here, you silly little thing. Come and give me a cuddle, and we'll forget all about it.'

Her entire body seething, Ellen, not trusting herself with what she might do or say if she stayed here a moment longer, shot Arthur a withering look, and said, 'You know what you can do with your cuddle, Arthur. Oh, I'm getting out of here. I can't bear to be in the same room with you.' Grabbing her coat from behind the back door Ellen shrugged her arms into the heavy sleeves, for once not noticing the stifling heat of the kitchen.

Behind her Arthur hovered anxiously. 'Hang on, love. Where d'you think you're going at this time of the morning?' Frantic now, he began gabbling. 'Now look, love, there's no need for this. You're blowing the whole business out of proportion.' Unthinking, he grabbed hold of Ellen's arm. With an angry twist she broke free and without bothering to look back, she strode out of the back door into the dark alley.

Never in her life had Ellen walked the streets in the dark, either in the morning or at night. Yet it would have taken a brave man to accost her in the mood she was in. Gradually, her anger turned into a new emotion, a feeling of elation, but more than that, for the first time she felt a rush of self-respect. No longer would she be dependent on Arthur; she didn't need him any more. She knew now she was well capable of looking after herself. But the feeling of euphoria was shortlived and quickly replaced by a wave of shame. Her footsteps slowed as a wave of remorse swept over her. Poor Arthur. It wasn't his fault. After all he had done for her and this was the thanks he got. Her steps dragged as reality returned. She had to go back. There was nowhere else for her to go. She had no one to turn to. Even if she had, she would never be so cruel as to just walk out without a word. She owed Arthur more than that, much more.

'We must stop meeting like this.' A deep voice cut through her thoughts.

Her head coming up sharply, Ellen felt her body relax when she saw who the man was. With a genuine smile, she said merrily, 'Good day, Mr Parker. And how are you this fine morning?'

Ted Parker tipped his hat back further on his head to see better, thinking at first he had mistaken Ellen for someone else. But the light from the end of the alley reassured him that this bright, seemingly carefree woman was indeed Ellen Mitson. Yet the change in her compared to yesterday's encounter was so marked that Ted wondered if she was unwell.

'You all right, Mrs Mitson? You seem different today. Has something happened?'

Ellen was standing so close to the man their breaths mingled in a fog of white mist. The semi-darkness covered them like a cloak and Ellen felt again the pull of attraction. In spite of the fact they were in an open space, that the dawn was just breaking and the sound of people's voices as they set about the start of a new day floated all around them, never had Ellen experienced such a feeling of intimacy. Gathering her wits, she spoke crisply. 'I'm fine, Mr Parker, but thank you for asking'. Ellen had to tip her head to see Ted's concerned gaze.

'Well, in that case, I'd best get off, else I'll miss my tram.' Again tipping his hat, Ted Parker made to walk on, puzzled by the sudden change in Ellen Mitson. Moments later his eyebrows rose in amazement when he felt himself being halted in his tracks by a small but strong hand on his arm.

'You own your own stall, don't you, Mr Parker?'

Thoroughly confused now, Ted looked down into Ellen's enquiring eyes. 'Yeah, that's right. But what . . .'

Linking her arm through his, Ellen smiled broadly. 'I was just wondering if you could do me a favour, Mr Parker. Oh, and please call me Ellen . . . Ted.'

Feeling more confident than she had ever felt in her life, Ellen hugged the muscled arm tighter as she walked with Ted towards the tram stop, chatting away as if she had known the handsome man all her life.

Her newly found confidence would have been shaken if Ellen had known she and Ted Parker were being sharply observed by a pair of malicious eyes.

CHAPTER FOUR

Agnes, her weathered face alight with mischief, handed over a penny change to the last customer from the early morning rush. 'There yer go, Edna,' she said. 'Sorry yer had ter wait, but Miss Fancy Pants decided ter take herself off somewhere.' Tapping the side of her nose Agnes winked, leaned over the counter then, lowering her voice, she added, 'Now I'm not one ter gossip, Edna, am I?'

Edna Brown, a regular visitor to the bakery, shook her head in agreement, while privately wondering who Agnes thought she was kidding. Everyone knew Agnes Handly was the worst scandalmonger in the district. But not wanting to miss out on a bit of juicy gossip she said vigorously, 'Nah, Agnes, yer ain't like that. An' yer know I can keep a secret. Come on, woman, spit it out.'

Looking over her shoulder towards the kitchen to make sure Arthur wasn't in earshot, Agnes preened herself and said gleefully, 'Seen her with me own two eyes I did. I'd just popped out ter see if the milkman was in sight, 'cos I was gasping fer a cuppa, an' what d'yer think I saw?' She paused, relishing the moment, a moment she'd been waiting for ever since that little madam had turned her world upside down. 'Her lady-ship, walking down the street, as bold as brass, with that Ted Parker. Arm in arm they was, talking and laughing for all the world to see, like they was a respectable couple walking out, and poor Mr Mitson, not knowing anything about what his wife's getting up to.'

Edna Brown looked at Agnes with distaste. She didn't like her, not many people did. Yet Agnes had once been popular, always good for a laugh and a chat – until young Ellen had arrived on the scene. Now Agnes was a bitter, middle-aged woman, whose only enjoyment in life was in trying to put young Ellen down at every possible opportunity. But Agnes hadn't finished yet.

'I don't know what ter do fer the best, Edna. I mean ter say. Should I tell Mr Mitson what's going on, or keep quiet? What would you do in my place?'

Engrossed in their conversation, neither woman heard the tinkle of the bell heralding another customer in the shop until an icy voice, dripping with scorn, snapped angrily, 'I know what I'd do, Agnes Handly. I'd keep me bleeding gob shut, before someone does it fer yer, yer spiteful old cow.'

Both women jumped as the familiar voice filled the bakery.

Whirling round, Agnes opened and shut her mouth

like a fish out of water. 'Oh . . . sorry, Nora, I didn't see you there,' she spluttered, her face reddening in the force of Nora Parker's anger.

The newcomer looked at the woman behind the counter, her sharp eyes taking in every detail of Agnes' body from top to toe. As usual, Agnes was dressed in the drab brown skirt and black shiny blouse she always wore in the shop. Her hair, scraped back from the plain face was a dull brown, liberally streaked with grey strands. For a split second, Nora Parker felt a spark of sympathy for Agnes. Everyone knew of her feelings for Arthur Mitson, but even twenty years ago, Agnes Handly had been a plain woman, and the passing years hadn't been kind to her. What chance had she against the youth and beauty of Ellen Mitson? Then Nora remembered the vindictive words she'd overheard, and any sympathy she might have had for Agnes disappeared in a renewed rush of anger.

Hugging her thick black shawl tight to her chest she snapped, 'That's bleeding obvious, otherwise yer wouldn't have been shouting yer mouth off about my Ted. And I'll tell yer something else, Agnes Handly.' The short, stout woman bristled furiously. 'My Ted could 'ave any girl he wants. He don't 'ave ter go sniffing round a married woman, like some men. So you mind what yer say in future, understand?'

Caught out, Agnes had no choice but to try and bluff her way out of the awkward situation. 'Now, 'ang on a minute, Nora. All right, so I shouldn't 'ave been talking about your Ted, but I know what I saw and—'

49

'I don't give a monkey's what yer think yer saw. If my Ted was with young Ellen, then it was all perfectly innocent. Not that you'd think that way. Yer've 'ad it in fer that young girl from the start, an' we all know the reason why ... don't we?'

Caught between the two sparring women, Edna Brown stood back to enjoy the spectacle of Agnes getting a taste of her own medicine, but her enjoyment was shortlived.

Desperate for some kind of diversion, Agnes turned on the hapless bystander. 'Is there anything else yer want, Edna?' Edna Brown squirmed uncomfortably before shuffling grudgingly out of the warm bakery.

Left alone, the two women eyed each other, neither willing to give ground. 'Well, d'yer want something, or is this just a social visit?' Agnes, back in control once more, glared at the equally angry woman on the other side of the counter.

Still fuming at hearing her beloved son's name muddied, Nora Parker wrestled with her conscience. There was nothing she'd like better than to tell Agnes Handly where to stick her bread, but Arthur Mitson's bakery was the best one in Hackney. Besides, it wasn't as if her custom was lining Agnes' pockets, and she had no quarrel with Arthur. Squaring her shoulders, she said waspishly, 'No, it ain't a social visit. If I was wanting a bit of company, I wouldn't come ter you for it. I'll 'ave a large cob, and half a dozen buns ... please.'

Her face sullen, Agnes wrapped the bread and buns and was placing them on the counter when Arthur came through from the kitchen into the shop, a worried frown on his face.

'Have you seen Ellen, Agnes? Oh, hello, Nora, I didn't see you for a minute. How are you?'

Shooting a warning glance in Agnes' direction, Nora Parker answered pleasantly, 'I'm fine, thanks, Arthur. And yourself?'

Forgetting his troubles for the moment Arthur smiled. 'Oh, same as always, Nora. Hot and flustered.' Not one for idle chatter, Arthur trailed off self-consciously.

Her heart going out to the kindly man and knowing Agnes would stick her poison in at the first available opportunity Nora said casually, 'I saw your Ellen a little while ago, Arthur. Me an' my Ted met her outside about . . . Ooh, ten, fifteen minutes ago. She said she fancied a bit of fresh air, so my Ted offered ter stay with her. He's like that, my Ted. Didn't want ter leave Ellen on her own, not round these parts, even if it did make him late fer work. Not that it matters what time he gets ter Hoxton, seeing as he's his own boss, like yerself, Arthur.' She smiled at Arthur with genuine kindness. Seeing the look of relief that crossed the plump face, Nora shot a gloating look at the seething Agnes thinking, 'That's scuppered your plans, yer spiteful old cow.'

The bell over the shop jingled again and all eyes turned to the door as Ellen entered the bakery. Sensing the strained atmosphere, Ellen looked from one face to the other, her conscience stabbing at her like a knife. Nora quickly came to her rescue.

'Hello, love. I was just telling Arthur 'ere how me

and Ted met yer outside and stopped fer a bit of a natter. I hope he walked yer back before he went ter work.'

Ellen shot her a grateful look. 'Yes he did, Nora, thanks.' Guilty at her earlier treatment of Arthur, Ellen strolled over to her husband's side and took hold of his hand. 'Actually I was trying to talk Ted into giving young Micky a job. I'm afraid I made a bit of a nuisance of myself.' Looking back at Nora, Ellen said sheepishly, 'Will you tell Ted I'm sorry for waylaying him in the street, please, Mrs Parker. He's much too nice to tell me off for putting him on the spot.'

Nora patted Ellen's arm affectionately. 'Don't be daft, love. He may be kind, but he ain't no fool when it comes ter his business, but I'll tell him what yer said.' Putting her purchases into a straw basket she smiled widely at Ellen. 'I'll have ter get a move on, or I'll be late fer me cleaning job. Not that I 'ave ter work . . .' She directed a triumphant look at the now dejected Agnes. 'My Ted's always telling me ter stay at 'ome and put me feet up, 'cos he earns enough without me working. But like I said ter him, What else would I do with meself all day? Nah! I like ter keep busy. Still, it's nice ter know there's someone ter look after yer when you're getting on in life; not like some poor cows with no family or friends ter fall back on. Anyway, I'll be off now. 'Bye love, 'bye Arthur.'

The deliberate snub to Agnes was not lost on Ellen, but Arthur, his mind put at rest, didn't notice. Squeezing Ellen's hand he asked tentatively, 'All right, love?'

Ellen smiled at him. 'Yes, Arthur, I'm fine now. I

just needed to get out for a while. I feel much better now.' Turning to Agnes she said, 'If you want a break, Agnes, I'll take over now.'

Her teeth gritted tightly, Agnes answered scathingly, 'I've only been working an hour. I think I can last a bit longer before I need a break.'

Ellen and Arthur exchanged amused glances, their differences forgotten. Relieved beyond measure that his fears had been unfounded, Arthur placed an affectionate arm around Ellen's shoulder. 'In that case, Agnes, I think me and Ellen will take our break now while you hold the fort. It may be just on eight, but we've been up since five-thirty.'

Humiliated beyond measure Agnes lowered her eyes and began to busy herself rearranging the already carefully stacked bread.

As soon as Ellen and Arthur had left Agnes stopped in her task. Praying there would be no more customers for a few minutes so she could have some time to herself she let her body sag. Then, like a woman twenty years her senior, she wearily sank down on the three-legged stool behind the counter, her mind in turmoil. When she had seen Ellen and Ted Parker together she had been sure she'd finally got one over on the young scut who had ruined her dreams of one day marrying the man who had been the centre of her life since she was nineteen – over twenty-three years ago. Twenty-three wasted years.

She had just turned nineteen when she'd come to the recently opened bakery in search of a job. At that time, Tom Mitson, Arthur's father, had been in sole charge of the baking while Arthur served in the shop.

Wanting to train his only son in the same line of work, Tom Mitson had taken Agnes on so that Arthur would be free to learn his father's trade. Tom had been a widower for five years and Agnes had become almost like a daughter to her employer. He had been a lovely man, kind and compassionate, always treating Agnes like family instead of an employee. She had been devastated when he had died of a heart attack at the age of fifty.

Arthur too had been beside himself with grief and, for a time, Agnes had thought the distraught young man would go to pieces. If Agnes hadn't been there for him, to offer a shoulder to cry on, to listen to his outpouring of grief any time of the night or day coupled with genuine affection and support, Arthur would have shut himself away and let the business, the business his father had spent so many years building, go to the wall. At the time, all Agnes had wanted was to see Arthur through his grief. Then, about a month after his father's death, Arthur had asked Agnes to stay the night and she had been only too happy to agree. The affair had been brief. While Agnes had fallen head over heels in love, it had soon become increasingly obvious that Arthur was regretting the affair. He would find excuses to avoid being alone with her and, being the timid man he was, he hadn't been able to pluck up the courage to address the problem. Loving him as she did, Agnes had ended it, simply to ease his peace of mind. She had imagined that, given time and space, Arthur would come to love her as much as she loved him. But that had never happened. Over the years Agnes had been forced to accept that Arthur would only ever see her as a friend and she had been content with the arrangement. Like most people, just being in close contact with a loved one had kept her happy.

Then he had brought the young, frightened girl into their lives, and Agnes had known immediately the reason why Arthur had never married. She had known where he spent most of his weekends, for he would regale her with all the news of his friends, and their beautiful daughter. Agnes had listened dutifully, glad he was spending his spare time with old friends. But how could she have imagined that one day the child Arthur was besotted with would end up as his wife. Shaking her head in misery, Agnes lowered her head into her hands as she remembered that she had encouraged Arthur to keep in contact with his friends, believing that by doing so there would be less chance of him meeting another woman.

When his friends had died, it was Agnes who had helped him, once again, to deal with his grief. And although she had been genuinely sorry that the couple had died in such horrible circumstances, nonetheless she had been grateful to be needed again. She had even welcomed his decision to bring the orphaned Ellen into his home. But the moment she had clapped eyes on the pretty young girl and seen the open adoration shining from Arthur's eyes whenever he looked at her, Agnes had known all the years she had devoted to the man she loved had been in vain. But what caused Agnes the most pain was the certain knowledge that she had forced the hasty marriage. If she hadn't started to spread rumours, Ellen would have grown up eventually and moved on and out of Arthur's life. But no, she had been so eaten up with jealousy she hadn't been able to stop her tongue from cultivating vicious gossip. Banging her hands on her knees in despair she whispered to the empty shop, 'Why couldn't you have kept your big gob shut? If you'd welcomed Ellen with open arms it would have been easy enough to bring up the suggestion of adoption to Arthur and he would have done anything to keep Ellen by his side.' And, in due course, she, Agnes, might have been able to persuade Arthur to make his family complete by marrying her. All this could have been possible, if she had made a friend of Ellen. Because, to be fair, the young girl had a kindly nature and would have been grateful to have an older woman to talk to, especially at a time when she was still getting over the loss of her mother. But Agnes, hurt beyond words and feeling betrayed, had turned into a nasty, spiteful woman. She knew too that Arthur wanted her out of the shop, but was too timid to sack her and that the new Mrs Mitson might not have any such qualms.

The change in Ellen since her marriage was incredible. During the past few months she had become more confident, more at ease with the customers, and had toughened up considerably. Judging by the fierce argument she had overheard about the coalman and the subsequent sighting of Ellen arm in arm with Ted Parker, Agnes was sure that Ellen was beginning to regret tying herself to an older man. The only hope Agnes had now was that the marriage would fail. Yet even if it did, unless she changed her ways she would never have Arthur.

Like Ellen, Agnes had also changed, but she had changed for the worse. She didn't even like herself and if she didn't, how could she expect anyone else to?

Was it too late to change? More importantly, could she change?

The bell sounded and immediately Agnes rose to her feet, a smile pasted on to her lips, ready to greet two of her regular customers.

Above the shop Ellen too was wrestling with her emotions. The short time she had spent in Ted Parker's company had been a revelation to her. She had felt like a different person. Ted had made her laugh like she'd never laughed before and the memory of her close proximity to the charismatic man was enough to send shivers of delight tingling up her back. Then the image changed to the look of utter relief on Arthur's face as Nora, bless her, had quickly defused what might have been a tricky situation. Well, she'd had her moment of reckless enjoyment, but it must never happen again. Not that anything untoward had happened between her and Ted, but she knew that in different circumstances things could have turned out very differently. She was painfully aware of the attraction she felt for Ted and, although she was still naive, she wasn't that inexperienced to realise Ted Parker felt the same way.

Later that night, as she lay awake beside the sleeping Arthur, she tried to recapture the pleasant memory of being in Ted's company, knowing that was all she would ever be able to have, a pleasant memory.

Yet instead of conjuring up the handsome features, the image that floated into Ellen's mind was that of a pair of striking blue eyes staring out of a blackened face.

CHAPTER FIVE

'Coo, Micky, are we rich? Can we get a place of our own now?' Molly, her blue eyes as wide as saucers, stared in fascinated awe at the silver coins lying in her brother's open palm. The open hero worship mirrored in Molly's eyes was a much needed balm to Micky's bruised ego. Now he was back at the place he called home, he forgot the feeling of hurt pride he had experienced on learning the deception Ellen had engineered in order to give him a job – and a very well paid job at that. He had been so proud, thinking he was helping the pretty young woman, until he'd realised she had only given him the work out of pity. All the way home he had felt a curious feeling of despondency, unable to understand why he felt so low when he had five shillings in his pocket. The money was a small fortune to someone in his position, so why, he had kept asking himself, wasn't he jumping for joy? Now he was with Molly, basking in

ANNA KING

her adoration, Micky found his self-respect returning.

Feeling quite pleased with himself he strutted up and down the cramped room. After all, he had every reason to be proud of himself. It wasn't even eight o'clock yet and already he had earned five bob. As soon as they had breakfasted on the currant buns Ellen had slipped under his arm on his way out of the shop he intended to try the markets to see if he couldn't earn another couple of bob. Of course, to earn even a shilling, he would have to work without a break for the remainder of the day. The job he'd had this morning was a one off: he wouldn't be that lucky again. And he said as much to his little sister who was still staring at him in awe, her cheeks bulging with the remains of one of the freshly cooked buns.

'Come on, Moll, eat up. The sooner we get down the markets, the sooner I can earn some more money.'

The hope in Molly's eyes dimmed. 'Does that mean we're not rich, Micky? Have we got to stay here for ever?'

Seeing the disappointment in his little sister's eyes, and hearing the resignation in her voice, Micky felt his elation deflating like a balloon suddenly deprived of air. Reaching out he caught hold of the small hands. 'No, we're not rich, Moll. But I promise you we ain't gonna stay 'ere for ever.' But Molly remained unconvinced. Gently lifting her chin so he could look her straight in the eyes he said softly, 'We'll 'ave ter stay 'ere fer a while longer, Moll. I don't like it any more than you do, but I'm doing the best I can.'

Her chin wobbling, Molly asked tearfully, 'Couldn't we get a room somewhere, Micky, just fer a few nights?

I hate it 'ere when yer not with me. I'm always frightened that man will get me, but I wouldn't be frightened if we was in a proper room with a lock on the door. Can't we, Micky, please? Just fer a little while.'

Swinging his head from side to side Micky muttered, 'I'm sorry, Moll, honest I am. I know five bob seems like a lot of money, but it won't last long if we go spending it on lodging houses, then we'll be right back here. And maybe even this place might be gone soon. If the council knocked the other 'ouses down, then they must be planning ter build something else here. That's why I want ter save up as much money as I can so we can get a proper place ter live fer good, not just fer a few days.' Pulling a face, Micky gave his sister a playful shove. 'Come on, girl, eat up. Unless yer want ter stay here on yer own while I'm down the market.'

The threat, although made in a joking way, galvanised Molly into action. 'All right, Micky, I'm hurrying,' she said anxiously, swallowing the last remnants of food in a loud gulp. 'You'll 'ave ter have a wash first though, Micky. You look filthy.'

Taken aback, Micky looked down at himself. He'd forgotten he was covered in coal dust. Then he had an idea. They may not have enough money for proper lodgings, but they could afford a trip to the local baths. Micky quickly added up the money he had put by. With the five bob he'd earned this morning, plus the one and threepence he had hidden behind a loose brick in the bedroom, he had enough not only for a much needed bath for himself and Molly, but also, if they looked carefully around the stalls, they might even be able to afford a change of clothing. In their hasty departure from the workhouse, Micky hadn't given a thought to the practicalities of life.

'Yer right, Moll. I ain't gonna get any work looking like this. Mind you, yer ain't exactly smelling of roses either. How about we treat ourselves ter a real bath, and a new set of clothes ... Well! Not new clothes, but we should be able ter pick up something on the rag stall. What d'yer say, Moll?'

Molly's eyes lit up. 'Oh, that'd be lovely, Micky. Will we 'ave ter have a cold bath? Or can we afford a hot bath with real soap and a soft towel?'

Micky cast a reproachful look at his sister. Hot baths with nice soap and soft towels were a luxury they couldn't afford, not at fourpence each – especially when they could have a cold bath with carbolic soap and a rough piece of cloth to dry themselves with for tuppence. Those opting for the second-class cubicles had to be in and out within ten minutes. Which, given the conditions, was all the time anyone wanted.

'Hang on, Moll. I just told yer we 'ave ter be careful with the money we've got. A hot bath with soap and proper towels will cost eightpence for the pair of us, that's unless we share a bath, an' I don't think that's allowed ... Oh, what the hell,' he grinned, wanting nothing more at this minute than to put the smile back on Molly's face. 'All right, we'll 'ave the best. After all, there's no telling when we'll be able ter afford it again. Besides, we deserve a treat. Just don't go getting used ter the good life, girl. Don't forget what Mum used ter say. Look after the pennies, and the pounds will look after themselves.'

At the mention of their mother, Molly's eyes filled with tears, her lower lip beginning to quiver as she whispered, 'I miss me mum, Micky, and me dad. I wish they was still alive and we was all back in our old house.'

Looking into Molly's tearful face Micky felt his own eyes begin to prickle. Sometimes, in those few seconds after waking, he would often forget the past, and expect to hear his mother shouting up the stairs for him to get up. Then harsh reality would set in. He would look at the sleeping Molly beside him, both of them lying on the filthy mattress, covered by blankets that were practically crawling. But it was the smell that sickened him the most. And not just the smell from the bedding, but from Molly and himself. A sudden resolution rose in his chest. If he had to work every minute of the day and night to get Molly out of this hell hole, then he would. In the meantime, he was going to give his little sister a day to remember.

At five o'clock that evening, Micky and Molly, tired but happier than they had been in a long time, returned to their dilapidated home. Two hours later Molly was fast asleep, leaving Micky to think back over their day.

First they had visited the second-hand clothes stall where Micky, after much good-natured haggling, had bought a thick jumper, a heavy black jacket and a pair of boots that still had plenty of life left in them. But his most cherished purchase was his first pair of long trousers. For Molly, he had splashed out on a red woollen dress and a grey coat. As she hadn't been pounding the streets every day as he had the past months, Molly's boots were still in reasonable condition. When it had come to the question of undergarments, however, the embarrassed Micky had left those essential purchases to his sister. Which would have been fine if Molly, never having shopped before, hadn't picked up a pair of grey long johns, calling out at the top of her young voice, 'Micky, will these fit yer? Come an' 'ave a look.' As amused glances came their way, Micky, mortified as only the young can be at being shown up in public, had quickly grabbed the offending garment, stuffing it into a tatty canvas bag someone had dropped in the street.

Their next stop had been the public baths in Mare Street. The attendant had looked at the two filthy children with open distaste. But Micky had stood his ground and when, some twenty minutes later, they had emerged clean in body and clothing, they had looked at each other and grinned widely. Their soiled clothing had been left in a cubicle, as a kind of present to the snooty attendant who had treated them so shabbily. Feeling very grown up in his long trousers, Micky had tried to maintain some kind of dignity. But Molly, her waist-length blonde hair freshly washed and dripping wet, had grabbed his hand crying joyously, 'Come on, Micky, race yer ter the market.' And Micky, forgetting his new status, had broke into a run, dragging the laughing Molly alongside him.

The exciting day had continued with Micky getting six hours' work in Well Street market. Even Molly had earned fourpence by fetching mugs of tea from the local café for the stall holders. By the time the traders had begun packing up for the day both children were exhausted. Yet it was an exhaustion tinged with happiness, for it was the first day since their escape from the workhouse that they had spent the entire day together.

To round off the day, Micky had bought fish and chips for their supper, and they ate the hot food straight out of the greasy paper.

The only damper was having to return to the hovel they'd occupied for the past months. In that time they had grown accustomed to the filthy conditions, grateful only that they had a roof of sorts over their heads. Now they were clean, it was doubly difficult for them to lie on the stained, damp mattress. But, as Micky had told Molly, it was either that or sleep standing up until they could afford decent accommodation. When Molly had fallen asleep, Micky counted the money he had left by the light of their last remaining candle, which reminded him he would have to buy some more tomorrow. Which also meant forking out more money. Sighing softly he removed the loose brick. Keeping sixpence back, he placed the rest of the money in his secret hideaway, a satisfied smile on his lips. Even with the visit to the baths and the new clothes plus the fish and chip supper, he still had almost six shillings left, thanks to the generosity of the market traders. Grimacing with distaste, Micky forced himself to lie down beside Molly. If he knew for sure how long they could remain here, he would do his best to make the place habitable. Second-hand furniture and bedding could be bought reasonably cheaply if you weren't that fussy. And anything would be better than their current living conditions.

The long day started to creep up on him, his eyes becoming heavier despite his efforts to stay awake. He wanted to make plans for tomorrow, but his tired body had other ideas.

His last conscious thought was of Ellen Mitson as he wondered if she had remembered his plea to ask around in search of a permanent job for him. He doubted she would have found anything for him yet. After all, he had only asked her this morning. Still, there was no harm in going to the bakery to enquire. Also he was anxious for the baker's wife to see him in his new finery. His face flushed in the darkness and with an angry shrug of his shoulders, he muttered, 'Soppy sod.' Blowing out the candle he turned on his side and let sleep overtake him.

CHAPTER SIX

It was a bright, sunlit day and Ellen was preparing to go shopping. The reason for her expedition was double-edged. She normally did her weekly shopping down Well Street market, but today, as she had for the past month, she was going to Hoxton instead. Passing through the bakery she stopped to speak to Agnes. 'I won't be too long, Agnes. Is there anything I can get you while I'm out?'

Agnes, in the process of serving a customer, looked up and, in a pleasant tone, said, 'No thanks, Ellen. I got my shopping yesterday.'

Buttoning up her light blue, three-quarter-length coat, Ellen said, 'Are you sure you can cope, Agnes? After all, Saturday is our busiest day.'

Agnes passed over a large crusty loaf to the bemused customer, whose face was etched in surprise at the friendly chatter between the two women who were normally at each other's throats. After all, half the fun of coming to this bakery was listening to Ellen and Agnes trade insults. Yet even though, on the surface at least, the women appeared to have patched up their differences, there was an undeniable air of tension, as if they were merely playacting.

'Don't yer worry about me,' said Agnes. 'I can cope fine on me own. You 'ave a nice day, an' don't worry about rushing back. After all, the trams'll be packed. You'd be better off going ter Well Street, but if yer've taken to going ter Hoxton, you'll 'ave ter fight yer way onto the tram. Couldn't be bothered meself. Still, I expect yer want ter see how young Micky's getting on now Ted Parker's given him a job.'

Feeling her cheeks growing hot, Ellen pulled on a pair of cotton gloves, adjusted her straw hat and said lightly, 'Well, yes, I am interested in how Micky's getting on, but Hoxton's a much bigger market than Well Street, and besides, it's nice to have a change of scenery now and then.'

Agnes nodded sagely. 'Course it is, love. You get off now, and enjoy yer day . . . Oh, by the way, your hair looks much better hanging loose; takes years off yer.'

Ellen nodded, a fresh rush of blood staining her cheeks, then held the door open for the customer, her sharp eyes noting the curiosity mirrored in her face. But she wasn't going to waste time gossiping, especially as whatever she said would be elaborated on. With a pleasant 'Good day, Mrs Stone' Ellen walked towards the tram stop, her nose sniffing the warm, spring air. It was amazing how the arrival of spring, with its warm weather and longer days, could lift one's spirits.

Stepping out quickly, Ellen was lucky to catch a tram straight away. As it was now ten-thirty, the morning rush was over and Ellen found herself with a choice of seats. Skipping up the circular stairs, she flopped down on a wooden, slatted bench, her gaze centred on the street below and the people going about their daily business on this fine day.

Once she had paid her fare, she was left alone with her thoughts and as she recalled the events of the past month, a tender smile came to her lips.

Not only had Ted Parker given Micky a trial run, starting with one day a week, Micky had impressed Ted so much that he now employed the young boy four days a week. And the change in Micky was nothing short of a miracle.

That first day he had come into the shop, wearing his long trousers and thick jacket, his face a mixture of self-consciousness and pride, Ellen's heart had gone out to the boy who was trying so hard to make an impression. Even Agnes had made a kind comment about Micky's appearance, causing the young boy to look at her suspiciously, as had Ellen, especially as it was only the previous day that Agnes had tried her best to make trouble between her and Arthur. If it hadn't been for Nora Parker's intervention, Ellen's moment of recklessness in waylaying Ted, which had been perfectly innocent, could easily have turned into a very nasty situation.

The following day Ellen had braced herself for further remarks, and had been taken aback when Agnes had arrived at her normal time and, for the first time since Ellen had known the woman, had greeted Ellen with a smile and a pleasant 'Good morning'. Then Micky had arrived, and he too had been greeted in the same vein. Ellen and Micky had exchanged bemused glances, and Ellen was trying to think up some small job for Micky to do when Ted had entered the shop and offered Micky a day's work on his stall down Hoxton Market. Ellen could still remember the look on Micky's face as he glanced from Ellen to Ted, not wanting to let Ellen down, but desperate for the chance of a real job. Ellen could also remember the joy that had spread over Micky's handsome features when she had told him there wasn't any work for him that day and to go along with Ted. He would break a few hearts, would Micky, when he got older. In fact he was already charming the women and girls that frequented Hoxton Market.

For the past month Ellen had visited Hoxton every Saturday and for the life of her she didn't know who she most liked seeing, Micky or Ted.

Taking a deep, satisfying breath of air, Ellen relaxed against the wooden seat. Everything seemed to be going well in her life and for that reason alone she felt a slight shiver of apprehension. Her misgivings centred solely on Agnes' sudden change of character. Not suspicious by nature, Ellen had been trying her utmost to establish a fresh acquaintance with the new, amiable side of Agnes, but it was hard going.

Then she shrugged impatiently. What was she worrying about? Maybe she was wrong and Agnes really had turned over a new leaf. According to Arthur, Agnes had once been a friendly, pleasant woman. He hadn't added that Agnes had only changed since their marriage; he hadn't needed to, that much had been evident. But maybe Agnes had accepted the situation and was now finally trying to make amends for her surly behaviour since Ellen had arrived at the bakery.

Her stop approaching, Ellen got to her feet, then, gripping the iron rail, she carefully descended the twisting stairs to the safety of the platform.

Joining the bustling crowd, Ellen made her way to Ted's stall, her stomach churning as it always did when she was about to see the man who had helped turn her life around. For if she hadn't bumped into him on that fraught morning, she would probably have returned home, still angry and frustrated, her minor triumph over the coal delivery soon paling into insignificance. Instead, something in Ted's character had brought out qualities in her she hadn't known she possessed. She had begun the slow process of growing into adulthood, her inner strength already coming to the fore. But since making a friend of Ted, she had found herself growing stronger each day. In an ironic twist of fate Ellen was following in her husband's footsteps. For where Arthur's life had revolved around his weekly visits to her parents' house, so was Ellen's life revolving around her weekly visit to Hoxton Market – and Ted. Approaching the fruit and vegetable stall, Ellen's face broke into a wide smile as she heard Micky shouting out to the passing crowd as if he'd been working the market all his life.

Standing back a pace so Micky wouldn't know she was watching him, Ellen looked on fondly, thinking as she did so how much Micky had changed from that first meeting when he had appeared outside the bakery, a bedraggled, filthy urchin who, even in dire need, had refused to take charity. Most people, Agnes for instance, would have quickly shown the young boy the door, or even called the police and turned him in for begging, a practice the police frowned on. But Ellen had seen past Micky's outward appearance to the dignity and character that lurked beneath his ragged apparel. And she had been proved right. She soon spotted Ted who had been hidden from her view by the large crowd. Unconsciously she adjusted her straw hat and flicked a long, thick strand of chestnut brown hair over her shoulder before walking towards the stall.

Ted was talking and laughing with two women, while at the same time filling brown bags with items of fruit and vegetables. One of the women was flirting openly with Ted, who was obviously enjoying every moment of the attractive woman's attention. The sight caused Ellen's stomach to constrict as if she'd been physically punched. All her earlier elation vanishing, Ellen, her heart thumping, her throat tight, turned to go. Then Micky spotted her.

'Oi, Ellen, hello. Ain't yer gonna buy anything today?'

Caught out, Ellen was forced to approach the stall, a tremulous smile on her lips. 'Hello, Micky. I was going to have a look around first, but don't worry, I'll be back later to get my usual order.'

Micky grinned. 'I'll get it ready fer yer, Ellen. Then yer can pick it up when you've finished looking round. Or I could drop it off on me way 'ome tonight; save yer carrying it all the way back home on the tram, won't it?'

'Thanks, Micky, that's kind of you. I might take you up on that offer,' Ellen said, her eyes flickering towards Ted, who was still enjoying the flirtatious banter with the two women.

Following her gaze, Micky's smile faltered. Pushing back his flat cap, he called out over-loudly, ''Ere, Ted, Ellen's here.'

Immediately Ted turned away from the hovering women, the grin on his lips widening. Teasingly he said to the woman who was practically draping herself over his body, 'See yer next week, darling. Don't do anything I wouldn't do.'

The blonde woman smiled brazenly. 'Don't leave much fer me ter do then, does it, Ted?'

Her face burning, Ellen fiddled nervously with the clasp of her leather bag. Then she looked at the woman and her spirits lifted once again. For the woman was looking daggers at her and Ellen, knowing her presence had caused a pique of jealousy, felt a surge of confidence.

'Hello, love.' Ted's deep, throaty voice brought the smile back to Ellen's face. Especially as he had dismissed the two women in favour of her company. 'Managed to get away from the sweat shop then?' He leant nearer, his body almost touching hers, sending a delicious shiver of delight down her spine. Then his hand reached out and touched the long, shining chestnut hair, adding softly, 'I prefer your hair like this. That other style didn't suit you at all, made yer look like an old married woman.'

Ellen's smile wavered. 'Well, I am, aren't I? Well . . .' she laughed self-consciously. 'Not exactly old, but I am married.'

Ted leant his head back as if to get a better view, then, his voice sombre, he said, 'Yeah, I know. I'm reminded of it every time I walk past the bakery.'

Her eyes met his and, for a brief few seconds, their gazes locked. Then someone pushed past them and the spell was broken.

Embarrassed by the chemistry that flowed between them and anxious to get the conversation back on a safer level, Ellen looked over at Micky and asked, 'How's Micky getting on?'

Following her gaze, and knowing what she was feeling, Ted replied, 'He's a natural. I admit I only gave him a chance as a favour to you, but it's turned out the other way round. I've lost count of the boys I've had working for me over the years, hoping I'd find someone reliable and honest, so I could set up another stall at one of the other markets. And with Petticoat Lane on Sunday morning, I could make a lot of money. But none of 'em was any good; well, not so much that, but there wasn't any I could have trusted to run me stall without me keeping an eye on 'em. Now I think I might just 'ave found the right bloke – 'Ere, just listen to him.'

Ellen turned her attention to Micky, smiling fondly as she heard him shouting out to the crowd with all the confidence of a grown man. 'Come on, ladies, yer won't find anything better than this stall if yer looking fer fresh fruit and veg.'

An elderly woman was busily inspecting a pile of

oranges. 'These fresh, are they, mate? I don't wanna get 'ome and find 'em as dry as me old man's throat on a Saturday night.'

'Fresh?' Micky picked up an orange and threw it in the air. Catching the large piece of fruit he said loudly, 'Picked 'em meself from an orchard in Kent at five o'clock this morning.'

The woman grinned, showing more gums than teeth. 'Yer cheeky devil. Go on then, I'll 'ave three, not that I believe a word of what yer say, but yer deserve a sale fer yer cheek.'

Deftly depositing three large oranges in the woman's shopping basket, Micky added, 'What about some nice juicy apples ter go with 'em?'

Fishing around in her purse the woman looked at Micky with a twinkle in her eye. 'I suppose yer picked those fresh this morning an' all?'

Micky winked, his cherubic face a picture of innocence. ''Course I did. I wouldn't lie ter a nice lady like yerself, now would I?'

Chuckling loudly the woman nodded. 'All right, lad, I'll 'ave a couple.' Again Micky had the apples in her basket before she could change her mind. But he wasn't finished yet. Knowing he was being watched by his new boss and Ellen, Micky, anxious to make a good impression, took the woman's money saying quickly, 'How about a bit of veg, love? Can't 'ave a good roast Sunday dinner without veg, can yer?'

Thoroughly enjoying the banter, the woman turned to another customer waiting to be served and cackled, 'Cheeky little beggar, ain't he? An' handsome into the bargain. Gawd, if I was thirty years younger I'd put a smile on yer face that'd last fer a week. Go on, I'll 'ave a cauli and half a pound of Brussels and that's me lot, mate. Yer'll 'ave me skint at this rate.'

Ellen and Ted exchanged amused glances, glances that were tinged with pride. As they were shoved once again, Ted, his eyes twinkling mischievously said, 'Look, we can't stand 'ere, we'll be trampled. How about 'aving a bit of lunch with me? I was gonna go for me dinner about now anyway.'

Ellen hesitated. There was nothing she would like more than to spend time in this man's company, but she was treading on dangerous ground. Then her head came up defiantly. Why shouldn't she enjoy herself? After all, nothing could come of her association with Ted. It wasn't as if she was planning to have an affair with the man. Even as the thought crossed her mind, an image floated before her eyes and such was the nature of her thoughts she blushed as if she had spoken her deepest secrets out loud. 'Thank you, Ted. I'd like that very much. Will Micky be all right on his own?'

Ted gave a hearty laugh. 'Get on with you. Ain't I just been telling yer how pleased I am with him? 'Course he'll be all right.' Taking hold of her arm he bent down and whispered in her ear, 'I suppose you know the lad's got a crush on you, poor little bleeder. Still, he'll get over it in time. At his age I was always falling in love with a different girl every week. Mind you, it's a different kettle of fish if it happens when you're older.'

Deliberately ignoring the last comment, Ellen's eyes darted to where Micky had a queue of women waiting to be served. Startled, she said, 'Don't be silly. He's just a boy and I'm a married woman.'

Ted snorted, 'You don't have to keep reminding me you're married. As for Micky, he's nearly fifteen, and you're not much older . . . Look, let's go and get something to eat, 'cos if one more person pushes me I'll land 'em one.' His disarming smile was evidence he would do no such thing. Then without warning he put his arm around her shoulder pulling her tight to his side, the sudden action sending a jolt through her entire body. For a second, a picture of Arthur swam before her eyes, but she instantly dismissed him from her mind. She wasn't doing anything wrong, she kept reminding herself, as she allowed Ted to lead her through the busy market towards a pub on the corner.

She was still telling herself the same thing when she emerged from the pub, slightly tipsy from the large gin and tonic she had swallowed without thinking. Not used to alcohol, the beverage had gone straight to her head.

Ted, amused at first, had become concerned at the thought of Ellen travelling home on her own in the state she was in, especially as it was his fault. Sitting her down on a bench outside the pub, he went back to the stall and told Micky he was taking Ellen home and would be back as soon as possible.

On the journey home, Ellen leant against Ted's side, revelling in the close, intimate contact of the man she was falling in love with . . .

Arriving at the bakery, Ted, his face troubled, now said, 'You'd better go in the back way and have a lie down before anyone sees you.'

Ellen giggled. 'Don't care if they do. I've had a wonderful day, well worth a telling off for. Thanks, Ted.' Fumbling in her bag for her key Ellen stumbled. Ted's arms came out circling her waist. The giggle that was forming instantly died as she stared up into the intense eyes, for once holding no trace of mockery.

Then his lips came down on hers. It was merely a touch, but the effect on Ellen was overwhelming. Instantly sober she pulled away, saying in a trembling voice, 'I'd better get in. Arthur will be worrying. Goodbye, Ted.'

Ted released her reluctantly. Well aware of Ellen's emotions he touched her lips with the tip of his finger saying tenderly, ''Bye, darlin'. See you next week.'

Her legs weak, Ellen let herself into the bakery. Quietly she made her way up the stairs to the bedroom, repeating over and over in her mind Ted's last words. He had called her darling. She knew the term was used frequently by East End men to any woman. It meant nothing – or did it? Hearing Arthur calling out to her as he came up the stairs, Ellen quickly lay down on the bed. She heard Arthur saying her name, but pretended to be asleep. For what seemed an age Arthur hovered beside the bed while Ellen fervently prayed for him to go. There was no way she could face him, not just now. When he finally closed the door, Ellen peered cautiously over her shoulder, sighing with relief at finding herself alone. Making herself more comfortable on the four-poster bed, she closed her eyes, intending to go over in her mind the events of the day and where she was going to go from here. Her emotions in turmoil, she vowed never again to visit the market. And if Ted came into the shop, she would treat him like any other customer. Yes she would, she told herself vehemently. But no matter how hard she tried to convince herself, she knew that come Saturday she would be back in Hoxton, to spend what little precious time she could with Ted.

CHAPTER SEVEN

After Micky had delivered Ellen's fruit and vegetables as promised, he hurried home, worrying as he always did if Molly was all right. He hated leaving her alone. It had been bad enough when he was doing a few hours' work here and there, but since Ted had taken him on four full days a week she was on her own from early morning until he got home. In all the months he had been praying for such an opportunity, Micky hadn't thought of what would happen to Molly once he was gainfully employed. As he broke into a run, he pondered on life's ironies. Here he was, getting what he and Molly had dreamed of since they had run away from the workhouse, yet neither of them had thought of the practical side of Micky working permanently.

Then there was the fear he might come back one evening and find the place they called home demolished and Molly taken into care. If that happened he would have no chance of getting her back. And, as if that wasn't bad enough, there was also the constant worry of the pervert Kenneth Wells hanging around.

'Molly, Moll, I'm home, mate.'

Instantly Molly's pretty face peered over the balcony. 'Ooh, I'm glad you're 'ome, Micky, it's really lonely being on me own.'

Scrambling up the rope, Micky gave his sister a hug. 'I know, Moll, but it can't be helped. Anyway, it's not so bad now the days are lighter for longer. And I've got a treat fer yer. I got us some pie and mash for tea. Ted gave me an extra tanner, 'cos he 'ad ter leave me looking after the stall on me own this afternoon. It was only fer a couple of hours, but he didn't 'ave ter pay me extra. I'd've done it fer nothing. He's a good bloke is Ted. Anyway, like I said, seeing as I got a bit extra, I thought we deserved a bit of a treat – you especially.' Reaching out a hand he stroked her cheek lovingly. 'You're a good girl, Moll, and brave. I know it must be horrible fer yer being on yer own all day. It wouldn't be so bad if yer could go out an' play, but yer can't, not with that . . .' He stopped abruptly. Molly didn't need reminding of Kenneth Wells. The poor little cow was terrified of even putting her nose out of the door in case he was lying in wait. Then there was the possibility of a truant officer spotting her. Laying out the hot food, Micky sighed. Gawd, but life was difficult.

They were halfway through their meal when Micky had an idea. 'Listen, Moll. It's the Easter holiday next week. How about yer come with me down the market? I mean, no one will notice why you're out of school, 'cos like I just said, all the schools will be closed down. What d'yer think?'

With a loud shout of pure joy, Molly flung her arms around her brother's neck. 'Oh, Micky, d'yer mean it? Will I be able to help yer out on the stall?'

Micky held her for a few seconds before gently disengaging her arms from the stranglehold she had on his neck. 'Hang on, mate. You can come with me, but yer won't be able to work with me.' Seeing the joy fading from the heart-shaped face, Micky said softly, 'Look, Moll, just think about it for a minute. No one knows about you. If I'd told Ellen and Ted I had a sister, it'd be all right, but if I suddenly turn up with you in tow, they might become suspicious and start asking awkward questions.'

Molly, her face solemn, said timidly, 'They might not, Micky. You could always just say you'd never mentioned me 'cos yer didn't think about it.'

Shaking his head Micky answered, 'Nah, that wouldn't work. It's been bad enough lying to Ellen and Ted that I've got a mum. I've got really friendly with both of them and they'd know something was wrong if I suddenly produced a sister. They're not stupid, Moll. Maybe neither of them would wonder why I'd never mentioned yer, but I don't think they would. Besides, now things are looking up, why take the chance?'

'Well, what am I gonna do all day down the market?' Putting the last morsel of pie into her small mouth she said excitedly, 'What if yer said I was a mate of yours, an' yer was looking after me during the school holidays while me mum was at work?'

His mouth full, Micky stared at his sister in amazement. She might be only eight, but she had the sense of a girl twice her age. Ellen and Ted wouldn't question Molly's presence if he followed her suggestion. Why hadn't he thought of it himself? Her idea was perfect.

Grinning widely he said, 'You sure yer only eight, Moll? Yer ain't a woman midget, are yer?'

Molly looked back at him in surprise. 'Don't be silly, Micky. You've always said if someone wanted something badly enough there was always a way round it. And if yer can't tell anyone I'm yer sister, then it's obvious yer could say I was just a mate you was looking after during the school holidays.'

Micky could only look at Molly in awe, mingled with pride and relief. Give her a few years and his sister would be able to look after herself – she might even end up looking after him too. Chuckling quietly Micky gave Molly an affectionate hug.

With the problem of the Easter holiday out of the way, the two youngsters talked until the evening turned into darkness. As always, her stomach full, her mind at rest, Molly was asleep by nine o'clock, leaving Micky to his dreams.

He now had nearly two pounds saved, enough to get them a room in a boarding house. Yet even though he was sure Ted would keep him on, after so long of worrying about money, Micky was afraid to touch his savings in case something happened and he lost his job. Then he looked down at the sleeping Molly. So young, so vulnerable, so brave, never complaining, other than of her fear of being left alone. In that instant

Micky made up his mind. On Monday he would take Molly with him to work. And once the school holiday was over he would look for a room, preferably with a landlady who didn't ask awkward questions. A frown crossed his forehead. That was something else he had to sort out. At some point he would have to get Molly into a school: he didn't want her growing up without any education. But that particular problem wasn't pressingly urgent. Even if he waited until he was sixteen, legally a man, he could still get Molly four or five years of schooling.

His head reeling with all the difficulties he had to deal with, Micky pushed everything to the back of his mind for the time being.

The minute he did that, his thoughts turned to Ellen. And as always, his stomach began to churn and he could feel his cheeks burning.

Even if he was older, he still wouldn't have a chance with her, not with her being married. And even if she wasn't, he knew he hadn't a hope in hell with Ted in the picture. He had seen the way they looked at each other and, each time he witnessed the growing affection blossoming between them, he experienced pangs of jealousy. Angry with himself, he punched his pillow. He was fond of both Ellen and Ted and at the same time he was jealous and for that alone he felt guilty. Ted had been good to him, as had Ellen. It wasn't fair for him to resent the man who had given him a job when no one else would. Not only that, Ted had bought Micky another change of clothes from the second-hand stall. And now Micky had a regular wage coming in, he was able to buy Molly two cotton dresses from a similar stall at the other end of the market. Both of them slightly faded, but to Molly, who had always been so particular about her appearance, the dresses could have been brand new, so delighted was she with them. They could even afford a bath every week, so what was he moaning about?

To take his mind off things that were so painful to him, Micky instead turned his thoughts to finding accommodation. No matter what lodgings he found Molly would still have to stay out of sight when he wasn't around, but at least he wouldn't have to worry about her, not once she was safely installed behind a proper door that locked. But for the next couple of weeks she would be with him every second of the day; more importantly she would be able to roam the market without fear and be able to smell and savour the spring air, instead of the fetid odour that pervaded the derelict house.

As Micky thought about his future, Ellen was doing much the same thing. Seated in her dining room with Arthur fast asleep in the armchair opposite her, Ellen put down the book she had been trying to read and leant her head back against the winged armchair.

The alcohol she had consumed earlier had long since worn off, leaving her with a throbbing headache and a guilty conscience to match. What had she been playing at leading on Ted like she had? She was now feeling deeply ashamed of her behaviour. Looking across at the sleeping man Ellen felt a surge of affection for her husband. She owed him so much, he deserved better. If only they could get away for a holiday. Oh, that would be marvellous.

For not only would it do Arthur, who to her knowledge hadn't had a holiday in the past twenty years, a power of good, it would also take her away from the temptation of Ted Parker. Excited by the notion, Ellen visualised her and Arthur, just the two of them, enjoying some time together, with nothing or no one to disturb them. Then common sense set in, ruining her plans. Arthur would never agree to close down the bakery for a weekend, never mind a couple of weeks. It wasn't that he couldn't afford to take a holiday, he was comfortably well off, but being the type of man he was, he'd be afraid of losing the loyal custom he'd accumulated over the years.

Arthur stirred, yawned loudly and smiled tiredly. 'Sorry, love. I don't seem able to stay awake once the day's business is over; must be a sign of old age creeping up on me.'

Quickly taking advantage of his words, Ellen left her chair and came and sat by his feet, resting her chin on his lap. Staring up into the plump face she said earnestly, 'Arthur, why don't we have a holiday? God knows you deserve one. What do you think, Arthur? Why, a couple of weeks by the seaside would do you a world of good.' Looking up at him anxiously Ellen felt her spirits drop at the look of agitation that crossed his face.

Running a shaking hand over his chin he replied, 'You know I can't just take two weeks' holiday, Ellen. I mean who'd look after the business? No, I'm sorry, love. It's out of the question.' Seeing the look of resignation on Ellen's features Arthur added kindly, 'Please, love, don't look like that. I'd love to go off for two weeks with just the two of us, but you must see it's impossible.'

Angry and frustrated, Ellen went back to her chair, her face sullen with disappointment.

'Look, Ellen, what if we had a weekend away? I could prepare the bread on Friday and leave it to rise overnight, like I always do and, if Agnes agrees, she can come in early Saturday morning and put them in the oven. As for the cakes, Agnes can make those by herself. In fact I could ask her to stay overnight, it would make it easier for her. I'd have to offer her extra money of course, but I'm sure she'd love the chance of running the place by herself. Then we can get away after the shop closes on the Friday we plan to go away and stay until Sunday night. I know it's not what you wanted, but at least that's better than nothing ... Ellen ... Ellen, love, say something.'

Staring at the wall, Ellen said dully, 'Forget it, Arthur. It wouldn't be worth the effort. By the time we got anywhere, we'd be lucky to have a couple of hours before it was time for bed. We'd have Saturday, but you'd want to get an early start on Sunday morning, so as you'd be back in time to prepare the bread for Monday. No, forget I said anything. If we can't get away for a proper holiday, then I'd rather stay at home.'

Judging by the set look on Ellen's face, Arthur knew he had found himself in a no-win situation, so he did what he always did and took the line of least resistance. Yawning excessively, he stood up and stretched.

'I think I'll have an early night, love. That's if you don't mind?' He peered at the downcast head, a sure sign his wife was not in the mood for talking.

'I'm sure I'll manage without your company until bedtime.' She glanced up at the mantel clock, adding scathingly, 'Though that'll be some time yet, seeing as it's only just on eight o'clock. Still, I'm sure I can find something to occupy me. I can read my book, or if I get really desperate, I could always ask Agnes up for a cup of tea and a chat. She is still downstairs, isn't she? She always stays late on Saturday to give the shop a good clean, all ready for Monday morning.' Throwing her head back she uttered a mirthless laugh. 'Good God! I must be desperate for company.'

Sheepishly Arthur said, 'I thought you two were getting on better lately.'

'Huh! You mean she's making an effort. She doesn't like me any more now than she did when I first arrived. But, yes, if she's willing to make the effort, then I suppose I should do the same and give her the benefit of the doubt . . . Oh, go to bed, Arthur. You're making me nervous hovering there like a lost soul.'

Tentatively Arthur moved forward to kiss Ellen good night, but Ellen was in no mood for his embrace, which she made evident by turning her head sharply, leaving Arthur's pursed lips landing inches from her ear. Dispirited, Arthur gave up trying to make amends and left the room, grateful for some time to himself.

The door had barely closed after him when there came a tap on the dining-room door. Without looking up Ellen called out, 'Come in, Agnes.'

Agnes entered the room. 'I just come up ter say I'm

leaving. Everything's done downstairs.' As she spoke, Agnes' eyes roamed the room. It was a modest size and comfortably furnished. The walls were papered with red and gold flock wallpaper, which complemented the dark red carpet. A highly polished cabinet took up most of the far wall. In the middle of the room stood a table big enough to seat six people, its mahogany surface covered by a green baize, tasselled tablecloth. There were various knick-knacks on the shelves, and on either side of the elaborate fireplace were two dark green, velvet armchairs. The mantelpiece itself held an assortment of figurines, that had once belonged to Arthur's mother. The centrepiece was a beautiful, gold-edged clock that had been in the Mitson family for over a century. Agnes had been in this room countless times over the years, yet each time seemed as if it was the first. It was a room she had once imagined would be hers and Arthur's.

Ellen watched Agnes' face closely, trying to imagine what was going through her mind. 'Thanks, Agnes. It's good of you to stay behind on Saturday.'

Agnes shrugged. 'It's what I've always done. Anyway, I'm off now.' Her eyes darted to the closed bedroom door. Ellen could plainly see the disappointment mirrored in Agnes' eyes as she realised she wouldn't be seeing Arthur now until Monday.

In a moment's compassion Ellen said quietly, 'Why don't you sit down for a minute, Agnes? I was going to make a cup of tea. Maybe you'd like to join me?'

Taken by surprise by the unexpected request, Agnes hesitated, but only for a few seconds. There was nothing or no one to hurry home to. She had been living on her own since her mother's death fifteen years ago. Which was why she stayed in the bakery for as long as she could, especially on Saturdays, in order to put off returning to the dreary terraced house to spend yet another lonely evening on her own. Lifting her shoulders she said, 'Yeah, all right. Ta, Ellen.'

'Well, come and sit down then, Agnes. Make yourself at home while I put the kettle on.' When Ellen had left, Agnes walked across the room, her steps slow and awkward, half expecting that Ellen was making fun of her and would return and retract the invitation. Seating herself in the chair Arthur had recently vacated, she perched uncomfortably on the edge. There was much Agnes disliked about Ellen, but she had to admit the young woman wasn't of a spiteful nature. If she had been, then she, Agnes, would have been given her marching orders long since. With this thought in mind she removed her black shawl and wriggled her bottom further back in the velvet chair.

'Here we are.' Ellen came bustling into the room carrying a silver tray. 'I've brought some cakes too. I hope you're hungry. I know I am.' Setting the tray down on the occasional table between the armchairs she said brightly, 'Help yourself, Agnes. Don't stand on ceremony.'

Ellen poured out the tea, then held the china cup to Agnes. Amiably she said, 'Actually, Agnes, I wanted to ask you a favour.'

Agnes, having just taken a sip of the hot beverage, spluttered and began coughing. 'A favour! From me?' Her initial thoughts returning, Agnes laid down her cup and asked suspiciously, 'You 'aving a laugh at me, Ellen? 'Cos if yer are, then it's a rotten trick ter play. Pretending ter be all friendly an' . . .'

'Just a moment, Agnes,' Ellen interrupted quickly. 'You know me better than that. I know we're not the best of friends, but I would never make fun of anyone out of spite.'

Relaxing slightly, Agnes picked her cup up and took a long swig before saying warily, 'Yeah, sorry, Ellen. It just came as a bit of a surprise, that's all. You asking fer my help, I mean.'

Anxious to put the older woman's mind at rest, Ellen, cutting two large slices of sponge cake, said tentatively, 'The thing is, Agnes, I've been trying to get Arthur to take a holiday, but it's like talking to a brick wall. As far as I know he's not had a holiday since his father died and that's over twenty years ago.' Handing over a generous slice of cake Ellen gave a short laugh. 'Hark at me telling you something you already know. After all, you've known Arthur much longer than me. By what Arthur's told me, his father was very fond of you, looking on you as part of the family. That's why I'm asking you for help. You're the only one I can think of to help me. Surely there's some way to persuade Arthur to take a holiday, without worrying about losing the custom he's built up over the years.' Staring at Agnes over the top of her cup Ellen asked, 'Can you help, Agnes? I mean, isn't there someone who could see to the baking while you ran the shop? And of course you'd be compensated for the extra work. You might even think about taking some time off yourself later on in the year, because

91

you've never had a holiday either. And with all the hard work you've put in over the years you deserve a break. But of course, that's up to you. So, what do you think?'

Agnes' mind was racing furiously. This was the last thing she had imagined Ellen would ask of her. Taking a bite out of the sponge cake she said, 'How long was yer thinking of being away?'

Now it was Ellen's turn to feel uncomfortable. Her voice hesitant she said, 'I was thinking of two weeks ... but I'd be happy with just a week,' she added swiftly as she saw the surprised look on Agnes' face.

'Two weeks! Bleeding 'ell. You ain't asking fer much, are yer? People like Arthur and me don't go on holiday fer a fortnight. A long weekend in Southend is as much as we can look forward to.'

Ellen's face fell in disappointment. 'That's just what Arthur said,' she replied dismally. 'Thanks anyway, Agnes, it was worth a try.'

'Hold yer 'orses, Ellen. I said a weekend was all most people have, I didn't say it was impossible. Give me a minute ter think, will yer?'

While Agnes consumed her cake, Ellen waited in trepidation. Then, putting her cup and plate down, Agnes nodded. 'I might be able ter help. I ain't promising, mind.' She peered at Ellen.

'Oh, no, I understand,' Ellen answered eagerly. 'I don't expect you to come up with an answer tonight, but if you could think of anything I'd be ever so grateful.'

Silence settled on the room again with Ellen holding her breath expectantly, then Agnes, coming to a decision, said briskly, 'I could ask Bill Cummins. He's been retired for two years now, but he might be grateful fer two weeks' work. Arthur knows Bill well. He's a good baker, is Bill. And if yer trust me ter look after the shop fer a couple of weeks, and Bill agrees . . . Well, I don't see as how Arthur could object, especially if yer work on him. He'd do anything ter keep yer happy, would Arthur.' A note of bitterness had crept into Agnes' voice. Rising to her feet she said, 'I'll go round ter Bill's 'ouse tomorrow, and see what he says. Don't get yer 'opes up though, but I'll do me best.' Getting to her feet she glanced at the book lying on the arm of Ellen's chair and asked, 'Good book, is it?' She picked it up, her eyebrows rising. '*Less Miserables*. That sounds like a barrel of laughs. What's it about anyway?'

Without stopping to think Ellen said, 'Actually it's pronounced, *Les Miserables*, and it's a bit complicated to explain.'

Immediately Agnes went on the defensive. 'In other words, I ain't clever enough ter understand.'

'Oh, no, that isn't what I meant at all,' Ellen said quickly, seeing the fragile truce disappearing. 'I'm having trouble with it myself. Victor Hugo's books are hard going. Basically it's about a young man who steals a loaf of bread to feed his starving family and ends up spending eighteen years in prison before escaping while on parole and a policeman who won't give up looking for him. That's the gist of it.'

Agnes' eyebrows rose as she handed the heavy tome back to Ellen. 'Eighteen years fer stealing a loaf of bread, that's a bit steep, ain't it?'

Ellen smiled. 'Well, he had extra time added on for trying to escape, but the story was written nearly thirty years ago and set in France. I imagine their laws are much harsher than ours. At least, I would hope so.'

Finding the conversation increasingly difficult, Ellen began to fidget nervously. Here she was, discussing a literary classic, when it was painfully obvious that Agnes' idea of a good read was a penny romance novel. An uncomfortable air pervaded the room as each woman tried hard to say something that would be of interest to them both, but it was no good. They simply had nothing in common.

Agnes was the first to speak. Standing up she said over-loudly, 'Well! I'll be off then. Like I said, I'll pop round ter see Bill tomorrow, an' I'll let yer know what he says on Monday, all right?'

Relieved Agnes was going, Ellen smiled gratefully. 'Thanks, Agnes. I really appreciate your help.'

Showing Agnes to the door Ellen hesitated slightly before putting out her hand in a gesture of friendship.

For a few awkward seconds her hand hovered uncertainly in the empty space between them. Then Agnes, her face betraying her embarrassment, reached out and clasped Ellen's hand.

'Yeah, well, I'll do what I can.' Agnes, her face averted in confusion, relinquished the soft palm.

''Bye, Agnes and, once again, thanks.'

Ellen had hardly closed the door when Arthur appeared from the bedroom. 'What on earth did you ask her up here for?' he demanded.

Swinging round, Ellen replied tartly, 'I thought you wanted an early night. As for Agnes, it's you that's

94

always moaning about me trying to get on better with her. And since she's been a lot friendlier lately, I thought it only fair to meet her halfway.'

Wearing an ankle-length, striped nightshirt Arthur looked a comical figure, but his face wasn't wreathed in his usual amiable smile. 'Yes, well, I've been thinking about that. I've known Agnes a lot longer than you, Ellen, and I don't trust her. If she's being friendly, then she's up to something, you mark my words.' Running a hand over his thinning hair, Arthur looked deeply disturbed. He admitted to himself that in the beginning he had prayed for Agnes and Ellen to get on, but he had now changed his mind. In fact, he wanted rid of the woman whose very presence always caused him to feel guilty and uncomfortable. He wanted to forget the past, and he couldn't do that while he was daily reminded of his brief, reckless fling all those years ago. His face reddening, Arthur mumbled, 'Look, Ellen, she's got to go. I know she's been on her best behaviour lately, but to be truthful, I always feel uncomfortable in her presence. It's time she went. She'd be better off. And I was thinking that maybe, once she's gone, I could offer young Micky some extra work when he's not working for Ted on the stall.'

Ellen's face was like stone. 'And who's going to tell Agnes her services are no longer required, Arthur? Because don't think I'm going to do your dirty work for you. If you want Agnes out of the shop, then you can tell her yourself. But I think it's a pretty dirty trick to play on a woman who's given the best part of her life to you.'

95

Ellen sat down, her face set. 'I'm going to read for a while, Arthur. And I'd rather be on my own. Goodnight.'

Agnes was at the shop door when she remembered she'd left her shawl upstairs. She was outside the door of the dining room when she heard Arthur's voice. And what he said made the blood drain from her face. She couldn't believe it. Not only did he want her out, but he was intending to give her job to that little guttersnipe Micky Masters. Her feet like lead, Agnes, her shawl forgotten, slowly descended the stairs. Once out in the street she didn't notice the chilly nip in the air. She didn't notice anything. All she could hear was Arthur's voice, and with each word she died a little inside. She was outside her house when she suddenly couldn't face another night on her own. Turning round she made her way to the nearest pub. Maybe a couple of gins would wipe away the hurtful words she had overheard.

But they would still be there in the morning. They would be with her for the rest of her life.

CHAPTER EIGHT

It was just after ten-thirty when Agnes staggered out of the Red Lion, her legs stumbling as she drunkenly tried to negotiate the cobbled road.

Passing the fish and chip shop she was suddenly reminded she'd had nothing to eat since the slice of sponge cake Ellen had given her and that wasn't enough for a woman of Agnes' healthy appetite. Finding the heady aroma irresistible, she weaved into the shop and ordered plaice and chips.

Too hungry to wait until she reached home, Agnes tore at the greasy paper and began cramming the delicious, greasy food into her mouth.

As she turned into the next street she saw a youth running in front of her. Normally she wouldn't have paid any attention. But even at this distance, she was sure she knew the young boy from somewhere. Her bleary eyes followed the running figure and when the boy passed under the street lamp on the other side of the road Agnes realised why the figure looked so familiar.

It was that brat, Micky Masters. Agnes followed Micky, not knowing why she was bothering, but powerless to stop herself. Finishing off the tasty meal, she threw the wrapping into the gutter, her eyes never leaving the figure in front of her. Then she stopped abruptly and ducked behind a wall as Micky furtively looked up and down the narrow street. Her forehead screwed in bewilderment as he stopped in front of a derelict house, before running inside.

A crafty smile crossed Agnes' lips. So that was it, was it? No wonder the boy was always cagey whenever the subject of his parents and home came up. The little bleeder was a runaway, though obviously not from the police or else he wouldn't have come regularly to the shop, or taken Ted Parker's offer of a job. Nah! He must be a workhouse brat on the run. Her thin lips spread into a grim smile of satisfaction. So, Mr bleeding Mitson was gonna give her job to Micky Masters, was he? Well, she'd soon put a stop to that idea. Then the smile dropped from her face.

What if he was just some orphan squatting wherever he could find a place to stay before moving on? Also she knew how fond Ellen was of the lad, not to mention Ted Parker. He was another one who had taken the young boy under his wing. Not quite so confident now, Agnes knew she had to have time to think before she did or said anything.

Then she let out a scream as a man stepped out in

front of her. Her first thought was of Jack the Ripper. He'd come back to his old haunting grounds!

'Dear me, I'm sorry I startled you, dear lady. I mean you no harm I do assure you.'

Agnes eyed the well-dressed man suspiciously. There was only one reason a man like this one was hanging round these parts, and that wasn't just to do a bit of sight-seeing.

Backing away she said harshly, 'Look, mate. If yer looking fer a tart, you've picked on the wrong woman. You'd best get yourself down ter Bethnal Green Road. There's plenty of 'em 'anging about down there.'

Kenneth Wells barely restrained himself from laughing in the old hag's face. As if any man would be interested in an old soak like her. The only reason he had accosted her was the fact she seemed to be interested in young Micky's business.

Stepping back a pace to remove any threat he might pose, he waited to judge the woman's reaction. The gesture worked. His sharp eyes noting the slight relaxation of the scraggy body, he raised his top hat, saying smoothly, 'Please, Madam, I'm a happily married man, and . . .'

Agnes laughed sneeringly. 'That ain't never stopped a bloke before, mate.'

Kenneth shook his head reproachfully. 'I do assure you, Madam, my intentions are quite honourable. The reason I'm down these parts is because I'm trying to keep an eye on my nephew and niece.'

Seeing the puzzled look cross Agnes' face he continued. 'You see, I noticed you too seemed interested in my nephew Micky, and I wondered if we might be of assistance to each other.' He stopped, then seeing he had her attention, hurried on. 'My brother and sister-in-law died just before Christmas, God rest their souls.' He bowed his head in a reverent manner. 'Naturally I asked their children to come and live with my wife and me. Young Molly was only too willing, poor little soul. Lovely child, she is. But Micky, now he's a different kettle of fish altogether. He refused point blank my offer of accommodation, saying he was capable of looking after himself and his sister. Well . . .' He spread his arm towards the derelict house. 'I ask you, dear lady. Does that look to you like a respectable place for a young girl to be left on her own while my no-good nephew walks the streets looking for work?'

"'Ang on a minute, mate,' Agnes interrupted him. 'I know Micky well enough, but he ain't never mentioned no sister before.'

Again Kenneth pointed towards the ruined building with his gold-capped walking stick. 'Of course he hasn't. He knows that if the authorities were informed of Molly's present mode of living, she would be taken away immediately. But, if I may ask, Madam, what is your interest in my nephew?'

Agnes hesitated. There was something about the well-spoken gentleman she didn't like.

Kenneth was quick to note her sudden distrust. Doffing his hat he said smoothly, 'As it seems we have something in common, may I buy you a drink? We can talk in comfort instead of standing out here on the street.'

Again Agnes hesitated, then nodded. It wouldn't

do any harm to listen to what the bloke had to say. And she'd get a few free drinks into the bargain.

Side by side they walked back towards the main road.

CHAPTER NINE

''Ere, what's up with Agnes? I ain't seen her looking so pleased with 'erself since before Arthur went an' got himself married. If I didn't know better, I'd think she'd got 'erself a bloke. I told yer my Bert saw her with some toff just before the Mitsons went away, but I didn't think nothing of it at the time. I mean ter say . . . !' Mabel Smith raised her eyebrows in disbelief. 'The poor cow would be 'ard pressed ter find an ordinary bloke, let alone one with a bit of class. What d'yer think, Nora?'

Nora Parker cast a disparaging glance first at the woman by her side, then to the object of their discussion. Both women had known Agnes for over twenty years and, as her neighbour Mabel had just commented, neither of them had seen the middle-aged woman looking so happy, nor as smart since the early days when Agnes had imagined that one day Arthur would eventually get around to proposing to her. Yet since the Mitsons had gone on holiday, leaving Agnes in charge of the business, a remarkable change had come over the once dowdy woman, a change that hadn't gone unnoticed by her regular customers.

Agnes, well aware of the speculation surrounding her and thoroughly enjoying her sudden elevated status, smiled sweetly at the elderly woman at the front of the queue as she put a large crusty loaf into a wicker basket. 'That'll be tuppence, please, Mrs Cox.'

'Thanks, Agnes ... Er, um, so how yer been lately, ducks? Got any news ter share with yer mates, love? Only we couldn't 'elp but notice how 'appy yer've been lately, an' we was wondering like, if yer had anything ter tell us? 'Cos I was only saying ter me daughter the other day, "Rene," I said, "if anyone deserves a bit of 'appiness, it's Agnes; especially after the way Arthur treated her."' The grey head bobbed up and down as if to add weight to her words. 'Now, I ain't just being nosy, love, you've gotta lot of friends round these parts ... Nah, it's true, ducks, honest.' The bird-like features of Mrs Cox crumpled at the look of scorn that suddenly flashed across Agnes' plain face. Shuffling her small frame awkwardly she murmured, 'Well, I can't stand 'ere gossiping all day. I'll see yer, ducks.' Nodding to the two other women waiting to be served, both of whom had been listening intently to the conversation, the red-faced woman hurried out of the warm bakery.

Agnes, her expression betraying none of the pleasurable churning in her stomach at finding herself the centre of attention, asked airily, 'Made up yer minds yet, ladies? Only yer've been 'ere long enough ter buy up 'alf the shop. Unless yer've just come in ter 'ave a nose round.'

Instantly the two remaining customers sprang to life, their faces turning hard at the insulting tone in Agnes' voice.

As Nora Parker made to come back at Agnes with a suitable retort, Mabel quickly gave the irate woman a discreet nudge in the ribs. Then, her features folding into a warm smile she said sweetly, 'Don't be daft, Agnes. We was just wondering who your gentleman friend was, that's all.'

Taken by surprise, Agnes' cheeks began to burn in confused embarrassment. Noting her uncomfortable reaction, Mabel hurried on gleefully. 'Ah, that surprised yer, didn't it? My Bert saw yer with him in the Nag's Head just before Arthur and Ellen went away. Proper toff my Bert said he was. Now yer can't blame us fer wondering who he is. I mean ter say, it's only natural we should be curious.' Agnes lowered her head in startled bewilderment, and Mabel smiled triumphantly at Nora before resuming her probing. 'Come on, woman, don't keep us in suspense. Who is he? Where d'yer meet 'im?'

Regaining some of her composure Agnes raised her head and stared hard at the two women. Women who had been coming into this shop for years and never before had they shown any genuine interest in her, apart from the time Arthur had brought Ellen here to live. Oh, they'd been out in force then, the nosy, hypocritical old cows. Making snide remarks and looking at her with feigned sympathy. How she had come to hate them all. These women with their boring, dependable husbands and snotty-nosed children, children who were now grown and rarely visited their parents, unless they were after something, apart from Nora, whose son Ted still lived at home and supported his widowed mother. The rest of them were still living in tiny houses, for ever in debt and having to watch every penny. And they had the cheek to feel, not only superior to her, but sorry for her as well! At least she owned her own house and she had a few bob in the bank, which was more than the majority of her customers could lay claim to.

Now she had a man in her life. And not just any man, but a man of means, a real gentleman.

The only fly in the ointment was Kenneth's wife.

Kenneth had been very open about his marital status right from the start and, as their friendship had blossomed, brought about by their mutual interest in young Micky Masters, Kenneth had confided in her that his wife's health, which had never been robust, was now so bad the doctors had told Kenneth to prepare himself for the worst. It was that evening that he had taken hold of her hand and, his eyes locked onto hers, had asked her gently if she would wait until he was free. A tingle of excitement ran up her spine as she recalled the intimate moment.

'Well, come on, woman, out with it.' The loud voice jerked Agnes back to the present and the naked curiosity that filled the faces of the two women. They were both smiling at her as if they were close friends, but their eyes slyly mocked her. Agnes recognised the look at once; after all, it was a look she had witnessed hundreds of times over the years. But now things had changed. Now she was the one holding the upper hand and she revelled in the new experience. It had been a very long time since she had felt any self-worth or respect for herself. Now she had both and she wasn't such a fool as to imagine that these women had suddenly become her bosom friends. Still, she was only human, and the desire to show off quickly overcame her reticence. But she must be careful how much she divulged. Kenneth had been most insistent about their relationship remaining a private matter between the two of them. But once Kenneth's wife was dead, there would be no more need for secrecy.

Assuming a superior air, Agnes straightened her back and, with her head held high, said, 'As a matter of fact I do have a gentleman friend, but I can't say any more at the moment.' She hesitated, then, unable to maintain her lofty attitude and desperate to talk about Kenneth, her mouth opened and the words she had fought to keep quiet came tumbling out in a rush of excitement. 'Oh, all right then, I'll tell yer. But yer've gotta promise ter keep it to yerselves.'

Both women edged closer to the counter, their faces agog with excitement.

Looking first over their shoulders to make sure no one else was about to enter the shop Agnes took a deep breath. 'Like I said, I can't say too much at the minute, but let's just say I might not be working 'ere fer much longer. My gentleman friend is very comfortably off, an' once we're married he'll expect me ter stay at 'ome, especially with the little one ter . . .' Agnes broke off, her face registering her horror at the near slip she had made in referring to Kenneth's niece.

But the inference hadn't gone unnoticed. Immediately Mabel exclaimed, 'Bleeding 'ell, Agnes. Yer ain't pregnant, are yer? Gawd love us, yer can't be, not at your age.'

Before the startled Agnes could reply Nora Parker snapped loudly, "Course she ain't too old, Mabel. There's plenty of women that's been caught out 'cos they thought they was too old ter get pregnant.' Cocking her head to one side she added slyly, 'An' yer only in yer early forties, ain't yer, Agnes?'

Agnes' face had turned scarlet, both in embarrassment and deep despair. It had been her life's wish to have a child of her own, but as the years had passed by she had reluctantly resigned herself to the fact that she would never have the joy of hearing a child call her mother. There was also the fear that one day soon Ellen would announce she was pregnant and that would be her undoing. The thought of watching Ellen's stomach swell, and Arthur strutting around as the expectant father was enough to make Agnes' insides knot in silent agony. She wouldn't be able to bear it, she knew she wouldn't. Yet now she was to have a second chance. Once Micky was out of the way leaving Kenneth the chance to rescue the little girl from the squalor in which she lived, then she, Agnes Handly, would become a mother to the orphaned child – once Kenneth was free to make her his wife. And maybe, just maybe, she might still have a child of her own one day. Though deep down she knew that her chances of becoming a mother at her time of life were very slim.

Gathering her startled wits she said bitterly, 'No, I ain't pregnant. Chance would be a fine thing, wouldn't it?'

The raw, naked pain on Agnes' plain face momentarily silenced both women, causing them pangs of guilt as they remembered how they had treated Agnes in the past. Nora Parker cleared her throat as if preparing to speak, but no words came. In those few moments it was as if a veneer had been stripped from Agnes' face, leaving in its place an anguish so painful to behold that both women dropped their gaze, a genuine feeling of sympathy engulfing them.

Nora was the first one to speak. For once at a disadvantage she said softly, 'Sorry, Agnes, we didn't mean any harm, did we, Mabel?' She looked to her friend for support.

'Oh, no, Agnes, 'course we didn't.' Her eyes flickering to Nora, Mabel continued uncomfortably. 'I mean ter say, we wouldn't be deliberately spiteful, honest.' Floundering now she glanced back at Nora, breathing a sigh of relief as her friend took over the strained conversation.

Anxious to change the topic of conversation Nora asked pleasantly, 'Well now, 'ow long is Arthur and Ellen away for?'

Her composure back in place once more, Agnes made a great play of rearranging the display of cakes on the counter before replying, 'They went fer two weeks, so they'll be back at the weekend.'

Their purchases bought and paid for, the women

prepared to leave, anxious to get outside so they could discuss Agnes and her gentleman friend in more detail. It was as they reached the door that Nora remarked casually, 'I still can't believe Arthur let Ellen talk 'im into 'aving a holiday. I wouldn't be surprised if they came back early, especially as Arthur's never been away from the place fer over twenty years. He's probably worrying 'imself sick his business will go ter rack and ruin while 'e's away. Mind you, I gotta say, Bill's baking ain't a patch on Arthur's, though don't tell Bill I said so. Anyway, see yer tomorrow, Agnes. 'Bye.'

No sooner had the women departed when the bell over the shop announced another customer, and it was one o'clock before Agnes had the chance for some time to herself.

With Bill minding the shop, Agnes took her dinner break in the kitchen. And as she ate a crusty cheese roll, she thought back over the past three weeks, her eyes and mouth softening at the memories. For the first time in twenty years she had a purpose for getting up in the morning, apart from going to work. Finishing her snack she wandered over to the mirror hanging over the sink and took stock of her reflection. And once more she marvelled at the difference a bit of hair dye and new clothes could make to a person's appearance. She looked ten years younger, but, she reflected sadly, no amount of hair dye and new clothes could make her more attractive. She was still as plain as she'd always been. Then she brightened. Kenneth obviously thought her attractive. In fact he had been lavish in his compliments on her new appearance. Idly smoothing down the ruffles on her new white blouse she then inspected her hair. She had toyed with the idea of letting it hang loose, but had quickly dismissed the notion. The last thing she wanted was to look like mutton dressed as lamb. She had, however, left a few wisps of hair framing her face, giving her features a softer look. The rest of her hair was neatly plaited and pinned to the back of her head. Turning her head this way then that, she was suddenly overwhelmed by a wave of frustration as she recalled all the wasted years. If only she hadn't been so stupid as to hope that Arthur would one day rekindle the romance of their early days. And where had her hopes and loyalty got her? Cast aside, her heart broken, her self-esteem shattered. If only she'd had the sense to move on when the affair with Arthur had ended she could have been married, maybe even had a family by now. If only! The two most tragic words in the world. But, by some miracle, she had been given a second chance of happiness and she wasn't going to waste it this time. Checking the mirror to make sure she had no crumbs on her mouth she suddenly recalled Nora Parker's comment about Arthur coming back early and the memory of those casually spoken words brought Agnes' head up sharply.

Arthur would never have consented to such an arrangement if she and Ellen, for once allied against the weak-willed man, hadn't constantly kept on at him, day after day, until the poor, harassed baker had finally agreed, just to get a bit of peace.

Pouring herself another mug of tea, Agnes' mind whirled anxiously, her thoughts going round and round her head like a pet mouse on a spinning wheel.

If she was to have any chance of a new life with Kenneth she would have to move quickly. Only last night Kenneth had pleaded with her again to put their plans into motion, but for some inexplicable reason she had continued to stall for more time. But now she realised there was no more time to prevaricate. Once Arthur and Ellen returned and, knowing Arthur, who must by now be champing at the bit to return home, they could well turn up any time now, she would have no opportunity to get Micky out of the way. She knew too, that, once the deed was done, she would have to leave her small terraced house. For once word got round, as it would surely do, she, Agnes, would no longer be welcomed in the East End. Her head drooped as the enormous consequences of what she was about to do hit her like a physical blow to her stomach. Then she stiffened her resolve. The plan was well worked out. Once Micky was out of the way, she would move into a small hotel, paid for by Kenneth, and there she would stay until they could finally be together. In the meantime she would put her house on the market with a reputable estate agency. Once the house was sold, the money earned would go into her bank account. She would feel easier in her mind once she knew there was a comfortable nest egg to fall back on if things with Kenneth didn't go well.

Not that she expected that to happen, she rebuked herself sharply, but she of all people knew that life didn't always work out as one expected.

Taking a deep breath, she swallowed the last of her

ANNA KING

tea and came to a decision. She would do it this evening. Yet even as she tried to convince herself she was doing it with the best of intentions, she couldn't stop the nagging guilt gnawing away inside.

CHAPTER TEN

Micky hastened his steps, a huge grin on his face. Everything was going well for him. He had been able to have Molly with him over the Easter holidays as he had promised her. No one had questioned her presence, accepting at face value his explanation that he was looking after the small girl as a favour to one of his neighbours. The change in Molly had been nothing short of a miracle. That time, as brief as it had been, had given Molly new hope for the future. Micky's grin widened, his whole body alight with happiness. Just this morning Ted had told him that next week he was going to trust Micky with the running of the stall in Hoxton, while he, Ted, looked for a regular pitch down Roman Road. It would only be for one morning, but if he did well Micky knew that Ted would eventually give him more responsibility. His step jaunty, Micky skipped along the pavement. He wouldn't let Ted down, not ever. Although

it would be some time before Ted would let Micky
run the stall by himself full time. He had even gone
so far as to say that come Micky's sixteenth birthday,
they would make permanent arrangements pertain-
ing to the running of the stalls. Whistling under his
breath Micky did a quick sum in his head. He would
be fifteen in May, so it would only be a matter of just
over a year before he would be given the chance to
be a proper stall holder. For the present though he
had to content himself with the knowledge that he
had a regular wage coming in each week. The only
thing that worried Micky was the fact that he was
deceiving both Ted and Ellen, the two most important people in his young life, apart from Molly. He'd
lost count of the times he had nearly blurted out the
truth to Ted as they worked side by side down the
market, but mercifully he had managed to keep his
tongue in check. Even though he was sure Ted
wouldn't turn him over to the authorities, Micky
wasn't sure of the law regarding minors. Maybe Ted
would get into trouble if he knew of Micky's living
conditions and didn't report it. No! Micky shook his
head. He couldn't risk it. Yet sometimes the need to
unburden himself was so strong he had to leave the
stall on some pretext for fear he might reveal the truth.
Anyway, with his future looking set he would soon
be able to look after Molly legally. His mind skirting
around the many pitfalls he would have to overcome,
Micky turned his attention to tomorrow, his half day
off. He hadn't told Molly yet, but now he had a few
pounds put by he was going to get the *Hackney Gazette*
and look for lodgings. He would have to be careful

of course. The first sign of a nosy landlady and he would be off like a shot. There were plenty of places around the East End where the owners of the boarding houses asked no questions. And all he and Molly needed was one room – with a stout lock, that was the most important thing of all. If everything went well, he and his sister should be safely housed by the weekend. His grin broadened still further as he imagined Moll's face when he told her he'd found somewhere for them both to live without fear.

As he approached the bakery he thought of Ellen and, as always when he thought of the pretty young woman, his heart gave a leap of happiness. He was old enough to know that Ellen was out of his reach, but that didn't stop him from loving her.

Passing the bakery he was startled to hear Agnes calling his name. Stopping, he turned to face her, his eyes wary. He hadn't set foot in the bakery since Ellen had gone on holiday, preferring instead to buy his bread from the bakers down Hoxton, rather than have to face that old bag. Now here she was framed in the doorway, her face radiating pleasure at seeing him. Micky paused. Life, since his parents had died, had hardened him and made him suspicious. But even if he hadn't changed, he would have been wary of the hospitable welcome when he knew Agnes didn't like him, had never liked him. He blinked, then looked again. She was still smiling at him as if he were a dear friend. Assuming a defensive stance he said guard-edly, 'Yeah, what d'yer want?'

Agnes, her heart thumping at what she was about to do, managed a watery smile. 'Well, that's a nice

115

welcome, I must say. And here's me saving the usual bread and cakes Ellen always puts by fer yer.'

Thrown off balance by the kind words and friendly face of the woman who had always treated him like something you'd scrape off your shoe, Micky remained where he was.

Agnes immediately noted Micky's suspicion and swallowed hard. This wasn't going to be as simple as she had first thought. Micky might be a mere boy, but he had the intelligence of someone twice his age. A feeling of desperation gripped her. The plan Kenneth had outlined must be accomplished. With a supreme effort Agnes gave a wry smile. 'Look, mate. I know we ain't exactly been the best of friends, but I'm trying. Can't yer give me another chance . . . eh?'

Still Micky hesitated. But his nature, kind by heart, was willing to give Agnes the benefit of the doubt. His eyes met Agnes' as if trying to gauge her true feelings and saw true remorse mirrored in her eyes. What he didn't suspect was the real reason behind the remorseful look. His body relaxed slightly, but his feet dragged awkwardly as he followed Agnes into the shop.

'Thanks, Agnes. Ta. I've been buying me bread an' cakes down the market, but they ain't as nice as they are 'ere.'

Her back to him, Agnes grabbed the parcel she'd put under the counter earlier on, then, her heart hammering so hard she was sure the boy must hear it and realise the truth behind her actions, quickly handed it over. 'There yer go, mate . . . Nah! Put yer money away, love,' she exclaimed as Micky reached into his pocket. 'It'd only go stale. Besides, Ellen never charges yer, does she?'

His face flustered Micky muttered, 'That was when I was doing odd jobs, I don't expect ter keep getting me grub fer nothing.'

Bustling quickly now in case someone came into the shop and witnessed the transaction, Agnes hurriedly ushered Micky out into the street. 'Sorry ter rush yer, love, but I want ter shut up fer the night.'

Still feeling awkward and ill at ease, Micky was only too pleased to leave. Then he paused. Looking back at Agnes he smiled and said shyly, 'Yer look nice, Agnes. An' thanks fer the grub. See yer.'

Agnes watched him go, her hand clutching her throat. Those few simple kind words had thrown her completely. As the minutes ticked by her troubled mind was screaming that what she was planning was wrong. She still didn't like the lad, but he'd never done anything to her, and just now, he had been so nice to her. And the words he had spoken had been genuine.

Then Kenneth's face floated before her eyes, and before she could change her mind she let out a loud shout. 'Stop 'im. Stop thief. The little bleeder's nicked me supper.'

Micky was halfway down the street when Agnes' strident voice reached him, and in that awful, heart-stopping moment he knew, knew that his earlier suspicions had been right. In the split second it took to realise he had been set up he thought of going back and facing Agnes and her lies, then he thought of Molly and his feet took flight, his hand discarding the parcel of food as if it had suddenly turned into a burning flame. And as he ran Agnes' voice followed him, high and screeching. Doors were flung open and people poured into the street to see what the commotion was all about. Then Micky was ducking and diving past them all, dodging their grasping hands.

Quiet now, Agnes watched until Micky disappeared from sight, a small crowd chasing after the young, terrified boy. To her surprise tears sprang to her eyes, making her blink. Then she stiffened as a loud voice boomed, 'What's up, Agnes? What's all the excitement about?'

Police Constable John Smith, the local bobby, loomed in front of Agnes as if he had been conjured out of thin air.

Gulping nervously Agnes stuttered, 'It's that Micky Masters. He's gorn an' nicked stuff from the shop. I just turned me back fer a minute, an' . . . an' the next minute he'd grabbed an armful of stuff from the counter and legged it.'

PC Smith's eyes narrowed. 'Now, Agnes, I know the lad slightly. He doesn't strike me as a thief. And anyway, why should he steal? He's got a good job with Ted now, he doesn't have any reason to thieve.'

Stepping nearer the trembling woman the policeman asked gruffly, 'Look here, Agnes, you sure it was young Micky? 'Cos I just can't see it myself.'

Agnes looked at the scepticism in the policeman's eyes and braced herself. It was done now, there was no going back.

Assuming an injured air she drew herself up to her fullest height and replied frostily, ''Course I'm sure. I ain't daft. Like I said, the boy came into the shop asking when Ellen was coming back, and while me back was turned he grabbed the parcel I'd laid out on the counter ter take home fer me supper and was gone before I could stop 'im.'

PC Smith pushed his helmet further back on his head, his eyes still sceptical. 'All right, Agnes. I'll see to it, but I gotta say I can't see Micky stealing, he's not the type.'

Her aggression coming to the fore, Agnes, feeling more in control of herself, bridled, 'You calling me a liar, John Smith? 'Cos if yer are then say it ter me face, instead of making sly comments.'

The veteran constable stared back at the small woman, his shrewd eyes noting the furtive look in Agnes' eyes before she dropped her gaze. 'All right, I'll take your word for it – for now. But I'll tell you something, Agnes Handly, there's something fishy about the whole business, so I hope you're right, for your sake.'

With a curt nod the police officer strode off in the direction Micky had taken, his hobnailed boots ringing out loudly on the cobbled streets as he moved quickly after the small crowd, all of them relishing the unexpected bit of excitement.

Micky, his face streaming with sweat and fear, ran on, but he had no chance of outrunning the baying mob chasing him. Not heeding where he was going, Micky turned a corner, then stopped; he had run into a dead end. Frantically looking around for a way out Micky began to cry. And that unexpected act of weakness was the final straw for the proud young boy.

Knowing he was trapped Micky angrily wiped the tears from his cheeks and turned to the excited crowd.

'I ain't done nothing. I didn't steal anything, honest. That old cow . . .'

A thick-set man moved forward grabbing Micky by the scruff of his neck. 'Yeah! That's what they all say, yer thieving little bastard. Let's see what the coppers 'ave ter say, shall we?'

Micky struggled wildly in the vice-like grip, then a loud voice of authority rang out. 'That's enough, Ron. I'll deal with this, let the boy go.'

All eyes turned to the uniformed man, their ghoulish enjoyment slipping from their faces as they realised the matter was now out of their hands.

The man called Ron, self-appointed leader of the crowd, reluctantly loosened his grip on Micky, the excitement disappearing from his fleshy features. 'All right, keep yer hair on. I was gonna take 'im down the station. Yer've saved me a trip.'

'Yeah, I'm sure you were, Ron. You certainly know the way, don't you?'

The deliberate reference to his shady past brought a flash of anger to the man's face, then he gave Micky a vicious push towards the stern-faced officer.

''Ere, take the thieving little bleeder. I'll tell yer something else an' all. It's the last time I try an' do the law any favours.'

'Well, I'm sure the force will be able to struggle on without your help, Ron. Now, on your way, the lot of you.'

One by one the crowd dispersed, their low mutterings fading as they returned to their homes.

Left alone with the police officer Micky looked up at the familiar burly man, his eyes pleading. 'I didn't steal anything, Officer, honest I didn't. She . . . I mean Agnes, she gave me the parcel. I offered ter pay fer it, but she said I could 'ave it fer nothing.' The tears began to spurt again, but Micky, in his agitated state, didn't realise he was crying. 'Please don't take me in, Officer. I ain't done nothing wrong. Ellen . . . I mean Mrs Mitson'll tell yer I ain't no thief . . .'

The officer looked at the tear-stained face with pity. There was something very wrong here. Although he didn't know the boy well, John Smith knew his patch, and the people on it. He had seen the young boy frequently, and knew of his friendship with the baker's wife. There wasn't much that went on around these streets that the veteran police officer didn't know about. He also knew Agnes Handly, and of the two he was rather inclined to believe the boy, though why Agnes should try and get the boy arrested was beyond him. But a crime had been reported and he had to take the boy in for questioning.

His voice low and sympathetic he said kindly, 'I'm sorry, son, I've got to take you down the station. But look, as soon as I've booked you in, I'll go round and have a word with Ted Parker and get him to come down, unless you'd rather I fetched your parents.'

Micky's heart leapt in fright. 'Oh no, don't . . . I mean, I ain't got a dad, an' me mum ain't been well . . .' Surprised at how easily the lies were tumbling from his lips Micky added, 'I don't want ter worry 'er, Officer. So could yer get Ted, please?'

Taking hold of the boy's arm PC Smith led him out

of the alley and into the main thoroughfare, his soothing voice erasing some of Micky's fear. 'Don't you go worrying, son. Ted'll sort this mess out, he's a good bloke, is Ted Parker.'

Wiping his face across the sleeve of his jacket Micky nodded dumbly, his spirits rising at the kindness in the policeman's voice. Quieter now he walked alongside the officer, his only thought being of Molly. As they entered the station in Mare Street Micky squeezed his eyes tightly shut and prayed silently – 'Please God, let Ted come quickly and make this nightmare go away so I can get home to Molly . . .'

Micky sat on a damp, smelly bunk bed, his eyes never leaving the closed cell door. He was finding it hard to breathe in the small, confined space. There wasn't even the luxury of a cell to himself, for lying on a similar bed only inches from his was a filthy, drunken tramp, whose snores were guaranteed to keep Micky awake all night. Not that he was planning on sleeping. Instead he closed his eyes, his mind saying over and over, 'Ted will be here soon.' He would. Ted wouldn't let him down. But the cell door remained shut tight, and the fear that had entered his heart the moment he had been thrown into the cell was fast turning into sheer terror. His only comfort was his unwavering faith in Ted Parker. He looked over at the tramp then dropped his face into his hands.

'Please, Ted. Hurry up. Come and get me, Ted, please. I'm so frightened. I've never been so scared in all me life. Please, Ted, come and get me . . . please.'

* * *

PC John Smith resumed his beat, his mind still on Micky Masters and the boy's refusal to give his address for fear of upsetting his ailing mother. Of course the woman would have to be informed of her son's arrest: he was bound by law to inform the next of kin of any prisoner. First though he would find Ted Parker. If anyone could help the young lad out of his present predicament, then Ted was the man to do it. He was only a few minutes away from Ted Parker's house when the local pub doors opened and a pile of men spilled out onto the street and proceeded to brawl. Sighing loudly, PC Smith waded into the fight. Luckily for him, two of his colleagues were soon on the scene and between them they managed to break up the fight, arresting four men in the process. With his hands full, the kindly police officer forgot all about young Micky. He only remembered when he returned to the station some hours later to sign off his shift. Guilt stricken, he raced to find Ted, praying that the man would be at home. His prayers were answered. Not a man to waste words, the officer, a friend of Ted's for over ten years, quickly explained the situation.

Within twenty minutes Ted was at the station, and with John Smith backing him up, the duty sergeant agreed to let Micky out on bail, providing that Ted, in the absence of a parent present, took full responsibility for the boy, and the charge levelled against him until the case came to court.

When Micky emerged from the cell, cowed and shivering, his handsome face blotched and swollen with tears, it took all of Ted's willpower not to sweep the stricken boy up into his arms. Then Micky looked up at him and, like a small child, ran towards the man he had come to love and threw himself against the strong, safe body. It was then that Ted, with a low groan of pity, picked Micky up and held him tight against his chest. And as he carried him from the police station, his voice softly whispering against Micky's ear, a feeling of rage against Agnes Handly and her foul accusations threatened to overwhelm him. Forcing himself to keep his emotions in check Ted took the still shivering boy to his home, vowing that, come tomorrow he would find Agnes and, if need be, shake the truth out of the lying, spiteful bitch.

The trauma of the past few hours had taken its toll on Micky, but not enough for him to have forgotten about his sister.

Wrapped in a warm blanket, with Nora Parker bustling around him and plying him with food and drink, it was difficult to get a word in as the irate woman continued to vent her anger against Agnes who had been the instigator in the whole sorry business.

Finally, conscious of the time and unable to keep quiet any longer, Micky caught hold of Nora's hand and, looking up at her beseechingly, he stuttered, 'Me sister. I've gotta get home ter me sister. She'll be so afraid ... She's on— only eight. An'... an' there's a man after 'er. A bad man. He ... he wants ter ... ter ...' His trembling voice trailed off, not able to speak of the vile intentions Kenneth Wells harboured against his little sister.

Ted and Nora exchanged glances, then Ted, drawing up a chair next to Micky, said quietly, 'You ain't got any mother, have yer, Micky?'

Fresh tears spilled from Micky's eyes as he shook his bowed head, ashamed to look Ted in the eye.

Glancing first at the startled Nora, Ted drew a deep breath and said kindly, 'I think yer've got some explaining ter do, mate.'

And Micky, too tired and scared to lie any longer, started to talk, his voice rising with agitation as he imagined Molly, alone, terrified out of her wits, wondering what had happened to him. But what really turned Micky's blood cold was the thought of Kenneth Wells getting his hands on the vulnerable child.

Before Micky had finished talking, Ted already had his coat on, his face grim. 'Come on, then. You'd better show me where you've been living. And after we've got Molly safely back here, there's gonna be some serious talking to be done.'

Micky lowered his gaze, thinking that Ted was angry with him for lying for so long. Then his chin was being pulled upwards, and Ted was smiling.

'Take that miserable look off yer face. You should 'ave told me what was going on from the start, but I suppose in your shoes I'd've done the same. Anyway, we know the truth now, and yer don't have ter worry any more. We'll sort it out . . . won't we, Mum?' He turned to look at the hovering Nora.

Her eyes misty, the normally stalwart woman flapped her hands at them crying, 'Of course we will, yer daft sod. Now go an' fetch that poor little mite. She must be scared ter death by now.'

Outside the house Micky tentatively caught hold of Ted's hand, a gesture he wouldn't have dreamed of a few hours earlier. But he needed comfort, needed to feel safe, and Ted made him feel safe. His throat tightening, Ted gave a loud cough before saying briskly, 'Well, come on then, let's go and get this sister of yours.'

As it was dark and nobody could see, Micky kept a tight hold of Ted's hand, as if he was afraid the man beside him would suddenly disappear. Twenty minutes later they were standing inside the derelict building and while Micky called out for his sister Ted looked around the filthy ruin in horror. The thought of two children living in these conditions for so long brought a lump of sadness coupled with anger to Ted's throat. His eyes sweeping the darkness he vowed silently that if it lay with him, Micky and his sister would never again have to live in such appalling conditions.

Micky climbed up the rope whispering, 'Moll, Moll, it's me, Micky. I'm sorry I'm so late, but I got into a bit of bother.' Silence greeted him. Screwing up his eyes he moved nearer the bed he shared with Molly, his stomach beginning to churn with fear. Blindly feeling his way towards the bed, he moved his hands over the smelly blankets expecting to come into contact with the small lump that was Molly, but the bed was empty. His eyes stretched wide in horror and disbelief as he opened his mouth and began to scream.

He'd come too late – Molly was no longer here. Someone had taken her, and he didn't have to think hard as to who had abducted his little sister. Unable to face the horror of what had happened to Molly,

126

Micky gave a low anguished groan. Red spots danced before his eyes – and then he was falling.

Falling into a warm, welcoming black hole where there was no feeling, no fear, just peace – lovely, wonderful peace.

CHAPTER ELEVEN

About an hour before Micky was rescued from the prison cell by Ted, Sadie North, a local prostitute was walking alongside a punter she had just picked up, chatting away nineteen to the dozen to keep the nervous man from changing his mind and making a bolt for it. She'd had a lot of men like the one shuffling awkwardly by her side, their shifty eyes darting from left to right for fear of being seen with the flamboyant prostitute. Middle-aged men who weren't getting any loving from their worn-out wives, women who were ground down by the daily existence of living, terrified of falling for another child to feed when there was barely enough to survive on as it was. The man who had picked her up on the corner of Mare Street had just staggered out from the Nag's Head, his courage bolstered by three pints of ale, and a small whisky; money that should have been used to feed his wife and children. Now the drink was wearing off and with it the beer-fuelled bravado.

Not for the first time Sadie wished she had somewhere local she could take her customers, instead of having to walk the streets in search of a dark alley. Her profession was sordid enough without having to perform her business down a darkened sidewalk. But her two-room flat that she was so proud of was her haven and her home, somewhere she could change out of her working clothes, and into respectable clothing and forget about her unsavoury occupation for a brief period of time. If she was lucky, a customer would offer to pay for an hour's pleasure in any one of the dozens of boarding houses and run-down hotels that asked no questions, but usually, like tonight, it was up to her to find somewhere to ply her trade. Still, she comforted herself with the thought that this man was to be her last punter for tonight.

Tucking the man's arm tighter to her side Sadie looked for somewhere suitable to conclude her business. Stopping outside the only building still standing among a pile of rubble that had once been a row of terraced houses, Sadie quickly pulled the man inside the pitch-black building. Safely off the streets and out of sight of any passers-by, the pot-bellied man regained his courage. Not bothering with the niceties of foreplay, the man grabbed Sadie's large breasts, his slobbering lips sucking at her neck and face. Anxious to get the familiar routine over with as quickly as possible, Sadie averted her face and lifted her skirts as the man began to unbutton his trousers, his breathing becoming ragged and harsh. Pressed up against the crumbling wall, Sadie gazed over the man's head, her eyes blank, her mind shutting out the act in which she was participating. Automatically murmuring encouragement to the sweating man, she urged him on, moaning and panting as if she was enjoying the experience as much as he, while her mind was wondering if she had enough food in the flat for her supper. Sadie waited impatiently for the man to finish. From experience she knew it wouldn't be long and, moments later, she was proved right as the man gave a loud shuddering sigh, his head falling onto Sadie's shoulder. Glad the unpleasant act was over, Sadie was about to ask for her money when a frightened scream from above their heads caused both parties to jump in fright.

Crouched on her bed, Molly, already scared and anxious at Micky's lateness, had heard the man and woman come into the building. She was used to tramps coming into the house, especially when it was cold and raining, but they never stayed for long, and Molly always remained as quiet as a mouse, as Micky had instructed her. But when the man had started to make loud, strange noises, and the woman had begun to moan and call out in a muffled voice, Molly, her heart beating fast, had crawled carefully over to the edge of the room. Not allowed to light her candle until Micky was home, Molly squinted into the gloom below, trying to make out the two shadowy figures in the darkness, her only source of light being a thin stream of moonlight shining through one of the many holes in the roof. But it wasn't bright enough to light the lower part of the house. Hearing the man's harsh breathing become louder coupled with the woman's low screams, Molly had curled herself up into a tight ball praying for her brother to come home. The sounds became increasingly louder, and Molly, thinking the man was hurting the woman and unable to keep quiet any longer, scrambled closer to the edge and screamed wildly, 'Stop it! Stop it! Let her go, you 'orrible man. You're a bad man. Stop hurting the lady.'

Recovering her wits, Sadie squinted her eyes up towards the sound of the childish voice. The man, quickly taking advantage of Sadie's distraction, rearranged his clothing and took to his heels. Hearing the sound of running footsteps, Sadie spun round, her face hardening as she realised she had been conned out of her money, bloody well-earned money at that, considering what she had to do for it. At any other time she would have given chase, but knowing there was a frightened child somewhere in the rotting building Sadie had no option but to let the man go. But it wasn't in her nature to let the crafty bleeder off completely.

'You stinking bastard. Don't think yer've got away with fleecing me. I'll catch up with you, you take me word. An' when I do, I hope your poor wife'll be with you. You won't be so bleeding cocky then.'

Panting with rage, Sadie glared down the dimly lit street, then her attention was brought back to the presence of the unknown child by the sound of muffled sobbing. Careful not to frighten the poor little mite more than she had been already, Sadie called out softly, 'It's all right, love. The bad man's gone, you can come out now.'

When no answer came, just the continual quiet sobbing, Sadie moved cautiously nearer the sound, her eyes raised. She saw the rope dangling from the old beams and thought of climbing it, then common sense quickly dismissed the idea. That particular route might be all right for a small child, but no way would it take her weight.

Standing directly beneath the rope she again called out, 'I know you're scared, love, but I ain't gonna hurt you,' but the sobbing only intensified.

Sadie was in a quandary. It was obvious the child needed help, but if she wasn't going to trust her enough to show herself, then there wasn't much Sadie could do. On the other hand, she couldn't just leave the child in this dump on her own. She wouldn't be able to sleep nights if she walked away and abandoned the child to the mercy of any passing pervert, and God knows there were plenty of them about. Trying a different tack she said calmly, 'All right, love. I don't blame you for not coming down. I mean to say, yer don't know me, but I don't want to just go off an' leave you, not after you helped me. After all, one good turn deserves another, don't it? You scared off that nasty man, didn't you? I don't know what I would've done if you hadn't of been here. But if you want me to go, then I will. Thanks for helping me, love, I'm really grateful.' Sadie paused, her ears pricked for any sound from above. 'I'm leaving now, love. 'Bye.' So saying she walked loudly on the spot to make it sound as if she was going.

Up above, Molly sat huddled on her bed, her young mind struggling to know what to do for the best. She was tired, cold and hungry, but most of all she was desperately frightened.

Even though she had no clock, Molly knew that her brother should have been back hours ago. She knew too that for Micky to be so late something terrible must have happened to him. And she couldn't even go and try to find him in case that horrible man was waiting for her to step outside the safety of her home.

In her young life she had only known two men. One was her father, whom she had adored and who had made her feel safe and loved. The other man was Kenneth Wells. He had been nice at first, until . . . Her immature mind quickly shut down on what the man had been trying to do when Micky had come running back that day. Micky had saved her. From what exactly, Molly wasn't quite sure, but she knew enough to know it was bad and nasty, and that just thinking of it made her feel sort of mucky inside.

From her limited experience of life she had imagined that there was only one bad man she had to avoid, but now she knew better. Her world, until now, had been very black and white for Molly. She stayed in the derelict building while Micky was at work, so that the bad man couldn't get her. Now she realised there were plenty more men of his type, and that new-found knowledge struck a chill into her heart. What if Micky didn't come home? What if something terrible had happened to him? What would she do then? She couldn't stay up here for ever. She desperately needed help, and down below there was a woman who might be able to provide that help. But if she showed herself Micky might be angry with her for disobeying his orders. But Micky wasn't here, was he? And if she had any chance of finding him she would need the help of a grown-up. If it had been a man downstairs, Molly wouldn't have dreamed of asking for help. But women didn't do nasty things to children; it was only men who did those nasty, dirty things. And the lady sounded nice. Still Molly hesitated, then she heard the woman's footsteps leaving, and in that moment Molly made up her mind. Scrambling to the edge of the floor, she leant over the edge, crying out in a trembling voice, 'Wait, lady. Don't go. I'll be down in a minute.'

Sadie watched as the small figure deftly slid down the rope with expert ease making it obvious the young girl had done it many times before.

Then the woman and girl were facing each other in the faint light of the moon shining through the rotting roof. Moving slowly, so as not to frighten the girl, Sadie gently took the small, cold hand and moved over to the empty doorway where, in the light shining brightly from the lamp post on the opposite side of the street, the two females took stock of each other. Molly's huge eyes stared in amazement at the lady dressed in a bright red dress with matching feathers stuck on top of equally bright auburn hair. Her mouth agape, Molly, momentarily stuck for words, continued to gaze at the gaudy creature, a sight she had never seen before.

Guessing what was going through the girl's mind, Sadie laughed merrily. 'Gawd 'elp us, love. Close your mouth before a moth flies in. I take it you've never seen anyone dressed like me before, 'ave you?'

Instantly contrite at having been caught out in her thoughts, and aware she was displaying bad manners, Molly stuttered, 'I'm sorry for staring, lady. Me mum always said it was rude to stare.'

Her face softening, Sadie asked kindly, 'And where is your mum, love?'

At the mention of her much missed mother, Molly's eyes, already moist, began to well up with fresh tears. 'She died . . . and me dad, an' all. An' . . . an' I don't 'alf miss 'em.'

Her face tender, Sadie crouched down and said softly, 'I'm sorry about that, love, I really am. But who looks after you now? You can't be caring for yourself.'

Sniffing loudly, Molly answered, 'Me brother Micky looks after me. He's nearly grown-up now, he'll be fifteen in a few weeks' time. But . . . but he hasn't come 'ome yet, an' . . . an' he's usually back by now.' She gave another loud sniff. 'And I'm scared something's happened to 'im, 'cos he'd never leave me on purpose. He's me brother, an' he loves me.'

When the strange woman's arms went around her shoulders Molly flinched then, needing physical comfort, the comfort her mother used to provide, she relaxed against the soft, sweet-smelling woman. Feeling the small frame nestled so trustingly against hers Sadie swallowed hard. It had been a long time since she had felt contact with another human body. Her punters didn't count. Contact with them was limited to the minimum amount of time possible. But that kind of contact was devoid of any warmth or affection; it was simply business. Now, with the child's head nestled in the voluptuous folds of her breasts,

135

Sadie felt a surge of tenderness and fierce protectiveness.

Hugging the small girl tighter Sadie thought quickly. She couldn't leave the child here to fend for herself; on the other hand there was the brother to think of. There could be any number of reasons why he was so late. And when, or if, he turned up and found his sister gone he would be frantic. She would have to leave a message of some kind. But how? She wasn't in the habit of carrying writing material on her person. Maybe the child could help. Tilting Molly's chin upwards she said, 'Now look, love, I can't leave you 'ere, so I'll have to take you home with me . . . Hang on, mate, don't be frightened . . .' she added quickly as she felt the girl begin to struggle in her grasp. 'What I was thinking was, we could maybe leave your brother a message, to let him know where you are. I can't just take you away without leaving some sort of note for him, can I? I mean to say, what'll he think when he comes home and finds you gone? Why, the poor little sod'll be out of his mind with worry. The problem is, I ain't got no paper or pen. How about you, love? You got anything we could write a note to your brother on?'

Molly chewed her lip thoughtfully, her confused mind torn between the desire to go with the lady, or to stay here in the dark and cold waiting for Micky to turn up. What if he'd had an accident? No one knew about her, no one would come and tell her if Micky was hurt or . . . Her mind shied away from the unimaginable possibility to explain Micky's absence.

Watching the girl struggle with her conscience Sadie

said wryly, 'Unless you'd rather I fetched the law, 'cos I can't leave you 'ere on your own.'

Instantly Molly's eyes filled with fear. Her body trembling she cried, 'Oh, no, please! Don't tell the coppers. They'd take me away an' put me back in the workhouse. An' ... an' it's 'orrible there.' Grabbing hold of Sadie's hands Molly hung on to them like a drowning man clinging to a life raft. 'We could write a note on me slate. Micky got it for me and some chalk so I could learn to spell and add up, 'cos I can't go to school any more. Wait a minute, I'll go and get them.' Scrambling up the rope she paused halfway and stared hard at the gaudily dressed woman, a woman Molly was now desperate to hold on to. 'You won't go, will you, lady? You will wait for me, won't you?'

Sadie nodded. ''Course I won't leave yer, you silly cow. Go on, get your slate and chalk.'

Molly was up and back down the rope in record time. ''Ere you are, lady. You'll 'ave to write the message, I ain't that good at writing yet. But I'm learning. After all,' she whispered sadly, 'I ain't got nothing else to do all day.'

Taking the slate, Sadie again moved out of the building into the street where the light was better, and after a moment's thought asked the hovering Molly, 'What's your brother's name again, love, I've forgotten. Come to think of it, I don't know your name either. In fact, we ain't been properly introduced.' Holding out her hand she said in mock formality, 'I'm Sadie North. How do you do?'

A shy smile lit up Molly's face as she solemnly took

the proffered hand saying, 'My name's Molly, and me brother's name is Micky, Micky Masters.'

'Hello, Molly, pleased to meet you. Now then, we'd best get a move on.' Raising her gaze to the darkening sky she added, 'It looks like it's going to chuck it down any minute.'

Finishing off the brief note that merely gave her name and address and that Molly was safe with her, Sadie put the stub of chalk in her beaded bag. Going back into the damp-smelling building, Sadie, with Molly close behind, looked around for somewhere to leave the slate so that Micky would be able to see it the minute he returned. The trouble was that with no proper lighting, except that from the street lamp on the other side of the road, and the weak stream of moonlight, it was difficult to think of where to place the slate where it would be easily seen.

Voicing her dilemma, Molly said earnestly, 'I know, lady, I'll put it on our bed. That's the first place Micky'll look for me.' Once again Molly scrambled up the rope, placing the slate at the foot of the double mattress.

She was about to descend the rope when Sadie called up, 'You'd better bring your coat, if you've got one. It's turning bleed— I mean it's turning bitter, an' it's starting to rain.'

'Oh, yes, I've got a coat, Micky bought me one at Easter. I'll get it. Hang on, lady, I won't be a minute.'

The desperate fear in Molly's voice caused a tight-ness in Sadie's throat, while at the same time she wondered what she was letting herself in for. For all she knew, this Micky character might be a thieving ruffian. Then she uttered a short laugh. What was she thinking? After all the years on the streets she was more than able to look after herself – she'd had enough practice. And if she could handle grown men, she didn't think she'd have much difficulty in managing a young lad of fourteen.

Terrified the lady might leave if she dallied too long, Molly grabbed her coat, bouncing on the mattress as she shrugged her arms into the thick sleeves. 'I'm coming, lady, I'm coming,' she called out anxiously, still afraid that the lady might change her mind and leave her here alone. As she bounded off the bed she noticed the slate fall to the floor. Hurriedly she laid it back upright at the foot of the bed, placing it directly under the moonlight so that it would be easy for Micky to see when he got back.

Once down in the lower part of the building Molly gazed up at the painted lady, her heart beating rapidly, still not sure she was doing the right thing.

Then Sadie stretched out her hand and Molly hesitated no more. Pausing only to look one more time down the street hoping to see the familiar figure of her brother racing towards her, Molly's face fell in disappointment. Clasping Sadie's hand tightly, Molly didn't utter another word as she went trustingly with her new-found friend.

Back in the building the rain Sadie had forecast began to pour down heavily. Most of the water missed the mattress which Micky had wisely pushed up against the furthest wall for just such occurrences. But the foot of the mattress was unprotected. As the rain poured through the hole in the roof, the rivulets quickly washed the carefully worded slate clean, completely obliterating the hastily chalked message.

CHAPTER TWELVE

Micky was inconsolable. Seated hunched by the fire-place in a worn, comfortable armchair back at Ted's house he stared miserably into the fire, watching the flames jump and lick at the heaped coal and wood laid in the grate, but inside he felt cold, so desperately cold.

It was now gone eleven and Nora, after much prompting and gentle bullying from her son, had finally, albeit reluctantly, gone to her bed leaving the young lad in the safe hands of Ted, but not before she had put a liberal dose of laudanum in Micky's cocoa. Just in case the lad got it into his head to try and sneak out to trawl the streets in another desperate attempt to find his sister. Then she and Ted would have two children to worry about, and Lord knows, one was enough!

Drawing up the matching armchair Ted pulled the chair closer to the silent youth until his knees were touching Micky's thin ones. 'Look, mate. There's nothing we can do tonight. I know you're half outta your head with worry – bleeding hell, I would be in your shoes – but yer've gotta look on the bright side. Maybe she just wandered off, you know, looking for yer, and . . .' Ted's words trailed off miserably. He was only making things worse by trying to give the lad false hope. Despite his attempts to comfort Micky, deep down Ted was imagining the worst. After all, the girl was only eight and, knowing their circumstances, would be unlikely to walk into the nearest police station to ask for help. Even so, Ted had gone back to Mare Street police station to ask if any lost young girl had been brought in by some kind passer-by. Then he'd had to answer some difficult questions as to why he was inquiring about a lost child, especially as he'd only just bailed out a young lad suspected of theft a couple of hours previously. Ted had hoped to find John Smith still on duty, but unfortunately that kindly man had gone back on his beat, and Ted couldn't waste time looking for him. His main concern had been to get back home to Micky whom he had left with his worried mother.

Receiving no response, Ted touched the slim leg lightly, then gave a tired smile. The laudanum had finally taken effect. Easy in his mind now he knew Micky would sleep for a good few hours, Ted took the opportunity to do the same.

But sleep didn't come easily to Ted. Not when his mind was filled with images of a young, vulnerable child in the hands of a pervert. Yet even with the horrendous images, the long day, coupled with worry, finally caught up with him. Exhausted beyond measure Ted's last thought was his planned visit to the bakery in the morning to find out just what that old witch Agnes had been up to, accusing and getting Micky arrested for stealing. And by God, he'd find out, even if he had to shake the truth out of the malicious old cow.

Agnes was in the scullery making herself yet another mug of strong tea in an effort to stay awake when the loud knocking resounded through the small terraced house.

Hurrying through the parlour to the front door, her smile of welcome was wiped from her face when, instead of a happy Kenneth holding a small child in his arms, there stood a man she hardly recognised, so contorted was his face with savage rage. Kicking the door shut behind him, Kenneth grabbed Agnes' arm in a vicious grip as he snarled, 'Where is she, you deceitful bitch? Where's my Molly?'

As the pain shot up her arm, Agnes tried not to cry out for fear of alerting the neighbours, if the loud banging at her door at this hour of the night hadn't already done so. Groaning pitifully she gasped, 'Please, Kenneth. You're 'urting me arm. I don't know what you're talking about. I did what you told me to, you know I did. If the kid ain't where she's supposed ter be, I don't know where she is. Why on earth would I?'

The pressure on her arm eased as Kenneth flung her to one side, striding past her into the parlour without so much as a backward glance at the quietly crying woman.

Timidly following him, Agnes looked at the tall, well-dressed figure with growing unease. It was the same figure who, only earlier that evening had held her in his arms, his face wreathed in smiles as he'd told her over and over how grateful he was to her for giving him the opportunity to rescue his niece.

Swallowing hard she moved nearer and when she tried to speak her voice came out in a croak. 'Are yer sure you went to the right place, Kenneth? I mean, maybe, you know, in the dark, like, you . . .'

Kenneth's fist came down hard on the mantelpiece making Agnes jump in alarm. Then she began to retreat as the murderous-looking man bore down on her.

'You stupid bitch. Of course I went to the right place. It's the only house still standing in that road.'

As he approached, Agnes stepped back further, her heart racing with fear. There was something wrong here, something terribly wrong. She could understand Kenneth being upset at not being able to find his niece, but nothing, at least, nothing normal, warranted this terrifying display of emotion.

'You were the only one other than me who knew where those brats were living. So I'll ask you again, and this time I want the truth, or so help me God I'll wring your scrawny neck.'

As he came nearer Agnes tried to run, then screamed in pain as she felt her hair being pulled viciously by the very roots from her head.

Instantly a loud thud on the adjoining wall broke the highly charged atmosphere in the small room.

'You all right in there, Aggie?' a strong voice called

from behind the parlour wall. And at the sound Kenneth came to his senses. That was all he needed, a nosy neighbour. With a supreme effort he released his hold on Agnes, then, with a great theatrical gesture he stumbled to the couch and slumped down, dropping his head in his hands – afraid to look at the hovering Agnes for fear he might not be able to contain his rage. Then he heard Agnes call back, 'Yeah, I'm all right, Doris. Just knocked me leg against the table. Thanks anyway.'

Breathing a sigh of relief Kenneth kept his face averted and whispered, 'Oh God, Agnes. I'm so sorry. I don't know what came over me. To go for you of all people, the only person whom I can trust implicitly. Will you forgive me, Agnes? I'll understand if you want me out of the house this instant. It's no more than I deserve after such despicable behaviour.' His hands still covering his face Kenneth held his breath as he waited for some response from Agnes, while cursing himself for his inability to contain his frustration. And it wasn't the first time. Good God, no! If he wasn't careful it would be the undoing of him one day.

Still deeply shocked and unnerved by Kenneth's actions Agnes felt behind her for a chair to steady herself, gratefully sinking down on the padded seat before her legs gave way beneath her. She couldn't believe what had happened. Kenneth, her kind, gentle Kenneth, a man who wouldn't hurt a fly, to have suddenly turned into a madman. If anyone had told her he was capable of such savagery she would have laughed in their face. Yet she had seen it for herself.

Then she heard a loud groan of anguish from the man sitting opposite and all her reservations vanished as Kenneth, looking at her with bloodshot eyes, eyes he had carefully rubbed until they had hurt to get the desired effect, gazed at her in mute contrition. And Agnes, firmly pushing any lingering doubt to the far recesses of her mind, went to the man she loved. With a cry of joyous relief she fell into Kenneth's outstretched arms sobbing, 'Don't worry, love. I understand. Finding yer niece gone like that would make anyone act crazy, especially when yer was so near to rescuing her from that filthy hovel. Now, don't you worry, darling. We'll find the girl, I promise. She can't 'ave got far. She probably got scared when Micky didn't come home and went out looking for 'im. I bet yer anything she's gone back to that place they call 'ome. After all, where else could she go? You probably just missed her. If yer'd waited a while longer, you might have caught her coming back.' Feeling herself being gently but firmly pushed from Kenneth's embrace, Agnes fidgeted with the laced-edged neck of her white frilly blouse, her thumping heart beginning to calm its erratic beat. 'Look, you sit and rest while I make us a nice cuppa, then we'll decide what to do, all right?' She looked at the averted face hopefully.

Conscious he had to make an effort, Kenneth looked up and smiled wanly. 'Thanks, Agnes. I don't deserve you, especially after the way I behaved earlier. I'm so ashamed. I don't know what got into me.'

Agnes' body relaxed. 'Now don't say another word about it, Kenneth. It's all done and forgotten. You just sit there while I fetch the tea. I won't be long.'

Left alone Kenneth allowed his true feelings to surface once more, his devious mind going over the past few weeks. Weeks he'd had to try and pretend he found the ugly old hag attractive. God! How stupid could some women be? Still, if the woman in question was as desperate for a man as Agnes was, she'd believe anything. His upper lip curled in contempt as he recalled how proud Agnes had been of the plan she had thought up to get Micky temporarily out of the way. She'd gone on about a book she'd just finished reading, a book that had given her the idea for getting Micky locked up for stealing some bread. A snort of derision came from his mouth. As if a woman of her limited intelligence could possibly understand the work of Victor Hugo. The stupid woman hadn't even been able to pronounce the title properly, pronouncing it as 'Less Miserables'. Up until that moment Kenneth hadn't had much occasion for humour, but he'd had to stop himself from laughing in her simpering face as she proudly tried to get her tongue around the French title. Obviously someone of higher intelligence had read the famous book and told Agnes snippets of the plot. But out of all the complexities of the story, all Agnes had remembered was the part about Jean Valjean stealing a loaf of bread. Stupid, ignorant cow! And he'd had to look impressed at her supposed knowledge.

Still, it had been worth it. Or so he had thought at the time. When he had met Agnes earlier that evening and she had told him that Micky Masters was safely locked up in Hackney police station, Kenneth had wanted to shout his elation to the very heavens. He'd had no intention of ever seeing Agnes Handly again. He'd had everything planned so meticulously. First he would go to the ruin and wait until Molly finally showed herself. He had expected a long wait as he knew the young girl was under strict instructions from that brat of a brother to keep indoors until he was home. But a child as young as Molly would eventually become frightened and venture out to find her brother, and then he would have her. How he had hurried through the streets, his mind filled with the delights to come once he had the girl safely installed in a secret place he had stumbled across quite by accident, and he was confident that she, like her predecessors, would entertain him for many months, or even years. It all depended on how young they were when he got them. But eventually children grow up, then, sadly, Molly would have to be got rid of, the same as all the others he'd taken over the years. But all that was in the future. Then, after all his scheming, all his fantasies, and, worst of all, the loving attention he'd had to shower on Agnes to keep her sweet, to then find the child gone had been a crushing blow.

He had searched the ruined building frantically when it had become apparent that the house was empty. His first reaction had been one of stunned amazement. Then the anger had begun to burn into a raging hate against the world. A world that didn't understand men like him. Needing to vent his anger on someone he had turned instinctively on Agnes. She was the only other person he could think of who could have taken the child. But now it was evident Agnes knew nothing of the girl's disappearance. More importantly he had almost given himself away. Any other woman with an ounce of pride would have shown him the door immediately, but not Agnes, who still obviously thought the sun shone out of his backside. Even so, he would have to be more careful until he had Molly. Even a woman as lonely and desperate as Agnes would become aware something was wrong sooner or later.

And he still needed Agnes – for the time being. Hearing footsteps Kenneth composed himself and smiled as Agnes reappeared bearing a tray carrying china cups and a plate of sandwiches.

'Shall I be mother?' Agnes simpered coyly.

Shuddering inwardly, Kenneth nodded. 'Please, my dear. Then I must be off. I won't be able to rest until I know my niece is safe.'

Agnes bent her head as she poured out the tea trying to hide her disappointment. She had hoped Kenneth might stay awhile, but it wouldn't be proper to suggest such a thing. Besides, she mustn't forget Kenneth had a wife to go home to.

'Is there anything I can do to help, Kenneth?' she asked wistfully. 'You know yer've only gotta ask.'

Kenneth shook his head. Downing his tea and ignoring the carefully cut sandwiches, he rose to his feet. 'I'm grateful, Agnes, but like I said, I must get off. I'll do what you suggested and go back, just in case Molly has returned.'

Rising with him Agnes walked alongside the immaculately dressed man to the door. 'Of course, Kenneth, I understand, and you've got yer wife to think of an' all, poor soul. I hope she doesn't 'ave too much of a shock if you don't manage to find your niece and bring her home with you tonight.'

For a moment Kenneth looked at her in puzzlement. 'Who . . . ?' he asked vaguely.

Agnes swallowed hard, her previous suspicions returning. 'Yer wife, Kenneth,' she replied, a tremor creeping into her voice. 'I expect she'll be worrying an' all, and that can't be good for a woman in her poor state of 'ealth.'

Immediately Kenneth's brow cleared. 'Good Lord!' he exclaimed, his lips parting to reveal white, even teeth in a wan smile. 'I nearly forgot about poor Margaret. I must get off. Goodnight, my love.'

Following him to the door, Agnes' forehead creased in confusion. Kenneth had just referred to his wife as Margaret, but she could have sworn he had told her his wife's name was Marjorie. Oh, stop it, she chided herself. She must have made a mistake. After all, the two names were similar.

On the doorstep Agnes held her face up for a kiss, and Kenneth obliged by giving the lovelorn woman a peck on the cheek.

Doffing his bowler hat, Kenneth was about to take his leave when a strong, sneering voice boomed in the night air. 'Well, well! If it isn't Kenny Stokes. I haven't seen your ugly mug around these parts for a couple of years. When did they let you out? If it was up to me I'd've thrown away the key, you filthy pervert. You still up to your old tricks, Kenny? 'Cos if you are, then you'd better be careful, as I'm going to be keeping an eye on you now I know you're out. And so will the rest of the nick once they know you're back on this patch.'

Under the street lamp, Kenneth's face drained leaving his handsome face bloodless. But more frightening to Agnes was the look of sheer terror that filled every inch of Kenneth's face.

Stumbling backwards, Kenneth cast a wary, frightened look at the glaring police officer before turning and, almost at a run, made off into the night.

'Well, nice company you're keeping these days, Agnes.' PC John Smith bore down on the startled woman. 'First you stitch up young Micky, now I find you with a piece of scum like Kenny Stokes.'

Her stomach churning, her heart racing, Agnes faced the stony-faced officer bravely. 'I don't know what you're referring to, John Smith. Copper or not, you've no right to be nasty to friends of mine, just 'cos you don't happen to like him. As a matter of fact, Kenneth and me are . . .' She gulped nervously. 'Well, if you must know, we're sort of courting. Only we've gotta keep it quiet, 'cos his poor wife's dying. And his name ain't Stokes, it's Wells, so there,' she added somewhat childishly.

To her horror, the uniformed man stared at her in amazement then threw his head back and laughed loudly. 'Bleeding hell, woman. Talk about there's no fool like an old fool. I don't know what that pervert's been telling you, Agnes, but I can tell you you're a bit too old for Kenny Stokes' tastes. About forty years too old, I'd say.'

Agnes opened her mouth to reply but no words came. All her earlier misgivings, all the suspicious thoughts she had harboured and squashed as soon as she saw Kenneth now came back at her with a vengeance. Yet still she refused to believe what the policeman was telling her, though deep down, in that special place where no one can hide the truth, not even from themselves, she knew with a sickening start that she was hearing the truth. And if that was true . . . Her knees buckled as the full horror of what she had done hit her like a physical blow. If John Smith hadn't moved quickly she would have fallen. When she came round she was in her armchair, John Smith's concerned face bending over her.

'Here, Agnes, old girl. Get this down you.' The smell of brandy wafted under her nose as she gratefully grabbed at the glass. Draining it in one go, she laid her head back, her eyes filling with tears. Dear God! What had she done? Closing her eyes her mind ran down the years to a time in her life that she had tried to obliterate. But, like all memories, sooner or later they surfaced, usually when least wanted or expected.

She was nine years old again, and she was lying on a comfortable sofa with her Uncle Cyril, a horsehair blanket thrown over them. Agnes' mother was in the room, smiling down at them, teasing Agnes for being such a miseryguts when she had such a special uncle who thought the world of her. And all the time under the blanket, in full view of her mother, her Uncle Cyril was touching her down below. Touching and hurting her, and she was powerless to stop him. For if she told, then her mum and dad would go to prison, and so would she for being such a bad little girl.

Her eyes flew open as John Smith said firmly, 'Come

on, old girl, tell me what you know.' The grim-faced officer was seated opposite her, just like Kenneth had done only a short time ago.

'Can I 'ave another drink, John? Gawd help me, I need it.'

Getting to his feet the constable answered kindly, 'It's your brandy, Agnes, but I want to know what's been going on with this Stokes bastard.'

Agnes nodded tiredly. Taking the replenished glass she took a long swallow, then, all the fight knocked out of her, she began to talk.

Micky stirred, a low whimper escaping his lips as he tried to wake himself from the nightmare, but his tired mind was too weak to obey his unconscious demand. Molly was calling for him, but he couldn't get to her. He tried – Oh God, how he tried – but it was no use. The closer he got to her, the further away she went, still calling his name, her pretty face awash with terror.

Then another face appeared in his dream. But this face was soothing, the eyes and lips assuring him everything would be all right. He just had to hang in there, he had to wait until she could get back, and then the nightmare would be over.

His body thrashed this way and that, but still he slept on. He could hear her voice so clearly, and after a while his body relaxed slightly. Then he called out into the darkness, 'Ellen, Ellen, come home. Please! Please, Ellen, come back.' Yet still he remained deep in slumber.

Opposite the young boy, Ted awoke with a start. 'Micky! Micky! You awake, mate?'

There was no answer from the slender form

huddled up in the armchair. Satisfied Micky was still asleep, Ted made himself comfortable while wondering if he had indeed heard Micky call out for Ellen, or if he himself had dreamed it. Either way, she was needed back here, as much for his sake as Micky's.

But would she come back if asked? There was only one way to find out. And Ted fully intended to do just that.

CHAPTER THIRTEEN

The Grand Hotel was in a prime position overlooking the sea front in the popular holiday resort of Southend. Visitors staying at the Grand were only five minutes away from the multitude of entertainment facilities which included theatres, amusement arcades and plenty of other activities to occupy the ever-increasing stream of holiday makers who had chosen Southend for their annual vacation. The Council boasted that their fair town had something for everyone, whatever their age. But, despite all the attractions of Britain's much loved resort, Ellen was bored out of her mind.

On this spring morning, Ellen was sitting out on the balcony adjacent to their first-floor room staring at the wonderful view of the sea front and sighed heavily. She had imagined that having some time to themselves would bring her and Arthur closer. Instead it had only served to emphasise how little they had in common. They had been fine back home – at least Ellen had thought so. Now she realised that it was only the fact that, during their short marriage, she and Arthur had spent very little time alone together. During the day they were both busy in the shop, and at night, tired out by the long day, and knowing they had to be up early, they normally only spent an hour or so in each other's company before retiring to bed. And then, she was usually reading while Arthur dozed off after his evening meal. Both of them had become accustomed to their daily routine, not realising they were, without knowing it, forming a kind of barrier between them, unconsciously masking the insurmountable differences in their personalities.

The holiday had started off well. The change of scenery and the chance to relax had been wonderful. Their days had been filled with exploring the seaside resort and all the sights it had to offer, but when they were alone in the hotel suite, or dining out at one of the local restaurants, it had soon become painfully clear to both Ellen and Arthur that their conversation was becoming more and more stilted and awkward. In some respects they were like a couple thrown together by chance and were now realising they had nothing in common. In all honesty Ellen had to admit that the sad state of affairs wasn't solely Arthur's fault; she was as much to blame for the tension that existed between them. The main trouble was that all of Arthur's conversation revolved around the bakery and the day to day running of his beloved business. Whereas Ellen, now she had broadened her horizons, due mainly to her friendship with Ted Parker and Micky, plus the various stall holders she had become friendly with over the past months, had plenty to talk about and humorous stories to tell. But whenever she tried to share her thoughts, Arthur would quickly change the subject and revert to his pet love – the bakery, the tradesmen, and of course, his loyal customers. It was as if he was trying to pretend that Ellen didn't have a life of her own now. And if he told her once more about the rise of prices in flour, yeast and everything else they needed to run the bakery she felt she wouldn't be responsible for her actions. Even that wouldn't have been so bad if the stories varied, but they were always the same. Yet Arthur continually regaled Ellen with his narrations as if imagining his wife was hearing them for the first time. And Ellen, heartily sick of hearing the familiar anecdotes again and again, had to restrain herself from screaming at him in frustration. The only thing that had saved her sanity was making the acquaintance of a middle-aged couple, May and George Bradley.

They had met at dinner in the hotel dining room and, after the initial embarrassment of being mistaken for father and daughter, the atmosphere had quickly changed. Much to Ellen's surprise, Arthur, who normally shied clear of meeting strangers, had taken to the pleasant couple with uncharacteristic warmth and enthusiasm. At first Ellen had been stunned to find her husband suggesting they make up a foursome, until she realised that Arthur too was aware that things weren't going well between them. And this knowledge only made Ellen feel more guilty. In a fit of desperation she had suggested they cut their holiday short and return home. She had been sure Arthur would jump at the idea, but there she had been wrong. For someone who had had to be dragged metaphorically kicking and screaming into taking a holiday, Arthur now seemed to be thoroughly enjoying himself. Or maybe he just wanted to keep Ellen away from London – and Ted Parker – for as long as possible. She was beginning to wonder if she had underestimated her husband.

She had imagined he was blissfully unaware of her growing attraction to the engaging stall holder, but now she wasn't so sure. He hadn't actually come out and said anything – that wasn't Arthur's way, for he hated any form of confrontation – but certain little things he had said, in a perfectly innocent manner, had caused a flutter of anxiety in Ellen's already guilty mind. If Arthur had indeed suspected anything, there was one thing of which Ellen was absolutely certain – those ideas had been planted in his mind by somebody. Arthur was intrinsically too honest and trusting to think of such a thing left to his own devices, and it didn't take a genius to figure out who that person was. She could just see Agnes making veiled remarks with her spiteful tongue. From the moment she and Arthur had married, Agnes had been looking for just such an opportunity to split her former lover and his young bride apart.

As this thought came to mind, Ellen's body gave an involuntary jump. Her heart began to beat faster as she imagined what it would be like to be free of

Arthur, and immediately she was once more assailed by guilt. But after the last disastrous ten days she knew she couldn't go on the way things stood. If she was bored and dissatisfied with her life now, how, in God's name, would she feel ten, or twenty, years from now? She shuddered at the thought. Arthur could live until his eighties or even nineties, by which time she would be in her fifties, an old woman, childless and bitter at the waste of her life. And as that thought crossed her mind, another one entered it. This must be how Agnes felt.

Ellen couldn't help but feel a pang of pity for her adversary. But she, Ellen, was still young enough to start again – if it wasn't for Arthur. Her eyes flew open in horror. What was she thinking? It was almost as if she were wishing Arthur dead so she could be free. No! No! She mustn't entertain such awful thoughts. She didn't wish Arthur any harm, it was just that ... well! She couldn't help but wish he would just ... just disappear. To go off somewhere, somewhere he would be happy, and in doing so set her free. A wry smile touched her lips. Maybe he would rediscover the feelings he had once held for Agnes and run off with her? The frivolous notion quickly vanished. 'I should be so lucky,' she muttered sadly. Getting to her feet she began to pace the small balcony, her thoughts in turmoil. She could always ask Arthur for a divorce, but even as the idea entered her mind it was gone. If she were to take such action, Arthur would be devastated. Not only that, he would also be deeply humiliated at being jilted by his child bride. It was what everyone who knew them was waiting for, and she couldn't do that to Arthur. Whatever his faults, he was a decent man and didn't deserve to be made an object of ridicule.

No! She would just have to put up with her life and make the most of a bad job. What was that old saying? She'd made her bed and now she must lie in it.

But she had been so young. Young and terrified of what was to become of her. She had jumped at the idea of marriage without giving a single thought as to what she was letting herself in for. If she'd had more experience of life she wouldn't have married a man twice her age just for a sense of security. But in that respect, Arthur hadn't been entirely blameless. As Agnes had so bitterly reproached him, he could have adopted her, or applied for legal guardianship. Ellen's eyes hardened. She at least had the excuse of innocence for her part in the hasty marriage; Arthur, on the other hand, had no such excuse. He had known exactly what he was doing.

Leaning her arms on the intricate iron railing of the balcony she squeezed her eyes shut. It was no use going over and over the same ground. The rights and wrongs of the past were done and couldn't be undone. That didn't mean to say the future couldn't be changed. Because the way things were now, it wasn't fair to either of them. Not for her, nor Arthur. He deserved better than a wife who didn't love him, not in the way a real wife should. And she deserved the chance for a proper marriage, with a husband she loved and children. She had always wanted to be a mother, but that would never happen while she was still tied to Arthur. Then there was Ted. With his laughing eyes and daredevil ways. Ted, a man who could turn her legs to water just by looking at her in that intimate way she both loved and feared. She knew he was just waiting for her to say the word, and he wouldn't think twice about taking her away from Arthur. Men like Ted took what they wanted without fear for the consequences. And that sort of man, if she was brutally honest with herself, was exactly what she craved. Only she wasn't brave enough to take that ultimate step. And that knowledge made her want to cry out in anguish and disgust at her own weakness.

She was rudely awoken from her daydream by the sound of her voice being called. Leaning over the balcony she groaned at the sight that met her eyes.

Standing outside the hotel looking up at her, his face beaming, was Arthur. Beside him, also smiling brightly, were the Bradleys, the middle-aged couple who had appeared like a godsend to Ellen. In their company Ellen could have a rest from the growing ordeal of making conversation with her husband. It had also meant she no longer had to entertain Arthur, much as one would with a young child, for, from the moment they had arrived in Southend, Arthur had clung to her side like a boy fearful of losing sight of his mother. If the Bradleys hadn't arrived when they had, Ellen didn't know how much longer her frayed nerves would have held out. With gentle persuasion she had encouraged Arthur to spend as much time as possible with their new-found friends, leaving her some much needed time to herself. He had objected at first, been almost frightened at the idea of branching out on his own without the presence of his wife to steer him in the right direction, and of course, to step into the conversation if it became stilted. Now it seemed he no longer needed her by his side every waking minute of the day, and for that reason alone, even if, after the holiday, she never saw either of them again, she would be for ever grateful to May and George Bradley.

'Ellen, Ellen, love. We're going down to the front to watch a game of bowls, maybe even have a game if we can. Do you want to join us?'

Ellen smiled back weakly. Watching a group of middle-aged men playing bowls wasn't her idea of entertainment; given the choice she'd rather watch paint dry. But if she could get Arthur and the Bradleys out of the way she could take a long stroll along the promenade, looking in the shops, relishing the time to herself. She might even go for a paddle, and hope Arthur didn't see her. He'd have a fit if he were to see her with her dress up around her knees showing her legs to all and sundry.

'Would you mind very much if I didn't, Arthur? I was looking forward to spending the day window shopping.'

Arthur waved his hand airily, his face a picture of husbandly indulgence. 'Of course I don't mind, love. If you're sure you'll be all right on your own.'

Biting down a moment's irritation Ellen smiled down at the trio. 'I'll be fine, Arthur. You get off, and I'll see you later for afternoon tea.'

With further waving and assurances they would

meet up later the trio finally walked off, disappearing into the swarm of people that filled the promenade. A sigh of relief escaped Ellen's lips. Getting to her feet she breathed in a deep lungful of sea air and walked back into the adjoining room, her eyes glancing at the mantel clock. It was now just after ten, which meant she had a whole five hours to herself. Grinning broadly she picked up her bonnet and bag and, like a child looking forward to a day off school, she made her way down to the foyer.

She was so engrossed in planning the precious time ahead of her she didn't hear her name being called at first until the receptionist called again.

'Mrs Mitson, there's a telegram for you. I was just about to send the bell boy to your room to deliver it.'

Taken by surprise Ellen took the brown envelope being held out to her, her mind whirling as she tried to think of who could possibly have sent a telegram. Nobody liked receiving the official-looking envelopes, for they usually contained bad news, and Ellen was no exception. Seating herself into a plush armchair in the foyer she carefully opened the envelope, and what she read brought her quickly to her feet.

'Is everything all right, Madam?' The male receptionist had appeared by her side, his face showing concern.

Gathering her thoughts, Ellen answered quickly, 'Yes! I mean, no, not really.' Folding the telegram she looked into the curious eyes of the smartly dressed man. 'There's been some trouble at home. I'm afraid we're going to have to cut our holiday short. Would you kindly prepare our bill while I fetch my husband.'

'Of course, Madam. I trust it's nothing too serious,' he said, his tone hopeful as if waiting for further information. But here he was disappointed, for Ellen, with an absent nod, swept out of the hotel in search of her husband.

'I still don't understand why we have to give up our holiday just because Ted Parker sends a telegram asking us to come back because young Micky's in trouble. I mean to say, it's not as if he's a relation, is it? What about his parents? Surely it's them who should be taking responsibility for their child. Unless they're incapable of looking after their own son. Still! They wouldn't be the first to neglect their offspring. Probably a couple of drunks, sponging off respectable, hard-working men like me.'

His fleshy face quivering petulantly Arthur failed to notice the anger building on Ellen's face.

'Besides, what could be so important that it couldn't have waited a few more days? I was really enjoying myself, and it was you who made such a fuss about taking a holiday in the first place. When I think of the inconvenience, not to mention having to let the Bradleys down, well . . .'

Ellen turned sharply to the red-faced, indignant man by her side and answered in no small voice, 'First of all, there was no mention in the telegram of you being needed, or wanted for that matter. You could have stayed behind with the Bradleys, I told you that, but of course you wouldn't hear of it, would you? Oh, not because you were concerned for me travelling back to London on my own, but because you were worried what it might look like if you had.'

Almost bouncing on the padded seat Ellen's voice rose a notch higher, much to Arthur's embarrassment.

'I wish to God you had stayed behind. You've done nothing but moan and whine about the inconvenience to yourself, with not a word of concern about Micky. Ted Parker wouldn't have gone to all the trouble of contacting us if it hadn't been important. But then, other people's troubles have never been high on your list of priorities, have they, Arthur? Unless of course you aren't put out in any way, then you're all smiles and affability. Well, I'm not like you. I care for my friends, and Micky is a friend. Maybe not a friend of yours, but he certainly is one of mine. And if he needs me, then I'm going to be there for him.'

Her steadily rising voice was attracting the attention of the other passengers aboard the train heading back to London, and immediately Arthur changed tack. Smiling inanely at two women seated on the other side of the aisle he bent his head to Ellen's and hissed nervously, 'Keep your voice down, woman. We don't want all and sundry knowing our business. We'll have plenty of time to discuss this unfortunate incident when we get home.'

Angrily Ellen shifted away from her agitated husband, a feeling of distaste rising inside her body that this two-faced, petulant man was her spouse. 'There you go again, thinking of yourself as usual. I should have come back on my own. After all, as you've so forcefully pointed out, Micky's problems are of no concern to you. And as I've already said, you could have stayed on at the hotel, I did tell you to. In fact I almost begged you to stay behind. But, oh no! That would have meant showing your true colours to your new friends, and that would never do, would it?' A slow shudder rippled through her body. 'God! Every time I think of the way you expressed genuine concern for Micky, it makes me feel sick. You were so convincing, I nearly believed you myself. But it was all an act, just so you could portray yourself in a good light for the Bradleys' benefit . . . Oh, get away from me . . .' Ellen pulled her hand away from Arthur's clammy grasp. 'I'm going to the dining car, and don't even think of following me, or I swear I'll really show you up.'

She glared down at the florid, quivering face and again felt a wave of shame – shame that this man was her husband. Arthur made no further move to stop her. Taking out the newspaper he had bought at the station he made a great study of burying his attention in the day's news.

Steadying herself against the rocking motion of the train Ellen entered the dining car and was immediately shown to an empty table. Suddenly realising she'd had nothing to eat since breakfast she ordered a pot of tea and a large cream cake. As she tucked into the delicious treat she reflected wryly that Arthur's stomach must be rumbling by now. If he hadn't been so preoccupied with having his holiday spoiled he would have made a beeline for the dining-car the moment they had boarded the train. For if there was one other love he had apart from the bakery, it was his stomach. But she had no fear he would follow her, not after the harsh words she had levelled at him.

Gazing out of the window as the train swept past the picturesque countryside Ellen wondered what could have happened that would make Ted take such drastic action as to send for her. Her hand flew to her mouth as an awful thought struck her. What if something terrible had happened to Micky? Oh, God! No, not that. An image of that sweet, handsome face floated before her eyes and her stomach lurched in alarm. Despite what Arthur said about the young boy not being any relation, Ellen felt differently. To her Micky was like the younger brother she'd never had. Ever since he had appeared at the door of the bakery, cold, hungry and ragged, yet maintaining an air of dignity in spite of his obvious plight, Ellen had felt an overwhelming responsibility for the young lad. And since Ted had taken him under his wing the change in Micky had been remarkable. He was a different person to the one she had first encountered, and Ellen couldn't help but feel a certain amount of pleasure and satisfaction that she had been instrumental in helping Micky forge a better life for himself.

But Arthur was right about one thing. Why would Ted take the drastic measure of sending for her unless matters back home were indeed serious? If so, then where were Micky's parents in his hour of need? Closing her eyes Ellen let the gentle rolling of the train lull her into a light sleep. Telling herself she could do nothing until they knew more about the situation, she let her body relax. She had a feeling she was going to need all her strength in the days to come.

CHAPTER FOURTEEN

Ellen, Ted and Arthur were sitting in the living room above the shop, the light refreshments Ellen had prepared and laid out on the dining table forgotten. The Mitsons listened in stunned silence as Ted recounted what had transpired during their short absence. When finally Ted stopped talking, Ellen stared at the dark-haired man she had missed more than she cared to admit, her thoughts whirling. So, poor Micky was an orphan on the run from the workhouse. Not only that, but he had an eight-year-old sister who was utterly dependent on him. Why, oh why hadn't he confided in her? But then, as Ted had pointed out, Micky had been too afraid of being sent back to the workhouse. Also the loyal young man hadn't wanted to take the chance of making trouble for his new-found friends. But all that paled into insignificance beside the horror of Molly Masters abducted by a known pervert, aided and abetted by Agnes Handly.

And that was what Ellen was finding so hard to believe.

Ellen knew her employee was capable of many things, but never in a million years would Ellen believe that even Agnes would stoop so low as to deliver an innocent child into the hands of a child abuser. There must be a mistake, there must be.

Arthur too was finding it hard to believe, but, unlike Ellen, Arthur's mind was working along very different lines. For years he had been trying to find a way to rid himself of the woman who caused him daily embarrassment and shame at the way he had treated her. Up until now he'd been unsuccessful in his quest, but now! His chest swelled, his heart began to beat erratically as he saw himself dismissing Agnes in a great show of moral outrage, preferably in the presence of an audience. No one would blame him. There was an unwritten code amongst the criminals of the East End. Stealing, extortion, violence and even murder were looked upon as a way of life because life was hard and people did what they could in order to survive. But there was one brand of low-life that even the most hardened of criminals wouldn't tolerate, and that was child molesters. The second most reviled person or persons were those who helped the sick, depraved men attain their innocent prey.

Arthur's mind was working furiously. This was the perfect opportunity for killing two birds with one stone. On the one hand he would be rid of the woman who had been a thorn in his side for years, and in doing so would raise his status in the community. No longer would he be looked upon as just good old Arthur. Dependable, dull Arthur. Tolerated and treated with the same kind of affection one would show to a faithful, aging dog. His chest swelled further as he envisaged the future. The new respect he would see mirrored in people's eyes, the deference he would command in the community. Of course he would have to make the dismissal of Agnes public, and the more witnesses to Agnes' humiliation the better. He frowned as a sudden thought struck him. After what had happened it was doubtful Agnes would dare show her face in public for quite some time. Then he relaxed. If she wouldn't come to him, then he would go to her, bringing with him as many observers as he could attract along the way.

The inner feeling of euphoria almost caused Arthur to rub his hands in glee. Fortunately he stopped himself in time. But in his vivid imagination there was no thought for the Masters children, even for the child Molly. It wasn't that Arthur was an unfeeling or unkind man, and if he were to witness a child being hurt he would step in to help if he could. But people like Arthur, who hadn't the gift of empathy, were incapable of feeling other people's pain, especially that of strangers. So wrapped up in his own private world was Arthur that everyone and everything was as of no consequence. His face and portly body rigid with self-importance, Arthur rose slowly to his feet. Sticking his chin out from the white starched collar of his shirt, he stuck his thumbs into the lapels of his jacket, rocked back on his heels and boomed pompously, 'Well, this is a fine state of affairs I must say. Though if the young man in question had been honest with us in the first place, none of this appalling business would have happened. But it has, and now we must try and minimise the damage.'

Ellen, brought out of her reverie with a start, could only stare open mouthed at the puffed-up features of her husband. Flickering her gaze at Ted she winced at the look of disgust that crossed his rugged face. Yet she couldn't blame him, for she too was experiencing the same sense of loathing.

Remaining seated she looked up at her husband and said icily, 'Minimise the damage! Is that all you can think of, Arthur? Why don't you just come straight out with it? What you really mean is how this is going to reflect on you, and the business. But don't worry, once word spreads they'll be queuing down the road from here to Mare Street, just on the off chance they might be able to pick up some juicy gossip. People are like that, not all of them, but most. They love to see other people's misery, it must be a distraction from their own dreary lives. Ghouls, that's all most people are, ghouls, and you're no better than any of them.'

Gripping the sides of her chair Ellen gritted her teeth as she almost spat the words at him. 'Ever since we arrived home and heard what Ted had to tell us, your only thought has been for yourself, and how my involvement with Micky might affect you . . .'

Aware of Ted's contemptuous glare Arthur's head snapped back on his neck. His colouring heightened further as he attempted to regain some home ground. 'Now look here, Ellen. I won't have you talking to me in that tone. Don't forget you are my wife, and as such will conduct yourself in a like manner.'

Ellen's face twitched in amusement at the unfamiliar tone. Their short acquaintance with the Bradleys had obviously rubbed off on Arthur. But where the Bradleys' way of talking was natural, Arthur merely sounded ridiculous. She could almost visualise him twirling the ends of a waxed moustache, if he'd possessed one. But the moment of humour was short-lived. For as she stared into the puffy face suffused with self-righteousness she realised that whatever feelings she had once held for Arthur were now gone. With his callous disregard for the plight of eight-year-old Molly, and the anguish Micky must be going through, he had killed the last vestige of affection and loyalty she had held for him as surely as if he'd severed them with a sharp blade. Worst of all, although she had never been in love with him, she had always respected and liked him as a person, and had held a great fondness for him. Now she found she didn't even like him any more, and she knew sadly that she would never feel the same about her husband ever again.

A sudden movement opposite her brought her attention back to Ted. The tall brooding man was on his feet. His eyes cold with contempt he turned his back deliberately on Arthur and, looking at Ellen, said shortly, 'Micky's at my house, if you want to see him. He's in a terrible state, poor sod. But who wouldn't be, in his shoes? You'd have to have a heart of stone not to feel for him right now.' Out of the corner of his eye Ted saw Arthur's lips twitch nervously and thought angrily, Yeah, that was directed at you, yer selfish, fat bastard. 'I haven't slept for more than an hour since Molly went missing.' He gave a short grunt of derision. 'Not that I can take any credit for that. Anyone with a bit of compassion would feel the same. Me mum's in a right old state, an' she don't even know the girl. But that don't make no difference. A child's a child whether you know them or not. And anyone with an ounce of decency would feel the same.' This time Ted made no attempt to disguise his contempt as he turned and stared coldly into Arthur's ruddy face. And such was the fury in Ted's eyes that Arthur stepped back a pace, his jowls quivering in fear and apprehension, knowing he was no match in either verbal or physical strength to Ted.

Inwardly squirming, Arthur made one last desperate effort to regain control of the situation. Directing his gaze at Ellen he said, 'Well, at least you won't have to concern yourself with Micky Masters any more. Now the truth's out, he'll be sent straight back to the workhouse, and if he's any sense he'll stay there until he's lawfully released . . .'

His words were cut off abruptly as Ted sprang across the room, his hands grabbing at Arthur's jacket in a vicious hold.

'Micky's going back to no workhouse, yer unfeeling bastard. He's staying with me an' me mum, and little Molly too when she's found. And I will find her. If I have to knock on every door and walk every mile of the East End, I'll do it.' Even as he said the words Ted knew he was grasping at straws where Molly was concerned. She could be anywhere. She might never be found. She wouldn't be the first child to go missing and never be seen again. But if he couldn't help Molly, he could provide a proper home for Micky. It wouldn't be easy. He'd have the authorities to deal with first. But if the worst came to the worst he'd up sticks and move away from the East End, because there was no way on God's earth he would let Micky go back to the workhouse; it would be like signing the boy's death warrant.

'Ted! Ted, for God's sake, let him go. This isn't solving anything. Please, Ted, stop it.'

Startled, Ted looked down at Ellen, then he felt her hands pulling at him and realised his own were wrapped around Arthur's flabby neck. Recoiling in shock, Ted's hands released their grip as quickly as if he'd been holding red-hot coals.

Severely shaken and gasping for breath Arthur staggered backwards, falling in a heap into the armchair he had so recently vacated.

The atmosphere was charged with tension. Then Ted, his face grim, turned to a pale-faced Ellen and said tersely, 'You coming with me or staying here? It's up to you.'

Faced with the option of going with Ted or staying here with Arthur, Ellen didn't hesitate. 'Of course I'll come,' she replied, picking up her cotton gloves and straw hat. Not looking back she said quietly, 'I don't know what time I'll be back, Arthur. Don't wait up for me.'

With Ted by his wife's side, Arthur could only watch helplessly as Ellen swept from the room.

* * *

175

Passing through the empty bakery Ellen forced herself
to put from her mind the unpleasant scene she had
just witnessed and focus her thoughts on Micky. Then,
her eyes bewildered, she asked Ted, 'I know there's
no love lost between me and Agnes, but I can't believe
she would do such a despicable thing. She must have
been duped into doing what she did.' Fiddling with
the clasp of her bag she lowered her gaze adding, 'I
want to see her, Ted. I have to know exactly what
happened while we were away ... I know, I know ...'
she held up a hand as Ted made to protest. 'I've
heard all the facts, but I want to hear Agnes' side of
it.'

Ted's face darkened. 'You go and see her if you
want, but I ain't going anywhere near the old bitch. I
wouldn't trust meself within a mile of her.'

It was only five minutes' walk to the row of terraced
houses where Agnes lived, and during the short
journey neither Ted nor Ellen spoke. It was as if they
had made an unspoken agreement not to mention
what had happened back at the bakery; that particular topic would have to be put on hold for the time
being. But it wasn't going to go away. Sooner or later
there was going to be a confrontation between herself,
Ted and Arthur, and it wasn't something she was
looking forward to. But for now Micky and his missing
sister were her top priorities.

As they approached the road Agnes lived in, the
first thing they saw was the burly figure of John Smith
standing guard outside the green door. The second
thing that caught their attention was the fact that the
front window had been smashed in.

'Afternoon, Mrs Mitson. Glad to see you back, love. Young Micky'll feel a lot better when he sees you, poor little sod. It was good of you to cut your holiday short.'

Ellen smiled wanly. 'To tell the truth, Officer, I was glad of the excuse. I know it was my idea to get away, but I was bored stiff after a couple of days.' Aware she was stalling for time, Ellen stepped forward, her hand gesturing towards the closed door. 'Could I see Agnes, Officer? Like I've said to Ted, I'd like to hear her side of the story before I make any judgment.'

Constable John Smith's face softened. She was a nice young woman was Ellen Mitson. She of all people would be justified in taking satisfaction from Agnes' present predicament. It was common knowledge how Agnes had tried her hardest to make life difficult for the new Mrs Mitson. Yet now, when Agnes needed friends, only Ellen was prepared to give her the benefit of the doubt. He himself had no liking for the acid-tongued woman, but after hearing her pitiful story, and seeing the genuine distress she was in, he had volunteered to stand guard outside Agnes' home, knowing the outcry that would ensue when word got around about what had transpired. He had no doubt Agnes had been tricked by a master craftsman, and was as much a victim as the child that had gone missing. Kenneth Stokes, or Wells, as he was now calling himself, had had plenty of practice in duping vulnerable women in his perverted search for fresh young bodies. PC John Smith, like his fellow officers, could only stand by and watch in frustration as men like Stokes got off time and time again. Men like him

177

were clever. They targeted poor families, worming their way into poverty-stricken homes, playing the benevolent gentleman, offering to take one of the children and find them a live-in job. Of course, the hungry, desperate mothers jumped at the chance of having at least one of their children taken care of. Of course there was no job and when Stokes and his kind were finished with their victims they would bring them back, cowed and too terrified to tell their parents what had happened to them.

Men like Stokes were the scum of the earth, not fit to breathe God's air. To make sure of their victims' silence, these so-called gentlemen would always leave a small amount of money to keep the parents quiet. But every now and then, an outraged parent on learning the truth had refused to be intimidated and had gone to the police, but rarely had the case ever come to court. For when it came to the day, with help from local bully boys, paid to instil fear into those brave enough to stand up to them, the parents in question would reluctantly withdraw their complaint. And no amount of police assurances were enough to convince them they would be kept safe until the trial was over. And who could blame them? John Smith thought sorrowfully. For every police officer stationed in the East End, there were ten villains who would cut their own granny's throat for the price of a pint of beer. In the twenty years Kenneth Stokes had been prowling the East End, he had been jailed only twice, both times sentenced to a poxy three years. But then, men like Stokes had money, and money bought the best solicitors.

'Of course you can see her, love. She needs all the help she can get right now.' Nodding towards the broken glass he added, 'As you can see, word's out already. If I hadn't turned up, things could have got a lot worse. Anyway, you go on in, love, while I have a word with Ted here.' He looked at Ted, saw the naked hatred in the dark eyes and shook his head, wondering if there was any point in trying to put Agnes' version of events to the normally cheerful stall holder. Well! He had nothing better to do, did he? It was worth a try.

Ellen passed through the green door and stepped warily into the small hallway. Swallowing nervously she called out, 'Agnes. Agnes, it's me, Ellen. May I come in, Agnes? I'd like to talk to you, if that's all right.'

Only silence greeted her words, but Ellen remained where she was. Obviously Agnes had heard her. Equally obviously, she was suspicious of Ellen's arrival. Knowing this, Ellen took another few tentative steps nearer the front room, talking all the while.

'I know you can hear me, Agnes. Agnes! Look, I don't blame you for being suspicious, but I promise you I haven't come to cause you any more trouble. I only want to help. I've always believed in making my own decisions, so until I hear it from your own lips, I'm not going to take any notice of the talk that's all around the streets.'

Still there was no answer. Then into the eerie silence came the sound of quiet sobbing, a sound that wrenched at Ellen's soft heart.

Her mouth dry, Ellen entered the front room, and there, curled up in a shabby armchair, was Agnes, her thin body wracked with heart-breaking sobs.

At the sight of her old adversary's distress, Ellen let out a low moan of pity. 'Oh, Agnes.' Dropping her bag on the dining table, Ellen knelt down by the armchair and laid a hand on the shuddering form. 'Look, shall I make some tea? I know it's an old cliché in circumstances like these, but it'll give me something to do while you try to compose yourself.'

Still there was no response from Agnes. It was only when Ellen put her hand on the thin arm that the body in the armchair suddenly came to life. With a frightening change in demeanour Agnes sat bolt upright, slapping Ellen's hand away viciously. 'I've already been taken for a mug, but I ain't a complete idiot.'

Her plain face ravaged by hours of crying, Agnes glared at the pretty young face staring back at her. And saw only pity and compassion mirrored in the clear blue eyes. Yet still she remained wary, and with good cause. With their past history why should Ellen Mitson worry about what happened to her?

Swallowing loudly, Agnes swivelled around in the chair, her gaze focused on the floor. 'I know why yer've come. Couldn't resist the opportunity ter gloat, could yer? Well, now's yer chance. So go ahead an' get it over with, then yer can piss off back ter where yer came from.'

Drawing herself up from her crouching position Ellen said quietly, 'I'll put the kettle on, it'll give me something to do while you think about what you've just said. And while you're thinking, ask yourself if

180

you really believe I'm the sort of person you've just described. If you decide I am, then I'll go and not trouble you again. But you and me know each other well, Agnes, and that's why I'm here. I don't believe for one moment you would deliberately conspire to hand an innocent child over to a pervert. All I ask is that you give me the same courtesy of the benefit of the doubt as to why I'm here. I'll be back in five minutes for your answer.'

Out in the scullery Ellen made herself busy, and when she returned carrying a tea tray Agnes was sitting upright, her red-rimmed eyes holding a tentative spark of hope.

Her voice quivering she asked, 'You really mean it? You really wanna 'elp me, hear my side of the story?'

Pouring out the tea Ellen smiled. 'That's why I'm here, Agnes.'

At Ellen's words Agnes' body slumped with relief. Now she had two allies – and that was two more than she had dared hope for. Maybe with John Smith and Ellen backing her up, there might still be a future for her in the East End.

As Agnes talked, Ellen listened and as the whole sordid tale unravelled she realised that her own problems seemed insignificant in comparison. Pushing all other thoughts from her mind, Ellen gave her undivided attention to Agnes.

CHAPTER FIFTEEN

'Put 'er outta yer mind, son. Yer only setting yerself up for a load of grief if yer carry on 'oping she'll leave 'er 'usband for you. It just ain't done, mate ... Well, not very often. And even then, yer've gotta 'ave a bleeding good reason fer wanting to get shot of an 'usband or wife. Yer can't just get a divorce 'cos yer fed up with yer spouse. Gawd 'elp us, if it was that easy, there wouldn't be very many married couples still together.' Nora Parker shot a quick look at her son, her heart missing a painful beat at the look of misery etched on his face.

Moving away from her only child Nora began setting out plates and cutlery for the fish and chip supper Ted had picked up on his way home, her thoughts racing in despair. Her Ted was a good-looking man, with a quick wit and overpowering personality and charm that had had the girls running after him since he was in short trousers. He could have had the pick of any woman, but who does he go and fall for? A bleeding married woman, that's who. Bustling around the small scullery Nora looked through to the sitting room where Ellen was sitting on the sofa, the pitiful figure of Micky Masters snuggled close to her side. So wrapped up in her thoughts was she, that Nora jumped when Ted's answer came.

'I'm a grown man, an' I'll make me own mistakes, just like I've always done, and not be frightened to face the consequences. Now, let's get this grub eaten before it gets cold. There'll be plenty of time to say your piece, 'cos you ain't gonna let it drop, no matter what I say. But not now, eh, Mum? Right now looking after Micky and finding his sister is more important than my love life, or lack of it!'

He grinned at Nora, and that lop-sided smile made even her, his own mother, want to reach out and grab hold of him. And in that respect she was lucky. As his mother, she could hold him any time she chose. With a wry smile she said affectionately, 'Give over. You'll never go short of female company, an' yer know it.'

Ted gazed down at her fondly, then winked. 'What can I say, Mum? I can't help being irresistible to women, now can I?'

But behind the jocular manner, Nora knew that there was only one woman he was interested in. And her looking barely older than the child she was comforting. A sharp slap on her backside propelled Nora forward, the impact almost upsetting the tray carrying their supper. Entering the living room she glanced up at her son and said waspishly, 'You'll smack my ars— backside once too often, me lad.

You're not too old ter get a good clout if I put me mind to it; just you remember that, mate.'

Handing out portions of the tempting food Ted chuckled. 'You don't have to mind your words in front of Ellen, Mum. I don't think she'll go into a swoon if she hears the word arse, would you, love?'

Ted's eyes were fixed on Ellen, and Nora, her heart sinking, saw the adoration shining from Ellen's eyes as she answered cheerfully, 'I very much doubt it. Working in the East End has toughened me up considerably. Mind you, I probably would have a couple of years ago before . . .' Her voice trailed off, her manner suddenly solemn as she remembered Arthur waiting at home on his own. But she felt so at ease here in Ted's home. She already knew Nora from the shop, and although their home wasn't a patch on her own rooms above the bakery, she felt more comfortable here than she'd ever felt anywhere else since her parents' death. Aware she was in danger of putting a damper on the evening, and realising that Micky needed to be in a positive atmosphere she said brightly, 'Goodness, I'm starving. I haven't had anything to eat since one cream cake on the train coming back, and that smell is heavenly.' Shifting her position to ease Micky from her side she said softly, 'Come on, Micky. Sit up properly and have your supper.'

His arms clinging to Ellen, Micky said tremulously, 'I ain't 'ungry.'

Gently but firmly Ellen extracted herself from Micky's fierce hold. 'Now look here, Micky. I know . . .' She looked at Ted and Nora. 'We all know how worried you are, but like I've already told you, that man hasn't got Molly. Agnes said . . .'

Micky twisted angrily away from her. 'I don't believe that old cow. I wouldn't believe anything she said. It was her fault I was nicked, just to get me outta the way so that pervert could get his 'ands on my Molly. He's been after 'er for months, but I looked after 'er. I protected 'er. But now . . . now . . . he's got 'er. An' . . . an' . . .' He broke off, his voice failing him as he dissolved into heart-rending sobs.

The three adults looked at each other helplessly, but it was Ellen who quickly took charge of the situation, making Nora realise that despite her youthful appearance, Ellen had a good head on her shoulders, which was more than could be said of some of the women Ted had brought home, none of whom had lasted long. But Ellen was speaking, bringing Nora's attention back to the two young people cuddling on her sofa.

In a strong, firm voice, Ellen took hold of Micky's shuddering shoulders and said, 'Now look, Micky, that man hasn't got your sister.' As Micky tried to pull away from Ellen's grasp, he found his face cradled in two soft hands, then his chin was lifted upwards and he was staring into Ellen's blue eyes.

'I don't blame you for not trusting Agnes, especially after the way she set you up for shoplifting. But think, Micky, think! If that man had got hold of Molly, then why would he have come back to see Agnes? And why would he have attacked her? Because he thought she had told on him. Either that, or she had changed her mind and got to Molly first. If that evil man had Molly, he'd have been long gone by now. He certainly wouldn't still be hanging around the East End.'

Micky's eyes flickered as he tried to take in Ellen's words. Part of him wanted to believe that Molly was safe somewhere, but his tortured mind was afraid to get his hopes up. Yet what Ellen was saying made sense. The only reason Kenneth Wells had sucked up to that old cow Agnes was to get his dirty hands on his beautiful, innocent sister. But if he didn't have Molly, then where was she? Oh Gawd, his head hurt, his stomach was churning, and he had a sensation in his chest he hadn't experienced since the death of his parents. He couldn't think straight. All he wanted to do was curl up in Ellen's comforting arms, and wake up to find his sweet Molly's face smiling at him.

'Micky! Micky, have you been listening to what I've been saying?'

Like an old man, Micky shrugged his shoulders and nodded wearily. 'Yeah, I heard you, and . . . and I want to believe what you're saying 'cos it makes sense. But if . . . if that's true, then where is she?' He looked at Ellen, then Ted and finally Nora, as if praying one of them would say something to reassure him, but they all averted their gaze, unable to endure the pain and terror in the frightened eyes.

Another awkward silence descended on the room. This time it was Nora who stepped into the breach. Clucking her tongue impatiently, she barked, 'Well, we're not gonna be able to think on an empty stomach. Now then, get that food inside you all before it goes stone cold. And while we're eating, we can 'ave a think an' maybe one of us'll come up with a brainstorm.'

Not bothering with the plates she had set out on

the table, Nora plonked the still warm, greasy parcels into everyone's laps. No one in the room would have thought they could eat at such an emotional time as this, but their empty stomachs soon proved them wrong. With the food consumed, followed by two mugs of strong, sweet tea, the occupants of the small, cosy room, their bellies full, their strength returning, began to talk.

Taking a long, loud slurp of her tea, Nora said, 'Now then, let's get our thinking caps on. From what Micky's told us, young Molly wouldn't 'ave left their 'ouse, unless she was really desperate. Now the way I see it, the poor little cow probably got frightened when Micky didn't come 'ome and wandered off trying to find him. She probably only intended to go outside so she could have a proper look up and down the street so she would see Micky as soon as he turned the corner into their road. We've all done it when we're waiting for someone. It's like if we keep looking outta the window, or out in the street, it'll make that person turn up quicker. Maybe she only intended to walk up to the top of the road, then lost her bearings. She's only eight, an' she ain't used to going out at night, an' what with it being dark ... Well, like I said, she probably got lost and she's hiding out somewhere waiting for Micky to come and find her.'

Nora smiled at the anguished face of the young boy, her smile fading at the look of utter hopelessness on Micky's deathly pale face.

Sitting on the edge of the sofa, his legs apart, his arms hanging limply between his knees he said flatly, 'What! For two nights? So where's she been sleeping?

And what's she been doing for food and drink? Who you trying to kid, Mrs Parker? I ain't stupid, you know.' His voice cracked and, sinking to a whisper he said, 'Someone's got her, and if it ain't that Wells bloke, it might be some other pervert. 'Cos he ain't the only man who likes little girls, is he?' Raising his head he looked directly at Ted and asked simply, 'Why are some men like that, Ted? I don't understand. Are they born like it, or do they change as they get older? Before this happened I couldn't wait to grow up. Now I ain't in such a hurry, 'cos right now I feel ashamed to be a man.'

Startled, Ted could only look to his mother for help, but on this occasion Nora wisely thought that this particular topic was best left to a man. Gathering up the greasy papers she said to Ellen, 'Give us a hand clearing up, will you, love? I think I've still got some fruit cake left for afters. That's if Ted ain't finished it off, greedy sod. He must 'ave hollow legs, 'cos the amount he eats he should be like the half side of an 'ouse.'

Ellen, as eager to leave the room as Nora, gratefully followed the stout woman into the scullery. 'What would you like me to do, Mrs Parker?'

Rinsing the mugs under the cold tap Nora looked over her shoulder saying, 'You can drop the Mrs Parker for a start. Me name's Nora to me friends, and I'd like us to be friends.' As the words left her mouth Nora was amazed she had uttered them. Only a short while ago she had been trying to think of ways to stop Ted from seeing the young woman who was smiling at her so openly. Yet, painful as it was to admit her son wasn't going to give up easily in his pursuit, and that ultimately there would be a high price to pay, Nora couldn't help but warm to Ellen. If only she wasn't married, she, Nora, couldn't have wished for a better daughter-in-law. But there it was, she reflected sadly, life was rarely easy, or fair. Which brought her mind back to the wretched boy desperately looking to Ted for answers that no ordinary person could possibly answer. From the other room she could hear Ted's low, soft voice and her heart went out to him, and the young boy whose world had been turned upside down in the cruellest way imaginable.

Nodding towards the open door she said flatly, 'It don't look good, does it, love?'

Ellen too looked towards the sitting room and said simply, 'No, it doesn't.'

They were seated at the kitchen table, neither of them anxious to return to the other room.

'Micky's right, you know.' Nora's voice was heavy, both with fatigue and worry. 'His sister ain't wandering round the streets looking for him. John Smith's got all the coppers on the beat looking out for 'er. And when it's a child gone missing, all coppers from miles around go that extra mile to find them. It ain't unknown for a lot of 'em to carry on looking even when they're off duty. Every derelict 'ouse'll be searched. Every man seen walking along with a young girl'll be stopped and questioned. An' it ain't only the coppers'll who'll be looking for her. Most of the East End knows what's 'appened by now an' they'll be keeping a look out an' all. So, if she was out there, and she ain't been found by now . . . Well! Like I said, it don't look good . . . 'Ere, you all right, love? Yer look clapped out.'

Ellen smiled tiredly, the long day finally catching up with her. 'I am tired, but I think it's more mental than physical tiredness. I still can't quite take it in. I mean Micky having a sister and living in a filthy ruin, both terrified of being caught and sent back to the workhouse. The poor, poor little souls. What they must have been through, and now this, it's just . . . just too cruel . . . Oh, I'm sorry . . .' Ellen dabbed quickly at the tears springing to her eyes. 'You've enough on your plate without me falling to pieces as well.'

Immediately all motherly concern, Nora made to comfort the distressed girl, but Ellen, sensing her intention, quickly composed herself. There would be plenty of time for tears later when she was on her own – and she still had Arthur to face! Thinking of the confrontation to come she gave her eyes a good wipe with her handkerchief and said shakily, 'No, you're right, God help them, it doesn't look good. But if the worst has happened, I only hope the poor little mite didn't suffer, and that she's found soon. At least then Micky can mourn her. Because the more time goes by the more he's going to suffer. But whatever the outcome, he'll always blame himself, and it's much harder to forgive oneself than to forgive others.'

Nora gave a derisive snort. 'Yeah, it is normally. But I doubt young Micky'll ever forgive Agnes Handly for her part in this whole sorry mess – my Ted too for that matter. Gawd! When he found out what she'd done! I've never seen him so angry, and I've seen him in many a foul temper, I can tell yer. It's lucky she's a woman, 'cos if it'd been a man, my Ted would 'ave beaten the shit outta him.' Darting a furtive look towards the front room, Nora lowered her voice and, leaning across the table added, 'I've tried ter reason with him, especially since I heard 'er side of it, but he ain't 'aving any of it. For what it's worth, I believe her. Like you, there ain't no love lost between me and Agnes, but I remember back when we were younger, yer wouldn't 'ave recognised 'er then. She was always good fer a laugh was Agnes. Oh, I know it's hard ter believe now, but she was a nice young girl. Felt a bit sorry fer 'er, to be honest. Stuck in that 'ouse, with her mum. Right old cow, she was, Audrey Handly. No wonder old Billy slung his hook when he did. Give 'im his due, he waited till Agnes left school. But the first week she brought 'ome a wage packet, he was off. No one ever saw him again . . .' Her words trailed off as she realised she was babbling. And the reason for her sudden discomfort was sitting only inches away from her. For the past hour, Nora's thoughts had been focused on Micky's troubles, but now, the worry of her Ted and Ellen Mitson came flooding back to torment her frayed nerves.

Seeing the elder woman's distress, and sensing the reason for it Ellen impulsively reached out and took hold of the plump hands lying on the table. 'It's all right, Nora. I know it must be awkward for you, having me here, I mean. But don't worry, I'll be going shortly . . . And, Nora . . .' She caught Nora's gaze and held it firmly. 'I don't intend making trouble. I'm a married woman, not happily married . . .' She tried to smile at her attempt at humour and failed. Dropping her gaze she whispered, 'I'd better be going. Arthur will be wondering where I've got to. You know how fussy he is.' Now she was the one babbling. 'I'll just say goodbye to Micky. I only wish I could take him home with me, but I can't. I doubt he'd come with me even if it were possible. No! Micky's far better off here with you and Ted. You can give him hope and stability, and that's what he most needs right now, especially Ted. Micky looks up to him and feels safe knowing Ted's around.'

'I know. He 'as that effect on people, does my Ted.' Nora's voice was filled with motherly pride as she followed Ellen back into the sitting room.

'Yer ain't going, are you, Ellen?' Micky, his bright blue eyes staring piteously out of a white, strained, pinched face. He would have run to her side if Ted's strong hand hadn't stilled his flight.

Gripping the thin shoulder Ted said, 'Now then, Micky. We've already been over this, ain't we? You know she can't stay here. You don't wanna get her into trouble, now, do yer?' Gently folding his fist into a ball Ted playfully brushed Micky's cheek. 'You stay here, mate, while I walk Ellen home. Me Mum will look after you until I get back, so don't you go giving her any trouble while I'm gone, d'yer hear?'

Ellen was shrugging her arms into the light blue summer coat she'd had on since leaving Southend, her head coming up sharply as she heard Ted's jocular words. Buttoning up the linen coat she glanced quickly towards Nora and saw plainly the anxiety etched on the plump face.

Turning all of her attention to the task in hand, Ellen, her heart thudding at the prospect of being alone with Ted, fastened the last button saying brightly, 'Oh, that's all right, Ted. It's still light outside, and besides, it's only a few minutes' walk from here.' Putting out her arms to the slight frame huddled up in the wide, comfortable armchair she said softly, 'Do I get a hug, Micky?'

The words were scarcely out of her mouth before Micky rushed into the warmth of the slim arms. Caught off balance momentarily Ellen stumbled, her hands grasping at Micky's wiry body in an attempt to remain on her feet. Then Ted was holding them both, and to the fearful Nora watching the sombre trio, they seemed to belong together. Even she, here in her own house, felt out of place. It was as if she was being shut out, put aside, and she knew then how Arthur must be feeling.

Jerking herself out of her reverie she said over-loudly, 'Be careful, lad. You nearly had the lot of you over.' Bustling around the room she added in an off-hand manner, 'Don't yer worry about Ellen, love. I'll walk her 'ome. Like she says, it's only a few minutes away, an' I need ter pick up a few things while I'm out.'

'And where yer gonna get anything this time of night?' Ted asked sardonically, knowing full well the reason why his mother was anxious not to let him and Ellen spend any time alone together. 'It's nearly half nine now, it'll be dark soon. So don't give me any old flannel about having ter get some shopping, all right? I'm walking Ellen home and that's an end ter it.' Giving the forlorn Micky's shoulder a firm squeeze of reassurance, Ted stood back as Ellen bent to kiss the pale cheek.

'I'll be back first thing in the morning, Micky, all right?'

Micky nodded listlessly, the pathetic action jerking at Ellen's already frayed emotions. Avoiding Nora's glance, she said, ''Bye, Nora . . . And thanks.'

Nora, now standing by Micky's side, merely nodded as the young couple left the house.

At the same time in the top floor in a tenement building in Shoreditch, Sadie North, her face devoid of make-up and wearing a pale blue woollen dress, was tucking her newly found charge into the brass-headed double bed Sadie had slept in alone since she'd bought it over fifteen years ago. Her policy of not bringing her punters home had never wavered. This two-room flat was her haven, her escape from the sordid world she lived in. When she had first moved in, the flat had been in a disgusting state; it had also been cheap. Over the years she had gradually renovated the two rooms, discovering she had a talent for spotting good, second-hand furniture. The final touch to her new home had been the purchase of two off cuts of carpet, which she had proudly fitted herself. No one else in the building had ever been invited into Sadie's domain, the other occupants of the tenement block preferring to keep themselves to themselves, which suited Sadie just fine.

But now she had been landed with an unexpected guest and was at a loss as to what to do about the child she had taken under her wing.

'I don't suppose yer've remembered the name of that bakery, or the names of your brother's friends, 'ave yer, love?' she asked hopefully. At the time, taking the child home with her had been the only option open to her, but she had hoped that Molly's brother, after reading the note left for him, would turn up to collect his sister. Now, after two days, Sadie had to face the possibility that something had happened to the boy. And the only way to find out was to track down Micky Masters' friends. Taking a deep breath she tried again. Tucking the eiderdown round Molly's neck she asked quietly, 'Your brother must 'ave told yer where he was working, love. If I know where to look, I can go and find him. You do want ter see him again, don't yer?'

But the girl remained mute, only her eyes showing her apprehension and fear, and it wasn't hard to understand why the child was so frightened.

That first night, the young girl hadn't stopped talking about her brother and every word and action had been filled with pride. Yet even then Sadie had detected a note of fear. And she had been right. For the next day Molly could barely remember her own name. The poor little cow was scared her brother wasn't coming back for her, not because he didn't want her, but because he couldn't. If that was the case then Molly must be hoping that Sadie would look after her. Her heart sinking, Sadie looked down into the large blue eyes staring out of a heart-shaped face. What on earth was she going to do if the brother couldn't be found? Smoothing down the bedcovers, she gently stroked the soft cheek saying, 'All right, love, don't worry. You 'ave a good night's sleep and perhaps you'll remember something in the morning. 'Night, love.'

''Night, Sadie,' Molly replied sleepily. 'God bless.'

Leaving the bedroom door slightly ajar, Sadie made herself a light supper, her mind whirling round in circles, wondering what to do for the best.

She'd already lost two nights' work, and while the rest had been very nice she wasn't going to earn any money sitting on her backside. Yet if she was to be honest with herself, these past forty-eight hours had been the happiest time of her life. For those short two days she had been able to pretend she was a normal, respectable woman and she realised she was in danger of taking that fantasy one step further and begin to think of herself as a mother. It was a dream she had harboured for over twenty years, but Sadie was nothing if not practical. She was a whore, a thirty-eight-year-old whore who had no desire for a permanent man in her life. Also, unlike many in her profession, she had never fallen pregnant, thus saving her from risking her life at the hands of the many back street abortionists that worked the East End.

Her inability to conceive may well have been due to being forced to go on the game at the tender age of twelve, urged on by her own mother, a blowsy, gin-soaked tart who had thought nothing of setting her only daughter on the sordid and often dangerous road of prostitution.

Brought up in a cramped, dirty bedsit where Bertha North had entertained her clients, Sadie had grown up watching different men come and go at all hours of the day and night. She had heard the groans and squeaking of the double bed from her straw-filled pallet tucked away into the furthest corner of the room. Sadie had never thought to question her mother when she had brought home her daughter's first client, for Sadie had never known any other way of life. Yet from that first, brutal encounter something inside Sadie had died. The only way she could survive in her new world was to build a protective barrier around her mind to block out the loathsome men that used her for their own pleasure without a thought for her as a person. And with each new punter her heart had hardened, until she was incapable of feeling any emotion.

Even when her mother had died from a venereal disease at the relatively young age of thirty-six, Sadie hadn't shed a single tear. She had paid for the cheapest funeral she could find, and, before the coffin lid had been nailed down, Sadie had looked down dispassionately at the bloated, ravaged face that could easily have been taken for a woman in her late fifties. Sadie had sworn then she would never end her days as a tuppenny whore.

With her mother gone, Sadie was left alone with no real friends or family to turn to. She had never known who her father was; then again, neither had her mother. From that day Sadie had started to make plans for her future. With steely determination she had promised herself that she would retire the day she turned forty, for she knew only too well that once a prostitute reached that landmark, it was a slippery slope into middle age then a sharp skid towards the grave. Sadie had seen too many old tarts, like her dead mother, desperately touting for trade, their looks gone, their bodies diseased, all alone in the world with only a gin bottle for company. With military precision she had estimated it would take that long to build up her growing nest egg, allowing herself a comfortable lifestyle until she was ready to embark on a new life.

Oh, she'd had it all mapped out. Her ultimate goal was to one day be able to set up a little business of her own. The precise nature of that business had yet to be decided, which was why she forced herself out onto the streets every night, desperate to earn as much money as she could before she reached forty, only two years away. Once her flat had been made into a home, every spare shilling she earned had been put into the bank for safe keeping and to earn interest. There was something else she'd promised herself, and that was to take herself out to the most expensive restaurant she could find and order the dearest meal on the menu. In short she planned to spoil herself rotten. Those plans and dreams had kept her going, kept her sane in her lowest, darkest hours, and God only knew there had been plenty of those. But her greatest pleasure would be the day she bundled up all the cheap, tarty clothes that had been her trademark for so many years and donate them to the Salvation Army. What that holy organisation would do with the obvious cast-off clothing of a prostitute was anyone's guess, for Sadie would be long gone before the bulky parcel was opened. Oh, yes, Sadie North had had her future well planned.

Then she had met Molly. And when, on the walk home that night, she had felt the small hand clasp hers so trustingly, it was as if a chisel had pierced a hole in the armour she had built around herself for so long. And the longer she spent with the sweet-natured girl, the wider the chink in her amour was spreading. Staring towards the open bedroom door Sadie felt her eyes misting over, and the shock of experiencing the first real emotion she could remember brought her sitting bolt upright. She had imagined she was no longer capable of such feelings, but a person would have to be made of stone not to be affected by the loving child. And though Sadie had tried her hardest to remain impervious to the little girl's innocent charm she now had to admit that, despite her best efforts, Molly had already wormed herself into Sadie's heart. And the longer Molly stayed, the harder it would be to give her up. And Sadie had had enough pain and let downs in her life; she wasn't going to allow herself to be hurt any more. First thing in the morning she was going to go to all the markets in the East End, and start asking questions. Market traders were a close-knit community; it shouldn't be too hard to track down Molly's brother – if he was still alive.

Hardening her defences once more, Sadie headed for the bedroom, undressed and, careful not to disturb the sleeping child, climbed into the double bed.

Then the small form turned over, snuggling against Sadie's voluptuous body and Sadie was lost. The feel of the warm body cuddling against her brought tears

ANNA KING

to Sadie's eyes, and this time she let them fall. There was something else Sadie had never experienced, and that was any form of genuine warmth and love.

She didn't know what tomorrow would bring. But for now she was going to cherish this precious moment, hold onto it for as long as possible, sadly acknowledging that tonight might be the last chance she would ever have to hold a child's warm body, innocent and trusting, next to hers.

CHAPTER SIXTEEN

'Please, Johnny, yer can't go off and leave me on me own. You know what will 'appen when yer've gone. I've already had me window smashed in. If you go it'll be me face next.'

Constable John Smith shook his head tiredly. 'I'm sorry Agnes, but I can't stop here for ever. I've already stayed too long as it is.'

Buttoning up his tunic the kindly policeman looked with genuine pity at the pathetic figure reeking of brandy, but what more could he do? Fixing his helmet firmly in place, he thought quietly before saying warily, 'Look, how about asking young Ellen if you can stay with her and Arthur . . . just until you get yourself sorted.'

Agnes' jaw dropped in amazement, then, her eyes hardening she spat out, 'Yer 'aving a laugh ain't yer?' A bitter sound erupted from her lips. 'Yer really think Arthur Mitson would offer to take me in when he's been trying to get rid of me for years? Nah! He'd laugh in me face and enjoy doing it.'

Taking his leave, PC Smith replied sympathetically, 'Maybe Arthur would, but Ellen wouldn't. She's a nice young woman, and she did offer to help if she could.'

Seeing the hope slowly enter her eyes, the uniformed man quickly pressed home his suggestion. 'Look, what if I come to the bakery with you? Arthur might be a bit more amiable with me alongside you. In fact, how about me having a word with him first, eh? And with Ellen siding with me, I can't see Arthur refusing, not with both of us pleading your case. You know what he's like, strength of character has never been Arthur's strongest point, has it? Poor old sod.'

Agnes' lips curled in disgust. 'Bleeding gutless, that's what Arthur's trouble is, always 'as been.' Rolling her eyes she added spitefully, 'Gawd help us. I must 'ave been blind all those years. If . . .'

Tired and impatient to get home to his long-suffering wife, John Smith interrupted Agnes' deliberate ploy to keep him talking. For a few brief moments he had considered inviting Agnes to stay at his modest house for the night. Horrified the thought had even crossed his mind John Smith rubbed his chin in agitation. His Sarah, wife of thirty years this coming August, was one of the sweetest-natured women he had ever known, but she was no mug. Giving up his spare time to help Agnes was one thing, bringing the said woman home with him was another matter entirely. Adopting a more professional manner he said crisply, 'Get your coat, and put a few bits in a bag for the night. If Arthur does dig his heels in,

I'll find you somewhere else to stay, I promise.'

Knowing John's word was always good, Agnes was soon dressed for the outdoors, a shopping bag containing her nightwear clutched tightly in her hand.

Thinking it more prudent to leave by the back door, the constable was caught off-guard as a chunk of brick sailed by his ear, hitting Agnes on the back of her covered head, causing her to cry out in pain. John swiftly put his bulk in front of the crying, terrified woman, his sharp eyes peering into the failing light, and focused on two shadowy figures lurking in the alley opposite.

'Get yourself off home before I run you in for disturbing the peace,' his authoritative voice boomed out into the silence of the night.

Then came the sound of running footsteps, and a sneering voice called out defiantly, 'Yer can't 'ave the bobbies looking after yer for ever, yer wicked old bitch. We'll get yer. You're gonna get what's coming to yer.'

Cursing beneath his breath, the constable could only watch helplessly as the would-be assailants ran off, their taunting threats still ringing in his ears. Taking a deep gulp of air he turned to the trembling woman hiding behind him and said brusquely, 'Come on, old girl. Let's get you to Arthur and Ellen's place before anyone else decides to take the law into their own hands.'

Cowering behind the safety of the broad, reassuring figure, Agnes tentatively reached out and caught hold of the policeman's arm, holding her breath, as if fearful of rejection, and when, after a few seconds, a heavy, warm hand covered hers, she let out a shuddering sigh of relief. A silence settled on the incongruous couple as they walked the short journey to their destination.

In the sitting room above the bakery, Arthur, his fleshy face sweating with anxiety, could still see the contempt in Ted Parker's eyes, still feel the tremor that had rippled through his body as he had gazed into those hard, cold eyes. A shudder racked him as the memory returned to haunt him. It wouldn't have been so bad if Ellen had spoken up for him: he was her husband after all. But no. Instead of performing her wifely duties she had sided with Ted Parker. Fresh beads of sweat broke out on his brow as he looked down at the dwindling remains of whisky in the cut crystal glass. Downing the last of the drink he rose unsteadily to his feet and staggered over to the sideboard, pouring another glass from the depleted decanter. Returning to his armchair he slumped down into the comfortable cushions, spilling some of the alcohol onto the carpet, but Arthur was too drunk to notice.

The one thing he had feared most had come to pass. He was going to lose Ellen.

If he was honest with himself the change in Ellen had been going on for some time. And he could almost pinpoint the time Ellen had begun to change. It had been when that brat Micky had first come knocking on the door. Because of him, Ellen had forged a friendship with Ted Parker in order to get the boy a job. From that moment on, Ellen had begun to grow further and further away from him. So when she had suggested going on holiday, Arthur, at first, worried about his business, had hesitated, mainly out of habit.

THE RAGAMUFFINS

But it hadn't taken him long to realise that a holiday might be his only chance to put their ailing marriage back on familiar ground. And for a short time the impromptu holiday by the sea seemed to have worked. Then the telegram had arrived, and Ellen had insisted she must return home that very day, her abrupt decision making it perfectly clear where her loyalties lay. And, as if he hadn't been humiliated enough in front of their new-found friends, the Bradleys, he'd had to endure a confrontation with Ted Parker in his own home.

Tears of self-pity pricked his eyes. Why was this happening to him?

Suddenly he was jerked back to the present by a hammering on the back door. Shuffling over to the slightly open window, he peered down, squinting to make out the figures standing below.

'Ellen, is that you?' he slurred, hopefully.

'Open up, Arthur, it's me, John Smith. I've got Agnes with me. Come on, man, I haven't got all night.'

The amount of alcohol Arthur had consumed had left him confused and disorientated. Not a big drinker by nature, Arthur was totally unprepared for the transformation he felt within himself. Filled with dutch courage he sauntered down the stairs, his expression set, determined that this time he would take control of the situation. Halfway down he tripped, grabbed the handrail to stop his fall, then, pulling himself up to his full height, he threw open the door and said, in what he hoped was a manly tone, 'Well, what d'you want?'

Hearing the aggressive note in Arthur's usually

placid voice, PC Smith hid a smile at Arthur's obvious attempt to be assertive. The constable gave a cough to cover his mirth before answering, 'Come on Arthur, let us in before the neighbours come out to see what's going on.'

Reluctantly Arthur gestured them in, trying to keep up the charade of masculinity. Unfortunately the weak-willed man couldn't quite pull it off. Faced with an officer of the law, albeit a man he had known for years, Arthur soon crumpled under the stern gaze. He heard himself agreeing to let Agnes stay until Ellen got home, noting with self-disgust the look of sympathy that crossed John Smith's face, a look that only served to remind Arthur how he appeared to the outside world. A bleeding mug! That's how people saw him, and usually they would be right. But not this time. Oh, no! There was no way Agnes Handly was going to get the better of him. If she thought she was going to spend the night under his roof, then she was going to be sorely disappointed. No sooner had the back door slammed behind the uniformed man, than the fixed smile dropped from Arthur's face, leaving in its stead the fury that was bubbling inside him. With eyes almost bulging out of his head, Arthur turned on Agnes, who had flopped gratefully into one of the armchairs placed either side of the fireplace. Grinding his teeth in anger he growled, 'Don't get yourself too comfortable, you ugly old cow.'

And Agnes, who for the first time that day had just begun to relax, heard the raw hatred in Arthur's voice and immediately the fear came surging back.

Arthur saw the look and his chest swelled with

renewed confidence. 'You can look surprised. You didn't think I was really going to welcome you back into this house with open arms, did you? 'Cos if you did, then you're even more stupid than I thought you were.'

Agnes remained where she was, her eyes hardening as she realised that the blustering façade Arthur had presented to the constable was merely the result of too much whisky. She should have known better. Like everything Arthur tried to do, getting drunk only made him appear more pathetic than he normally did. His newly found courage would disappear as soon as the drink wore off. Until then she wasn't moving. Grimly churning inside, Agnes remained quiet as the maddened man raged on.

'Bleeding hell, I always knew you were desperate for a man. You proved that when you carried on hanging around my neck when I made it perfectly obvious I wasn't interested in you any more. But I kept you on here out of the goodness of my heart, when what I should have done was to send you packing. But I didn't think even somebody like you would be that desperate that you'd hand over a little girl to a pervert just to keep him interested in you.'

As Arthur's cruel words continued to beat inside her head, Agnes, her knuckles white, gripped the side of the armchair as she slowly raised herself to her feet, her lips settling into a tight grim line. Taking one step towards him she kept her voice low, but there was no disguising the menace in her tone.

'Yer bloody hypocrite. 'Ow you can stand there and preach when you're no better yerself. For two years

I've 'ad to put up with the thought of you in bed with a mere child. 'Cos that's all she was when yer married 'er. All that putting on a front as the respectable businessman to make excuses for marrying a poor little orphan out of the goodness of your 'eart just to cover up your true colours. You think that everyone round these parts was thinking what a kind man you was, when all the time they've been sniggering behind your back. And yer've got the nerve ter call me names. All right, what I did was a terrible thing ter do. But as God is my witness, I didn't know what that man was like. If I had, I'd've turned him over to the nearest copper. 'Cos yer wrong, Arthur. I'd never see a child hurt, never, and if you think I would, then yer never really knew me – just like I never really knew you. Or maybe I did, and wouldn't believe it. People are like that, yer know. They can be very blind to a person's faults, especially when they're in love. And I did love you, Arthur. Now I see yer was just a dirty old man, and yer still are.'

Advancing on the startled man Agnes continued her barrage of abuse, her fears forgotten. Arthur backed away, his face reddening as Agnes went on relentlessly, her voice dripping with scorn. Shocked into silence, Arthur could only stand mute, shocked at the venom in her voice.

'When I think of her living here before yer married her. Carrying on all the time. Did yer think no one knew?' Arthur blanched as the true meaning of her words began to pierce through his fuddled mind. Oblivious of his distress Agnes hissed, 'How old was she when yer first fancied her? Seven? Eight? Or do you like 'em younger? All those years you was playing the dutiful friend, when all the time you was only going round there just to get yer 'ands on the kid.'

Stung into action at the outrageous thought Arthur leapt forward, his hand grasping Agnes' arm in a vicious grip. Ignoring her cry of pain Arthur hissed, 'I've never slept with Ellen now or in the past, not in the way you mean, you filthy-minded bitch.'

Spittle sprayed from Arthur's lips over Agnes' face, but she didn't flinch, for despite Arthur's murderous countenance Agnes knew she was in no danger. Arthur was, and always would be, a coward at heart, ready to back down if faced with a stronger character, and Agnes wasn't a woman to be easily intimidated – especially by the likes of Arthur Mitson. So wrapped up in their own private war were they, neither heard the door open, or were aware Ellen and Ted had entered the room until Ellen's anguished voice cut through the heavy atmosphere like a knife.

'Arthur . . . please . . .'

Releasing his hold on Agnes Arthur whirled round to find the couple staring at him in surprise. But whereas Ellen's face portrayed hurt, the expression on Ted Parker's face could only be described as triumphant.

And in that moment, Arthur realised his world, as he knew it, was finished. But worse still was the knowledge that he had condemned himself out of his own mouth. Knowing anything he said now would be futile Arthur turned and, stopping only to grab the depleted whisky decanter, he walked with as much dignity as he could muster into the safety of his bedroom, closing the door quietly behind him.

Ignoring the dumbfounded Agnes, Ted took hold of Ellen's arms, his face alight with excitement. 'Why didn't you ever tell me? Don't yer know what this means? You ain't properly married. You can walk out now, and there's nothing Arthur can do. I ain't no expert on divorces, but I do know yer can get a marriage annulled if it ain't been ... well, you know ...'

But Ellen, her face burning with embarrassment at having her most personal and intimate secrets aired in public, had no intention of giving the avidly watching Agnes any further information about her private life. Pushing Ted's arms away she said firmly, 'I can't talk about it now, Ted. No matter how badly Arthur's behaved, he doesn't deserve this public humiliation. I want you to go, Ted.'

His face screwing up in bewildered lines Ted said, 'What are yer talking about, love? Don't you understand, you're free. We can be together now. Look ...'

Ellen turned on him. 'I asked you to leave, Ted. This is Arthur's home, and whatever you say, I am still his wife until the law says otherwise.'

Looking into Ellen's determined face Ted's mouth tightened. 'All right. If that's what you want, I'm going. But don't leave it too long, Ellen. I love yer, but I ain't gonna wait around for ever. You get things sorted with Arthur, and soon.'

When Ted slammed out of the room Ellen turned wearily to Agnes. 'It's all right, Agnes, I know why you're here. We met Constable Smith on the way home. You can stay for the night, but I'm afraid you'll have to sleep downstairs. I'm sorry I can't offer you a bed, you'll have to make do with the armchair in the kitchen. I know it's a bit battered but it's quite comfortable, and after all, it is only for one night. Now I'm going to bed. I've had just about enough for one day. Goodnight, Agnes.'

When Ellen entered the bedroom Arthur was standing by the window, his hands clasped behind his back, his body ridged. But although his body was still, his mind was churning. All he could hear was Ted Parker's voice filled with glee, mocking him for his inability to be a proper husband to his young wife, and try as he might, Arthur couldn't get those words out of his mind. But if Ted Parker was gloating over the true state of affairs between himself and Ellen, that old bitch Agnes must be over the moon at the news. No doubt when the fuss concerning the Masters children was forgotten, his one-time lover would waste no time in regaling the whole sorry business to all and sundry – that's if Ted Parker didn't beat her to it.

His head drooped in despair. It wasn't fair. All his life he'd tried to be kind and easygoing, and where had it got him? Ridiculed and despised by all who knew him, that's where! Even Ellen was turning against him. Oh, she might have sent Ted Parker packing tonight, but for how long? Slowly turning he looked to where Ellen was getting ready for bed. She normally undressed in the adjoining bathroom, immersing herself in the flannel nightdress that covered her from neck to ankle before getting into bed. And the fact that she felt comfortable disrobing in front of him only inflamed his already maddened, whisky-fuelled mind. Did she think he was made of stone? Or maybe she imagined he was incapable of acting like a normal red-blooded man, a man like Ted Parker!

Unaware of her husband's thoughts Ellen said tiredly, 'Would you mind sleeping in the spare room tonight, Arthur? I think we both need some time alone.'

And those words, spoken without rancour, were for Arthur the final straw, and something inside him snapped.

Not recognising his own voice Arthur answered, 'Yes, I would mind as it happens. You've made a right mug of me today, and I've had enough. D'you hear me, I've had enough.'

Ellen's eyes widened in surprise as Arthur advanced towards the bed, and for the first time a flicker of alarm tugged at her chest. Clutching her nightdress close to her breasts she tried to keep her voice light.

'Don't be silly, Arthur. Look, we're both tired, let's not start an argument now. We can talk properly in the morning . . . Arthur. Arthur, what are you doing?'

His face grim, Arthur growled, 'I'm getting undressed for bed. My bed, with my wife.' Stripped to his undergarments Arthur gave a low, mirthless laugh. 'Yeah, my wife. And I think it's about time you started to act like a wife.'

Thoroughly frightened now, Ellen began to rise from the bed. 'Stop it, Arthur. Look, you're drunk, you don't know what you're doing. Please, Arthur, you're beginning to frighten me . . .'

A heavy hand pushed her back onto the bed, then Arthur was on top of her, his heavy bulk crushing her into the mattress.

Tears stung her eyes as Ellen tried futilely to push Arthur away, but it was no use. Feeling as if she were in a nightmare, Ellen could only lie helpless as sweaty hands roamed over her body. But she couldn't stifle the cry of pain as a red-hot pain seemed to tear her insides apart.

Arthur heard the cry, but he was too far gone to stop. Then it was over, and with it came stark reality.

With a soft moan of despair Arthur rolled off the trembling body. 'Oh, God! Ellen, I'm so sorry. I don't know what came over me. Please . . . please, Ellen, say something.'

But Ellen, traumatised by the violent assault, could only lie still, her face turned into her pillow, while Arthur sat on the edge of the bed, his large frame heaving with sobs of remorse.

And when, some time later, he staggered from the room, Ellen remained still. It was as if she had lost the use of her limbs. Only her mind remained active. And her thoughts were more painful than her bruised body.

All her secret dreams of one day being with Ted, living with him, bearing his children and growing old together were gone for ever.

For with that one brutal act, Arthur had bound her to him for life.

CHAPTER SEVENTEEN

'Now, Mrs Knight is gonna keep an eye on yer while I go to work. All right? Be a good girl. I'll be 'ome as soon as I can.' Sadie rested her hands on Molly's shoulders as she tried to reassure her that she wasn't about to run off and leave her behind.

Molly, her blue eyes filling with tears, answered tremulously, 'I promise, Sadie. I'll be good. You will be coming 'ome, won't ya?'

A gruff voice from behind laughed, ''Course she'll be coming 'ome, yer daft little thing. Now, how about getting out from under me feet.' Waddling over to the open door, the heavily pregnant woman called out loudly, 'Billy, Charlie. Get yerselves in here.'

Two laughing, scruffy boys raced into the room, almost knocking Molly over. 'What d'yer want, Mum?' they cried in unison.

'Take Molly out ter play with yer for a while. I'll call yer when yer tea's ready.'

Before Molly could protest, the boys grabbed a hand each and dragged her out of the door. The last sight Sadie had of Molly was a sad, pleading look from big, blue eyes filled with unshed tears.

'Don't worry, Sadie, she'll be all right with them two.'

Struggling to appear unconcerned, Sadie replied, 'Yeah, I know, Lil, they're good lads. You know, I've only had 'er a couple of weeks, but it seems like she's always been 'ere. Anyway, I know I've said it before, but thanks for looking after 'er for me. Gawd knows what I'd've done without your help this past fortnight, 'cos I couldn't 'ave left 'er on 'er own, not the state she's been in. Right then, I don't know what time I'll be 'ome, but I won't leave it too late. After all, I've got someone else to think about now; bloody nuisance!'

The offhand remark didn't fool Lily Knight for a moment. 'Don't be daft. The boys'll be looking after 'er more than I will, and besides, I need the money yer pay me after that old git ran out on me as soon as he found out there was another one on the way.' Lily Knight wiped her face with a grimy cloth, then, her face suddenly guarded, she said hesitantly, 'Look, mate, I know it's none of me business, but yer ain't getting too fond of the kid, are yer? Only yer know 'er brother could turn up outta the blue an' take 'er away, an' I don't wanna see yer get 'urt.' Lily Knight's voice trailed off as a flash of anger crossed Sadie's face. Undaunted she took a deep breath and added,

'Now don't yer go giving me daggers, Sadie North. We've known each other too long fer playing silly buggers, and I know yer ain't been exactly breaking yer neck ter find that brother of young Molly's, 'ave yer?'

Swallowing hard Sadie lowered her gaze. 'Nah, yer right, Lil, I ain't. I did fer the first few days, yer know I did. But without knowing where ter look, it was a waste of time. All I know from what Molly told me that first night was that 'er brother did odd jobs in a bakery, then got a job down the market a couple of days a week. D'yer know how many bakeries there are round these parts? Bleeding dozens of 'em. It's the same with the markets. Yer know 'ow those market traders operate. They go from one market to the next, working different days at each one. Then there's the fly pitchers, an' if young Micky's taken up with one of those shifty bleeders, I'll never find 'im. Besides, maybe he ain't the loving brother Molly thinks he is. After all, a lad that age don't wanna be lumbered with a little sister hanging round his neck. For all I know, he might 'ave pissed off for good, and if that's the case, then he could be anywhere.'

Yet even as she spoke, the words sounded hollow to her ears. No one could engender the kind of love Molly had for her elusive brother unless that love was reciprocated.

Avoiding her friend's kindly stare, Sadie, her voice softer, said, 'I had me whole life mapped out, then I had ter go and find Molly hiding in that filthy hovel. She was so scared, Lil. But even then, when she 'eard me with that punter and thought he was hurting me, she tried ter help me. And I've gotta say, I don't think I could 'ave been that brave in her circumstances. She's a good kid, Lil, and she's me last chance of ever 'aving a kid of me own. And I'll tell yer something else. Tonight's me last night on the game. I've got enough put by ter get a place for the pair of us, somewhere decent. She ain't gonna grow up like we did. She's gonna 'ave everything we missed out on. As fer her brother . . .'

She shrugged. 'Well, I'll just 'ave ter take me chances, won't I? Anyway, I'd best be off. The sooner tonight's over the better, 'cos ter tell yer the truth, Lil, I ain't got the stomach for it any more. Every night before I get into bed with Molly, I scrub meself from top ter bottom. She's so clean and innocent, and when I think of how I've spent the evening . . . Well! Like I said, I think I'm sort of contaminating her. That's why I'm giving it up, and I'll tell yer something else, I ain't gonna miss it. All these years I've managed ter turn off me feelings while some slimy bastard's mauling me, I can't do that any more. In fact I'm in two minds whether ter go out tonight, but seeing as I've got me glad rags on I might as well earn as much as I can, 'cos like I said, after tonight I'm gonna become a respectable woman. Can yer imagine that, Lil? Me, Sadie North, hard as nails, going soft over some kid I didn't even know existed two weeks ago.' She smiled at her closest friend, her only friend, but the smile held a distinctive air of defiance, as if daring Lily Knight to contradict her.

But that worldly woman knew better than to cross swords with Sadie, besides which she was genuinely fond of the brassy, straight-talking woman she'd been friends with for over ten years. She'd been a good mate to Lily Knight, slipping her a few shillings now and then simply because Lily's husband was a lazy good-for-nothing waster who'd never done an honest day's work in the last five years. It had been the best day of Lily's life when he'd walked out for good, but she didn't know what she'd have done without the odd shilling Sadie always left on her kitchen table whenever she visited. Now it looked like she was about to lose her dear friend, and she was going to miss her, and not just because when Sadie went, so would the much needed few bob she had come to rely on.

Nodding, Lily replied as lightly as she could manage. 'I don't blame yer, Sadie. Don't forget I was on the game meself once, though not as long as you. Anyway, yer get off, an' don't worry about young Molly. Me boys'll take good care of 'er.'

'Yeah, I know they will. Thanks, Lil, see yer later, or maybe sooner.' Sadie winked. 'Yer never know, I might change me mind an' come straight back 'ome.' As Sadie walked across the forecourt of the block of flats, she could hear the loud happy sound of children playing. Resisting the impulse of making sure that Molly was all right, Sadie turned and made her way to the High Street.

'Come on, Molly, you can do it.' Billy Knight, his impish face throwing out the challenge, said, 'Me and Charlie 'ave done it lots of times. We don't let scaredy girls in our gang. 'Course if you don't wanna play with us, you can always go running back to our mum.'

Molly, her stomach churning as she looked at the planks covering a large hole on a building site, swallowed nervously.

'I'm not scared,' she answered defiantly.

Then, tentatively testing her weight on one of the broad planks, she inched her way across to where Charlie Knight was waiting, a huge smile on his grimy face. Halfway across, the planks started to bow and creak, causing Molly to wobble. A loud cry of derision came from both boys and instinctively Molly put her fears to one side. With a look of determination, she made it safely across. With a loud shout both boys slapped Molly hard on the back to show their approval. 'Well done, Moll, you're the first gel to have got across without crying.' Their acceptance of her caused a warm feeling to course through Molly's slim frame. 'Come on, Molly, we'll show you our camp.'

Molly followed the boys happily, finally assured of the knowledge that she was among friends. For a few seconds she stopped and lifted her face to the sun, savouring the feel of the warmth on her skin. It was so good to be out in the fresh air, to be able to run and laugh with children of her own age, even if they were boys. A wistful look flitted over her face as she thought of Micky. Then Billy Knight shouted at her to hurry up, and with the resilience of a child, she ran after the two boys, thoughts of her missing brother pushed firmly to the back of her mind.

Sadie was sitting at an empty table in the Red Bull public house in Mare Street nursing a gin and tonic and fervently wishing she hadn't bothered coming out tonight. Apart from one old regular, she hadn't had one offer in the past two hours. She was about to leave when who should walk in but the punter who had run off that night she had first encountered Molly. Never one to let go of a grievance, Sadie immediately made a bee line for the unsuspecting man.

'Hello, mate. Remember me?' She stood directly in his path and had the satisfaction of seeing the look of fear leap into his eyes. 'Yeah, that's right, yer miserable old bastard. Now then, we've got some unfinished business, ain't we? Like the matter of the five bob yer owe me. I don't do freebies, at least not fer fat old bastards like you. So come on, hand over me money, 'cos I ain't leaving 'ere till I get paid what's owed me.'

The man, accompanied by two friends, floundered for a moment, then, emboldened by the presence of his companions who were watching the scene with great interest, drew himself up and said contemptuously, 'I ain't paying you a penny, yer old tart, though hang on a minute, on second thoughts, I will pay yer – here!' With much laughing from the onlookers in the pub the man took a coin from his pocket and held it out to the furious Sadie. 'There yer are, one penny. That's all you're worth, yer clapped-out old bag.'

Feeling very pleased with himself, the man dropped the coin at Sadie's feet and with much back slapping from his friends he sauntered to the bar. But he hadn't counted on a woman like Sadie North. He hadn't gone more than a few steps when he was spun round and, before he could utter another word, a heavy fist caught him square on the chin, sending him spinning across the room before he landed on the sawdust floor in an undignified heap.

Standing over him Sadie laughed, 'No one gets one over on me, yer little toe rag. You can keep yer penny. By the looks of yer, you need it more than I do. Oh, and by the way, give my sympathies ter yer wife. I've seen bigger fingers than your cock. In fact I didn't even know you'd done it till yer'd finished, and that didn't take long either. See ya!'

As she turned to go, the man, furious at being made to look a fool in front of the entire pub, stumbled to his feet and shouted after her, 'I ain't surprised yer can't notice when you're being screwed, 'cos an old slag like you would only notice if yer was shagged by an elephant. Maybe your new recruit will make yer more money. I saw yer take that little girl outta that old house. You teaching her all yer old tricks, 'cos if yer are, put me down for a visit. At least then I wouldn't begrudge paying . . .' The words were hardly out of his mouth when Sadie came rushing back at him, but this time the landlord, not wanting a full-scale riot in his pub, came out from behind the bar and grabbed Sadie roughly.

'Leave it, I don't want any trouble in 'ere, Sadie. Now go 'ome, there's a good girl. He ain't worth it. Go on, get yerself off outta 'ere, otherwise I'll have ter throw yer out, and I don't wanna do that.'

Her face still twisted with fury, Sadie shrugged off the restraining arms, and with one last murderous glare at the portly man standing within the safety of his group of friends, she slammed out of the pub.

At the back of the snug, a shabbily dressed man who had listened avidly to the heated exchange quietly followed Sadie from the pub.

Storming down the road, the irate woman, still fuming from the vicious verbal assault, didn't notice she was being followed. Heading straight for home she was back at the block of flats within fifteen minutes.

Careful not to be seen, Kenneth Wells, né Stokes, watched Sadie disappear into the building.

So that's where young Molly had gone. At least he assumed the girl spoken about was his Molly. It was too much of a coincidence to be anyone else. Of course he might be wrong, but he didn't think so. There was only one way to find out for sure. Come tomorrow he would return and watch and wait. Making sure of the name of the road, he walked off whistling, a satisfied smile on his lips.

'I wish you didn't have to go out ter work, Sadie. I get scared something might happen to yer, like my brother.' Molly, her blue eyes reflecting her fear, stared at Sadie. 'I mean, I like living with you, Sadie, but I miss me brother. What if he's trying ter find me? He'll be so worried, 'specially with that nasty man . . .' Aware she had said too much, Molly clamped down on her tongue, but Sadie wasn't to be deterred so easily. Apart from their initial encounter, this was the first time Molly had revealed anything about her past life.

'What man, love?' she asked gently, careful not to frighten the child into silence once more.

Molly's childish emotions were running high. More than anything she wanted to tell Sadie about the man she still had nightmares about, but she was afraid to say too much in case Sadie decided to take her to the police. And if that happened, she would end up back at the workhouse, and she'd never go back there, she'd rather die first. But when Sadie lay down on the bed and took her into those warm, comforting arms, Molly found herself talking, and once she'd started, it was as if a dam had broken inside her. Between tears she told Sadie everything, starting from her parents' death to running away from the workhouse, and ending up in the ruins of the house in Morning Lane where Sadie had found her. But most of all she talked about her brother Micky and how much she missed him. She also revealed the whereabouts of the bakery, and of the kind woman who had given Micky work, and found him a job working on a stall with a man called Ted Parker.

And as Sadie listened, all her dreams of starting a new life with the golden-haired child crashed around her ears. She had imagined Molly had accepted that her brother wasn't coming back for her, but now she saw she had been deluding herself. Yet worse than that, she had put her own interests before those of Molly. Now she knew where to look she had no option but to make enquiries about Micky Masters. For if the boy was still alive, it would be the utmost cruelty to keep brother and sister apart. Even so she hoped the boy had abandoned his sister, and was immediately ashamed she could even think such a terrible thing. With a sinking sensation in the pit of her stomach she held the weeping child in her arms until she finally fell into an exhausted sleep.

Tenderly tucking the small form under the blankets, Sadie looked down on the beautiful little girl and, amazed, she felt tears prick the back of her eyes. She hadn't cried since she was twelve, after her first initiation into the seedy world of prostitution, and she hadn't shed a tear since. She had imagined any form of emotion had died on that awful night when her mother had handed her over to her first customer. Even after all these years she could still see his face, sweating and excited at the prospect of having a virgin. For even though she had only been twelve at the time, it was relatively unusual for a girl of her age to still be a virgin, especially in her new profession. She could even remember how much he paid. Five pounds, a fortune back then. But child prostitution was a lucrative business, even now. She could still see the large, white five-pound note, handed to her delighted mother when the man had finished with her. After a while the price went down. Child or not, she had become soiled goods.

With a heavy heart she left the sleeping Molly and settled herself in the sitting room she was so proud of. Looking around the room she saw the polished furniture, the deep piled carpet and the flock wallpaper she had put up herself, but for once the sight gave her no pleasure. She finally had to admit to herself she had been living in a fool's paradise. When she left these rooms she would take all her possessions with her to her new house, but given the choice she would give up all she had worked so hard for in exchange for Molly. It was the early hours of the morning before she climbed into bed. And, like Molly, she fell asleep with tears streaking her face.

CHAPTER EIGHTEEN

Arthur Mitson's modest bakery had never been so busy. In the past two weeks, a steady stream of customers had poured through its doors, but despite the constant ringing of the till, it was glaringly obvious that the owners of the thriving business appeared far from happy.

Along with the regulars had come the gossip-mongers, their curiosity fuelled by the story in the *Hackney Gazette* about the little girl that had gone missing, presumed abducted by a pervert well known to the police. Yet although every one of the idle curious were genuinely concerned about the fate of the missing child, the true reason behind their constant visits to the bakery was in the hope of meeting Agnes Handly, the woman who, according to the papers, had been in cahoots with the man it was said had snatched the eight-year-old girl.

Even though the newspaper articles had stated that

the former assistant at the Mitson bakery had gone to ground, it didn't stop the thrill seekers from visiting the place where the evil Agnes Handly had once worked – and she must be evil to have done what she had. But their efforts to elicit information from the young woman serving behind the counter had come up against a blank wall. Yet they continued to come. Unable to learn the truth they'd had to be content with the rumours that were circulating the streets surrounding the bakery, and a very juicy piece of gossip it was. As with most rumours, no one was quite sure where the original story had started. Some said it was old Ma Wilson who had started the ball rolling.

Apparently, the elderly widow had been woken by a frantic knocking on her door late one night. At first, fearful of being murdered in her bed, the terrified woman had stayed huddled beneath her quilted eiderdown praying whoever it was would get tired and go away, but the banging had continued relentlessly. It was only when she heard her name being called that she had ventured trembling from her bed and cautiously peered out of her window to see Agnes Handly's worried face staring back at her. Relieved to see the familiar face, the elderly woman had let the agitated Agnes into her house, asking what had led Agnes to her door at this hour of night. And the answer she had received was nothing short of sensational.

Playing down her role in the abduction of the Masters child – something Ma Wilson knew nothing about, for she rarely ventured out of doors, nor did she read the newspapers due to her failing eyesight

– Agnes had described her terror at the mounting
mob of outraged people baying for her blood, and
how John Smith had taken her to Arthur Mitson's
home for her own safety – only for her to be terrorised
by the very man the policeman had handed her over
to for help.

'. . . I'm telling yer, that's what I heard.' A plump
woman was holding court outside the bakery, her face
alight with excitement. 'An' that's not all.' The woman
stopped for breath, making her moment of impor-
tance last as long as possible. Then, seeing she had
the undivided attention of the group of women
surrounding her she carried on, 'It turns out old
Arthur's never done the business with young Ellen,
yer know, in bed . . . !'

A woman in the small crowd gave a derisive laugh.
'Is that all? Bleeding 'ell, Flo, I'd've been more
surprised if he 'ad. I mean ter say, he's a nice enough
bloke, but he ain't exactly the sort of man ter make a
young girl go weak at the knees, or any other woman
for that matter, now is he? Nah! I've always thought
him and Ellen had what they call a marriage of
convenience . . .'

'Cor blimey! Hark at you, Gladys Brown. Marriage
of convenience, my arse. You've been reading those
fancy magazines again, ain't yer?' Another woman
broke into the conversation. 'Anyway, I don't believe
a word of it. I mean ter say, Arthur might be a boring
old fart, but he's still a man, ain't he? Yer can't tell me
he's been sharing a bed with a pretty girl like Ellen
for how long is it? Two years, an' kept 'is pecker
tucked in 'is underclothes. Unless, of course, he can't

get it up any more. An' let's face it, he can't 'ave had much practice, poor old sod.'

The woman called Flo, seeing her audience slipping away from her, raised her voice, desperate not to have her moment of glory taken from her. ''Ang on, I ain't got ter the best bit yet. Unless yer ain't interested in what else I 'eard.'

The group of women fell silent, their curiosity getting the better of them. Satisfied she had their attention once more, Florrie Baxter hurried on.

'Like I was saying, Arthur an' Agnes were 'aving a row when he told 'er he'd never touched Ellen in that way, when who should walk in but young Ellen and Ted Parker. Well! Agnes told Ma Wilson all hell broke loose. First Arthur stormed out of the room, then Ted pulled Ellen into his arms like they was a couple of sweethearts, and told her that her marriage wasn't legal . . . Well, not that exactly, but he was all excited, saying she could divorce Arthur on account of the marriage not being consummated; I think that's the word he used. Anyway Ellen told him ter go and according ter Agnes' version, Ted Parker told Ellen he loved her, but not ter keep him 'anging on too long, 'cos he wasn't gonna wait fer 'er for ever.'

Stopping for breath the delighted Florrie saw she had a captive audience and carried on quickly before someone else took it into their heads to steal her thunder.

'So off he goes in a right old temper, but Agnes didn't 'ave a chance ter talk ter Ellen 'cos she went straight ter bed. I gotta say, she's a nice girl, is Ellen, 'cos even though she must 'ave been in a right state herself, she still thought of Agnes. Told her she could sleep downstairs fer the night. And let's face it, she could've chucked her out, 'specially the way Agnes has treated Ellen since she married Arthur. Anyway, Agnes didn't fancy sleeping in a chair downstairs, 'cos it'd turned chilly that night. So she stayed where she was, thinking she'd be able to slip away quietly in the morning, and Arthur and Ellen wouldn't be any the wiser. She was just drifting off ter sleep when she heard raised voices, an' yer know how nosy Agnes Handly is.'

She nodded to the spellbound group, not realising the hypocrisy of her words. As her eyes roamed over her audience she noticed a woman she'd never seen before. Unlike the others, this particular woman, although listening intently, didn't appear to be as engrossed as the others. Mentally shrugging, Florrie Baxter finally got to the crux of her tale.

'When she 'eard Arthur shouting, she didn't take much notice at first, 'cos he'd been drinking, an' yer know what men are like when they've had a few. But then she 'eard Ellen trying ter calm him down, then, according ter Agnes, Ellen started crying. Well, Agnes got worried, so she went over ter listen at the bedroom door, an' you'll never guess what she 'eard . . .' She paused for effect, delighting in the rapt faces of the women crowding round her. 'Only Arthur saying that it was time Ellen began ter act like a proper wife, and poor Ellen crying and begging Arthur to stop and that he was frightening her. The last thing Agnes 'eard was Ellen cry out, like she was in pain, then it all went quiet. Agnes was just wondering what ter do when she 'eard Arthur coming towards the door. According ter her, she was frightened Arthur might rape her too' – a coarse laugh erupted from her thin lips – 'Bleeding wishful thinking if yer ask me. So she grabbed 'er things an' ran as if she 'ad a rocket up her arse. That's how she ended up at Ma Wilson's. She knew the old girl wouldn't 'ave 'eard about that business with the little girl and that pervert she'd got herself tangled up with. When Ma Wilson woke up next morning, Agnes had gone without so much as a thank you or by yer leave. No one knows where she is now. If she's any sense she'll stay right away from the East End. People 'ave long memories round these parts. The only chance Agnes Handly 'as of coming back 'ome is if that poor little girl's found safe and sound, please God! Though if Agnes' story about Arthur forcing 'imself on Ellen is true, I hope fer 'is sake Ted don't find out, 'cos if he does, there'll be murder done.'

With no more news to impart the woman fell silent, her brief moment at the centre of attention over.

Slowly the women began to disperse, all except for the stranger who had been listening to the lurid story in silence.

Sadie remained where she was, then, anxious not to attract unwelcome attention, she began to pace up and down, giving the impression she was waiting for someone. Then, curiosity getting the better of her she stopped and looked into the shop window, only to give a nervous start as she saw the young woman, whom she surmised was the object of the conversation she had overheard, staring straight back at her. Flustered, Sadie quickly moved away. Her mind spinning she

231

wondered what she should do for the best. Under the circumstances she didn't think it a good idea to approach the baker's wife at the moment. If what she had heard was true then the poor cow had enough on her plate to deal with. Knowing she was prevaricating, and hating herself for wasting valuable time she made a decision. Glancing to her right she saw the woman who had been holding court and made her way towards her.

Florrie Baxter was only too eager to have a sympathetic ear, and, after having to listen to the same story again, Sadie finally managed to get a word in, getting to the real purpose for striking up a conversation with the garrulous woman. Fifteen minutes later she was on a tram heading for Roman Road market where she had been reliably informed Ted Parker ran his stall. For reasons of her own she hadn't asked about Micky Masters, telling herself it was best if she didn't let anyone know she was looking for the boy. But no matter which excuse she tried to assuage her guilt, deep down she knew she was still hoping the boy would be long gone, and then she would be able to keep Molly with her without raising anyone's suspicions as to why she was trying to locate the boy. It would also stop any awkward questions being asked.

But whatever the outcome, she must put her own feelings aside and do what was best for Molly.

When she alighted from the tram, she slowly made her way down the long lines of stalls, her feet dragging, a sick sensation in her stomach. It would have been quicker to ask the first stall holder where to locate Ted Parker, but she was in no hurry to find him. The longer it took her to find him, and ask about Micky Masters, the longer she could hold onto her dream of keeping Molly, of having a daughter to share her lonely life with.

'I bet they're having a field day out there, nosy cows. Still, I'm not complaining, we've never been so busy.'

Arthur, coming to relieve Ellen so she could have her lunch, attempted a jocular tone, but the icy look on his wife's face chilled him to the bone. The morning rush was over so it was safe for them to talk, until the next customer arrived.

His fleshy face reddening he said pleadingly, 'Please, Ellen, love. I've apologised over and over again. I was mad with rage at seeing you with Ted Parker, and hearing what he said about you being able to leave me and go with him. I was almost out of my head with worry that I was going to lose you, but I swear to God, I never meant to hurt you. You must know I'm speaking the truth. God Almighty, we've been married and sharing a bed for over two years, and I've never laid a finger on you. Now be fair, there's not many men would have done that. I'd cut off me right arm if I could turn back the clock, but I can't. What's done is done. But I swear to you, it'll never happen again. Ellen . . . Ellen! Please, love, say something. It's killing me having you look right through me as if I wasn't there. What more can I do for you to forgive me? Just say the word and I'll do whatever you ask.'

Taking off her apron, Ellen came out from behind the counter. Without looking at him she said in a cold, flat voice, 'It's not your right arm I'd like to cut off, Arthur. And no matter what excuse you use to try to justify what you did, the truth is you raped me. I know a husband can't be charged with raping his wife, the law doesn't recognise a woman's rights in that matter once she's married, more's the pity. You say you're sorry and it'll never happen again, and that much is true.' She turned to face him, and Arthur flinched at the dead look in those once sparkling eyes. 'Because I'll tell you now, Arthur, if you ever attempt such an act again, I swear I'll pack up and move out without a backward glance, and you'll never see me again.'

Arthur stared after the retreating figure, his entire body filled with an emotion he couldn't put a name to. The Ellen he had married was gone for ever. It was as if she had died. He felt what he could only term as a kind of bereavement. As the bell over the door tinkled, a wild thought entered his mind. Please God, let that one, never-to-be-repeated act result in a pregnancy. Only then would he be able to put his tortured mind at ease. For two long, agonising weeks he had been expecting Ellen to pack her bags and leave – and it wouldn't have taken a genius to work out where she would go.

But if she were to have a baby, then surely she would stay with him, if only for the sake of the child.

Putting his best smile on he asked the waiting customer, 'Yes, love, and what can I get you today?'

It was one o'clock and Sadie was sitting in the pie and mash shop drinking her third mug of tea. She was aware of the curious glances in her direction, not surprising since she'd been sitting in the same booth for the past two hours. Ignoring the other occupants of the café she sipped her tea, her eyes staring unseeingly out of the window. She'd had no trouble in locating Ted Parker. The first stall holder she had spoken to had pointed him out to her. Her heart beating like a drum, she had slowly approached the stall, her eyes darting back and forth in search of a glimpse of the young boy she had set out to find, but the tall, dark-haired man appeared to be working the stall alone. At any other time, Sadie would have appreciated the rugged good looks of Ted Parker, but not today. Today, the only thing on her mind was trying to find a way to keep the child she had grown to love.

But instead of enquiring of the boy's whereabouts she heard herself asking for a pound of apples and half a dozen oranges; Molly needed the good nourishing food she had long been denied. Oblivious of Ted's good-natured banter, Sadie paid for her purchases and, needing more time to get her thoughts in order, decided to treat herself to her favourite meal of pie and mash. She had just finished her third mug of tea when a man slid into the booth, sitting himself down comfortably on the bench opposite her. Raising her eyes she saw the dark-haired market trader staring at her with marked curiosity.

Without preamble he said, 'I hear yer've been asking about me. D'yer mind telling me why?'

Knowing men as she did, Sadie knew that, despite the man's good-natured tone, he wasn't the type to be fobbed off easily. With the ease of a man comfortable in himself he beckoned over the waitress and ordered a meal, a mug of strong tea, and another one for Sadie. By the way the waitress hovered coyly over him it was obvious that not only was he well known in the café, but that he was also very much a ladies' man. Ten, fifteen years ago, she would likely have felt the same attraction, but with the life she'd led, men no longer had the power to excite her.

'Well. You gonna tell me why you've been looking fer me, or do I have ter tie you down and beat the truth outta you?' Ted grinned amiably. 'Oh, thanks, darlin',' he said as the piping hot dinner was laid before him. The waitress darted a quizzical look at Sadie, then squealed with pleasure as Ted slapped her smartly on the backside. Giving her a broad wink he said laughingly, 'Bring us over another tea in five minutes, there's a good girl.'

Her cheeks turning a bright pink the waitress hurried to her next customer.

Tucking into his meal Ted said lightly, 'I'm still waiting, love. You must 'ave a good reason fer wanting to meet me, and seeing as I'm a curious bloke, I'd like ter know why, and you ain't leaving till you tell me.'

Behind the friendly tone, Sadie knew the man was deadly serious. Not knowing where to start, she swallowed nervously, then, deciding the best course of action was just to blurt out the truth, she said quietly, 'I've been looking fer a boy called Micky Masters and I was told he works fer you. I've got his sister Molly staying with me.' Even though she had been expecting some sort of reaction she wasn't prepared for the electrifying effect her words had on the market trader.

His dinner forgotten, Ted leant forward, his flippant manner replaced by one of desperate urgency. 'Listen, love, I don't know who you are, or if you're telling the truth. There's a lot of people who'll be grateful ter you for ever, including me. But if you're pissing me about, then you've got a bleeding sick sense of humour.'

Immediately on the defensive Sadie shot back angrily, 'Don't you talk ter me like that. What d'yer take me for? I found Molly hiding in a filthy ruin, and I took her home with me. All she talked about that night was her wonderful brother Micky, an' I thought I'd look after her fer the night then set about finding 'er brother the next day. Only it didn't work out like that, 'cos the following morning I couldn't get a word out of her. And believe me I tried. I mean, I didn't mind having 'er stay the night, but I certainly didn't bargain on 'aving 'er still with me a fortnight later. Apart from knowing 'er brother's name, and that he did some odd jobs for a nice lady in a bakery before getting a job with a man called Ted Parker who ran a fruit and veg stall. But she didn't say where the bakery or market was for that matter. And like I said, the morning after I couldn't get anything else outta 'er. I didn't 'ave anything else ter go on. It ain't easy trying ter find someone when yer ain't got a clue where ter look. I reckon the only reason she clammed up was because she was frightened something bad had happened ter her brother. In her little mind she was probably scared of being sent back ter the workhouse an' hoped that if she kept quiet and behaved herself I'd take 'er in and look after her.'

Impatiently pushing away his plate Ted said scathingly, 'Don't give me that. Bleeding hell, the story was splashed all over the front page of the *Hackney Gazette* for the first three days after Molly went missing. She's not headline news any more but the paper's still asking fer anyone who's got any information ter come forward. They've even offered a reward . . .' Ted's eyes suddenly narrowed. 'Is that what this is all about? 'Cos if it is then you're outta luck. You ain't the first one that's tried to collect the reward . . .'

He wasn't given the chance to finish his sentence, for Sadie, emotionally drained, her anger reaching boiling point, spat out bitterly, 'You bastard! I ain't interested in the money. I didn't even know there was a reward . . . Oh, yeah, yer can look at me like that, yer smug git, but it's the truth. And the reason I didn't know about it is because I don't buy the newspapers; there wouldn't be much point seeing as I can't read.' Her breathing rapid, Sadie carried on. 'If yer must know, I was hoping I wouldn't be able ter find Molly's brother. I know I said I was annoyed at first at being lumbered with her, but the truth is, I've grown ter love her. I thought, given time, she'd forget her brother, 'cos apart from that first night she hardly ever mentioned him. And like I said, I was 'oping, in time, she'd grow ter love and be happy with me. But last night, as I was tucking 'er into bed, she suddenly started crying for her brother. And once she'd started it all came tumbling out. The name of the bakery where he used ter do odd jobs, and she told me your name, but she couldn't remember the market where you worked; though once I knew your name it wasn't hard ter find you.' Her voice dropped to a whisper as she tiredly pushed back a strand of hair from her face.

'So there it is. First thing this morning I left Molly with a friend and came looking. I went ter the bakery first, then I lost me nerve and asked someone if she knew of a Ted Parker.' She bravely gave a watery smile. 'Seems you're well known, because the woman I asked knew exactly who you was and where I could find you . . .' She raised her shoulders, 'So 'ere I am, and before the day's out Molly'll be with her brother and everyone will be 'appy . . . except me.' Her voice began to tremble as the strain of keeping up a normal appearance finally got the better of her. Her eyes suspiciously bright, a sob caught in her throat as she said, 'It'll break me 'eart to let 'er go, but I've gotta think of Molly, and 'er brother . . . Oh, shit! Let's get outta 'ere, please, before I make a complete mug of meself.'

Throwing down some coins on the marble table Ted took Sadie's arm and led her from the café. Once out in the fresh air Sadie began to regain control of her emotions.

'So then, where is this Micky? I thought he was working fer you.'

'He is. Sometimes he puts in a full day's work, then there's times like today when he can't settle, and off he goes to search the streets for his sister. He often doesn't come 'ome till gone midnight, almost dead on his feet. He used ter be such a happy kid, but he ain't smiled since Molly went missing.' Ted paused before asking, 'Did Molly say anything about a man called Kenneth Wells?'

239

ANNA KING

Sadie shook her head. 'No, I don't remember her mentioning anyone of that name. Though she did say something about a nasty man she was afraid of. Is that the man?'

Ted nodded grimly. 'Yeah, that's the perverted bastard. It's also why Micky's been almost outta his 'ead with fear that Wells had got hold of her. Look, give me ten minutes ter find someone ter take care of me stall, and then I'll take yer 'ome with me ter wait fer Micky. It'll give me the chance ter fill yer in with the rest of the story.' He hadn't walked more than a few steps when he turned and asked, 'I know it's none of me business, but what was yer doing in that derelict house at that time of the evening?'

For the first time in her life Sadie was suddenly ashamed of her profession. Then, lifting her chin proudly she replied, 'You're right, it ain't none of your business. But if yer must know I was entertaining a client. To put it more bluntly, I'm a brass; there, satisfied now, are yer?'

Ted walked back towards her, a smile on his face. Then to her surprise he lifted her off her feet and planted a kiss on her cheek.

'From where I'm standing, darling, you're eighteen carat pure gold.'

Then he was striding off, whistling happily, leaving Sadie feeling she had suddenly become someone special, and that feeling caused her chest to swell with emotion and pride. Her step lighter she began to browse among the stalls until Ted returned for her.

CHAPTER NINETEEN

At almost the same time Sadie was entering the pie and mash shop, three other people were also consumed with thoughts of Molly, each one for very different reasons.

Micky Masters had been pounding the streets since six o'clock that morning. After a sleepless night, his mind forming indescribable images of his sweet Molly in the hands of that dirty old man, he had finally given up hope of getting any rest and, careful not to wake Ted or Nora, crept out of the house, praying fervently that this might be the day he found his sister. The condition he might find her in was pushed firmly to the furthest recesses of his mind.

Walking the same streets he had trodden the last fortnight he stopped every person he encounted to ask if they had seen a girl answering his sister's description; the answer was always the same. Most of the people he stopped looked at the ashen-faced boy who seemed to have aged years in the short time his younger sister had gone missing, and smiled at him pityingly, wishing with all their hearts they could do something to help, but powerless to do more than pat the young man on the shoulder and try to reassure him his sister would be found soon while knowing that those chances were slim to the point of impossibility. After all this time there was no doubt in anyone's mind that Molly Masters was dead – and those brave enough to look straight into the boy's eyes saw that he knew it too, but would never rest until the body was found and given a decent burial. Yet for every person who stopped to offer some kind of sympathy or hope, there were at least three others who hurriedly crossed the road, or disappeared into the nearest shop to avoid the desperate young boy. As one woman remarked to her friend, the world could be a cruel place at the best of times, but a boy of Micky Masters' age should never have to experience the kind of pain he was suffering. She added grimly that when that Wells bloke was caught he should be handed over to the fathers and mothers of the East End. They'd make sure he never harmed a child again – not with his balls cut off he wouldn't.

Micky trudged on, his steps slowing as the sleepless night and five hours of walking began to catch up on him. His eyes felt hard and gritty, and every bone and muscle in his body ached, yet still he carried on. But if his body was bone weary his mind continued to taunt him.

It was all his fault. If he hadn't gone into the bakery with Agnes that night, he wouldn't have ended up in prison and Molly wouldn't have been left unprotected. He should have been suspicious of Agnes' sudden show of friendship, but she had seemed so genuine. Even so, based on past experience with that old bitch, he shouldn't have been so trusting. But the fact remained he had, and he would never forgive himself. Molly had trusted him unconditionally, and he had let her down. As he walked on, his head felt suddenly light and his vision became blurred. The next thing he knew his legs buckled at the knees, and if it hadn't been for a kind passer-by catching hold of his thin body, he would have fallen onto the hard cobbles.

'Come on, mate, let's get yer 'ome an' some grub inside yer, 'cos I bet yer ain't eaten today, 'ave yer? An' yer ain't gonna do yer sister any good if yer land up in the 'ospital.'

Micky peered up at the man holding him upright, trying to recall his name, but he was so exhausted he could barely remember his own. Without uttering a word he offered no resistance as the concerned man half-walked, half-carried the youngster to the Parkers' home.

Agnes was also feeling the strain. If anything had happened to the young girl she would never be able to live with herself again. She was honest enough to recognise her own faults and admit she had turned into a bitter, lonely woman. She was also aware that she didn't have one single person in the world she could call a friend, and that knowledge cut her deeply. Her life could have been so different if she had never gone to work for Arthur Mitson, and in doing so fall in love with a man who had used her for comfort after the death of his father, then dumped her without a second thought. She could have been happily married to a man who loved her, and children – oh, how she had longed for children. For years she had kept hoping that one day either Arthur would renew their relationship, or, failing that, she'd hoped that she would meet someone else. And with each passing year her hopes faded until she was forced to admit she would never hear a child call her Mum. Mum! Such a simple word, yet so precious. Was it any wonder, starved of love as she had been, she had been so easily duped into believing the lies Kenneth had told her? How he must have laughed at her eagerness to please him, and she, stupid fool as she was, had fallen hook, line and sinker for his plausible patter. And in doing so had put an innocent child at risk of an ordeal she had suffered herself as a child at the hands of her uncle.

The only consolation she had was the fact that the smooth-talking bastard didn't have the girl. If he had got his filthy hands on Molly, he would never have come to her that night in a rage at being deprived of his prey. But despite the intervention of PC John Smith, she knew that men like Wells – she couldn't think of him by his real name of Stokes – didn't give up easily. Somebody had Micky's sister, and she had to find her before Wells did. But that was easier said than done. Sitting on a bench in Victoria Park she reflected on recent events.

Like Micky, she had also been walking the streets for weeks. But unlike Micky Masters, Agnes was searching for the man who had effectively destroyed the lives of so many people, including herself. She was at present living in a one-room flat in Shoreditch, too frightened to return to her home, for fear of further reprisals. Even if the child was found safe and sound, there was always the chance she could return and find her home burned to the ground in retaliation for what many people deemed her part in being in league with a pervert.

Finishing the sandwiches she had brought with her, she rose reluctantly to her aching feet. It was just gone eleven. She would visit a few pubs before returning to her dingy room for a couple of hours' sleep, before venturing back out onto the streets once more. Making sure the black crochet shawl she had worn covering her head and most of her face since that night she had landed at Ma Wilson's door in case someone recognised her, she summoned up her waning strength and ventured forth once more. Stopping at a back street pub she ordered a large gin to keep her strength up. She was about to leave when the pub doors opened and a smartly dressed man sauntered in. Her jaw dropping in disbelief, her head swivelled round to follow his progress, unable to believe her eyes. The hair colouring was different, the once smooth face was now sporting a moustache and a goatee beard, while the upper part of his face was almost obscured by a pair of tortoise-shell eye glasses. But despite his best efforts to alter his appearance, Agnes recognised him straight away, and it took all of her willpower to stay where she was and not run across the pub and attack him with all the strength she possessed. A surge of rage swept through her. Her basic instinct was to scream his true identity to the entire pub before smashing her empty glass right into that smug, evil face. After that she would leave him to the mercy of the pub customers, and if there was any justice they'd tear him limb from limb. Her lips white with fury she gripped the empty glass. She had to think and think hard. Every fibre in her being wanted to avenge what he had done to her. For not only had he ruined her life, he had used her in the most despicable way known to man. No! She must keep her head. Even though he hadn't managed to get the child that night he had attacked her, there was always the possibility he had somehow tracked her down since. If that was the case then the only way to find the child was to follow Kenneth wherever he went.

Until then she would have to put all thoughts of revenge on hold. Her day would come, of that she had no doubt. Careful to keep her shawl half covering her face she ordered another gin and waited.

Taking a last look in the full-length mirror in the boarding house, where he had been staying since that nosy bastard John Smith had appeared on the scene, the well-dressed man gave a satisfied smirk at the image that stared back at him. For weeks he'd had to dress like a working-class man, a scruffy, unwashed male of the lowest order in his books, in order to avoid being recognised. Now that period of time was nearly over. It had been hard to contain his frustration once he had ascertained that the slut Sadie North was the cause of all his misfortunes. His first instinct had been to confront the blowsy prostitute, but after witnessing the violent altercation in the public house he had quickly changed his mind. Instead he had followed the furious woman to a block of flats not too far from the pub. It was an area he was familiar with, so he didn't have to worry about finding it again. All night he had lain awake, thinking hard as to how he would get his Molly back – if indeed the child referred to *was* his Molly!

A sudden noise from the landing snapped him out of his reverie.

Briskly now, he took one last look in the mirror. Then, shutting the door behind him, he left the seedy building, his steps taking him back to the building he had visited last night, and was rewarded by the sight of Molly leaving the tenement building in the company of two young boys whose ages he judged to be between ten and twelve respectively. Five minutes later a plain, smartly dressed woman wearing a black skirt and a white silk blouse appeared at the door of one of the first-floor flats, looking the image of respectability. The sight of her threw him, for she bore no resemblance to the painted whore he had followed the previous evening – until she opened her mouth. From his position he heard her say clearly in a strong, common voice, 'Righto, Lil, wish me luck, mate. I ain't looking forward ter it, but now I know where ter look, I gotta try an' find Molly's brother. I think I'll try the bakery first, an' if I don't get no luck there, I'll ask after this bloke Ted Parker. 'Cos if young Micky was working fer 'im two weeks ago, he likely still is. Mind you, don't say anything to Moll about where I've gone. I don't wanna get 'er 'opes up, poor little love. Anyway, see yer, Lil.'

A slovenly, heavily pregnant woman came out into the street, her arm going round her friend's shoulders in a gesture of comfort.

'Don't worry, Sadie, love. Look on the bright side. If yer find the brother, yer might end up with two kids ter look after, just like a ready-made family. An' the best bit is, yer won't 'ave a bleeding 'usband getting under yer feet.'

From his vantage point, Wells saw a dispirited look pass over the prostitute's face.

'Thanks, Lil, but I don't think there's much chance of that, do you?'

Giving her friend another awkward pat on the back the pregnant woman re-entered her flat. Unaware she was being watched, Sadie's shoulders slumped for a brief moment, then, with a look of determination etched on her freshly washed face, she began to walk towards him. Quickly darting out of sight, he waited until she had disappeared before approaching the flat she had just left, unaware that he too was being closely scrutinised.

Agnes hadn't taken her sharp eyes off the hateful figure since she had followed him out of the pub. She too had overheard the exchange between the two women, and it didn't take a genius to figure out what was going on. Somehow, Kenneth had found out who had Molly, and where. Now she knew too. But what to do with the knowledge? Clutching her shawl tighter around her head she saw Kenneth knock at the ground-floor flat, and within a few minutes he had disappeared inside. Her eyes darting frantically up and down the street she looked in vain for a copper. Most days you couldn't walk more than a few feet without practically falling over one of them. Of course, when you really wanted one, there were none to be seen.

Unlike Wells, she hadn't seen Molly run off to play with the two boys. As far as she knew, the girl was inside the flat. Knowing how plausible Kenneth could be, Agnes had no doubt he would at this moment be spinning the same tale he had spun to her. She only hoped the woman who had been left in charge of Micky's sister wouldn't be as gullible as she had been. And if he couldn't persuade the woman to hand over the child to him, her supposed uncle, Agnes had no doubt he would take her by force. What was she to do? She was no match for a grown man if it came to a struggle. But if she left to find a copper, he could be long gone by the time she found one. Of course she could always scream for help. There must be plenty of people at home at this time of day. She nodded, her mind made up. That's what she'd do. If he came out of that flat with the little girl, she'd scream at the top of her lungs. Her plan of action settled, she leant back out of sight against the brick wall and waited.

Inside the flat, a none too clean mug of tea held in his hand, Kenneth Wells, disguising his distaste at his surroundings, turned on the charm he had perfected over the years and smiled at the straight-faced woman.

'So, Lil . . . If I may call you Lil?'

Lily nodded wordlessly, a clear look of distrust on her face. Kenneth saw the look and cursed silently.

The only reason he hadn't gone to Sadie North was because he had deemed her too worldly-wise to be easily taken in. Also it was obvious she had become fond of his Molly. Why else would she have taken her in and cared for her these past two weeks? Now it was becoming alarmingly clear that this woman, Lily Knight, wasn't going to be a pushover either. Keeping a tight rein on his temper, he put down the mug onto an equally grimy, sticky table, and curved his lips into what he assumed was a disarming smile.

'I don't blame you for being suspicious. Indeed, it does you credit that you should take your duties in looking after my niece so diligently, but you must try and see it from my point of view. I've been going out of my mind with worry, thinking the worst. It was bad enough when I knew Molly was being looked after by that young tearaway Micky – he's a bad lot, that one. I was never very close to my brother, I will admit, that's why I was unaware of my brother and sister-in-law's deaths. The authorities traced me eventually, but by the time I arrived at the workhouse, that scallywag Micky had already made his escape, taking Molly with him. It would have been far better if he had left her behind, but he was always a selfish boy. Anyway, what's done is done. Micky can look after himself, but I would be failing in my duties as Molly's legal guardian if I left her with a known prostitute . . .' Too late he realised he had said the wrong thing.

Her face cold Lily waddled over to the door and flung it wide. 'Yer must think I was born yesterday. People like you, with yer smart clothes an' fancy talk think us cockneys are all thick – well, we ain't. We might not be able ter talk posh, but we can smell a rat when we see one, an' you, mister, stink like a rotting corpse. D'yer really think I'd fall for that load of old cobblers? If yer was really Molly's uncle, yer'd 'ave brought the law with yer, or somebody from the authorities. Nah! I know who you are. You're the nasty man Molly told Sadie about. Scum, that's what men like you are, scum. An' yer've got the nerve ter look down on decent people just 'cos we're poor. Now! Get outta my 'ouse. And 'ere's something ter think on. I know what yer look like now, an' the minute Sadie gets back, we'll be straight down the cop shop. Now, piss off, yer disgusting bleeder. Go on, get outta my 'ouse.'

Still believing people like Lily Knight could be bought off if offered the right price Kenneth pulled out his wallet and threw down two white five-pound notes. Lily merely glanced at the two pieces of crisp paper. She had never seen so much money in her entire life, and probably never would again, but she'd rather cut off her arm than sink to the level of selling a child, any child. Her voice dripping with scorn she spat out, 'Go on, get yer stinking carcass outta my 'ouse, an' yer can take yer blood money with yer, yer smarmy bastard.'

The velvety veneer slipped from his face like paint stripped from a wall with a blow torch. His upper lip curling in anger he snarled, 'Don't go getting on your high horse with me, you fat slag. Do you imagine I don't know what you're after? Here! There's another five pounds. That's what you're really after, aren't you? More money. You're all the same, people like you. You'd sell your own mother if the price was high enough. So don't go pretending moral indignation on me, because it won't wash. Go on, take it,' he pointed scornfully to the small pile of money. 'You can split it with your friend when she gets back. Because let's face it, that's more than a pair of old slappers like you will ever earn in your line of work . . .'

The look on Wells' face turned to fear as, with a cry of pure rage, the woman grabbed a carving knife from the table and, holding it in front of her bulging stomach, she rushed at him, raising the wicked-looking blade so that it was only inches from his face. Instinctively he grabbed hold of her wrist, but not before the knife slashed across the back of his right hand. He had imagined it would be an easy task to disarm her, but he hadn't bargained for the tenacity of the East End women, especially when those women were mothers. And like all mothers, Lily fought her assailant with every bit of strength she possessed to protect the innocent child he had come for. But for all her fury, she was still a woman, and a heavily pregnant one at that. Yet still she would not relinquish the knife, her only form of defence. Gasping and sweating, Kenneth lifted his arm high, bringing it down viciously across Lily's perspiring face. Lily had often been hit by her husband, especially when he'd come home drunk, so she was accustomed to being used as a punch bag. In normal circumstances she would have weathered the blow, but, with her bulging stomach weighing her down, she was caught off balance and fell to the floor with a sickening thud.

His breathing still rapid, Kenneth tried to calm himself down and concoct another plan, for after today he would never get another chance to get his hands on Molly. Edging cautiously towards the still form, Kenneth, bracing himself for another attack, carefully turned the woman over, then reeled back in shock. For there, almost hidden by her huge belly, the carving knife she had tried to use on him was now embedded between her ponderous breasts. The sweat was pouring off him now. Then he heard the sound of laughing children approaching and with a swiftness of thought that surprised even himself, he practically threw himself across the room and behind the open door.

Billy Knight was the first to enter the room, as always a grievance on his lips about something his brother had done to upset him, only to come to an abrupt stop at the sight of his mother lying motionless on the floor, covered in blood, the wooden handle of the kitchen knife protruding from her chest. It was a sight that rendered him speechless with shock. Then he was being shoved out of the way by his older brother Charlie.

'Mum . . . Mum, Billy's nicked me conkers . . . Mum . . . Mum . . . !' The two boys were framed in the doorway, their eyes wide with horror and disbelief.

Blissfully unaware of the horrific scene, her view hidden by the two boys, Molly playfully pushed Charlie, laughing, 'Get outta the way, Charlie. I need ter go to the lav.' Using her elbows she tried to push the solid form out of her path, but he remained as if turned to stone. ''Ere, what's up? What's 'appened, Charlie? Where's yer mum?'

Suddenly stung into life, both boys rushed towards their silent mother crying piteously, 'Get up, Mum ... Please, Mum, get up ...'

It was only then that Molly saw Lily and like the boys she was momentarily struck dumb with shock. Then she opened her mouth wide and let out a blood-curdling scream of pure terror. The sound seemed to galvanise the boys into action. Charlie, older than his brother by a mere ten months, took charge.

'You, Billy, run for 'elp, quick.' When his brother stayed huddled over his mother, Charlie grabbed him roughly by the back of the neck shouting, 'Hurry, Billy. Yer gotta get a doctor. Go on, run, Billy, run ...' His voice broke, and shoving his brother out into the street he turned to Molly who was still screaming. 'Shut up ... shut up.' The harsh words were a brave attempt to adopt an adult demeanour. 'Look, get some sheets ... or towels ... Anything. We've gotta try an' stop the bleeding ... We've gotta do something ...' But for all his bravado, he was still only a child, a child terrified of losing his mum. His voice breaking on a sob, his eyes bright with tears, he looked for help to Molly. But Molly, although now silent, remained rooted to the spot. By now people were pouring out into the street to see what all the noise was about.

Still in his hiding place, Kenneth cursed his bad luck. Within seconds the place would be crawling with people, and if that fat cow was dead, then he'd hang. But he wasn't just going to stay hidden behind the door, for once that crowd entered the flat he'd be discovered in seconds. Slamming the door shut he sprang forward at the unsuspecting Charlie, and with a clenched fist hit him hard around the head, the blow sending the boy falling across his mother's bleeding body. Then he turned to the petrified Molly. Picking her up with his good arm, he covered her mouth with the hand Lily had stuck the knife into, adding to Molly's terror as she tasted his blood on her lips.

The sound of voices was growing louder and nearer. Like a trapped rat he looked wildly around the tiny room to a narrow hallway. With his prize firmly held in a vice-like grip, he bounded out of the room, his eyes lighting up at the sight of the open window leading out to the back yard. He had just climbed through the narrow window when a small group of people burst into the room behind him. Dropping onto the uneven slabs beneath the window, Kenneth ran as if the devil himself was on his tail, the limp body of Molly, who had fainted, slung over his shoulders. Keeping to the back streets he managed to avoid being seen. Only when he was sure he was safe did he stop to staunch the wound in his hand with a linen hand-kerchief which he always wore in his breast pocket, before moving Molly's position from over his shoulder and into his arms, looking for all the world like a doting father carrying his sleeping child home.

Hailing a hackney cab, he clambered in, giving the cabbie an address in Essex. A satisfied smile of relief on his lips, he sat back on the leather seat, his eyes devouring the still form of the young girl. It had been the devil of a job to get her, but get her he had – and she was going to pay for all the trouble she had caused him.

* * *

When Molly screamed Agnes had jumped with fright, not having heard them come back. Then all hell seemed to break loose as a boy raced sobbing from the flat calling for help. Inching forward Agnes approached the open doorway, but before she could look inside the door slammed in her face. Running to the side window she witnessed Kenneth's assault on the boy, and him grabbing who she could only assume was the elusive Molly. Pushing open the door she too stopped in her tracks at the sight that met her eyes. Then she heard running footsteps and, following the sound, saw Kenneth make his escape with the girl through a window at the back of the flat. Although not as agile as she once was she managed to scramble out of the window and, careful to keep at a safe distance she followed the retreating figure, while at the same time keeping a look out for the law, or even a couple of strong men who would be able to stop Wells making off with the unconscious girl. But luck wasn't with her today. Nor for the bloodied woman left for dead, or maybe already dead, and the boy, also lying unconscious over his mother's body as if trying to protect her from further harm. The only way she could help the little girl was to find out where Kenneth was taking her. And as soon as she knew, she'd go straight to the law.

Then they were out of the back alleys and into the high street. And there was that pervert, looking to all intents and purposes like a loving father holding his child close to his chest. She saw him hail the cab and looked desperately around her for some kind of assistance. At this time of day, the high street was fairly busy, but before she could enlist any help, the cab was driving away, leaving Agnes crying in frustration. She couldn't believe he had got away with the child so easily, not in broad daylight. But as her mother used to say, 'the devil looks after his own', and if ever there was a personification of evil, it was Kenneth Wells and all men of his ilk.

Then she had the first piece of luck she'd had for weeks. For as the cab drove past her she heard Kenneth's voice through the open window, giving the cabbie the address he wanted taking to.

Repeating the address over and over in her mind, fearful of forgetting it, Agnes saw two policemen strolling down the high street.

She was only a few feet away from the uniformed men when she stopped suddenly, an idea forming in her mind.

She knew where to find Kenneth now. What if she went to the address she had now committed to memory, and rescued the child by herself? After all, she would have the advantage of surprise on her side, for Kenneth had no idea that anyone knew where to find him. And what if she was able to get the child away and back to safety? For not only would she be saving the girl from a known pervert's clutches, but she too would be able to return to her own home without fear. She had passed the two officers, her mind jumping forward, the unplanned thoughts gathering momentum by the second. Returning to the cheap boarding house, she quickly took some money from a box hidden under a loose floorboard, and hurried back out onto the streets. Within minutes she was settled in the back of a cab, an experience new to her, but for once she wasn't concerned how much money the journey was going to cost her. By the time she had asked directions and waited around for trams it might take hours to get to the destination she was heading for, and time was of the essence.

Aware she was trembling, Agnes slowed her breathing and tried to relax, knowing however that she would never have any peace of mind until the child was safe. It was all up to her now – the way it should be, for it was because of her the child was in danger. Clenching her hands together to stop them shaking Agnes was suddenly thankful her journey was going to be a relatively long one. It would give her time to think.

Ted and Sadie heard the commotion before they had even turned the corner that led into the block of flats. Exchanging fearful glances they both quickened their step. At first they couldn't see anything for the crowds of people milling around the courtyard, then, one of Sadie's neighbours caught sight of her and hurried forward.

'Oh, Gawd, Sadie, love. Yer'll never guess what's 'appened. Poor Lil's been done in, an' little Charlie's been bashed round the 'ead an' all. And we can't find your Molly, she . . .'

Sadie pushed the woman aside, her heart thumping with fear. With Ted behind her, she pulled at the people swarming around the door of the first-floor flat, then stopped dead in her tracks at the sight that confronted her. With a muffled scream she leapt forward.

'Lil! Lil! Oh, God! Please . . . please, don't be dead
. . .' Dropping to her knees, she gently cradled her
friend's head in her lap. 'Come on, Lil, mate. It's me,
Sadie. Come on, yer silly cow, stop pissing about . . .
Lil . . . Lil . . .'

Her vision blurred as tears rained down her face,
then two small bodies were tugging at her, their
childish shrills of fear penetrating Sadie's own grief.
Her arms going out automatically she pulled the two
stricken boys to her, holding them tightly against her
heaving chest.

Over all the din came the sound of police whistles,
and someone in the crowd shouted that the ambulance cart was on the way, but to the deeply shocked
Sadie, the sounds all seemed to blur together in a
confusion of unintelligible noises. Raising her head
she looked over the boys' heads and saw Ted Parker
staring down at her. Then he too seemed to jump and
dance before her eyes. Holding Billy and Charlie tight,
she lowered her gaze and gently rocked the two
youngsters back and forth, not knowing if she was
comforting them or herself in the instinctive gesture.

There was a question she wanted to ask the boys,
a question that was screaming around inside her head,
but couldn't bring herself to say the words, for fear
of what the answer might be.

Clutching the boys tight, her eyes clouded over as
she looked around the familiar faces. Some she only
knew by sight, others she didn't recognise, but the
only face she wanted to see, longed to see, wasn't
there.

CHAPTER TWENTY

'I don't bloody well believe it. I mean, how the fucking hell can anyone just walk in off the street and stab a woman, a pregnant woman at that, knock one kid unconscious and make off with another one in broad daylight, and no one see anything? I could understand it if it had happened at night, but Gawd Almighty, in the middle of the day? And where's all the nosy neighbours when yer need them?' Ted stormed. 'That bloke must lead a charmed life, that's all I can say ... Bastard!'

'Calm down, Ted. We're doing everything we can ...'

'Oh, yeah. Like what?' Ted cut in angrily. 'Yer said the same thing when the kid first went missing, an' yer've done bleeding sod all, as far as I can see.'

The policeman's mouth tightened. 'Now that's enough, Ted. I know you're upset so I'll let that slide. But you know full bloody well me and the rest of the nick have been working our bloody guts out trying to find that kid. And we're not getting paid any overtime for it, either.'

Ted stared back into the angry face and let his gaze drop. Shaking his head from side to side he nipped on his bottom lip before replying quietly, 'Yeah, I know, Officer, I know.' Running a hand through his thick hair he said, 'But I was so close. So bloody close. If I'd only been ten minutes earlier I might have been in time to stop that maniac. Then Molly would be where she belongs, with her brother, and that poor cow wouldn't've been knifed, an' ...'

The constable laid a comforting hand on Ted's shoulder. 'I understand, mate ... It's a right bloody mess, ain't it?'

John Smith sighed tiredly. Since the Masters girl had gone missing he'd hardly had a decent night's sleep. Added to his daily workload he'd taken Agnes Handly under his wing as well. The other men had laughed at him, saying they'd begrudge looking after that old trout in the line of work, but to waste his own time? Well, they'd said, rather him than them. But the seasoned policeman had just smiled and carried on with his work quietly, refusing to be drawn into any conflict with his colleagues. And even if they didn't understand, or share his ideals, they respected the bulky man and kept their counsel.

Now, as of one-thirty this afternoon, 27 May 1898, the whole of the Metropolitan Police force was on full alert. There was no talk about overtime now, paid or otherwise. There was a madman on the loose, but the criminal they were looking for was far worse than any madman, for this particular one was a child molester, the lowest of the low. A man who brought shame on his own sex, for no one was more reviled than a man who sought out innocent children to pander to his sick, perverted sexual desires, and the sooner he was caught and locked up the better for every decent person alive. Every policeman in London was drafted onto the streets, knocking on doors, pulling in every pervert known to them. But all to no avail. A couple of Sadie North's neighbours had come forward giving a description of the smartly dressed man seen entering Lily Knight's flat, but apart from that, they had no more information to give. Now, two hours later, the entire police force were out pounding the streets looking for the man known as Kenneth Stokes, alias Wells, and his accomplice, Agnes Handly. John Smith had tried to tell his superiors that Agnes Handly was as much a victim as anyone, but no one would listen, and the constable knew better than to pursue that line. Though it would have been helpful if he could find Agnes. She might know more than she thought, but, like the elusive Stokes, Agnes was nowhere to be found. Though not for a second did John Smith imagine she was with the man they sought. For he firmly believed that unfortunate wretch was more sinned against than sinning.

'Look, I'm sorry, mate.' Ted was talking again, his face tired and drawn, more from worry than lack of sleep. Also he was experiencing a great feeling of deflation. As he had said to the policeman, he'd been so near to finding Micky's sister. He remembered the journey to Sadie North's home, and how he had imagined seeing Micky's face when he returned his sister to him. Never for a moment had Ted envisaged the horrific scene that had greeted him instead. The woman, Lily Knight, was now in hospital fighting for her life, unaware her baby, brought into the world prematurely by the vicious attack on its mother, was dead. Sadie North was at her friend's bedside with the two Knight boys whom she had taken under her wing for the time being.

Then there was Micky.

Micky, once so full of life, so full of hope for the future, even nursing a crush on Ellen, and thinking nobody noticed. Now he was over at the bakery, crying his eyes out in her arms. In his hour of need he had reverted to childhood and in Ellen he saw only a mother figure, someone to cling to. She was the first person he had asked for when Ted had returned with his grim news. Ted had been apprehensive about taking the boy over to the bakery, but Arthur, give him his due, had welcomed Micky in with open arms, even offering to keep him for as long as he wanted to stay. And that had been suspicious in itself. But any business he had with Arthur and Ellen would have to wait for now. They had a lifetime in front of them – unlike Micky's sister if they didn't find her soon. He knew the police were doing everything they could but he was still angry at the lack of progress and despite his better judgement he couldn't resist having another dig.

'I ain't 'aving a go at you, Johnny, but it doesn't look as if the rest of the law's exactly breaking its neck trying ter find the kid. I mean, like I said before, I could understand him getting away if it'd been night, but how the 'ell could he walk the streets with the kid without someone noticing? He must 'ave taken a cab. If I was a copper, that would 'ave been the first thing I'd've done – question the cab drivers. Or maybe he had a carriage waiting? But however he got away he had ter be out on the streets for a while, and the kid would've called fer help, wouldn't she?'

Like Ted, the constable was also tired and frustrated and his patience, held under control through years of experience, finally snapped.

'Now you listen to me, mouth almighty. You haven't got a clue about what's going on. And I don't have to justify myself or the rest of the force to you or anyone else, but I will anyway, if only to shut you up. For your information almost every man wearing a uniform has a daughter or niece and they'd be on the warpath even if they weren't officers of the law. That's what's the matter with people like you. You seem to think policemen are a breed apart from the rest of the human race. Well, they're not. They're just like any other man, with feelings and anger. They cry and laugh just like you, but because they wear a uniform people imagine they're above human feelings. And another thing, don't call me Johnny. It's "Officer" to you, mate. As it happens we've already spoken to most of the cab drivers near the location of the flats, and one of the drivers remembers a man carrying a little girl. He thought she was asleep. As for her calling out? Huh! You don't know anything about children either, do you? Just imagine if you were eight years old and had just seen a friend stabbed and covered in blood. It must have been like a nightmare to her. Then the man she's petrified of is suddenly there. Do you really think she'd have called for help? She must have been terrified of making a sound in case the man hurt her. Though the poor little cow didn't even have the choice, seeing as she was unconscious. One more crack about the police and you'll feel the weight of my hand, no matter how big you are. And it won't be the first time, will it?'

At the sudden change in the constable's voice Ted jumped. Then, as long-ago memories resurfaced he smiled sheepishly. 'Yeah, I remember.' His lean frame relaxed for the first time that afternoon. 'How old was I? Twelve, thirteen? You caught me nicking an apple off a fruit stall up Mare Street. I didn't even 'ave a chance ter take a bite outta it, did I? Gawd, but yer gave me a fright when you grabbed me by the scruff of the neck. I'd already had a good look up and down the road before I got up the nerve to pinch that apple, an' I didn't see you. And when you suddenly appeared, I thought you was some sort of magician. I can still see it now. All me mates were watching, 'cos they'd dared me to do it, but they soon legged it when you showed up. But I knew wherever they was hiding they'd still be watching, so I put on a front, pretending I wasn't scared. Gawd! I was so cocky, wasn't I? Giving you a load of lip, till yer grabbed me by the ear and marched me down the length of the market. Then yer asked if I'd rather 'ave a clip round the ear, or be taken 'ome to me mum an' tell her what I'd done. Well! I didn't 'ave much of a choice, did I? 'Cos I was more frightened of me mum than you. Then I spotted me mates hiding behind the wall of the church. Well! I couldn't let them see how scared I was, so I put on me swagger and told you to go ahead and clout me.' As the memory became clearer Ted slapped his knee in mirth. 'I didn't know what'd hit me. I thought me head was gonna fall off. I wasn't so cocky then, was I? That clout sent me cross-eyed and bandy-legged. Me eyes were rolling, I could've sworn I heard bells ringing, an' I staggered 'ome looking and walking like a half wit with me mates following 'aving a good laugh at my expense.'

As the memory came flooding back Ted threw back his head and laughed uproariously.

Listening to Ted's infectious laughter John felt his own lips beginning to twitch and within seconds the two men were rolling with mirth. It was just what they both needed after the trauma of the last couple of hours. They were still laughing when a loud knock interrupted their merriment. Immediately the laughter stopped as if turned off by a tap. Exchanging apprehensive glances the constable was the first to move. Throwing the front door open he saw two of his colleagues standing on the doorstep.

'Well, what's happened?' he said over-loudly, his nerves causing a hardness in his voice.

The elder of the policemen raised his eyebrows before answering. 'We've got the cab driver that took a man and little girl to a house near Epping Forest. Inspector Lewis has already left, but we thought you deserved to know what's happening, especially after all the hard work you've put into finding the kid.'

Standing behind John Smith Ted couldn't help but notice the deference in the officer's tone, nor the way both men were looking to the older policeman for guidance, even though they were all of the same rank.

His blunt features tight with repressed anger the constable cursed quietly. 'Well, that's no surprise, is it? It's always the same. We work our arses off while he sits behind his desk shuffling papers, bawling out us lowly constables when things go wrong, but he's first in the queue if there's any glory to be had. Any excuse to get his picture in the papers, lazy bastard!'

Again the waiting officers exchanged startled glances. For as long as they'd known the middle-aged officer they had never even heard him raise his voice, let alone act in this manner. But if anything his outburst only increased their respect for voicing what the rest of the station thought of their inspector.

Reaching for his helmet from the hall table John said to Ted, 'Looks like we've finally had some luck, and about time too. Let's just hope it doesn't turn out to be a wild goose chase. Anyway, I'll let you know everything as soon as I get back.'

The words, although kindly spoken, were nonetheless a dismissal, and Ted wasn't used to being treated in such a fashion. His lips tightening he retorted, 'If yer think I'm just gonna wait here twiddling me thumbs when you know where that filthy swine is hiding, you've got another think coming. If yer won't let me come with yer then I'll find out where he is on me own.'

Knowing Ted wasn't the type to make empty threats John sighed. Turning to the waiting two men he said, 'Wait a minute, will you? I just want a quick word with Ted.'

Closing the door slightly so the curious men couldn't overhear the conversation, he faced Ted squarely. 'Look, mate, I understand how you must be feeling. There's no one wants to catch that piece of vermin more than me, but I can't let you come with us, you must know that. My inspector would have my head on a plate if I brought a civilian along with us.'

His face grim Ted reached behind the constable and threw the door wide open. 'Don't let me keep you, your mates are waiting fer you, and I've got business to see to meself.'

Knowing it was useless to argue further John Smith took his leave.

Within minutes Ted was striding down the street, making his way to the high street situated near the building where Sadie North lived. But once there he was bitterly disappointed, for the cabbie who had taken Stokes and Molly on their journey was nowhere to be found. Frustrated, angry, and reluctant to face Micky without some concrete news, Ted pounded the pavements for nearly half an hour before plucking up the courage to face the young man who had become so dear to him.

Arthur turned the closed sign on the bakery door, sighing with a mixture of tiredness and relief that another day of curious strangers and listening to sly innuendoes was over, at least until tomorrow, when the whole sordid experience would start all over again. And all because they were hoping to see the infamous Agnes Handly, supposed partner in crime of Kenneth

Stokes. It made Arthur wonder at the stupidity of some people. Surely they realised Agnes wasn't going to return to her job, not with the entire police force trying to track down her whereabouts. Then again, there was no accounting for people's peculiarities. His only consolation was that today was early closing.

But his ordeal wasn't over yet. He raised his eyes. There was a time, not so long ago, when this had been his favourite part of the day. Then he would climb the stairs, a smile on his face, to the rooms above to be greeted by a cheerful Ellen and a hot meal waiting for him. And as they ate he and Ellen would talk about the day's events, with Ellen recounting some amusing tale concerning some of their more awkward customers. But not any longer. Oh, his dinner would still be waiting for him, but he would have to eat his meal alone, for Ellen no longer sat at the table with him. She was civil to him, as she would be to any stranger. There wasn't even the opportunity to sit down to resolve their differences, no chance for him to try to explain what had made him act the way he had that night – not with Micky Masters temporarily in residence. Then there was Ted Parker dropping in at any hour of the day or night as if he owned the place.

Yet by far the worst part for Arthur was the way Ellen's face lit up like a beacon whenever Ted walked into the room. And it wasn't only Ellen who came to life on seeing Ted; Micky too would run to him, clinging onto the charismatic man, gathering strength from Ted's presence, while he, Arthur was left alone and ignored as if he wasn't even in the room. And each time Arthur witnessed the obvious attraction between his wife and the local market trader, a man half Arthur's age, his stomach would churn with fear. He was living on a knife's edge, expecting Ellen to announce she was leaving him, and there would be nothing he could do to stop her. But if it came to that, he wasn't about to make it easy for her and Ted Parker. He'd never agree to a divorce.

Yet he remembered vividly that night when John Smith had deposited Agnes on him, and she'd confronted him about his relationship with Ellen, insinuating he was as bad as the man who had abducted Molly Masters. But the ultimate shame was finding Ellen and Ted standing in the doorway. Nor could he forget the triumphant, gloating look on Ted Parker's face. If he'd been a man of Ted's calibre he would have stood his ground and faced him down. But no, not him. Instead he had grabbed the whisky decanter and scuttled away like a frightened rabbit into the bedroom. Even with the door closed, he could hear Ted telling Ellen their marriage was a sham, and as he'd listened Arthur's self-esteem had hit rock bottom. He'd felt like a nobody, somebody who was worthless, useless and practically non-existent.

He hadn't planned what had happened that night. He had forced himself on Ellen. He still couldn't comprehend how he could have committed such a despicable act. He'd wanted so badly to feel like a proper man, and also to make their marriage a proper one in every respect. Yet never in a million years would he have made love to Ellen if he hadn't been so full of anger and drink. Even so, he'd hoped Ellen would forgive him eventually. But instead of putting a halt to the flourishing relationship between Ellen and Ted, he had driven her further into his rival's arms.

'You all right, Arthur?'

Arthur jumped at the sound of Nora Parker's voice. Plastering a smile on his face he replied heartily, 'Yeah, I'm fine thanks, Nora. And thanks also for helping out in the shop, I really appreciate it. Here.' Opening the till, he handed Nora half a sovereign for her work of the last few days.

Nora took the money. 'Thanks, Arthur. It's nice being back at work. I mean Ted doesn't keep me short, but there's nothing so rewarding as earning yer own money. D'yer want me back tomorrow? Only I'll 'ave plenty of time ter spare now Micky's moved in here. I know it's only a temporary arrangement, but in the meantime I'm available ter help out if yer want me.'

'That'll be very helpful, Nora. I was thinking of hiring someone to run the shop now Agnes has scarpered and Ellen's preoccupied with young Micky. So yes please, Nora. It'll be a godsend with you in charge of the shop and the takings. It's comforting to know there's someone I can trust.'

As Nora reached the door she hesitated, wondering if she should say something to ease Arthur's mind. But what? Everyone, including herself, had predicted that the marriage wouldn't last. But never had she imagined it would be her son who would ultimately blow Arthur's world apart. There were a hundred things she wanted to say, but the words stuck in her throat. Instead she patted Arthur's arm affectionately saying, ''Bye, Arthur, I'll see yer in the morning.'

''Bye, Nora, and thanks again.'

After he had locked up Arthur spent another fifteen minutes doing mundane jobs in the shop, leaving it until the last minute before he would have to go upstairs and face Ellen. With nothing left to do he made his way up the stairs, his feet dragging as he mounted the steps, wondering with dread what kind of reception he would receive.

'You're late. I've had to put your dinner back in the oven to keep warm. Sit down and I'll get it for you.'

As Arthur waited for his meal he reflected sorrowfully that Ellen hadn't even asked why he was late; as he feared, she was no longer interested in his life.

Tucking into his dinner he looked to where Ellen was sitting by the fireplace embroidering a linen handkerchief, something she had never been interested in before. In fact she had taken up numerous new hobbies, and Arthur knew they were merely a diversion so she wouldn't have to talk to him any more than was absolutely necessary. But Arthur wasn't going to give up on his marriage without a fight, however feeble his attempts were.

As he spooned a forkful of shepherd's pie into his mouth he asked casually, 'Where's Micky? He hasn't gone out wandering the streets again, has he?'

Without looking up Ellen replied, 'No, he's in bed. He was nearly hysterical after hearing the latest news so I sent for the doctor. He gave Micky something to make him sleep. Hopefully he's stay asleep until morning. He's absolutely exhausted in mind and body.'

'Oh, well, that's something, I suppose. Where is he by the way? I presume you've put him in the box room.'

This time Ellen looked up at her husband. With a coolness in her voice she said, 'No, he's sleeping in our . . . I mean my bed. I did think of putting him in the spare room, but if I had, there'd be nowhere for you to sleep. Unless you were hoping to share my bed again, and let me tell you, Arthur, that is never going to happen. Of course if you want your bed back, then I'll move into the box room with Micky. It'll be a tight squeeze, but I'll be able to sleep nights without worrying you'll take it into your mind to try it on again.'

Suddenly Arthur lost his appetite. Pushing his plate away he meet Ellen's gaze and, with a voice filled with emotion he said, 'Please, Ellen, won't you ever forgive me for that night? I mean, be fair. In the two years we've been married I've never ever bothered you in that way. Besides, even if I was over rough, by law I had every right to make love to my wife . . .'

Ellen's head jerked up as Arthur's words hit her with the force of a physical blow. Her voice dripping with scorn she said, 'Why don't we call it by its proper name – rape! Because that's what you did to me, Arthur. You raped me, violated my body like a dog rutting a bitch in heat, and with the same selfish indifference to my feelings.'

Seeing the look of disgust on her face, Arthur felt the blood rush to his cheeks. But this time, instead of trying to appease Ellen, he felt a surge of anger wash over him, and before the voice of reason could stop him he turned viciously on his wife.

'I don't suppose you'd have objected if it'd been Ted Parker, would you? Oh, no. Not on your life you wouldn't. D'you really think I don't know what's going on between you two? How far has it gone? Was I really the first one to bed you . . .'

Before he could say anything more, Ellen was standing in front of him, her face filled with fury, her arm raised. Caught unaware Arthur never got the chance to dodge the powerful blow Ellen landed on his face. Reeling back in shock Arthur could only stare in amazement at the woman gazing at him with hate-filled eyes. There was no resemblance to the Ellen he had known since birth, and her next words confirmed his worst fears.

'Get out of my sight, Arthur. I don't know you any more, and I don't even want to try. We're finished. The only reason I've stayed these past two weeks was because I wanted to be sure there weren't any reper-cussions from that night. And this morning I found out there weren't, so there's nothing to keep me with you. Get out, Arthur, just go; I can't stand even being in the same room as you.'

And Arthur, his brief, angry outburst squashed the moment Ellen had retaliated, turned, and almost ran from the room.

CHAPTER TWENTY-ONE

As Arthur stormed out into the street he collided with Ted who was obviously heading for the place he had just left. As their bodies touched, Arthur felt Ted's hard, muscle-toned physique against his own flabby frame, and this only served to remind him once again of his inadequacies. For a moment Arthur felt a surge of rage against this man, against all the people who looked on him with derision or pity, but most of all he raged against God. All his life Arthur had strived to be a good man, a decent human being, wanting only to be liked and respected, but no matter how hard he had tried, somehow he'd always failed. And now he couldn't lie to himself any longer. There would always be two types of men in the world. Men like him, and men like Ted Parker. And the Ted Parkers of this world always got what they wanted, leaving their crumbs to men like him. The worst part of the scenario was that men like Arthur would always be grateful for their leavings.

'You all right, Arthur, mate?' Ted was staring at him, a puzzled look on his face.

Composing himself Arthur fought to control himself. He'd lost Ellen, that much was plain, but that didn't mean he was going to stand meekly by and let Ted Parker take his wife without some sort of fight. Even if he lost everything, he could still retain his dignity. Pulling himself up to his fullest height, Arthur replied tersely, 'Of course I'm all right. Why shouldn't I be?'

Ted shrugged his shoulders. There was clearly something troubling Arthur, and it was probably due to him. Still, he wasn't going to be a hypocrite and pretend to be a concerned friend at this late stage. 'All right, I was only asking.' Jerking his head towards the closed bakery he asked briskly, 'Is it all right if I go up ter see Micky?'

Arthur stared at him coldly. 'Why ask me? You'll do what you want regardless of what I say. I mean, it's only my home, though you'd never know it the way you come and go as you please.' Bobbing his head he added, 'Well! What are you waiting for? It's not as if you don't know the way, is it?'

Ted's eyebrows arched in surprise at the baker's manner then said dryly, 'Yeah! I know me way right enough. Cheers, Arthur.' He turned on his heel then stopped. 'Will I see yer later?'

Arthur uttered a mirthless snort of laughter. 'Oh, I'll be back, Ted. I don't know what time, it all depends on how long I stay in the pub. If I'm enjoying myself I might stay until closing time. On the other hand if I get bored I could be back home within the hour. But

I don't suppose it'll bother you either way, unless of course you'd like to spend some time alone with Micky.'

Now there was an unmistakable sneer in Arthur's tone. But Ted, impatient to share his news with Ellen, simply turned his back on Arthur and began to walk round to the back door that led to the rooms above the bakery. Arthur watched his rival enter his home, his hands forming into balled fists at his side, furious that he had been dismissed so casually especially as he'd thought he had handled Ted with a dignified show of strength. Oh! How he would have loved to run after the tall, athletic figure and beat him to the ground, recognising with despair that he was inca-pable of such an act. His shoulders slumped, he walked towards the nearest pub.

'Ted!' Ellen cried with genuine pleasure.

Resisting the impulse to pull her into his arms and rain passionate kisses over her lovely face, Ted had to content himself with a gentle hug and a chaste kiss on her cheek.

'Have you any more news, Ted?' She hovered by his side, her face and manner showing her anxiety. They were in the living room now, and, ignoring Ellen's query, Ted asked, 'Where's Micky?' His eyes roamed around the room, expecting the youngster to suddenly appear.

'The doctor gave him some sleeping powders. He said Micky shouldn't wake up until morning, but he left me some more, just in case.' Taking Ted's hand Ellen led him to the settee and pulled him down beside her onto the soft cushions and laid her head against his shoulder. 'You mustn't blame yourself for what happened. There was no way you could have known that odious man had already found out Molly's where-abouts.'

Ted gently touched her lips with his fingers. 'Shush, love. There's something I've gotta tell yer . . . Oh! By the way, I bumped into Arthur on me way in. He was in a funny mood. You two 'ad a row?'

Ellen kept her face averted. 'No, of course not. I think all this business with Micky and his sister is getting him down. He doesn't like any deviation from his routine.'

Ted snorted. 'Huh! Well, he's gonna 'ave ter get used to things changing, isn't he? . . . All right, all right, don't get yerself agitated,' he said quickly as he felt Ellen begin to fidget awkwardly in the circle of his arm. 'I ain't gonna say anything till young Molly's been found. After all . . .' He planted a kiss on the top of her shiny hair. 'We've got all the time in the world, ain't we?'

Relaxing again Ellen murmured, 'You said you had something to tell me.'

Ted clapped his hand to his forehand. 'Gawd! I nearly forgot why I came round, except for the obvious.' He grinned affectionately, the smile wavering as he remembered the reason for his visit. 'The thing is, love, the coppers 'ave found the cabbie who picked up Stokes and Molly; that's to say, he picked up a man and girl fitting the descriptions. The time factor fits an' all.' Ellen was now sitting upright, her eyes bright with renewed hope, leaving Ted to wonder if he had done the right thing in telling Ellen before Molly had been found, but it was too late. 'Now look, love, don't go getting yer 'opes up just yet.'

'But like you've just said, it looks promising. How did you find out?'

'Johnny Smith was at my place when two of his mates called with the news. Apparently their inspector had already left for the address the cabbie gave them about half an hour before Johnny found out. Anyway, I wanted ter go with 'em but he wasn't 'aving any of that. 'Course I wasn't best pleased, so I went ter the cab rank meself and asked around, but the bloke I was after wasn't there. His mates weren't sure if he was still down at the station or off on another fare. So I thought I'd pop round ter keep yer up ter date, then go back an' see if he's back yet. If he ain't, I'll find out where he lives and go round. I hope I won't 'ave ter wait that long though. With a bit of luck the coppers 'ave already found the pair of 'em, and are on their way back home right this minute.'

Neither of them heard the bedroom door open until a weak voice whispered, 'I wanna come with yer.'

Startled, Ellen and Ted jumped apart.

'Micky, what on earth are you doing out of bed?' Ellen exclaimed in alarm.

Then Ted was hurrying towards the pale young boy, just catching him as his legs gave way beneath him.

'The only place you're going is back ter bed, mate,' he said firmly as he swept the frail figure up into his arms.

'No, I ain't. I'm coming with yer, an' yer can't stop me,' Micky protested in a pitifully weak voice.

'Don't be daft, yer silly bugger, yer can hardly stand let alone walk, and I ain't got time ter carry yer.' Looking at the tears beginning to form in the boy's eyes Ted's voice softened. Taking him into the bedroom he lowered him gently onto the bed then sat down on the side. 'Look, mate, I know yer've 'eard it all before, but this time there's a real chance of finding Molly. But I ain't gonna lie ter yer. You ain't stupid, so I ain't gonna treat yer like a kid. Like I said, there's a good chance the police are already on their way back with your sister, but then again this Stokes is a wily bastard. He's been getting away with the same sort of thing fer years. We've just gotta pray that this time he's finally run outta luck. And I know yer want ter be there when he's found, but you must know yer just ain't up ter it. Even if I was ter help yer, you'd only slow me down.'

Ellen stood by the door, her hand held against her throat. 'Ted's right, Micky. You're much too weak to go with him. But as soon as he knows anything, he'll come straight here, won't you, Ted?' Her eyes fixed on the solemn-faced man.

Ted held her gaze for a moment before turning his attention back to the agitated form laid out on the bed. ''Course I will.' Taking hold of Micky's hand he said, 'I'm gonna ask yer a question, Micky, an' I want a straight answer, all right?'

Micky's head nodded listlessly.

'Right then. Do you trust me?'

''Course I do.' The answer came back without hesitation.

'Good! Then yer know I'll do everything in my power to find Molly an' bring her back to you.'

280

Micky's eyes blinked rapidly as he fought to stay awake. 'I know yer will, Ted. But . . . but I'm so frightened, Ted. Even if yer do find her, what if that man's already . . .' He gulped loudly, unable to utter the words that had filled his mind since Molly had vanished.

Ted bowed his head and gripped the small hand tighter. 'I know, mate, I know. But we've gotta look on the bright side. At least up till this morning Molly was safe, an' that bloke will be too busy hiding from the law ter think of anything else, and as I said ter Ellen, they've got a good chance of catching 'im.' Turning his head he said to Ellen, 'Make him a cup of cocoa, will yer, love, it'll help settle him.'

Grateful for something to do, Ellen hurried off. She was pouring hot milk into a mug when Ted entered the kitchen.

'Put another one of those powders the doctor gave him into his drink.'

Ellen, her gaze anxious, said, 'I can't, Ted. The doctor said he was only to have one dose every four hours, and it's only been a couple of hours since he—'

Ted interrupted impatiently, 'Yeah, I know. He also said the medicine would probably knock him out till the morning, an' he was wrong about that. Anyway, it can't do him any harm, can it?' Seeing the doubt in Ellen's eyes he pressed home his point. 'Look, the poor little sod's doing his best ter stay awake, frightened ter close his eyes 'cos he feels guilty being tucked up safe while his sister's out there somewhere with a madman. I'm only thinking of Micky, and what's best fer him. So you tell me, d'yer think it's better fer him ter toss an' turn all night, his mind filled with pictures too horrific ter imagine, or give 'im another sleeping powder ter knock 'im out, an' give his mind a bit of peace, at least till tomorrow?'

Against her better judgement Ellen had to admit Ted's logic made sense. Reaching into a drawer she took out another of the sleeping draughts the doctor had left and poured it into the hot cocoa. Giving it one final stir she held it out to Ted saying, 'You give it to him, Ted. I can't face him just now. I know I'm being a coward, but I'm afraid if I go into that room I'll break down, and that's the last thing he needs right now.'

'Don't be too hard on yerself, darlin'. If it wasn't fer you, he'd be in a worse state than he is right now.' Putting his hand out he touched her face lovingly. 'I'll take this into him, then be on me way.'

But it was another fifteen minutes before Ted left them. In spite of his hurry to be out doing something, Ted hadn't the heart to leave the boy until he was sure the medicine had taken effect and Micky was fast asleep.

For Ellen there was no such escape. The only thing she could so was sit by Micky's bedside and pray. She never imagined she would be able to sleep at such a time, but if she didn't know how fatigued she was, her mind and body did. Within an hour of Ted's departure, she too was afforded the luxury of sleep.

CHAPTER TWENTY-TWO

'What an almighty cock-up. When I get my hands on that lying cabbie, he'll wish he'd never been born. Sending me on a wild goose chase, a man of my standing. He's made a laughing stock of me, that's what he's done.'

Inspector William Lewis, his hands clasped behind his back, paced up and down in front of the house he'd been sent to, his fleshy face almost purple with rage. A dozen officers stood awkwardly a few feet away, their heads lowered for fear their inspector would see the glee in their eyes at witnessing the posturing man brought low. But what was really the icing on the cake was the waiting journalists, summoned by Inspector Lewis himself to capture his triumph when he arrested the known child molester and kidnapper. He'd also requested a photographer to be present at his moment of glory, but his plans of becoming a hero had gone badly wrong. For the house he had ordered his men to break into by kicking in the front door, so as not to give Kenneth Stokes any chance of escaping, had been the worst decision he'd ever made in his twenty years in the police force. For the said house was owned by the local magistrate, and that distinguished man, outraged by the onslaught on his home, not to mention the intrusion on his privacy, was in no mood to listen to reason. Instead he had threatened to make a formal complaint to Inspector Lewis' superiors.

His head swinging from side to side, looking for someone to vent his rage on, his eyes alighted on the small group of journalists and the two photographers, both of whom had already taken a number of pictures, unknown to the livid senior officer. Flinging out his arm to his assembled men Lewis thundered to no one in particular, 'Get rid of these vultures. I want them out of here. Do you hear me? Get them away from here – now!'

A group of uniformed men began to advance on the newspaper men, but they needn't have bothered. The men from the newspapers had already gathered enough information and pictures for a good story for tomorrow's newspapers. Grinning broadly, for they too disliked the glory-hunting inspector as much as his own men did, they began to depart, watched by the waiting officers who were enviously wishing they could leave too. They'd been hanging around for over half an hour, and all because their inspector was too proud to admit defeat, hoping instead that something, anything might happen to save his face.

Then, from their ranks, a solitary man stepped

forward and approached the furious man. As if one, they held their breath in admiration as John Smith planted himself firmly, and without fear, in front of his superior and said clearly, 'Could I have a word, Sir?'

The plain-clothes man looked up sharply, his eyes narrowing as he saw who dared to confront him. Of course, John Smith. They had joined the force in the same year, but there the similarity ended. He, William Lewis, had always intended to rise in the ranks, whereas John Smith had been content to remain out on the street as a lowly constable. Yet Lewis knew that PC Smith could have made it to the top if he'd wanted to, for he was an intelligent man, and a bloody good copper to boot. With this in mind the inspector motioned John further back from his men. He was anxious to hear what Smith had to say, for whatever it was it would be something worth listening to, and he certainly hadn't come up with any other plans despite furiously racking his brains. Even so, he didn't want his men to hear what Smith had to say. There was still time to save face if Smith could come up with a good idea. If he had, he, Lewis, would find some way to take the credit, so it was imperative their conversation was not overheard.

Rocking back on his heels he gave the impression he was doing John Smith a favour by listening to him, but despite his best efforts, PC Smith knew the man too well to be either deceived or impressed.

'Well, come on, man, if you've got something to say then spit it out,' he barked.

Unaffected by the man's tone John said in a calm,

clear voice, 'I think we should search the forest, Sir. It's obvious Stokes deliberately gave the cabbie the wrong address. He must have known we'd question all the hackney cab drivers and this was most likely his way of throwing us off the scent and thumbing his nose at us into the bargain.'

Lewis tipped his trilby hat further back on his head and said shortly, 'I've already worked that much out for myself, Constable. In spite of what you and the rest of the men think of me, I'm not entirely stupid. So if you've nothing further to say, I suggest . . .'

Not at all intimidated by his superior John Smith continued. 'It's my opinion Stokes knows this particular area. Look at the facts. He hires a cab and gives the driver the address of the local magistrate. Maybe that was just a coincidence, but I don't think so. Like I said, he's trying to rub our noses in it, and what better way than to humiliate us by leading us to that particular house. Look around you, Sir.' John waved his arm towards the surrounding area. 'There's only eight houses in all, and we've spoken to every home owner. Every one of them is either a respectable businessman or professional person, that's only to be expected in a place like this. Yet the address we were given was the biggest and most expensive one, owned by a man who could make life very difficult for us if he has a mind to do so. Like I said, it might just be a coincidence, but it's the sort of prank Stokes would play, and if that's the case, then like I said, he must be familiar with the area. Shall I go on, Sir?'

Lewis struggled with his pride before indicating with a nod of his head that John Smith should continue.

'All right then. We know he doesn't live in any of these houses, so I think he has a hideaway somewhere in the forest. Think about it, Sir. It's the only possible solution. He was definitely dropped off here, he was on foot, with a child and no apparent transport, yet nobody saw him. He couldn't vanish into thin air, so he must be nearby somewhere.

'And the only place he could be is in the forest. Don't forget, Sir, we've never been able to find out where he lives. Every time we've picked him up with a child, it's always been in some seedy boarding house or hotel. And as despicable as Stokes is, he's no fool. He's had years to find or even build a place to bring his victims to without fear of being found, and what better place to hide than in Epping Forest.'

Inspector Lewis nipped nervously on his bottom lip. What Smith said made sense. But if he was right, it would take more than his handful of officers to find Stokes' hideout. It would take considerable manpower to search the vast expanse of Epping Forest, not to mention the time factor. Even with a hundred officers it might take days, maybe even longer. As Smith said, Stokes was no fool. An image of Kenneth Stokes' smug, sneering, mocking face floated before his eyes and his face hardened.

'All right, Smith, we'll try it your way.' Taking a gold hunter from his inside pocket he flipped open the case. 'It's nearly four now, that leaves us a good four hours if the light holds, but we're going to need more men.' Clicking the fob watch closed he continued. 'Send one of the men back for more officers, and by that I mean every man available, on duty or off. It'll mean leaving the streets empty for the rest of the afternoon, but I reckon the good people of the East End will be able to fend for themselves until nightfall.'

'Right you are, Sir.' John Smith touched the tip of his helmet as a salute. 'I'll see to it straight away. And, Sir . . .'

'Yes?' The word seemed to explode from Lewis's lips as he tried to keep a tight rein on his rising temper. It galled him to have to ask for help from one of his men; it was doubly galling to take advice from this particular constable. But he was wise enough to know that if anyone could find Stokes and the Masters child, that man was John Smith.

Undaunted, John said, 'Even if we round up all the shift we're still going to be short of manpower. We need to call in Scotland Yard for additional help, but we won't be able to manage that today. In the meantime I think we should ask for volunteers to help in the search. Feelings are running high in the East End, and I doubt we'd have any trouble in finding men to help us.'

His lips pursed tight, Lewis gave a curt nod of his head, cursing himself for not thinking of Smith's suggestion himself. It was the perfect and most logical solution to his immediate problem of the shortage of men.

Stirring himself to action Lewis strode towards his waiting officers, then stood to one side as Constable Smith instructed the men as to the course of action.

As the men began to enter the forest the sound of an approaching carriage caught the inspector's attention. Thinking it was more reporters arriving he walked forward, holding his arm up to stop the hackney carriage going any further. His face grim he yanked open the carriage door, ready to give the intruders short shrift, but he didn't get the chance to speak before a tall, rugged-looking man leapt down.

'Thanks, mate. There yer go,' he said tossing half a crown up to the cab driver. 'Hang about a minute, will yer, mate? Just till I see what's happening.'

'Righto, guv,' the driver answered happily, not wanting to leave the scene of the unfolding drama.

'Just a minute, where do you think you're going?'

Ted glanced down at the hand gripping his arm, then looked coldly at the man barring his way. 'If you want ter use that hand in the next couple of weeks I'd take it off me arm if I was you.'

Lewis bridled visibly. He'd had enough humiliation for one day without some nosy sightseer giving him grief. Assuming his superior demeanour he barked, 'Don't take that tone with me, mister. My name is Inspector Lewis, and there is a police investigation going on here. So you can just get back in that cab and . . .'

Ted shook off the offending arm with ease. 'I don't care if you're the bleedin' pope. This is a public place, and I've got as much right here as you have.'

The two men faced each other, neither one of them prepared to give way, then Ted's head whipped round as he heard his name being called.

'Ted, am I glad to see you!' John Smith appeared, his presence diffusing the situation. Ignoring the hostile atmosphere he clapped Ted on the shoulder. 'We think Stokes is hiding somewhere in the forest.

289

I've already sent one of the men back to get more help, so you can take his place.' Conscious of his inspector's growing wrath John introduced Ted. 'This is Ted Parker, Sir. He's sort of guardian to Micky Masters, the brother of the child Stokes has abducted.' Then turning to Ted he said, 'We've been expecting more journalists and the inspector is the only man with the authority to stop them entering the forest.' The blatant lie uttered in a respectful tone did much to soothe his inspector's anger while giving the man a loophole to redeem himself, a chance that the man seized gratefully.

Clearing his throat Lewis said, 'I'm sorry, Mr Parker. As Constable Smith said, I thought you were another reporter. I apologise for my earlier actions.' The words sounded as if they were being ground out, as they indeed were, but he knew that men like Ted Parker weren't easily intimidated, if at all.

But Ted had already forgotten the surly man's presence. 'You're joking, ain't yer? Bleeding 'ell, Johnny, it'd take an army to search that place. You sure he's in there?'

This time the constable didn't take Ted to task for calling him by name. There were much more important issues at stake. 'No, we're not sure, but it's the only lead we've got. Look, let's get going, I'll fill you in as we go.'

'Just a minute, Constable.' The authoritative voice stopped both men in their tracks. 'I'm going to take Mr Parker's carriage back to the station. I should have gone sooner instead of sending an inexperienced officer. I'll be of more use there than here. I'm leaving you in charge in my absence, Smith. Don't let me down.'

Striving to keep a straight face John replied, 'I'll do my best, Sir.'

Both men waited until Lewis had driven away, then John said in an uncharacteristic manner, 'Arsehole.'

Coming from the usually staid officer, the word caused Ted to forget the urgency of the moment. Throwing back his head he gave a huge burst of laughter, and John, his lips twitching, joined in as together they walked into the vast forest of Epping.

Dusk was falling when two market porters, willing volunteers in the search for Molly Masters, stumbled upon an old hut, almost obscured by a clump of trees. Obeying the instructions they had been given not to try and apprehend Stokes without police back up the men shouted for attention, trying desperately to curb the overwhelming temptation to ignore the police order and kick the door in themselves, and waited for the police to arrive. They didn't have long to wait. Within minutes, two uniformed officers came crashing through the undergrowth and, without any preliminaries, put their shoulders to the door, aided by the excited men who had first stumbled on the hut.

With the combined weight of the four men the door flew open, its hinges shattered by the onslaught as the men crashed into the hut, falling over themselves by the sheer number of their bodies. They were stumbling to their feet when more men, uniformed and civilians alike, converged on the hut, their faces lit up exuberantly. But their joy was short-lived, for although it was clear the two-room hut had recently been used, it was now uninhabited. And the disappointment of the men, who had been combing the forest for hours, after putting in a full day's work, was so great they could have wept. As word spread through the densely shrouded woods, the euphoria that had gripped the search party quickly evaporated as they realised that once again the lunatic they had been hunting had eluded them, and, with the deepening dusk, they knew they could do no more this night.

'That's that, then,' Ted said tiredly. Like the other men, he too felt like crying with disappointment and frustration. But Ted had more reason than the rest of the men to feel such devastating numbness in his body, for this was the second time in one day when his hopes of finding Molly Masters alive and well had been dashed to the ground.

'Come on, Ted. There's nothing more any of us can do today. Let's go home and get some sleep. We're going to need as much rest as we can get, because we're going to be back here at first light tomorrow morning. And by then we'll have more officers, and probably more volunteers too once the word spreads. It won't be just us now: Scotland Yard will be quick to get in on the act, and the top brass will send every available man up here.'

John Smith led Ted away from the hut, his face drawn with fatigue. Like every man in the search party he had been on his feet since dawn. He should have gone off duty hours ago, but when the life of a child was at stake, time became immaterial. Looking around him in the fading light he said earnestly, 'He's still here somewhere, I know he is, I can feel it. He must have put a lot of time and trouble in getting that hut fit to live in; he'd even put a padlock on the front door to prevent anyone from going in. He must have left in a hurry, because he didn't have time to put the lock in place.'

'You don't know fer sure that hut's got anything ter do with Stokes,' Ted said wearily. 'For all we know it could belong ter some gamekeeper, or . . .'

'Nah!' John cut in sharply. 'It's Stokes, I know it is. And if he's got one hiding place in here, what's to say he hasn't got another one? I know this bloke, Ted, he's clever. He's been at this game for over twenty years, and in all that time we've only managed to put him away twice. But this time it's gonna be different. We'll get the bastard, Ted, I swear it, by all that's holy and good in this world, I swear we'll get him, and when we do, I promise he'll never hurt another child again.'

A junior officer approached John, beckoning him to one side. Ted looked on absently as the two men spoke in whispers. Then John was back by Ted's side.

'Inspector Lewis has just sent word that the Knight woman's dead – and her baby. So it's murder now. And no amount of fancy lawyers are going to get him out of this mess, not this time. It's the hangman's noose for Kenneth Stokes, and nobody deserves it more than that evil bastard.'

Ted swung his head from side to side in anguish, the guilt almost tearing him apart. Now he had two more lives on his conscience. He should have acted quicker, instead of poncing about trying to find someone to look after his stall. Those precious minutes could have prevented the tragic events.

'Don't take it so hard, Ted. I know how you feel, but there's nothing you could have done. The best thing we can do now is go home, get some rest, and come back in the morning.'

But Ted didn't budge. He couldn't face going back home without Molly, couldn't bear to see the look of desolation in Micky's eyes when he knew that he, Ted, had failed him again.

'You go, John ... Officer, I'm staying. I noticed a pub on me way 'ere. It ain't far, I'll get a room fer the night.' Raising his head he stared hard at the man by his side. 'I can't go 'ome; not yet, not without Molly. D'yer understand, I can't go 'ome, not till we find her, I just can't.'

Knowing it was futile to argue with the distraught man, and too bone-weary to try, John patted Ted on the back. 'You do what you feel you must, Ted. I'm off home to my wife and bed. I'll see you in the morning. Oh, and I'll get someone to stop by the bakery. Ellen will be worried if you don't show up. Take care, Ted. Goodnight.'

Ted, unable to move, remained leaning against one of the hundreds of oak trees that populated the forest. He could have stayed there all night, but his mind alerted him to the fact that if he didn't move soon he might well have to spend the night, and suddenly that idea didn't seem so appealing. Following the last of the demoralised men back to the road, Ted walked to the pub he had noticed earlier and booked a room for the night.

Two hours and several pints of beer later he stared

up at the ceiling and rubbed his eyes. They felt as if they were filled with sand and grit. He desperately needed sleep, if only for a few hours, but every time he closed his eyes he saw Micky's white, pleading face.

'I'll find her, mate. I promise I'll find her, and bring her back ter yer. Trust me, Micky . . . Please God! Let me find her. Let her live, God. She's only a little kid. Don't let that madman hurt her. Please, God, keep her safe till I find her.'

His prayer seemed to echo and hang in the empty air, mocking and taunting him. Choking back a sob he turned his head into the pillow and closed his eyes.

CHAPTER TWENTY-THREE

An owl hooted in the dark causing a small huddled figure to jump in alarm. Her heart beating rapidly Agnes tried valiantly to control her rising fear. Nothing had turned out as she had planned; everything that could go wrong had gone wrong. Now she was trapped in what she could only describe as a living nightmare. Every sound, even the smallest rustle in the long grass was intensified in the eerie silence of the night, conjuring up frightening images to a woman already teetering on hysteria.

Stifling a scream Agnes tried to focus on the circumstances that had brought her to this predicament.

Somehow, in the busy traffic, her carriage had overtaken the one Kenneth and the child were travelling in. So it was that she arrived at the destination five minutes before the second hackney cab. Ordering the driver to stop before the carriage reached the house, Agnes had quickly alighted, paid the fare, and scurried into the woods, intending to watch Kenneth arrive and make sure he was safely inside the house before raising the alarm. She'd already decided not to carry out her original plan of trying to rescue the little girl herself. It had been a comforting thought and one she had relished, herself hailed as a heroine, her picture in the papers, the exoneration of her blackened name, but most important of all, the safety of the child Kenneth now had in his clutches. But she had reluctantly realised that such an act was beyond her capabilities, and one only found in the penny novels she was so fond of reading. No! The safest and most realistic course of action was to wait until he was home and feeling safe, then raise the alarm at one of the nearby houses.

She couldn't believe her eyes when Kenneth, clutching a silent, fair-haired girl by the hand, had waited until the cab had departed, then, looking left and right, he had scooped the girl up into his arms and headed for the forest. He had passed within feet of her, and Agnes hadn't realised she had stopped breathing until a loud burst of air was expelled from her lungs. It hadn't been just the fear of Kenneth spotting her that had left her breathless, it had been the sheer audacity of him. It was true the area was sparsely populated – she had counted only eight houses – but still, somebody could have seen him enter the forest with the girl.

And for the next few minutes she had braced herself for a shout from one of the householders, challenging him, but no such sound came, and Agnes realised that it was down to her to save the Masters girl. For if she left to seek help, Kenneth could vanish deep into the forest, a place he seemed familiar with judging by the ease and confidence he displayed. He appeared to know exactly where he was going.

It was a good half hour before she had seen the hut, and she would never have found it on her own. Neither would anyone else.

Kenneth had chosen his hiding place well.

The hut was situated amidst a clump of trees far away from the dozens of paths and open spaces used by the public. She'd watched as he'd unlocked the padlock, opened the door, and pushed the girl inside, but not before Agnes had caught a glimpse of terror in the child's eyes. Not once had she uttered a sound until Kenneth prodded her in the back, then had come a soft moan, a pitiful sound that had wrenched at Agnes' heart.

She had experienced a rush of anger, a quick burst of courage, but the feelings were shortlived, much to her shame. And so she had waited and done nothing, telling herself that if she heard the girl cry out or scream then she would put her own safety to one side and start screaming herself. But the child had remained silent, and Agnes had stayed where she was, trying to work out what to do for the best. Her life had been uneventful until she had met Kenneth, so she had never had the opportunity to test her courage. Like most people she had daydreamed about performing an heroic act, like pushing a child out of the way of a runaway carriage, thus saving it from the hooves of wild horses, unheeding of her own safety. She had also fantasised about running into a burning building to help people trapped inside, and the subsequent adulation that followed any act of heroism. She had truly believed that in the right circumstances she would forget her own fears and jump in to help without stopping to think of her own safety.

Now that time had come and she had found herself wanting. She had been forced to examine what she was really made of, and that knowledge brought her head low; the sense of guilt and shame was overwhelming. But not even the deepest sense of self-loathing could spark her into action. The minutes had ticked away while she struggled with her inner self, trying to dredge up some courage to do something, anything, rather than just stand here helpless while God only knew what horrors that evil bastard was inflicting on a helpless child.

Then had come salvation in the form of the search party.

Before she knew it the forest was crawling with coppers and volunteers. Her first instinct was one of relief. She had been on the verge of calling attention to herself when instinct stopped her as she realised what it would look like if she was found here, only feet away from the place Kenneth had the child hidden. They would think she was in it with Kenneth; they already thought it. Nobody would believe the truth, and looking at the whole sordid business from their view she couldn't say she blamed them. So she had stayed where she was, frightened to move for fear of attracting attention. Then those two men had stumbled on the hut and raised the alarm, and she had slipped away, hiding among the trees, hoping no one would see her, all the while sending up a prayer of thanks that Kenneth Wells, as she knew him, would at last be caught, and the Masters girl freed from her terrifying experience.

She couldn't believe her eyes when the hut door had been broken down and there was no sign of Kenneth or the child. Her mouth agape, she had stood rooted to the spot, thinking she was going out of her mind.

Long after the men had left she had remained hidden. With the light fading rapidly the men had searched on until it was too dark to continue. But they would be back. She had heard John Smith's voice, and had been tempted to call out to him. He alone would have believed her, she trusted him, but again she had hesitated too long. For the next voice she recognised had been that of Ted Parker, and she knew only too well what he thought of her. It had been fortunate that all eyes had been focused on the hut, for if not then surely someone would have spotted her, even in the fading light. It was at that moment she had realised what her options were. If she called out the volunteers might see her first and turn on her; and from what she'd seen and heard, those men far outnumbered the police. But if she stayed quiet she would be left alone in the forest all night, and the very notion of that prospect terrified her. She was still trying to summon up the courage to call out to John for help when she'd heard him tell Ted the news about the Knight woman and her unborn baby. But it wasn't the shocking news of the murder of the pregnant woman that had stilled her tongue, it was the tone in John's voice, a tone deep with anger and hate – it could have been a stranger talking, for if she hadn't known for sure it was John, she wouldn't have recognised his voice. And for the first time her faith in the kindly policeman faltered. Maybe now he too would turn against her, and she was startled to find how deeply hurtful that idea was. So she had stayed quiet.

Now she was stranded until morning, afraid to close her eyes in case some animal crept up on her in the dark. Afraid too of dreaming, for surely in her dreams she would see the child, hear her silent screams for help.

She didn't know she was crying until she felt the salty water trickle over her dry lips.

Then a light had come on in the hut.

Kenneth Stokes was elated. At last he had Molly Masters just where he wanted her, locked away from the outside world where no one could disturb them. Never had he wanted a child as badly as he had wanted Molly, and the more obstacles that had been placed in his way, the more he had wanted her, not least because he had got one over on everyone who had tried to stand in his way. Especially that smug bastard John Smith. After such a long, frustrating wait, he was in no great hurry to put his mark on the golden-haired girl. Instead he savoured the moment, alternating between taunting the child and whispering vile words of what he intended to do with her. Mercifully she was so traumatised by the unexpected abduction and seeing Mrs Knight lying covered in blood, his words had disintregated into mere, unintelligible sounds that floated over her dulled senses.

However, his initial euphoria was shortlived.

At first he thought his mind was playing tricks on him, until he'd peered out of the window. He didn't know how he had been tracked down so fast, but he had prepared for such an emergency. Scooping Molly out of the chair, he leant down, pulled back a strip of carpet, inserted his finger into a hole in the wooden floor beneath and yanked open a trap door. Within minutes he was safely hidden in the basement below, the carpet-covered trap door shut tight. He had no worries of being discovered, for who would think of looking for a basement under an old hut in the forest?

After being released from his last imprisonment he had thought long and hard about the time he had spent behind bars. The experience hadn't been a pleasant one, for even amongst thieves and murderers, men like him were treated as the lowest form of life. He had endured countless beatings, often within sight of the so-called prison guards, supposedly there to guard against such incidents, who had turned a blind eye to his sufferings, often delivering a blow or punch themselves. Even now, years later, he could still remember the degradation, the pain, suffering and fear he had been forced to endure. There had even been times he had genuinely been afraid for his life.

One thing he knew: he would never, ever go back into prison again. But nor had he considered giving up his pursuit of children for his own depraved purposes. There then had remained the problem of where he could take his victims without fear of discovery. Then, one afternoon, when he had been out walking aimlessly in the forest he had stumbled, quite by accident, upon the hut. On closer inspection he had found the two-room hut deserted, and by the squalor and disarray of the place it was obvious it had been unoccupied for some time. He could only assume that the dilapidated hut had once been home to a gamekeeper. And in the owner's absence it seemed that numerous tramps had availed themselves of the opportunity of having a roof over their heads.

During the time it had lain empty the door had been broken down, the windows smashed, and the wooden floor littered with empty beer bottles. But far worse, above the stale smell of beer, tobacco and rotting food, was the overpowering stench of human waste. Whoever had occupied the hut had obviously used it as a toilet. Kenneth, fastidious by nature, had been appalled at the way some people lived. Even animals didn't live in their own filth. Then he had heard a scurrying noise and jumped as two large rats emerged from the fire grate, their wicked black eyes staring at him fearlessly. He had retreated from the hut, a linen handkerchief covering his face.

He had hurried away, fearful of catching something, and returned to the hotel he had been staying at. Yet the memory of his find wouldn't go away. It hadn't taken him long to see the possibilities of the abandoned hut. Because of its location, the likelihood of someone chancing on it was almost negligible. Take him for example. He'd been walking in the forest for years, usually on the look out for unsupervised children, and he had never seen the hut until that day. As the germ of the idea grew in Kenneth's mind, so did his excitement.

He did not relish the task of cleaning the hut, although he knew he had no choice but to undertake the unpleasant task himself. He had enough money to hire builders and cleaners, but he couldn't take the risk of anybody knowing about the hut. The first thing he had done was to padlock the door and board up the window to prevent any passing tramp from entering what he now looked upon as his private property. Once the hut had been made secure, he'd had to start on the interior. On the first three visits to his new hideaway he had flinched at its appalling state and returned to his comfortable hotel, unable to tackle the gruesome task. Again he'd been strongly tempted to find someone willing to do the job for him, which wouldn't have been hard, providing the pay was good enough.

Weeks came and went, during which time he couldn't get his mind off the hut, his thoughts alternating between being eager to put his plans into motion to make the hut habitable, and repelled by the filthy conditions he would have to tackle to make it so. The longer he put it off the more anxious he became that someone else might chance on the hut, see the new padlock, find it empty, and become curious enough to make enquiries. That thought had been enough to galvanise him into action. Once he had taken up residence he would soon find some plausible reason for his being there, if anyone should stumble upon his new home and ask questions. Not that he was worried. If he'd been a tramp it would be a different matter, but not many people questioned a man of obvious wealth and refinement.

For someone as fastidious as himself the task of cleaning up other people's mess had been a living nightmare. On two occasions he had been physically sick, then, as the days passed he had stayed longer on each visit until he had become desensitised to the squalor. One blessing was that the previous legal owner had taken his furniture with him, leaving only a stained, flea-ridden mattress, a table and two hard-backed chairs, all the worse for wear, but easy enough to get rid of. It would have been difficult if he'd had to dispose of two fully furnished rooms.

The table and chairs had been chopped up and distributed in the forest, the mattress, which could have crawled out of its own accord, he had dumped as far away from the hut as possible. Then he had brought in furniture to replace the items he'd destroyed. The procedure had been simple enough. He'd hired a horse and carriage, loaded the furniture into the covered vehicle and ridden into the forest. No one had taken any notice of him, for gentlemen riding in the forest weren't an uncommon sight. Still, he'd kept a watchful eye out before entering the denser part of the forest.

The clean up of the hut had taken him the best part of a fortnight as he couldn't bear to be inside for more than a couple of hours at a time. He had left the floors until last, intending to scrub the wooden floor before laying some remnants of carpet. Because, he had told himself, if he planned to spend some considerable time in this place, he might as well have some creature comforts. It was then he had made the startling discovery. Hidden under a thick, hessian mat was a brass handle set in a square section of the floor. His heart beating with growing excitement he had pulled on the brass ring, lifting it up with bated breath. Bracing himself for what he might find, and with a gas lamp held in a shaking hand he had descended the rungs of the ladder, some of which were badly rotten causing him to stumble several times. Safely jumping off the last step he had swept the lamp around the basement, hardly daring to believe his luck. Like the two rooms above, the basement needed a good clean, but elated by his find, he didn't even flinch at the prospect of further work.

It had taken another few weeks to transport more furniture, for he didn't want to arouse any suspicion if by chance someone noticed his frequent trips into the forest, but it had been worth it. Every minute he had spent getting the hut habitable, every piece of filth he'd had to handle, had all been worth it.

He had been just thinking about his good fortune when he'd heard the commotion in the wood. Glancing at Molly he had seen a spark of life creep into her eyes and he had grinned.

'Don't go getting your hopes up, my sweet Molly, dear. They're not going to find you; no one's ever going to find you.'

Grabbing her he put a hand over her mouth, just in case she plucked up the courage to scream, and ran with her into the second room. Within a few minutes he had the trap door open, clambered down the repaired ladder and thrown her unceremoniously onto a mattress before scrambling back up the ladder to secure the trap door. It was an exercise he had practised countless times. He had replaced the brass ring with a hole he had drilled into the wooden floor, blocking it with the plug of wood he had removed from the same place. All he had to do when he wanted to use the basement was lift the carpet, push the plug out, and with his finger pull up the door. Once inside he simply put the plug back in place to fill the hole. He had also nailed a piece of carpet to the edges of the trap door so that when he closed it from below, the carpet concealed any sign of the trap door. It was highly unlikely anyone would ever even think of looking for a trap door in the simple hut, but Kenneth had learned never to take any unnecessary chances. He had no idea who had built the basement, or for what purpose, nor did he care.

Bound and now gagged, Molly could only listen to the sound of heavy footsteps and men's voices, her tormented mind flitting from hope to despair. Then there was silence, and the last remnant of hope died. When he was sure the last of the men had left, and safe in the knowledge that Molly was helpless, Kenneth had taken the opportunity of a couple of hours' sleep; it had been a long, fraught day, and his hand was stinging from where that old slag had used a knife on him. When he had woken he had listened intently, still cautious. When he was satisfied it was all clear he had advanced on the sleeping child, an evil smile curving his lips. But he recoiled in disgust at the stench of urine and faeces emanating from the still form. Maddened with rage he viciously kicked the chair, knocking both child and chair backwards. Molly awoke seconds before she landed on the floor with a sickening thud.

'You bitch, you filthy bitch.' The nasty man was glaring down at her, his face twisted with anger. 'You did it on purpose, didn't you? Thought you were being clever, didn't you? Well you're not getting off that easily.' Wrinkling his nose he ripped the gag from her mouth, untied the rope holding her to the chair and snarled, 'You stink like a sewer, you . . .'

Eyes wide with fear Molly whimpered, 'I'm sorry, Mister, I couldn't 'elp it. I . . . I tried ter . . . ter 'old it, honest, I did but . . . but I could . . . couldn't . . .'

'Shut up, just shut your mouth and do as you're told.'

Terrified into silence Molly did as she was bid, her small heart beating inside her breast like a trapped bird.

'Get up that ladder, and be quick. Go on, do as you're told, or by God you'll pay dearly. And take the lamp, I've got my hands full.'

Her legs stiff from being bound so long, Molly stumbled then quickly regained her balance, her fear outweighing her pain.

Keeping his distance Kenneth followed her up the ladder, the handkerchief still held to his nose. In his other hand he carried a suitcase. Once upstairs he pointed towards a small chest of drawers hissing, 'There's a bowl of water and soap on there. Get yourself cleaned up, then wash those filthy clothes, and be quick about it.' Opening the suitcase he took out a long, white nightdress and threw it at her feet. 'When you're finished put that on ... Well! Get moving.'

Molly's feet almost left the floor in a hurry to do as she was told.

While he waited Kenneth picked up a wicker chair and flopped into it, his face cold as he stared at the mess the search party had made. The furniture had all been knocked over and the floor was covered with muddy footprints. Then he winced. Looking down at his hand he saw blood seeping through the makeshift bandage. Cursing, he carefully pulled the bandage off, his lips tightening as he saw the cut was still bleeding, indicating that his injury was worse than he had first imagined. For the first time, Kenneth felt a jolt of alarm. He had taken great care to clean the wound, covering it with a strip of linen he had torn off one of the dresses he had bought for Molly; he liked his children to look nice. But at this moment Molly was the furthest from his mind. The only person he could think about at present was himself. Pulling the lamp nearer he scrutinised his injury, and what he saw frightened him, for the wound was not only bleeding, but the pain was beginning to cause him great discomfort. Again he cursed the woman who had attacked him.

Thinking hard he went over his options. Obviously he needed proper medical care, but the nearest hospital was miles away. Then he smiled. Of course, there was an old retired doctor living nearby. He had met him on several occasions during his visits to the forest. With time on his hands the elderly doctor often took long walks in the forest, as did many people. They had only exchanged pleasantries on those meetings, even though the doctor had tried to engage Kenneth in long conversations. Kenneth, on the other hand, had kept their meetings as brief as possible, talking long enough not to arouse suspicion as to his frequent excursions into the forest, but pleasant enough to not arouse any suspicions. Now he was glad he had made the effort. Looking at his fob watch he saw it was nearly eleven and frowned. He hadn't realised he had slept that long. The old boy would probably be in bed by now. Still, he could always knock and concoct some tale as to his predicament.

Looking at Molly he pondered what to do about the girl. Obviously he couldn't take her with him. He would have to tie her up again, though he doubted she would attempt to escape. She'd be too frightened to venture out into the darkness on her own.

'You nearly ready?' he shouted impatiently.

Molly, who was desperately trying to get herself cleaned up, afraid of making the man more angry, quickly completed her ablutions, put the wet clothes on the floor in the corner and pulled on the night-dress he had given her. Her lips trembling, she walked towards him.

Kenneth stared at her hungrily, then another sharp pain brought his mind back to his immediate needs.

'Now, listen to me. I've got to go out, but I'll be watching this place, so don't go getting any ideas, do you hear me?'

Molly nodded dumbly, too scared to move, let alone try and find her way through the black night into the forest.

'Now, I'm going to trust you. You come and sit down

and you stay there until I get back.' Warily approaching him, Molly let herself be lowered into the wicker chair. 'Don't forget, I'll be watching. If you so much as put your head outside the door, I'll see you.'

Keeping his eyes on the pitiful figure, Kenneth inspected the door, cursing loudly as he realised it had been torn off its hinges then propped back into place, the padlock dangling uselessly on its chain. It would be a long time before he could repair the damage. He would have to wait until he was sure the police had given up interest in the hut, and that could be a long time. In the meanwhile he had the basement, and that was all he cared about.

He thought again about tying the child up, then dismissed the idea. She was already rendered helpless by her fear of him, and what he would do if she dared disobey him. And that form of intimidation was far more binding than any rope.

Picking up the lamp he went towards the door, and was startled when the child cried out, 'Don't leave me in the dark, Mister. I'll be good, honest, I will . . . just do— don't leave me in the dark.'

Grinning cruelly, he bent over the terrified little girl. 'You've been a bad girl, Molly. Fouling yourself as you did. And bad girls have to be punished. Don't make it worse by talking back to me. All right?'

The fair head bobbed, then dropped onto her chest.

Kenneth hesitated. This was how he liked them best. Mentally beaten into submission, willing to do anything to keep him happy. Then he moved towards the door. She would be even more compliant by the time he returned.

Propping up the door as best he could from the outside Kenneth hurried through the forest, anxious to get his wound seen to – and even more anxious to get back to the waiting child.

Left alone in the darkness Molly didn't move. It was as if her limbs, even the very core of her being, had been frozen. Her tortured mind however was still free to feel, to fear, and to pray.

'Please, Micky, come and get me. Or Sadie, why haven't you come for me? I'm so scared. Please, someone, help me. Come and get me, please come and get me before the bad man comes back.'

CHAPTER TWENTY-FOUR

Agnes watched in disbelief as she heard and saw Kenneth leave the hut. It was impossible, she told herself. She'd seen with her own eyes the police and members of the search party enter the hut and find it empty; she hadn't believed the evidence of her own eyes then either. Blinking rapidly she clutched at her throat. Was she losing her mind? What other explanation could there be? After all, it was only a small wooden shack. The police couldn't have failed to spot them if Kenneth and the child had been in there. But she'd seen them go in, of that she was sure. She shook her head as if to clear it. She was desperately tired, both mentally and physically. Was she mad? There was only one way to find out, and that was to search the hut herself.

She waited until the light from the gas lamp Kenneth was carrying had faded, then, taking a deep breath, she gingerly pushed the broken door with one hand while holding it upright with the other, and peered in. The room was pitch black, the only light was a thin stream from the moon, but it wasn't enough to enable her to see into the shack. Feeling a little foolish, and on edge in case Kenneth was lurking somewhere in the woods, she called out softly, 'Molly? Molly, are yer in there, love?'

Silence greeted her. Then she heard a movement and, encouraged by the sound she called again, 'Molly? You there, mate? Don't be frightened, I've come ter take yer back 'ome.'

The sound came again, and this time Agnes looked in the direction of the source. Realising she would have to enter the hut Agnes moved the door away from the entrance, propping it up against the inner wall. With the door removed, the thin stream of light from the full moon dimly illuminated the interior. It was very faint, but it was enough to see the shadowy figure of a small form hunched up in a ball in a chair.

'Molly?' Agnes whispered. 'It's all right, love. I ain't gonna hurt yer,' she repeated, realising the child was probably too frightened to answer. 'Don't be scared, Molly, I'm 'ere ter 'elp yer.'

The huddled form sprang to life and ran towards her. Even in the dim light Agnes saw the elfin face light up with relief at the sight of her, and swallowed hard. She couldn't remember the last time anyone had been so pleased to see her. Then reality set in, and with it the fear came flooding back. There was no time for pleasantries. Kenneth could be playing a cruel trick on the child, pretending to leave

314

and then return, hoping to catch her out in some minor misdemeanour. It was just the sort of thing he was capable of.

'Come on, love. There's no time for talking, we've gotta get outta 'ere before that wicked bas— man comes back. Quickly now . . . Molly! Are yer listening ter me?'

But Molly, her initial joy over and terrified into submission by her abductor, afraid this lady was a friend of his, trying to trick her, stayed where she was. Reading her mind, and knowing time was of the essence, Agnes sprang forward and grabbed the child by the hand, pulling her across the small space of floor. Within minutes they were in the forest and Molly stopped struggling and gripped Agnes' hand tightly for fear the lady would let go of her and leave her alone in the frightening darkness of the forest.

With only the watery light of the moon to guide them the pair stumbled blindly through the woods until Agnes decided they were far enough away from the hut to stop and rest. Gasping for breath she squeezed the tiny hand holding hers so trustingly now and said, 'It's all right, love, I think we're safe enough now. But we ain't gonna be able to find our way outta this place till morning. 'Ere, let's sit down and 'ave a rest and a natter.'

Sinking onto the damp grass, the child cuddled by her side, Agnes talked rapidly, trying to put the girl's mind at ease. 'I know your name, but yer don't know mine, so I'll introduce meself. My name's Agnes, I know yer brother Micky . . .'

Instantly she felt the child's hand attempt to pull

away from hers, and with a sinking heart she
realised why. Keeping her voice light she continued,
'Oh, I know what Micky's said about me. That I was
a miserable old cow that was always 'aving a go at
'im, am I right?' The small hand stilled, encouraging
Agnes to go on. 'He was right an' all. I am a miserable old cow, but I ain't wicked, not like that nasty
man. And when yer went missing I tried me best ter
'elp find yer. That's why I'm 'ere. I followed Kenn—
that man what snatched yer,' she quickly corrected
herself. It wouldn't do to let the child know that she
knew him by name. 'What we'll do is cuddle up ter
keep warm, and wait fer morning, 'cos we'll only
get lost if we try ter find our way out in the dark.
Oh, I can't wait ter see Micky's face when he sees
yer . . .'

The girl jumped in her arms. 'Micky's alive? He
ain't dead then?'

Pulling her closer Agnes swallowed the lump that
had formed in her throat. ''Course he ain't dead, yer
silly thing. Why, he's been out walking the streets
since yer went missing, half outta 'is mind he's been
with worry. He's been staying with Ted Parker an'
his mum. I expect he's told yer all about them, ain't
he?'

Agnes felt Molly's head nod against her shoulder
and her slim frame slump with relief at the news her
brother was alive and well.

For a time there was silence between them, then,
Molly, her voice low and trembling whispered, 'What
about Mrs Knight, Sadie's friend? The . . . the bad man
hurt her. She . . . she was lying on . . . on the floor and

316

there was . . . was blo— blood all over her. She's gonna be al— all right, ain't she?'

Agnes tightened her hold on the shivering girl and leant her chin on the blonde head. She'd overheard John Smith telling Ted the woman was dead, and Stokes was now wanted for murder, but she couldn't tell the child that, not after what she'd been through. As the thought entered her mind Agnes' stomach lurched. Had she been in time? Kenneth had had the girl alone for hours. Dear God! If he'd harmed Molly while she'd been hiding, thinking only of her own skin, she'd never forgive herself. She had to ask, but she'd have to go careful.

Clearing her throat she said, 'I don't know, love, we'll 'ave ter wait and find out.' Again silence descended on them as Agnes tried to work out how to phase the question she had to ask. Keeping her voice casual she asked, 'That nasty man. Did . . . did he do anything to yer? I mean did he hurt yer?'

She waited with bated breath for the girl to answer.

'No . . . Well, he frightened me, and . . . and he said he was gonna 'urt me if I didn't do like he told me. And he was really angry 'cos I . . . I messed meself. But I couldn't 'elp it . . .' Her voice trailed off tiredly.

'So he never sort of . . . yer know, did anything yer didn't like . . .'

Stifling a yawn, Molly answered softly, ''Course he did. He took me away from Micky and Sadie. An' I wanna go back ter me brother, then we can all live together.'

In the darkness Agnes breathed a sigh of relief. She felt as if a great weight had been lifted from her shoulders. At last, after all these years, she had finally done something right. As for Micky and Molly going to live with this Sadie character, whoever she was. Well! Ted Parker would have something to say about that – and Ellen too for that matter.

'Tell yer what, love. You try and get some sleep, yer ain't got nothing ter worry about now. I'll look after yer, I promise.'

There was no answer. The girl, feeling safe in Agnes' arms, had already fallen asleep. Carefully taking off her shawl, Agnes wrapped it around the scantily clad child. Without the woollen garment Agnes shivered, but she welcomed the coldness of the night. It would help to keep her awake.

Kenneth had only walked for ten minutes before he changed his mind about seeking out the doctor's help. The pain in his hand had momentarily clouded his judgement. Then he remembered the search party would be back at first light, and even though they had already questioned everyone in the vicinity, there was no knowing if they would do the same tomorrow. In spite of the throbbing of his hand he couldn't take the chance of the police asking questions again. And if they knocked on the retired doctor's door and he told them about a man visiting him with a cut hand, the game would be up. Cursing his stupidity he quickly turned on his heel and headed back to the hut, the gas lamp illuminating his path. It was only a cut, another few hours wasn't going to make any difference. As long as he kept it clean, it should heal by itself in a few days. In the meantime he had much more pleasant pursuits to look forward to. His face illuminated by the lamp was one of pure evil.

His hand forgotten now, he quickened his pace. As he approached the hut he saw at once that the door, which he had closed, was now gone leaving the hut wide open. With a loud cry that bordered on a scream he ran forward, only to come to a dead stop. He didn't have to look round the two-room abode to know that Molly, that little bitch, had run off. Like a madman he paced the room, pulling at his hair in rage and disbelief. None of his previous children had ever had the courage to disobey him. He had held them prisoners, not only by physical force, but by mental intimidation. Who would have thought that Molly Masters, that terrified, cowed little chit of a girl, would have the nerve to disobey him? Unable to sit still he continued to pace back and forth around the confined space, his features contorted with rage.

Gradually his anger abated, his steps slowing as he began to think more rationally. What was he worried about? She couldn't get very far, could she? Right now she was probably lost, stumbling around in the dark, terrified out of her wits. He would lay bets that she would welcome even his presence in her predicament. All he had to do was wait until about five. The search party wouldn't be back until six, six-thirty at the latest. She couldn't be more than a fifteen-minute walk away, and by five she'd be asleep with exhaustion. He knew the forest like the back of his hand; he'd find her long before anyone else turned up. Satisfied in his mind he hadn't lost her, he settled back in the chair, a smirk on his lips.

'Just you wait, you little cow. You'll pay dearly for putting me to all this trouble, you wait and see.'

Agnes awoke with a start, unable to believe she'd fallen asleep. Dawn was just beginning to break, and with it their last chance to escape from the forest and the man who had turned her world upside down, and nearly ruined Molly Masters' into the bargain. Gently shaking the child awake Agnes said softly, 'Come on, love. Time to get going.'

Molly woke instantly, her body stiffening, then relaxing as she realised she was safe.

'That's a good girl.' Agnes, already on her feet, helped Molly to hers. 'Now listen, love, I ain't got a clue where we are, so we'll just 'ave ter walk round till the police come back. We might get lucky and find our way ter the road, but I wouldn't like ter bet on it. What we've gotta do is keep quiet. No talking or making any more noise than we 'ave to, 'cos that man is gonna be looking fer yer. Now, now . . .' Agnes gave the little girl's shoulders a reassuring hug, as Molly jerked violently at the mention of the 'nasty man'. 'He ain't gonna get yer, I won't let 'im. Besides, he doesn't know I'm with yer, does he? He thinks you're on yer own. So he's gonna be cocky, ain't he? Well, the laugh's gonna be on him. Now let's get going, and remember . . .' She gave a conspirational wink, 'Keep quiet, and yer ears open, and before yer know it, this place'll be crawling with coppers.'

'All right, lady,' Molly whispered. 'An' then I'll see

Micky and Sadie, an' Mrs Knight and Billy and
Charlie. They're me friends; I'll be quiet now.' She
smiled up at Agnes and squeezed her hand.

Agnes' heart missed a beat at Molly's words, but
now wasn't the time to tell the child the truth. Instead
she gripped the tiny hand tighter and began to creep
slowly through the forest.

Sadie sat by Lily's bedside, her warm fingers clasped
around the cold hand of her friend. She had been
sitting in the same spot for hours. Her eyes, red from
crying, were dry now, but the pain inside her wouldn't
go away. Because of her, Lily, her only friend, was
dead, and her children left on their own.

Her body, stiff from sitting in the same position for
so long, now moved as a hand came to rest gently on
her shoulder.

'Why don't you go home, love? There's nothing
you can do here. You'll make yourself ill. You've had
nothing to eat or drink since you came in and . . .'
The nurse's words trailed off as Sadie turned and
looked up at her and the anguish mirrored in the
red-rimmed eyes caused the nurse to lower her gaze.
She had been a nurse for over twenty years and been
through the same sad ordeal more times than she
could remember, but it never got any easier to deal
with someone who had lost someone close. Be it a
mother, brother, husband or wife, or in this case, a
dear friend, the pain experienced by the people left
behind to grieve never ceased to create a feeling of
inadequacy inside her.

Like a woman twice her age Sadie rose unsteadily

to her feet. Brushing the kindly nurse gently to one side she said solemnly, 'Thank you fer all yer kindness, Nurse. I appreciate it, even though I never said so at the time. I'll be off now, I've gotta see ter Lily's boys like I promised.'

The nurse looked at the tired woman with sympathy. 'Don't do anything rash, dear. I know you promised to take care of your friend's children, but I've witnessed many a deathbed promise, and while the person concerned genuinely means to keep that promise, it isn't always possible to keep that vow made under the most distressing of circumstances. So don't feel too bad if you change your mind. Taking on two children, especially children who are no relation to you, could be very difficult.'

At the nurse's words, Sadie sprang into life. 'Thanks fer the advice, Nurse, but Lily was me friend. More ter the point, she's dead because of me. That's something I'm gonna 'ave ter live with fer the rest of me life. The least I can do is ter look after 'er boys, I owe her that much. Besides, I never make a promise I can't keep.' Gathering up her strength she continued firmly, 'Now then, where's the boys? Or should I say my boys, 'cos that's what they are now.'

The nurse stepped to one side, her expression worried. 'It might not be that simple, dear. You can't just take them, you know. You'll have to go through the authorities.' Seeing the look of anger flash over Sadie's face, the nurse, who was used to irate patients and their families, continued in a calm voice. 'It's no good you looking at me like that, I don't make the rules. If you were a relative it would be a different

322

matter entirely.' She paused, a conspiratorial expression coming into her eyes. 'Then again, you could be their aunt for all anyone knows, or a cousin perhaps. If that's so, then the authorities will be only too pleased to wash their hands of them. There are enough homeless children roaming the streets as it is. I'm sure they would be only too pleased to be spared the time and expense of placing them in the workhouse. You'd have to fill in a form, of course, stating your relationship to the children, but that's merely a formality. The authorities rarely check up on the relevant documents, they're much too busy elsewhere.' Arching her eyebrows the nurse gazed expectantly at Sadie.

Immediately picking up on the nurse's meaning Sadie bristled. 'Well, of course I'm their auntie. I wouldn't saddle meself with two kids if I didn't 'ave to, would I? You give me that form ter fill in then take me to me nephews, wherever you've put them ... Only ...'

'Yes, dear?'

A wave of embarrassment swept over Sadie, then she shook off the feeling angrily. This was no time for false pride. Her chin thrust out defiantly she said tersely, 'I can't read or write. Well, not properly.'

The nurse's face relaxed. 'Oh, is that all? You come with me, dear, and we'll fill in the form together, if that's all right with you?'

Sadie nodded, a wave of gratitude flooding through her tired body and with it a sudden burst of fresh emotion. As she went to follow the uniformed figure she said in a shaking voice and on the point of tears,

"Ang on a minute, Nurse. Could . . . could I 'ave a bit of time with me mate? Just . . . just ter say good—goodbye properly.'

When the nurse left the ward Sadie stood for a few minutes before approaching her friend for the last time. Leaning over the still figure, the wrapped bundle of her dead baby placed in her lifeless arms, Sadie kissed Lily on the forehead, and with that simple act fresh tears spilled from her reddened eyes.

'Goodbye, mate. I'm gonna miss yer. But I'll take care of your boys, like I promised. I probably won't be as good a mum like you was, Lil, but . . . but I'll do me best. Oh, Lil . . . Lil. I'm so . . . so sorry. Pl—please, please, Lil, forgive me. I loved yer, yer soppy cow. Only . . . only I didn't realise it till . . . till now.'

Her body began to shake with renewed grief, and though it was genuine, there was a thread of guilt tormenting her. She would keep her word to her dead friend, but she felt no affection for the Knight boys. To her they were just two scruffy kids who happened to belong to her friend. The only child she wanted, had ever wanted was Molly. Now she was gone for ever. For even if found, and Sadie prayed fervently she would be, for the alternative was unthinkable, she would never be able to keep her. If . . . no! Not if, she silently corrected herself, *when* she was found, she would be returned to her brother and would live with him and the Parkers, while she would be left with two grief-stricken, bewildered boys of whom she knew absolutely nothing. With tears blinding her vision she felt an arm go round her shoulder and let herself be led from the room. Sobbing uncontrollably her mind kept repeating over and over again, 'Oh, Molly. My sweet, sweet Molly. Be safe, my angel. Wherever you are, please be safe. I don't care if I can't have you with me like I wanted, as long as you're safe.'

CHAPTER TWENTY-FIVE

'Arthur, where have you been all night?' Ellen stood in the doorway of the bedroom tying her red dressing gown tighter around her waist, her long hair falling loosely around her face and shoulders.

The sight of her brought an ache of pain and loneliness in Arthur such as he'd never felt. He had stayed at the Hope and Anchor until closing time, something he had never done before.

But no matter how much he had drunk, his mind had remained clear. After leaving the pub he had wandered the streets for hours trying to convince himself that he and Ellen would somehow weather the storm that had entered their lives in the shape of Ted Parker. During those dark hours he had done a lot of soul searching, and he hadn't liked what he'd seen. But he had tried to convince himself that he had always acted out of chivalry. Now, seeing her looking so young, so fresh, a flash of clarity came to him. Ellen didn't belong to him – she never had and never would. Agnes had been right when she'd accused him of marrying the young girl for his own selfish reasons, instead of adopting her, as any decent man with true honourable intentions would have done. But whatever happened in the future he would still have the memories of the time they had spent together. They had been the happiest days of his life and he would treasure them always. Now he had to undo the harm he had caused and let Ellen go while she still had some affection for him. The fact that he had already lost her was clear, but despite that awful night when he had forced himself on her, a memory that had tormented him day and night, Ellen might still stay with him out of kindness and some sort of misguided loyalty – she was that kind of woman, a rarity in this day and age. But, oh God! It would be the hardest thing he'd ever had to do in his life. Afraid his habitual weakness would let him down, he began his rehearsed words before he changed his mind.

Clearing his throat gruffly he began buttoning up his coat again, careful to avoid Ellen's searching stare. 'I'm joining the search party for young Molly. It was the talk of the pub last night, and made me realise how selfish I've been. I should have been thinking of the missing child, instead of my own feelings – but then that's what I've always done, think about myself.' Keeping his face averted he continued. 'Oh, I never did it deliberately, but nevertheless I did. I've been a selfish beggar, but it's not too late to rectify the harm I've done, especially to you ... No, don't, Ellen, let me finish,' he said quickly as he heard the rustle of her slippered feet approaching. 'This is hard enough as it is. I'm afraid that if I look at you, I'll change my mind, so just stay quiet and listen, please.'

He sensed rather than saw Ellen stop in her tracks, but she was near enough for him to smell the subtle perfume she always wore, and it was nearly the undoing of him. Buttoning and unbuttoning his coat, his fingers shaking with nerves he said, 'I should never have married you, Ellen. It wasn't fair on you. The plain truth is, I took advantage of a vulnerable, innocent young girl. I even convinced myself I was acting like some kind of knight in shining armour.' He gave a nervous laugh. 'Can you imagine a more ludicrous image? Agnes saw right through me, and my selfish motives, and she was right.' He shook his head slowly as his guilty conscience continued to torment him.

'She's another one I hurt. I never intended to, but I did. It's like I've been wearing blinkers for most of my life, but walking the streets at night, alone, with no distractions, it was as if those blinkers were suddenly lifted, and I saw myself as if for the first time. Oh, I don't mean my weakness and lack of gumption, I've always known that. Maybe that was part of my reason for wanting to make you my wife. I thought people might look on me with some respect for marrying a young, pretty girl. But I was wrong again. They were laughing at me behind my back all the time. Probably making bets on how long it would be before you came to your senses and walked out on me. Well, I can't right the wrong I did Agnes, but I can you.' Now he did look at Ellen. She was standing as still as a statue, her hands holding the neck of her dressing gown together. 'I heard what Ted Parker said that night, about you being able to get an annulment on the grounds that the marriage hadn't been consummated, and he was right, though I wouldn't have thought he would know of such legal matters. But that's beside the point. We can't do anything about it now, not while Micky's sister is still missing, but once she's found, we can start putting the wheels in motion to getting the marriage annulled.'

As his words sank in Ellen stammered, 'But . . . but, Arthur, that isn't true, we . . .'

Raising his hand Arthur said quietly. 'What happened that night is between you and me, and I for one certainly don't want my despicable action becoming public knowledge. I know there's been gossip, started no doubt by Agnes, but like I said, only we know the real truth. So what do you say, Ellen? I'm giving you the opportunity to leave me, I'm letting you go, love. But you'd better make your mind up quickly, because . . . I don't know if I'm strong enough to . . . to . . .'

In spite of his valiant efforts to stay in control, his voice cracked and tears stung the back of his eyes. Desperate not to let Ellen see his distress he made for the door. Swallowing hard he said huskily, 'I'd best be off. The search party is gathering outside Hackney police station at six o'clock, I don't want to miss them. I don't know what time I'll be back. Perhaps it would be better if the shop remains closed today. I'm sure people will understand why. Goodbye, Ellen.'

Before Ellen could speak Arthur was gone. Her legs shaking, Ellen sank down gratefully onto the first chair she came to, her mind hardly daring to believe what her ears had heard. She was free. It was what she had wanted since the first time she had realised she was in love with Ted, so why wasn't she feeling any joy? Why did she feel like crying instead? Lifting her eyes to the closed door she whispered, 'Oh, Arthur. Poor, poor Arthur. I'm sorry.'

Yet even as she spoke the words, a feeling of relief and elation flooded over her. Soon she would be a free woman. The pathway to a life with Ted had been cleared. But how could she feel these emotions when young Molly was still missing? Her mind in turmoil, she crept into the bedroom and looked in on the sleeping boy. The extra sleeping draught had done the trick. Carefully she climbed onto the double bed and put her arm around the thin shoulders affectionately. Laying her head against Micky's back she closed her eyes and hugged the young boy with all the fierce, protective love a mother would feel for a son.

Creeping as silently as possible Agnes led Molly through the mass of trees that seemed to close in on them no matter which way they went. Agnes had been sure she would remember the way she had come in once the dawn broke, but she was wrong. She was hopelessly lost, but on no account must the child know they were probably going round in circles. Every so often Agnes would stop and give the little girl a reassuring cuddle, as much for her own benefit as for the child's. Grimly Agnes listened in hope for the sound of raised voices and trampling feet, but there was nothing apart from the birds twittering and the occasional rustle of a small animal scrambling through the undergrowth. At first both woman and child had jumped at the slightest sound, but now, after nearly an hour, they had become used to the noises of the forest. Stopping for a rest Agnes leant against one of the many oak trees that populated the woods keeping Molly tight by her side. If only she had some way to tell the time. It seemed to have been light for well over an hour now, and still there was no sight or sound of the search party. Surely they'd be here soon. She couldn't keep going on the way they had been. For all she knew they might be heading further into the forest, rather than out of it. The best thing would be to stay where they were and wait to be rescued.

Besides, the child was nearly dead on her feet. Not that she had complained, the poor little love. There weren't many children of her age who could be so brave in the circumstances, not after what she had been through. A rush of affection flowed through Agnes as she looked down at the pretty, heart-shaped face – a feeling that was quickly replaced by guilt as she remembered that it was she who had helped that evil bastard get his hands on her. Then her head came up defiantly as she tried to justify herself. All right, so she had been stupid enough to play into Kenneth's hands, but he himself had been thwarted by the intervention of the woman called Sadie, the woman Molly had spoken about during their seemingly endless trek.

Agnes could still feel Kenneth's hands round her throat when he'd discovered the child gone, thinking she had had some part in the removal of his intended prey. Sinking down onto the grass, she cradled Molly

in her lap, her thoughts turning to the other woman
Molly had spoken of with affection, Lily Knight, the
woman Kenneth had murdered, together with her
unborn baby. Her only comfort now was the knowledge that, as John Smith had said, the man she had
known as Kenneth Wells would hang for his crimes.

In spite of her thoughts she remained alert for any
unusual sounds, but as time passed and with it the
undoubted arrival of the search party got closer, Agnes
began to relax a little. So when she heard a rustle she
didn't stir, thinking it to be yet another wild animal
running about in its natural habitat – until Molly let
out a high, piercing scream. Too late Agnes tried to
rise, only to be knocked down by a heavy clenched
fist to her forehead. Stunned she lay still, unable to
move, her vision blinded momentarily by the cruel
blow. But she could still hear, and the words, spoken
by the familiar and now hated voice, chilled her to
the very bones of her body.

'You stupid, ignorant old hag. Did you really think
you could get the better of me?' He let out a laugh
that to Agnes' fuddled mind sounded on the verge
of hysteria. 'I should have known the kid wouldn't
have the nerve to make a run for it without help. But
I never thought it would be you. Did you really think
you'd get one over on me? Better people than you
have tried to outwit me and failed. I've been caught,
oh, yes, I'll grant you that, but there was never
enough evidence to keep me in jail for long. But those
days are over. They'll never catch me again.' He was
so close Agnes could smell his sour breath. 'And I'll
tell you why, seeing as you won't be able to pass on

the information, because I'm going to kill you, just like I killed that other slag who tried to keep me from my Molly.' He let out a high-pitched laugh. 'You know what's so funny, Agnes? Well, I'll tell you. Molly and me were in that hut all along. I heard the so-called search party break down the door, all full of themselves thinking they'd cornered me, and what did they find? Nothing, absolutely nothing. And this is the best part. You listening, you pathetic old cow?'

Agnes' head was beginning to clear but she remained inert, biding her time, hoping to lure Kenneth into a false sense of security. For if he thought she was incapable of movement there was a chance, a slim chance, but a chance all the same, that she might be able to catch him unaware, long enough to let Molly escape. Her heart leapt in fright as she realised she hadn't heard any sound from Molly since that awful scream. But Kenneth was still talking.

'They didn't find me because I was underneath the hut in the basement. Yeah, that's right, that run-down old hut actually has a basement. But no one will ever find it. Who would think of looking for it in a dilapidated old hut? I don't know how it came to be there, perhaps the hut was built over it, but who cares? I only found it by chance, and I've hidden it well. And now, my pitiful old friend, it's time to say goodbye. Time's getting on, and I don't intend to be out in the open when the good people of the East End and the coppers start arriving.'

Agnes was fully conscious now, still dizzy, but alert to the situation. Opening her eyes she saw the madness in his eyes, eyes that widened in shock as

Agnes grabbed hold of his coat and screamed at the top of her voice, 'Run, Molly. Run . . . run, sweetheart.'

Taken off guard, Kenneth relaxed his hold on Molly, but the terrified child remained rooted to the spot, as she had on seeing Lily Knight's blood-soaked body.

Then Agnes screamed again, 'Molly, love. Run . . . Please, run . . . run.'

And this time Molly did as she was bid. Stumbling and running blindly she ran sobbing, not knowing where she was going, expecting the nasty man to catch her at any minute.

Seeing Molly run gave Agnes a strength she didn't know she possessed, a strength brought about by sheer desperation and a desire to save the life of a child she hardly knew. As she continued to wrestle with Stokes, she saw out of the corner of her eye that his right hand was bandaged and bloodstained, and the sight gave her fresh hope.

So that was why she had managed to hold him at bay for so long: he had the use of only one hand. Twisting and turning she managed to bring up her knee, ramming it with all her remaining strength into his groin. As her knee found its mark, Kenneth let out a scream of pain and rage, but Agnes wasn't finished yet. As Stokes reeled back, she grabbed his injured hand and savagely ground it into the dirt beneath the grass. Almost out of his head with pain Kenneth lashed out with his good hand, catching Agnes a crushing blow under her chin. Her head jolted back before crashing onto a large, sharp stone.

Kenneth watched as Agnes' body jerked once then lay still.

Cursing and doubled up in pain he was about to make sure she was dead when he heard shouts and the pounding of men's boots approaching. Still racked with pain he gave Agnes' inert body one last savage kick before heading back to the hut, and safety. He knew Molly was now lost to him for ever, but there were plenty more Mollys in the world. He doubted she would tell anyone about the basement. Even if she did, who would believe her? They'd likely put any such tale down to childish hysteria, particularly when they didn't find it. At the very worst the police might search the hut again, but it would be a perfunctory procedure. And the only other person who knew was Agnes, and he was sure she wouldn't be doing any talking. A groan of pain burst from his lips as he staggered back to the hut. Ten minutes later he was safely settled down in the basement, confident his hideout would never be discovered.

The pain in his groin was easing, but his hand was throbbing badly. Glancing down at the dried blood and dirt that streaked the bandage he cursed profusely. That old cow had reopened the wound, and rubbed dirt into it. Well, she wouldn't be doing any more harm now, would she? His glee was shortlived as he prised the linen cloth away from the wound, for it had stuck deep. It was just as well he had furnished the basement with creature comforts. Finding a bottle of brandy he took a deep swallow, then another to dull the pain before redressing the wound. Scrutinising the injury closely he sighed with relief. It looked clean, and it had stopped bleeding.

A loud noise brought his head upwards. So they were back, were they? Well, let them search the hut as long as they liked, he could stay down here for days, weeks even, if the worst came to the worst. He had enough food and drink to last him that long. Taking the brandy bottle with him he lay down on the double mattress and raised the bottle. 'Cheers, lads. You work your arses off. I'm quite comfortable where I am,' he said mockingly before finishing off the remainder of the brandy and falling into a deep sleep.

Molly heard the men as they entered the forest. Following the sounds of the deep voices she stumbled across Agnes. Sobbing with relief at finding the nice lady she threw herself across the still body crying, 'Wake up, lady. The policemen are here. Wake up, lady, please, wake up.'

She was still trying to stir Agnes when Ted and John, followed closely by four other men, came across them. With a loud shout of triumph Ted bounded forward, scooping Molly up into his arms, holding the dishevelled, small body tight against his chest. Then he looked down at Agnes, his lips curling in disgust. Rounding on John he snarled, 'I told yer she was in on it, but yer wouldn't 'ave it, would yer?'

Before John could answer, Ted, still holding Molly protectively with one arm, stooped and grabbed the inert figure with his free hand.

'Come on, yer wicked old bitch. Get up and face the music.' When the figure stayed silent Ted pulled at her arm roughly. 'Stop messing about, yer ain't fooling no one ...' Then he staggered back as the fragile figure in his arms began to beat at his face and neck with clenched fists.

'Stop it! Leave her alone. She ain't done nothing wrong. She saved me from the nasty man. She's a nice lady, she is, she is. An' she's me friend. The nasty man found us, an' ... an' he tried ter 'urt her like he 'urt Mrs Knight. But she hit him an' told me ter run, so ... so I did. Then I 'eard yer coming, just like she said yer would. Only the nasty man must 'ave 'urt her bad, 'cos she won't wake up ... she won't wake up ...' She broke off sobbing and threw her arms tight around Ted's neck crying, 'Make 'er wake up, Mister. Make 'er better, please, make 'er better.'

Ted looked helplessly at John Smith, and the uniformed man was quick to notice the look was threaded heavily with guilt.

'You get her out of here, I'll send one of the men for an ambulance cart. Because in case you haven't noticed, Agnes is badly injured.' His voice was heavy with sarcasm, which wasn't lost on Ted.

Nodding dumbly he pressed his face against the blonde head nestled on his shoulder. 'Yeah, all right.' He went to walk away then stopped. Looking to where Johnny was now kneeling beside Agnes he said, 'I'm sorry. Yer was right all along, I ...'

John didn't even look up as he barked, 'Just get the child away from here.' Then, ignoring Ted, he shouted to the waiting men, 'Spread out. He can't be far away.' Instantly the men sprang into action, their faces beaming with relief that the child had been found. As Ted walked towards the edge of the forest to where police wagons were waiting, he heard a resounding cheer echo through the forest as word quickly spread that the little girl had been found safe, and every man he passed patted him on the back or shoulder.

Ted acknowledged the men's camaraderie and walked on. The only thing on his mind was to get Molly back to her brother as soon as possible. But mixed with his elation at finding Molly there was a deep feeling of guilt for the contemptible way he had treated Agnes.

He was nearing the roadway when he came face to face with Arthur. 'Thank God!' cried Arthur. Then he smiled at Ted. 'Take her home, Ted. Ellen's waiting for you, for you both. I'll stay here and help in the search to find Stokes.' Then he did something Ted wasn't expecting: Arthur put out his hand in friendship, and Ted took it.

They gripped hands tightly and looked deep into each other's eyes – and what Ted saw there said more than any words could.

Then Arthur was gone, marching into the forest with three other men. Ted watched until they disappeared from view before taking Molly to one of the waiting police wagons.

CHAPTER TWENTY-SIX

As the police wagon made its way back to Hackney more and more people began to come out of their homes to watch its progress, proving beyond question the unequalled validity of the East End grapevine. And the reception they received couldn't have been more tumultuous than if the Queen herself was riding amongst them. Ted and the constable driving the wagon found themselves the heroes of the hour, and, despite their best efforts, neither man could stop his wide, soppy grin. Molly, on the other hand, seemed oblivious of the attention she was receiving; the only thought in her mind was seeing her brother again. Despite Ted's assurances that Micky was waiting for her, Molly wouldn't believe it until she saw him with her own eyes. Being possessed of a kind nature she couldn't help but think of the two ladies who had tried to help her and been hurt in the process, but her prime concern was to see Micky. To hear his voice again, even if he started to tease her, or even shout at her, although Micky had rarely shouted at her. When the wagon stopped outside a bakery she looked up at Ted, puzzled.

'Why we stopping 'ere, Mister? The lady . . . I mean Agnes, said Micky was staying with you an' yer mum. You don't live 'ere.' Squirming in Ted's grasp Molly cried in alarm, 'Yer've been lying ter me, ain't yer? And that old lady what 'elped me get away from the nasty man. Yer've both been lying ter me. Something's 'appened ter him, ain't it? That's why 'e didn't come back fer me that night, 'cos he couldn't . . .'

Ted easily caught hold of the flailing arms, saying warmly, 'We ain't been lying ter yer, love, honest. He was staying with me and Mum, but then he decided he wanted ter be with Ellen, you know, the lady that Micky used ter work fer?'

But Molly was no longer listening or struggling. Instead her eyes as wide as saucers stared past him to the alley that ran down the back of the bakery. Then, with an ear-splitting scream that caused Ted to flinch, she shouted, 'Micky!'

Ted's head swivelled on his shoulders as he followed her line of sight, and there, looking incongruous and pitiful, clothed in one of Ted's nightshirts that hung down to the boy's ankles, stood Micky, a look of disbelief on his face, as he stared back at the girl he had thought he'd never see again. Beside him, her hand on his shoulder, stood a smiling Ellen, looking as though she was trying her hardest not to let her emotions get the better of her. But, like Ted and the young constable, she couldn't stop the trembling of her lips, nor the tears of joy that were slowly rolling down her cheeks.

Then Micky was half running, half stumbling, as he ran to his sister. Molly had already jumped down from the wagon and ran, her little legs pumping furiously as she raced towards her brother's outstretched arms.

'Molly ... Oh, Moll, I thought yer was dead.' Micky's voice shook as Molly propelled herself into his arms, the impact of her body catching the still drowsy Micky off balance. But Molly hung onto his neck for dear life, and down the two of them went, then lay on the bumpy, cold cobbles, holding each other tight, afraid to let go for fear that someone or something would separate them again.

More people were still spilling out onto the streets, mainly the women, for their menfolk were out with the search party, and on each of their faces was the relief and joy that only a mother could feel for the safe return of a child, any child. The young constable who had driven Molly and Ted home saw the crowd begin to gather and quickly took control.

'I think we should get 'em indoors, Sir.' Jerking his head towards the groups of women heading their way he said, 'They mean well, but under the circumstances it'd be better if the children could spend some time alone together before facing ...'

His words were rudely cut off as a man wearing an overcoat, already busily scribbling on a large pad of paper, tried to pass them, but the constable blocked his path. 'Now, now, Sir. Leave the youngsters in peace, they've been through enough without being pestered by you lot.'

But the journalist wasn't to be put off so easily. Here was the story of a lifetime, and he was determined to get first-hand information and interviews before any of his rivals turned up.

'Come on, mate. Just a few words with the kids. It ain't often stories like these 'ave an 'appy ending.'

'I said no, and I mean no. You'll have plenty of time later to get your story. Right now they need a doctor, not a nosy reporter badgering them with a load of questions . . . Hey, you there.'

A loud bang and puff of smoke caught the constable's attention. Muttering angrily he headed towards the man about to take another photograph of the children still locked together on the ground. It was a poignant sight, and one that would earn the photographer a good deal of money. He was preparing to take another one when the uniformed man blocked his path.

With the policeman's attention diverted elsewhere the reporter grinned and started towards the alley.

'No yer don't, mate.' Ted swung the man around, pushing him backwards.

'Now, 'ang on a minute,' the man protested, then stopped as he stared into Ted's face. It was the face of a man not be trifled with, and the reporter knew when he was beaten. Besides, his associate had already taken a photo of the Masters children, while he himself would write the headline above it, plus a story to accompany it. He had been one of the first journalists to cover the story of the missing girl and the murder of Lily Knight, so he had more than enough information to warrant the front page of his newspaper.

Throwing up his hands in defeat he grinned good naturedly. 'All right, all right. No need ter get stroppy.' Tipping his hat to the back of his head he said, 'I know when I've met me match. You'd better hurry up and get the pair of 'em indoors before the rest of the bloodhounds turn up. They're front-page news at the moment, the pair of 'em, an' yer can't keep 'em all away – as big as you are,' he laughed.

Ted smiled back. 'Don't bet on it,' he said then he was striding down the alley to the three people that needed him most at this time; two of whom he already loved, and the third ... Ted gave a mental shrug. He didn't think he'd have much trouble in learning to love Molly Masters.

Bending down he lifted both children into his arms with ease. Then with a loving glance at Ellen he followed her indoors, kicking the door behind them with his foot, and the sound of the door closing gave him the feeling of security. Soon, very soon, their privacy would be invaded. It was only to be expected. The doctor had already been sent for. But until he arrived Ted had the children and Ellen all to himself. And he was going to make the most of that time.

For the next five days Agnes drifted in and out of consciousness, thus preventing the police from questioning her as to the whereabouts of Kenneth Stokes. The exhaustive search of Epping Forest had proved fruitless. It seemed as if the hunted man had disappeared from the face of the earth.

The only other person who might have helped them was the child, Molly Masters, but she too had had little information to help them find the man who had abducted her. It had been left to John Smith to tackle the delicate task of questioning the little girl, much to the chagrin of his inspector who had already had his nose put out of joint when the case had been taken over by Scotland Yard.

In the presence of a doctor, John had tried to get Molly to tell him where Kenneth Stokes had taken her, but each of his questions had been met with a stone wall. It was as if events from the time she had been taken from Lily Knight's house until Agnes had led her to safety had been blanked from her mind. The doctor had explained to John that such cases where a child was concerned was perfectly normal. The trauma Molly had been through had left a profound and lasting effect on the little girl. The doctor had gone on to say that in his experience some people, both adult and children, had recalled unpleasant memories given time, while others never had – it all depended on the individual concerned.

Which didn't help the police at all.

At the moment the Masters children were staying at Ted's house, with Nora Parker fiercely guarding the children from prying eyes and nosy reporters, of which there were an abundance.

There was also a heavy presence of newspapermen gathered outside the Hackney hospital where Agnes still lay unconscious from the savage attack on her by Stokes.

The police were on guard outside the private room in which Agnes lay. One of the few people allowed in to sit with her was Ted Parker. It was on the fifth day as he sat by her bedside, the guilt about the way he had treated her still heavy on his mind, when her eyes opened.

Seeing Ted by her bed, Agnes' eyes widened in fear, and this alone caused Ted's stomach to churn in shame. Quick to put her mind at ease he caught hold of the frail hand lying outside the starched sheets and said gently, 'It's all right, Agnes. I ain't gonna hurt yer. I was wrong about yer, and I feel ashamed of meself when I think of the times I've gone fer yer. Johnny Smith kept telling me yer wouldn't 'ave anything ter do with the likes of Stokes, but I wouldn't listen. I should 'ave, 'cos he was right. Yer saved Molly from that pervert, an' nearly got yerself killed doing it.'

Agnes felt the tenderness in Ted's touch and voice and relaxed. She tried to speak but her lips felt as if they were glued together. With a weak movement of her head she looked at the pitcher of water on the locker by her bed. Ted saw her distress and instantly poured the liquid into a glass. Lifting Agnes' head from the pillows he held the glass to her dried, cracked lips.

Gulping eagerly at the cool water Agnes spluttered and coughed, the action causing her to screw up her eyes in pain. Ted laid her back on the pillow, his face taking on a look of genuine concern.

"Ang on, Agnes, I'll get a nurse or doctor. They've been waiting fer yer to come round.'

Agnes caught at Ted's hand.

'No, wait a minute,' she croaked painfully. 'Yer said Mo— Molly's all right?'.

'Yeah, she's fine, Agnes. And it's all thanks ter you, yer . . .'

Impatiently Agnes squeezed Ted's hand, motioning him to be quiet.

Quickly picking up on her signal he sat down again and said earnestly, 'What is it, Agnes? You trying ter tell me something?'

Agnes nodded her head gingerly. Looking towards the closed door then back to Ted's anxious face she whispered, ''Ave they found 'im?'

She didn't have to name who she was referring to. Alert now, Ted moved closer to the bed. 'No, they ain't. It's like he's vanished into thin air. But you know something, don't yer, Agnes?'

Agnes's eyes fluttered and closed, and for a heart-stopping moment Ted thought she'd fallen back into unconsciousness. Then she spoke, but her voice was so weak Ted had to lean his ear against her mouth to hear what she was trying so hard to convey.

'The hut, Ted. He's hiding in the hut.'

Deeply disappointed, Ted drew his head back, gently stroking her hand. 'Nah! They've looked there, Agnes. If he was there, he ain't now.'

Again Agnes became agitated, her grip on Ted's hand tightening.

''Ere, don't go upsetting yerself, love. It ain't your fault, yer . . .'

Desperate to make herself heard Agnes motioned for Ted to come closer. Again laying his ear against her mouth he listened, humouring her as she spoke disjointedly. Then he sat bolt upright as her words sank in.

'A basement! Nah, there can't be. The coppers would've found it by now if there was one. They've had the place upside down, they . . .'

'No, it's there . . . he . . . he told me.' Agnes swallowed painfully. 'More water, please, Ted.'

Ted moved like lightning to get the water. If Agnes was telling the truth it would explain a lot of things. But more important still, if Stokes was hiding in a basement beneath the hut in the forest, he wanted to be the one to find him.

Her thirst quenched, Agnes tried once more to make Ted believe her. 'Thanks, Ted.' Her claw-like hand gripped his, and Ted didn't flinch at her touch, as he would have in the past. 'Listen . . . I ain't . . . ain't going off me 'ead. He thought he was gonna kill me, otherwise he'd never 'ave let me in on his little secret. You go there, Ted. You go and look. Don't . . . don't tell the law . . . just go and see if he's still there.' Her eyes nearly closed, her grip on his hand loosening, she pleaded, 'Yer know what I mean, Ted?'

Ted nodded grimly. Yes! He understood all right.

Leaning over her he did something he never thought he would: he kissed Agnes on the forehead, and the gesture was made with true affection and gratitude.

At that moment the doctor entered the room followed by John Smith. 'The policeman on guard said he thought he heard voices. Has she come round?'

Ted stood up, his hand still holding Agnes'. 'Yeah, she did. But she didn't make much sense. Still, it's a good sign, ain't it?' The hand in his relaxed as Agnes, drifting back into sleep, realised Ted had understood her message.

John looked Ted straight in the eye. 'You sure she didn't say anything – like where we could find Stokes?'

Ted shook his head. 'Nah! Sorry, Officer. Like I said, she didn't make much sense. I couldn't understand what she was trying ter say.' Adopting a casual manner he grinned saying, 'Anyway I gotta get off, I've got a business ter run – see ya.'

John Smith watched Ted go, a quizzical look in his eyes. Then he shrugged. If Ted was up to something, as an officer of the law maybe it was best he didn't know about it.

Kenneth Stokes lay on the mattress, his face and body contorted in agony, leaving him as helpless as a newborn baby. Yet despite the pain and fever that racked his body, his mind remained crystal clear, trying desperately to understand what was happening to him.

He remembered cleaning and changing his bandage, and drinking a bottle of brandy while listening to the heavy boots pounding above him. He had fallen asleep and woken up to find his injured hand formed into a rigid clench he had no control over. When he had tried to rise from the mattress he had felt unwell accompanied by fleeting pains in his back. Putting the symptoms down to the likelihood his wound had become infected, he had struggled to change the dressing, but even that relatively simple task had proved difficult. He didn't know if he had passed out or simply fallen asleep afterwards, but when he awoke he found himself drenched in sweat.

Reaching for a jug of water he'd put by his side he tried to sit up but found each movement tortuous. But he truly became alarmed when, after managing to pour himself a drink, he found it difficult to swallow. He had slept again, his only notion of time being his fob watch, and even this was denied him as he couldn't control his good hand to light the lamp on the table by his bed. Still, he put his illness down to a severe cold, made worse by the infection in his hand.

But on the fourth day he awoke to find his jaw, which had begun to feel stiff, had worsened to such an extent that his teeth were clenched together so tightly he could barely open his mouth. Then the spasms had started, and Stokes could lie to himself no longer. He'd always prided himself on being an intellectual man, a man who had continued to further his education even after he'd left the hallowed halls of Eton. One of his favourite pastimes was reading up on medical matters, a knowledge that had often come into use when trying to inveigle his way into the homes of ignorant parents, who were only too pleased to have a nice, generous doctor who seemed happy to help their sick children for no recompense. Now that knowledge was striking terror into the very fibre of his being.

Lockjaw.

Another spasm struck, causing the upper part of his body to arch painfully, quickly accompanied by a sudden increased pressure on his clenched teeth. When it was over Kenneth lay back sweating in pain and fear. He knew another spasm could kill him, and there was nothing he could do to help himself.

Damn that slut. If she had handed over Molly, none of this would have happened. It wasn't him that had picked up the knife. He'd had no choice but to protect himself and had been stabbed in the process. Even then he might have been all right if that other old hag hadn't rubbed the wounded hand in the dirt. The flimsy bandage hadn't been thick enough to stop the dirt from penetrating through the inadequate covering. That's what had done it, he was sure. Damn them both to hell.

Then he heard footsteps overhead, and a spark of hope leapt into his eyes. He no longer cared if he was caught. He had enough money to buy the best lawyers. If by some miracle the Knight woman was still alive, he could plead self-defence, and the same went for Agnes Handly. Oh! What did it matter? As long as he was found and received medical attention.

There was still time – surely there was still time!

But would whoever was in the hut find the trap door? The fear came flooding back. No one would ever find him unless they knew where to look, he'd made sure of that. Then he heard the unmistakable sound of the trap door opening.

Ted walked slowly around the small hut, his sharp eyes fixed firmly on the wooden floor. He had looked under the three rugs and the wide strip of carpet in the largest room, but had found nothing. Now he was beginning to wonder if Agnes' mind had been turned by the experience she had gone through. Yet she had seemed so sure. Sinking down onto a chair he thought carefully. He'd bet that Agnes' mind was as sane as his, and if that was the case then some-where in these small rooms a trap door lay hidden. His eyes fixed on the floor, he stared again at the strip of carpet. He'd already looked under it once, but knowing the man Stokes, he would be careful to make sure his secret hideaway wouldn't be easily found, if there was one. Getting down on his knees he looked again under the carpet, sighing and feeling he was wasting his time in going over the same ground, but he was here now and he might as well be thorough. It was tacked down in each corner but the carpet was loose and easy to look under. This time Ted ran his hand over the floorboards beneath but found nothing out of the ordinary. Leaning back on his heels Ted nipped at his bottom lip in disap-pointment. Nothing, absolutely nothing.

He was about to leave when he remembered Agnes' words, the desperate look in her eyes, and the surpris-ingly firm grip on his hand when the doctor and John Smith had entered the room. Muttering 'Oh, the hell with it,' he got down on his knees. If he had to crawl over the entire floor on his hands and knees and look at every floorboard, then that's what he would do: he owed Agnes that much. For a start he'd have that carpet up. There was nothing under it, he'd already checked, but it wouldn't do any harm to have a closer look. Not having any tool to take out the nails that were holding the carpet in place, he pulled at the rough material with both hands and was rewarded with a sudden tearing of the frayed material. Pulling the carpet back he looked at the wooden flooring. With the floor bare, Ted ran his hand again over the

351

surface the wood, not expecting to find anything but feeling impelled to do his best before returning to Agnes. Running his hand in the opposite direction he felt a slight, almost imperceptible groove in the flooring.

Telling himself not to get his hopes up, nonetheless Ted couldn't stop a growing feeling of excitement mounting. On closer inspection he saw what looked like a wooden plug blocking a circular hole. Hardly daring to breathe Ted poked the plug with his finger then leant back as the plug fell away to reveal a hole. His excitement mounting Ted hooked his finger through the hole and pulled, then fell back as a large square of the flooring gave way. Ted had to restrain himself from shouting his glee out loud. Even though it was light outside, the area below the hut was cloaked in darkness.

Getting to his feet Ted quickly found a gas lamp, then there followed a frustrating search for something to light it with. Then he found a box of matches in the empty grate. Gingerly descending the ladder Ted started to wonder what he was getting so excited about. All right, so he'd found out where Stokes had kept Molly, and maybe others, but it was obvious by the darkness that the man he was looking for had long gone. His initial euphoria subsiding, Ted continued further down, then he let out a muffled shout as an overpowering stench hit his nostrils.

'Bleeding 'ell!' He stopped halfway down the ladder, undecided whether or not to investigate further, then he heard a peculiar sound coming from below. The unfamiliar noise reminded Ted of an animal grunting, and without thinking he made his way down to the bottom of the ladder. Holding his jacket over his nose Ted waved the lamp around the gloomy underground room, noting the items of furniture here were of much better quality than that above. He turned, the lamp lighting up the room, then gasped out loud as the light centred on the mattress, and the grotesque figure lying on it. Surprised and shocked, Ted inched nearer the bed, holding the lamp high so he could see better. And what he saw appalled him.

The man lay in obvious agony, his torso raised from the mattress, his head at an unnatural angle. But it was his face that shocked Ted the most, in particular the lips that were stretched wide over clenched teeth, giving the appearance of a mirthless, unnatural grin.

As if in a trance Ted approached the contorted body, his own face solemn. The stench was emanating from the incapacitated man, but such was Ted's shock at finding him here, he no longer noticed the rank, unpleasant smell.

'Are you Stokes?' Ted spoke in a clipped, brusque voice, even though he already knew the answer, if only by the quality of the man's clothing, now fouled but still that of a man of means. Besides, who else could it be? But he had to be sure.

With apparent agony the man tried to speak through his rigid, clenched teeth. 'Yeees . . . He— help me. Pl— please . . .'

Ted remained still, his face expressionless and Kenneth felt a moment of relief. Someone had found him. It didn't matter what the law would do to him, at least he'd be alive. Then he looked up into the stranger's eyes, and what he saw reflected there killed any hope of redemption.

Ted lowered the lamp and pulled a chair nearer the double bed and sat down. 'So you're the scum that snatched young Molly, an' Gawd knows 'ow many other poor little cows. Not ter mention murdering Lily Knight an' her unborn baby, just so yer could get yer 'ands on an innocent little girl. An' yer really think I'm gonna 'elp yer? You must be fucking mad.' Ted rose abruptly. Standing over the man he had grown to hate, Ted was about to speak further when Stokes' body went into another, more violent spasm, the suddenness causing Ted to stagger away from the twitching form. He waited until the spasm was over then, for the last time, looked down at the man who had caused so much pain and misery and said in a voice filled with deep loathing, 'Die, you bastard. And die hard, 'cos it's no more than a piece of filth like you deserves.'

Then he turned and climbed back up the ladder, aware that Stokes' eyes were following him with silent pleading. But Ted didn't hesitate. Stepping off the last rung of the ladder he closed the trap door, pulled the ripped carpet back into place, turned out the lamp and left the hut.

He never looked back.

Left once again in the darkness Kenneth knew he was going to die. Yet not for one moment did he think to ask forgiveness for his dreadful sins. For in his eyes, he had done nothing wrong. Another spasm attacked his weakened body, the first of many before he finally died, choking on his own tongue. And his death was exactly that which Ted had wished on him. For Kenneth Stokes took a long time to die.

CHAPTER TWENTY-SEVEN

The children were asleep. Ted had left reluctantly, by Ellen's wishes, leaving her alone with Arthur and the children. It was ten o'clock and Ellen could hardly believe all that had happened during the last five days. Cautiously she lifted the net curtain and peered down into the street, then quickly let the curtain drop.

'Still out there, are they, love?' Arthur had entered the room with two mugs of cocoa in his hands.

Ellen smiled tiredly. 'Just a few. Journalists, I expect. I feel sorry for them in a way. After all, they are only trying to make a living.' Taking one of the mugs she added, 'I don't think I'll need any rocking tonight. I'm so tired I can hardly keep my eyes open.'

Arthur grunted in reply. 'Me neither. It's a pity we couldn't find that pervert though. For all we know he might have snatched some other child while we were chasing round in circles in the forest. God! I hope not. Mind you, it was a miracle the hut was found at all, the way it was situated. Johnny reckons Stokes must have mingled with the search party. There's no other way he could have got out of those woods because, don't forget, only Johnny and a few of the older police officers know what Stokes looks like. I don't blame the police for calling off the search. It was obvious after the third day that the man was long gone. At least we got Molly back, and in time, according to the doctor, so that's something to be thankful for.'

Ellen smiled over the top of her mug. 'Yes, indeed that is something to be thankful for. To be honest I'd begun to think the worst, but Micky never gave up hope.'

An awkward silence descended on them until Arthur coughed and said, 'We should talk about the future, Ellen. I know you're worried about hurting me, but I brought it on myself, and now it's time to make amends.'

'Really, Arthur, there's no rush. It's barely been a week since Molly was found, and we've hardly had time to catch our breath.'

Arthur shook his head and, in a resigned voice, said, 'The longer we put things off, the harder it's going to be. Ted's already becoming impatient, and I can't say as I blame him. By the way ...' He paused uncomfortably, shifting in his chair before continuing. 'I expect you've told Ted about that night, not that I'm blaming you, I'd just like to know when to expect a thrashing.'

Her face flushed, Ellen replied quietly, 'I told him

we'd been together once, but that we'd both known it was a mistake, and decided to carry on as we had before, in a platonic relationship. Ted agreed that that part of our marriage would be best left between the three of us, so you needn't worry on that score.'

Arthur gave a nervous laugh. 'Well, that's a relief I must say. Now look, Ellen, I know you're tired, we both are, but as I said before, we need to talk. I've been thinking a lot these past few days and I've come to a decision.' Reaching out he took hold of her hand. 'I'm leaving the East End . . . No, don't stop me,' he added as Ellen made to speak. 'Like I said, I've had a lot of time to think things over and I believe it's best for all of us if I leave.' Looking into Ellen's shocked face Arthur saw something else mirrored in her eyes – relief. Arthur lowered his gaze for a moment so that Ellen wouldn't see the pain his words were costing him. A brisk note entered his voice as he went on. 'What I propose to do is leave you the business, and set up somewhere else.' Fumbling in his pocket he brought out a crumpled letter. 'This came a couple of days ago. I would have told you, but with all the commotion going on, it went completely out of my head.' Unfolding the paper he said, 'It's from Mr Bradley, you remember, the couple we met in Southend,' he said as Ellen looked puzzled.

'Oh, oh yes, of course, I remember. What does he have to say? Not bad news I hope?'

'No, no, far from it. He wrote that he and his wife were sorry we had to cut our holiday short, and he's invited us down to stay with them in Chislehurst, when it's convenient. I didn't pay it much attention at first, but now it would be the perfect answer. It will give me the chance to get away. I've already written back explaining the situation and now I'm waiting for a reply. Of course they may take back the invitation when they realise it'll only be me for company.' He laughed self-consciously. 'But I hope not. I was planning to go away, but I wasn't relishing the notion of going somewhere strange by myself.'

He fell silent and his silence brought a wash of guilt over Ellen. But before she could say anything Arthur got up abruptly. 'To be brutally honest, the fact is I just haven't the gumption to stay around once you and Ted become common knowledge. I've been the butt of too many jokes in my life, and I'm tired of them. I know it will look like I'm running away, which I am, but I'd rather they all had a good laugh at my expense when I'm well out of earshot. At least then I'll be able to salvage a bit of pride.'

Ellen didn't know what to say. All Arthur had said made sense, but it wasn't fair to expect him to leave his business and home when in essence he'd done nothing wrong. Yet it would solve a lot of worries if Arthur was no longer around. The selfish notion bowed Ellen's head in shame.

'I'll give it a week, then, if I don't hear from the Bradleys, I'll make alternative arrangements.' Arthur was speaking again, almost rambling, to cover the awkwardness between them. 'In the meantime I'll go on sleeping in the spare room, speaking of which ...' He yawned loudly. 'I think I'll retire now, I have to be up early in the morning. I have my customers to think of, though I'd appreciate it if you kept my plans to yourself, and Ted of course. Then, when the time comes, I'll just slip away quietly. You'll have to take on another baker of course. Bill Cummons would be only too happy to be offered the job, and he did do a good job while we were away on holiday; that's if you want to carry on with the business. I hope you do, it's been in the family a long time. Anyway, good night, love, see you in the morning.' Stopping outside the spare room he said quietly, 'You know, Ellen, I may not have all the qualities of a man like Ted Parker, but I'm a bloody good baker.'

Ellen didn't reply, her throat was too full. Putting out the lamp she crept into her bedroom and climbed in beside Molly; Micky was sleeping on a bedroll on the floor. Since they had been reunited, they hadn't let each other out of their sight for any longer than necessary. By mutual agreement it had been decided that the children should move back in with Ellen; and though Nora had protested at first, for she had grown used to having the children with her, she had been relieved at heart. At her age she had become set in her ways, and having two children under her feet was beginning to take its toll, though not for the world would she have admitted it.

Snuggling up against Molly's warm body Ellen stared at the far wall thinking over what Arthur had proposed. If she had any loyalty at all she'd at least try and talk him out of his plans, but she wasn't going to. She would keep quiet and let Arthur go, because that's what she wanted; but she'd never have a moment's peace or experience true joy until she knew for certain that Arthur was settled and happy, and for a man of her husband's character, that could take a very long time.

The hospital room was eerily quiet, with only the swishing of the nurses' uniforms as they passed by on their way to and from the main ward. At this time of night, with most of the patients asleep, it was a peaceful place to be, a safe place that induced a feeling of security.

'I'd better be on me way, Agnes, before the Sister realises I'm still 'ere and kicks me out on me ear.' Ted patted the thin hand. 'I'll be back tomorrow.'

Agnes, trying hard to keep awake, squeezed his hand. 'You sure he's dead, Ted? I mean yer not just telling me that ter make me feel better, 'cos I'd rather know the truth.'

Ted kept hold of her fingers, replying grimly, 'Yeah, he's dead all right. If not right now, then he will be soon. No one's gonna find 'im where he is. Even if some tramp comes across the hut, whoever it is ain't gonna be looking fer a trap door in a run-down hut, are they? And Stokes ain't in no condition ter call out fer 'elp. Nah, he's a goner, so yer just rest an' get yerself better.'

In a hoarse whisper Agnes wheezed, 'An' yer don't . . . don't feel guilty . . . fer leaving 'im ter die, I mean?'

A muscle in Ted's face twitched but his voice was deadly calm as he answered. 'No, I don't. Any more than I'd regret having a rabid dog put down, though I think I'd show the dog some pity. They ain't got no control over what nature made them.' Smoothing

361

down the covers of the bed he lingered for a minute before asking, 'Agnes, will yer tell me something? It's about Arthur and Ellen. You know what went on there better than anyone else, an' I was wondering like if . . .'

Agnes' fingers scratched at the sheets in agitation. 'Don't take . . . any notice of what I said . . . about Arthur . . . forcing 'imself on Ellen. It . . . it ain't true. I was . . . just . . . just being spiteful, that's all. Just . . . just a spiteful old . . . old woman . . .'

Ted's lean frame relaxed at her words. He had heard the rumours, but had been too afraid of tackling Ellen about them for fear of what her answer would be. He hadn't trusted himself not to give Arthur a good beating if the rumours had contained any truth. Now he was glad he'd kept his own counsel, because if he hadn't, maybe Arthur wouldn't be as accommodating as he was being. Ellen had explained what had happened, but he had wanted to hear it from Agnes, just to be sure. And he had to admit it took a different kind of courage for a man to admit he had lived and slept with an attractive young woman for over two years, and never had any physical contact with her, especially when it wasn't true. Arthur could have made it hard for them to start a new life together. He could have insisted on dragging Ellen through a public divorce, but, whatever his reasons, he was making it easy for them, and for that Ted owed him a debt of gratitude. That's not to say he wasn't disappointed that Arthur had been with Ellen first, but it had happened, and in all fairness to the man, he had been married at the time. Anyway, it was a subject he didn't want to dwell on. It was in the past; he had the future to look to now. A future with Ellen, Micky and Molly. He might have to wait a while, but it would be worth it in the end.

CHAPTER TWENTY-EIGHT

It was Christmas Day and the rooms above the bakery were full to bursting. Ellen and Ted had decided to have their Christmas dinner here rather than at Ted's house, which hadn't pleased Nora Parker at first, until Ellen had asked if the older woman would help her prepare and cook the large meal, professing to be out of her depth at cooking for such a large gathering. Now, as Nora basted the enormous turkey, she thought, not for the first time, that it was the strangest Christmas dinner she'd ever been to. Putting the bird back into the oven Nora wiped the sweat from her face and took a large gulp of sherry as she mentally counted the number of people she was catering for, just to make sure she hadn't left anyone out. There was Sadie and the two boys, Ellen, Ted, and Micky and Molly, plus herself and John Smith. A look of sadness flitted over her face as she recalled the memory of poor Sarah Smith. Just a bad cold, John had told her when she'd enquired after his wife. But the cold had turned into pneumonia. Within a few days Sarah was dead, leaving John shocked and grief-stricken at the suddenness with which his beloved wife had been taken from him.

That had been over two months ago, but John still hadn't come to terms with his bereavement. It had taken her, Ted and Ellen to persuade the solemn man to have his Christmas dinner with them instead of sitting alone in an empty house brooding. Taking a few steps from the kitchen she peered into the sitting room where the table was already set for the festive occasion.

'Need any 'elp, Nora?' Sadie North, dressed in a simple blue blouse and black skirt, looked at Nora hopefully. Nora understood exactly how Sadie felt and her mood softened towards the former prostitute. She and Sadie hadn't exactly hit it off at first, but were now friends, due to their association with Molly. Sadie and the Knight boys had visited frequently since Molly had come to live with her brother and Ellen, but this was the first time she and the boys had been invited to what was essentially a family occasion, and it was obvious Sadie was feeling a bit awkward.

'Yeah, thanks, Sadie, I could do with an extra pair of 'ands.' Sadie gratefully followed Nora back into the kitchen. ''Ere yer go, love, get that down yer,' Nora said gaily, handing Sadie a glass of sherry.

'Cheers, Nora.' Sadie took the drink gratefully. 'What d'yer want me ter do?'

Waving her hand in the air Nora said, 'Nothing,

thanks. I just thought you was looking a bit left outta it.'

Sadie leant her buttocks against the table. 'Is it that obvious?'

Nora laughed. 'Don't worry, mate, I don't think anyone else has noticed, 'specially the two lovebirds.' She nodded towards the other room where Ted and Ellen were standing together, smiling like doting parents as the four children played with the toys they had received for Christmas.

Following Nora's glance Sadie asked hesitantly, ''As there been any news of Arthur ... I mean, about getting the annulment? 'Cos Ellen and Ted can't get married till it's all sorted. It must be hard fer you, I mean, with your Ted living at your 'ouse one minute, and here the next. It must be confusing fer the kids an' all.'

'Nah.' Nora waved her hand airily, the sherry beginning to take its toll. 'Kids tend ter take things at face value. They're much easier at dealing with changes in their lives just as long as they feel safe. Anyway, according ter Ellen it won't be too long now. They're just waiting fer the solicitors, that's probably what's 'olding everything up. Mind you, just between the two of us, I think the reason it's taking so long is 'cos Arthur's been dragging his feet, at least he was till he met the widowed sister of that Bradley woman. Like I said, up till a couple of months ago Arthur kept stalling every time Ellen wrote ter him, making up any excuse to delay signing the final papers. Now suddenly he's doing all he can ter hurry up the whole business. Of course he's making out he's doing it fer

Ellen's sake, but I've known Arthur since he was in short trousers.

He's the type of bloke that can't cope on his own. First he depended on 'is dad, then when he died he latched onto Agnes. I don't know the whys and wherefores of how he dumped Agnes, but I do know he started to spend more and more time with Ellen's parents after Ellen was born. From that time on he became besotted with Ellen. Yer see what I mean about him not being capable of living alone. Ellen and her parents became like a sort of family ter him. Now he's taken up with this widowed woman he's got someone else to look after him. I wouldn't be at all surprised if he announced he was getting married again, once the annulment has been finalised.

My Ted's already been ter the solicitors. Gave them a right rollicking he did, but them sort ain't easily frightened. Most likely they're making as much money as they can outta the whole thing while they still can. Gawd knows how long it'd take if they was trying ter get a divorce. Most likely be too long in the tooth to care,' she ended on a raucous laugh, then put her hand to her mouth in dismay. 'Bleeding 'ell, I'll be pissed if I 'ave any more. 'Ere, 'elp me get this turkey outta the oven, before it dries up.'

Ted and Ellen looked up at the sound of loud laughter coming from the kitchen.

'Sounds like Mum's been at the sherry again,' Ted grinned widely, his arm tightening around Ellen's waist. 'You all right fer a drink, Johnny?'

John Smith glanced up absently, his thoughts wandering to a time when he and Sarah had shared many a Christmas together. Jolted out of his reverie, John put on a brave face for the young couple's benefit, though he was already regretting accepting their kind offer. Now he was here, he mustn't put a damper on the proceedings.

'Thanks Ted, I'll have another beer, please.'

While Ted fetched the beer, Ellen sat down on the arm of John's chair, saying gently, 'You must miss your wife terribly. I just want you to know that we won't be offended if you want to leave early, though it would be wonderful if you could stay for the day.'

John patted Ellen's hand affectionately. 'You're a lovely girl, Ellen. Ted's a lucky man, and so am I for having such good friends. It's a pity Agnes couldn't be with us, though I can understand why she wanted to get away, poor soul.' A look of sadness clouded his eyes. 'All her life Agnes wanted to be popular, to feel important, much the same as Arthur did. Then when she achieved that aim she couldn't handle it. It must have been very hard for her to suddenly find herself the centre of attraction. You would have thought she'd have gloried in having her name splashed all over the newspaper, and people who'd previously poked fun at her suddenly swarming round her, wanting to be her friend.

There's an old saying that goes, "Beware of what you wish for, 'cos it might come true." And that's what happened to Agnes. All that she wished for came too late. That's why she went away, she couldn't handle being in the limelight. But I think the real reason she upped sticks was because she didn't think she deserved the praise and fame that came after she'd put her life on the line to save Molly, because she still blamed herself for her part in the whole sordid episode.'

He fell silent, and Ellen waited, sure the solemn man had more to say, and she was right.

Toying with his empty glass John looked up at Ellen and asked, 'I don't suppose you know where she is, only I can't bear to think of her in some strange hotel or boarding house all alone on Christmas day.'

Ellen shook her head. 'No, I don't, Johnny, I wish I did. If we knew where she was Ted would have gone to fetch her home. The last we heard from her she wrote to say she was having a nice time and would be back soon – that was nearly a month ago.'

'What you two looking so gloomy about?' Ted handed John another beer. 'It's Christmas, everyone's happy at Christmas.'

John took the bottle of beer gratefully, hoping the alcohol would help cheer him into the festive proceedings.

'We were just talking about Agnes, and how we'd hoped she would have come back in time for Christmas,' Ellen answered.

The smile on Ted's lips wavered at the mention of Agnes. He most of all wished she could have shared the special occasion with them. He still hadn't shaken off the guilt for the awful way he had treated her, and he had a feeling he never would.

He was saved from further self-recrimination by his mother's voice calling loudly, 'Come on, you lot. Get yerselves up ter the table. Ellen, if yer could fetch the vegetables, Ted can start carving.'

Nora and Sadie were carrying a large platter upon

which rested the golden browned turkey and a large portion of roast potatoes. Putting the heavy tray onto the table Nora said, 'It's a good job Ted brought over the extra chairs, else some of us would've had to have our dinner standing up.'

Ellen had just finished saying grace, a ritual that was greeted with muffled glee by the Knight boys, until they were given a quick clout to the backs of their heads by an embarrassed Sadie, when they heard a loud knock on the back door.

'Good Lord, who could that be?' Ellen had risen to her feet.

'Sit down. I'll go and see who it is.' Ted pushed her gently back onto her chair. 'Don't start without me, will yer?'

Bounding down the stairs, he saw a large white envelope lying on the mat, and pulled open the door. There, on the doorstep were several gaily wrapped parcels. His head swinging from left to right he saw a figure walking quickly away and called out, 'Hey, Agnes, where yer going, yer silly cow?'

Agnes stopped in her tracks and turned to face Ted. 'I'm sorry, Ted. I didn't mean ter spoil yer Christmas dinner, only I just got back and I wanted ter leave the presents fer the kids.'

Ted caught at her arm and pulled her into the house, along with the parcels. 'Get inside, fer Gawd's sake, before we freeze ter death. Anyway, why didn't yer let us know you was back home? Yer know we would 'ave wanted yer with us at Christmas. I don't know why yer went away in the first place.'

With much pushing and prodding, Ted propelled the embarrassed woman up the stairs. Pushing open the door he shouted merrily, 'Look who I found lurking outside.'

A great cry of pleasure went up as the assembled group saw who it was. But it was Molly who ran into Agnes' arms. 'Oh, I'm glad yer came, Agnes. It wouldn't 'ave been the same without you, would it, Micky?'

Her face flushed, Agnes looked around the room, a sudden warmth spreading through her chilled body. She had been afraid she wouldn't have been welcomed, especially on a day primarily reserved for family. But she saw now she had been wrong. She hadn't been intruding. All these people were genuinely pleased to see her. It was an experience she wasn't used to, and she had to swallow the lump in her throat before answering, 'Yer sure I ain't disturbing yer?'

Ellen started towards her, but it was John who pulled up the one remaining chair and placed it beside him. 'Here you go, old girl. You sit with me.'

Her legs unsteady, Agnes sat down as Ellen said grace once again for the benefit of the late visitor. With the formalities over, Ted began carving the turkey, while Nora and Sadie made sure the children had enough vegetables on their plates, much to their disgust. But before the assembled group could start on the tantalising meal Ted rose to his feet. Looking around the table to make sure everyone had a drink he raised his glass.

'Merry Christmas, everyone. To friends and family,

all together on the best day of the year.' His eyes swept around the table, but it was Agnes his eyes lingered on as if he were speaking to her alone. And that kindly gesture created in Agnes a feeling of belonging – a feeling of being loved, and for a moment she feared she would break down. Then she felt a strong hand grip hers and looked up into John's face and the moment passed.

There was a tinkle of glasses touching, then a resounding 'Merry Christmas' filled the room before the hungry group began their meal.